Youth and Theatre of the Oppressed

Youth and Theatre
of the Oppressed

Edited by Peter Duffy and Elinor Vettraino

YOUTH AND THEATRE OF THE OPPRESSED
Copyright © Peter Duffy and Elinor Vettraino, 2010.

First published in 2010 by PALGRAVE MACMILLAN® in the United States—a division of St. Martin's Press LLC, 175 Fifth Avenue, New York, NY 10010

Where this book is distributed in the UK, Europe and the rest of the world, this is by Palgrave Macmillan, a division of Macmillan Publishers Limited, registered in England, company number 785998, of Houndmills, Basingstoke, Hampshire RG21 6XS.

Palgrave Macmillan is the global academic imprint of the above companies and has companies and representatives throughout the world.

Palgrave® and Macmillan® are registered trademarks in the United States, the United Kingdom, Europe and other countries.

ISBN: 978-0-230-61917-3

Library of Congress Cataloging-in-Publication Data

Youth and theatre of the oppressed / edited by Peter Duffy and Elinor Vettraino.
    p. cm.
    ISBN 978-0-230-61917-3 (alk. paper)
    1. Drama—Therapeutic use. 2. Theater and youth. 3. Drama in education. I. Duffy, Peter, 1971- II. Vettraino, Elinor.

RJ505.P89Y68 2010
616.89'1523—dc22   2009029402

A catalogue record of the book is available from the British Library.

Design by Scribe Inc.

First edition: March 2010

10 9 8 7 6 5 4 3 2 1

Printed in the United States of America.

To my wife, Patti Walker. This project, along with most things in my life, would never have become a reality without you. To my daughter, Evelyn, I hope this book makes some small contribution to ensure that the world you and all children grow up in will be a healthy, peaceful, free, equitable, and inspiring one.

—Peter Duffy

For my wonderful husband, Peter Vettraino—"thank you for believing"—and for Elvis and Moose.

—Elinor Vettraino

I am not; I am being. As a traveller, I am passing from one state to another. I am not; I came and I go.

—Augusto Boal, *The Aesthetics of the Oppressed*

Contents

Acknowledgments ix

Foreword xi
Peter Duffy and Elinor Vettraino

Our Role in Crisis xv
Julian Boal

Introduction: Why This? Why Now?: A Contributors' Discussion 1

Part I   Theatre of the Oppressed in Educational Settings

1   Puppet Intervention in the Early Childhood Classroom:
    Augusto Boal's Influences and Beyond 17
    Andrea Dishy and Karina Naumer

2   Exploring the Stigmatized Child through Theatre of the
    Oppressed Techniques 45
    Johnny Saldaña

3   Silent Screaming and the Power of Stillness: Theatre of the
    Oppressed within Mainstream Elementary Education 63
    Elinor Vettraino

Part II   The Political Life of Youth

4   Viewpoints on Israeli-Palestinian Theatrical Encounters 83
    Chen Alon and Sonja Arsham Kuftinec, with Ihsan Turkiyye

5   TELAvision: Weaving Connections for Teen Theatre of the
    Oppressed 97
    Brent Blair

6   In Search of the Radical in Performance: Theatre of the
    Oppressed with Incarcerated Youth 125
    Diane Conrad

7   Rethinking Interaction On and Off the Stage:
    Jana Sanskriti's Experience 143
    Sanjoy Ganguly

8   Acting Outside the Box: Integrating Theatre of the Oppressed
     within an Antiracism Schools Program   159
     Warren Linds and Linda Goulet

Part III   Theatre of the Oppressed Practice with Youth

9   Staying Alert: A Conversation with Chris Vine   187
     Peter Duffy

10   From *I* to *We*: Analogical Induction and Theatre of the
     Oppressed with Youth   203
     Peter Duffy

11   Ripples on the Water: Discoveries Made with Young People
     Using Theatre of the Oppressed   217
     Christina Marín

12   Let's Rock the Bus   229
     Mady Schutzman and B. J. Dodge

13   The Human Art: An Interview on Theatre of the Oppressed
     and Youth with Augusto Boal   251
     Peter Duffy

Afterword: Snacking on the Moment: The Drama of "Working
     Through" Oppression with Kids   263
     Glenn M. Hudak

Contributors   271

Index   279

Acknowledgments

To my parents, you have been my constant and unfailing supporters. I wouldn't be where I am without your loving guidance. To my brothers and sisters, thank you for being the best kind of family—my friends. To Elinor, thank you, thank you, thank you! You have my undying gratitude. Lastly, to all the contributors to this book, thank you for your inspiring conversation, your generous sharing of your expertise and experience, your faith and patience with the project, and your dedication to the important work you do. I am a richer person for having worked with you.

—Peter Duffy

It's difficult to know where to start because so many people have helped me in the realization of this book. First of all, my thanks go to Peter Duffy for asking me on board with this project. This has been a longtime coming for him, and I am privileged to have shared in this journey. I also want to thank the contributors for their input and energy; without them, this text wouldn't exist. I also owe a debt of gratitude to my research mentor Dr. Divya Jindal-Snape, who has been unswerving in her support. My husband's wisdom and support for me in this project has been invaluable, and further thanks go to good friends and family—Tracey, Craig (and Joshua), Pauline, Sean, Linley, John, Brian, Lynn, Linda, Jayne, Lesley, Ruth, Mark, and Amanda—thanks for the feedback and encouragement. I also need to thank Cindy and her team in Dundee for the endless Grande Americanos as I was writing—you kept me going! And lastly, I can't finish without thanking Augusto; I have learned a huge amount from his teachings and his openness. I hope that this text truly does him justice.

—Elinor Vettraino

Foreword

Peter Duffy and Elinor Vettraino

When this project was first conceived, it had a very different look to it. Originally, it was going to be a book chronicling work Peter was doing at the time with a group of high school students in central Maine. He was a high school English and drama teacher and cocreated an interactive theatre company with a core of about twenty high school students. Their goal was to generate interactive theatrical experiences that dug deeper than the model of audience members asking questions of actors in role about the choices they made. They employed Image Theatre, Forum Theatre, and even Rainbow of Desire to create pieces that challenged the assumptions of students and their teachers, parents, and administrators. The troupe traveled to schools from Maine to New York City creating pieces of theatre with and for student bodies that deconstructed the oppressions of youth, parents, and teachers and challenged participants to look deeper into, to borrow from Paulo Freire, how their world was named.

When Peter and the troupe were creating this work, they kept seeking out resources that would support and challenge what they were creating together. They found a lot of material on Theatre of the Oppressed (TO) but precious little about TO and youth specifically. When Peter first started talking to Augusto Boal about the work the students and he were doing, Boal told him that he had yet to employ TO methods with young people. Up until that point, all of his work had been with adults. Boal did end up doing a fair amount of work with incarcerated teens and other groups of young people, but it was never his primary interest. Because of the lack of published work on the topic, it became Peter's goal to dedicate himself to starting a larger dialogue about the work that youth and youth workers, educators, and theatre artists were doing in conjunction with TO.

The more he discussed the book project with colleagues, the clearer it became that the necessary text would be a volume of international perspectives that explored addressing the oppressions of youth through TO. Peter connected with a colleague and friend, Elinor Vettraino, who became the coeditor for this revised concept. As a practitioner in Scotland working with children and teacher education students, Elinor shared Peter's vision for a text that connected practitioners' insights and experiences with questions and critical dialogue. This text, *Youth and Theatre of the Oppressed*, is the culmination of this necessary project.

The volume does not set out to be a *how-to* but more of a *how-come?* It seeks to pose more questions than it answers. It seeks to investigate critically the practitioners' praxis and to start a dialogue about the intersection of TO and youth. The book's goals are to provoke thoughtful dialogue, question established conventions, and further the exciting international conversation about TO and youth. This dialectical approach to the text will hopefully spark questions within the reader and provide possible frameworks to experiment within the reader's own work.

The editors hope that the book remains true to the spirit of the arsenal of TO. TO's purpose is to encourage the collective to develop possible alternatives to oppressive forces in their own lives. In its own way, this book shares the goal of engaging the collective by aiming to create generative conversations among its readers that look deeply into the issues of community—whether in India or Indiana—and to work with young people to name their world, untangle the knot of oppressions, and develop with them possible action plans for their own futures.

There is little doubt that young people deal with often-inconceivable oppressions. When we learn their stories, we discover worlds that haunt us and bring us to the point of utter disbelief. We hear of gun-toting child soldiers, youth plagued by famine, young people whose parents were stolen by HIV, child prostitutes, and youth trying to learn about justice while growing up in war-ravaged countries. We learn of those blinded by the lure of materialism and instant gratification, adolescents who spend too much of their days alone or without stable adults in their lives, youth who are abused and neglected in horrifying ways, children who dare not to dream. We meet learners who are sent to institutions that rarely value them as individuals and who must learn how to conform to the standardized ways of teaching and learning in order to get by. We hear stories of young people who are so obsessed with their weight that they will do anything to remain thin. We meet children who have so internalized the oppressor that they become the oppressors of their peers. Such stories can make one numb and feel impotent in the face of this *unfortunate inevitability* of history. This book suggests, however, that this need not be the case. In each chapter, we meet individuals who are working against racism, bullying, poverty, institutions, and governments to create *forums* for the voiceless to discover their voice and the powerless to act on their power. This book acknowledges the complicated lives of young people and gives examples of people working with youth to turn these tides.

The book is divided into three parts. In each part, the authors' approaches to their work make use of TO techniques in a methodological sense. They also explore the relationships between the philosophy of TO and contexts in which they operate. Three overriding themes emerge from these contexts: TO in educational settings, TO and the political life of youth, and TO practice with youth.

Part I, "TO in Educational Settings," examines institutionalized oppressions in formalized places of learning. Schools homogenize in order to run smoothly, and this process creates environments where shy and marginalized students become easy prey for their peers and teachers alike. The chapters in this section demonstrate the versatility of the TO techniques from preschool-age children right to adolescence. Each chapter focuses on student voice and individual power.

Part II, "TO and the Political Life of Youths," uncovers young people's responses to the political agendas they daily face. Many of these political forces are not unique to the lives of young people; however, the power to impact on these issues often lies within the adult world. The chapters within this section amplify the similarities of the political forces waged against young people across the globe, which highlights the fact that they are not alone in their struggle.

The chapters within Part III, "TO Practice with Youth," offer an exploration of broader issues in connection with TO work. Contributors critically reflect on approaches and adaptations of techniques that have evolved over many years in many contexts. The final words in this part are given to Augusto Boal, who offers his own reflections on the intersection between TO and youth.

Boal has said that the TO is a mirror where we can see our psyche and can penetrate it to modify our own image. The three parts of this book offer a mirror to practitioners to discover ways in which their practice can be enhanced through reflection on the praxis of others. Boal was fond of quoting Antonio Machado's proverb, "Caminante el camino no existe, el camino lo hace el caminante al caminar," which, loosely translated, means "the road does not exist; the traveler creates the road by traveling." As a final thought in the context of employing TO with youth, there is no road. We hope to create this road together.

Our Role in Crisis

Julian Boal
Original translation by Ruth Cave

We are in a time of global economic and social crisis. The funds announced to save our financial system (but is it really our own?) are so enormous that I cannot believe it is possible for anyone not to feel the obscenity in the contradiction of, on the one hand, the paying off of banks' debts so quickly effectuated by the same governments worldwide that, on the other hand, deny the existence of resources to pay for investment in hospitals, schools, pensions, and so on.

Around the world, many people have taken up arms against the systems that they believe have created this crisis. For example, most of the groups that want to do Theatre of the Oppressed (TO) have taken up the fight against corporations and, as part of that, do not want to work for big business—and in my opinion, rightly so. But what about projects that work in schools or in government? While this is not a book about TO and schools, many young people's conceptual development of education comes from their experiences of schools, so it is an important aspect to discuss here. But just as oppression exists in the corridors of power within big business, so it exists in the corridors and classrooms of schools throughout the world. It is not about where you do the work you do but about *what* you do and *how* you choose to engage with the work. We cannot be lulled into thinking that we are doing right in the world just because we are cultural workers; cultural workers often work for the same states that legitimizes oppression.

It is striking to see how the criticisms that Paulo Freire leveled at schools mirror those that Augusto Boal levels at theatre. Both authors vigorously denounce the partition of roles and space established by these two institutions. "Those who know" stand facing their complementary opposite, "those who don't know." The gap that separates the two will never be bridged because this gap is absolutely necessary for the survival of those two institutions. Freire's criticism of the "banking approach" to education cannot but be seen as contiguous with Boal's criticism of the "obscenity of the word spectator."

Over time, these two thoughts have been dulled down. They were transformed from dynamic and powerful tools into methods that became a formulaic approach to emancipation. Doing this has removed any form of critical engagement within these two schools of thought—Boalian and Freirian—and instead reduced the concepts to the strict application of defined steps within a methodology. The benefits of these steps would be measured by extremely arbitrary criteria, such as the number of times the audience intervened. The number becomes the criterion, but what can this number tell us about the quality of the exchanges, of the reflections that were ignited, and of the emancipation possibilities that started to rise or not to rise?

How far away are we from the time when Brecht could announce that his task was not to work *immediately* for the largest audiences but that he preferred to work first with a limited number of workers in order to enable them to become a circle of connoisseurs capable of, by themselves, transmitting their enthusiasm for theatre and the valuable discoveries they made by being involved with it? Because those working with TO in communities are often beholden to funders and grant subsidies, the luxury of time does not exist, and we become, sometimes without realizing it, worshippers of the "number." I do not believe that any interesting work can be done with youth without a critical reflection on the concrete conditions that allow this work but at the same time set boundaries to it.

Schools have a dual nature. They prepare young people for churning out learned ideas, and sometimes children reproduce what they have been taught more than they create. Intertwined with this is the space that schools create for young people to reflect on their own condition: the fundamental premise of conscientization. Theatre is the best place in which anyone can experiment with what it is to be someone else. Theatre gives anyone the possibility to be in someone else's shoes and assume all social positions. By performing these other social roles, we discover that what we thought was a completely natural phenomenon, for instance, being a man, is also partly, or maybe entirely, a role that is socially constructed. If it is society that constructed those roles, then we can imagine a society in which those roles will be different.

All the chapters within this book are testimony to the analysis of the tensions that exist between oppression and emancipation. These tensions are always present, regardless of how hard institutions, communities, and individuals try to be free of them. This is for no other reason than because everything within our societies, including us, is constructed by and for oppression; this, in turn, brings the need and possibility for emancipation. In this book, you will not find a "how-to" methodology to follow in order to achieve libratory and quantified results because all the contributors here are speaking about their specific practices and experiences, all of which are rich, complex, and quite different.

If the world today is in crisis, then so should our role be. If our response to this crisis simply ends up as a lament for the drying up of our subsidies and grants, our response will not be at the level required to match the enormous tasks in front of us now. But if we decide to put ourselves in crisis, to think about what our role really means, to reflect on the real significance that the words *oppression* and *emancipation* can have today, and to and see without complacency what means we have at our disposal to challenge oppression, then this crisis might be salutary for us. We have to be humble and recognize the modesty of our means so that our ambition to transform the world transforms first the tool that is ours.

Introduction

Why This? Why Now?

A Contributors' Discussion

Throughout this text, you will meet practitioners all working with young people and using Theatre of the Oppressed (TO) as a vehicle for exploring the lives hidden within their stories. What follows is an amalgamation of a number of conversations that many of the contributors had over the period of the development of this book. These conversations explore the "Why this?" and "Why now?" questions that we had when putting the book together. The book is separated into three parts: "Theatre of the Oppressed in Educational Settings," "The Political Life of Youths," and "Theatre of the Oppressed Practice with Youths." The conversations woven together here offer some indication of our thoughts behind our work.

* * *

Peter: I'm just wondering how, if at all, TO can be introduced in any sort of formal capacity into general education settings such as elementary schools or high schools. What are your thoughts on the possibilities here? What are the issues for you in relation to attempting to embed TO into educational practice within schools?

Johnny: One of the first things that occurs to me is that preservice educators have to first become acquainted with Boal's TO through a dedicated course in the subject.

Elinor: I agree with Johnny on this one. I think it needs to start with teacher education programs.

Brent: There are several aspects of this dilemma, but pedagogically, in relation to training I have carried out with my group in the past, we felt that TO could absolutely be introduced in formal capacities through curricular adjustments in the standards and guidelines based on evidence of Theatre in Education/Drama in Education (TIE/DIE) practice as beneficial to the overall learning environment. We also felt that this could happen through local visiting artists bringing theatre to the schools and through professional development workshops in TO with teachers. This not only invites all levels of teachers to utilize TO techniques within the curricular program without having to change the standards, but it also makes it formal in the sense that school administrators promote and encourage teachers to attend by paying their workshop fees, for example.

Johnny: At Arizona State University, we require that all preservice theatre teachers take Theatre for Social Change (THP 482) and read related literature (e.g., by Michael Rohd) in other drama education courses. Once teachers become aware of this form of theatre, they are more likely to incorporate it into their classroom curriculum. They most often see how relevant it is to today's young people.

Andrea: Karina Naumer and I wrote about our puppet intervention project, which we carried out in early elementary schools. The project is particularly created for a classroom setting; it's not a presentational format or performed in a theatre so it lends itself quite well to being integrated into the classroom and school focus. It's only for intimate classroom settings. Even though there are bits of puppet show in it, the students come and replace puppet voices in a moment of conflict or in a moment that they feel they should. In this case, the TO is completely embedded in the practice as it is not connected directly to a curriculum. Having said that, if it is very specifically about a story the students are reading, it would take the children's learning deeper into character work as well as plot development and those sorts of preliteracy concepts.

What's particularly different about what we did with this age group in this long-term experiment, what we call puppet intervention, is that the students did not always step in for the oppressed character. We had to flip some of the models a bit because students often wanted to correct oppressor behavior because they could see that was the *bad* behavior. The irony is that even though students embraced working in this style, it didn't mean that when a problem erupted among students in their regular, everyday lives—you know, so-and-so stole so-and-so's pencil—it didn't immediately jump to the *bad* behavior that they just corrected two seconds before. So we were struggling with that, though many teachers said the puppet intervention scenario was one that they constantly referred back to, and the kids had a group understanding or group vocabulary of the situation. They were able to say, "You just did that just like that puppet did. That isn't a good thing." We were only in a classroom setting in which that thrived.

Peter: I think you're raising a really interesting point, Andrea, and it's something that I found as well. If you think about internalized oppressions and the way our bodies have been trained to react to situations, that's a lifelong training. It's unrealistic to think that a few days of a residency are going to contradict that learning. Instead, I think we need to work with the students to create the language they need to recontextualize the behavioral framework they have so that they can see other possibilities. Often, it's about opening up options and asking, "What else could you do?" It doesn't necessarily change behavior, but it can give students an opportunity to show each other what other alternatives exist.

Elinor: I agree. I think that the power to transform your own difficult situation into something that is liberating is very much underestimated. In a sense, it's allowing your mind the freedom to create through your body a positive vision of what your situation could be like if you had options or took opportunities to behave in a way that was different from your reality. Often, the possibilities are there, but we are too conditioned to believe in them or see them; I find that particularly with young children who are conditioned to respond in particular ways to adults especially in formalized institutional settings like schools.

B. J.: Yeah, permission to imagine something else. The last time I used TO within a school setting was after school with sixth, seventh, and eighth graders, and we made a play about issues in their school, which, in reality, was about the system as oppressor. We didn't have breakout sessions; we had a kind of forum where the administrators stopped the students on their way to class and said, "You have to button up your shirt and look a certain way." The students, as Andrea said, always wanted to stand in for the oppressor, or they wanted to have vengeance. They wanted to be able to talk back to the vice principal because they were never allowed to do that, so it became sort of a Rainbow Forum and it got us to thinking that maybe Rainbow is the way to go.

Diane: That schools are the oppressor has been very much my experience working with high school–aged youths who are deemed "at risk." I spent a few years as a classroom teacher—teaching drama at the junior and senior high school levels—and since have done TO-based research with high school students and incarcerated youth. Young people have told me, on a number of occasions, how oppressive schools are for them. That's what brought me to work in a youth jail. Schools are like prisons for some kids. It's true that it's very challenging to do TO work in school settings because of all the constraints regarding what students can say, the expectations around their behavior, the content of our explorations, and so on. These elements are all heightened to the extreme in jail. If you can do TO in jail, you can do it anywhere!

Brent: One of the many teen communities I am always attempting to work with are the students in the culture of violence, trauma, and abuse—most especially young teens locked up for life sentences for crimes committed during their youth. But I see barriers to this. First, the work opens people up to the possibilities of life, but the reality is that they will probably never be released from prison, so the letdown after the project is over is frequently too depressing for most involved. Second, depending on location, probation staff, the state, the county sheriff's office, and so on are typically not friendly to any kind of humanizing work that doesn't state as its primary purpose the transformation of these "teens at risk" into more "decent" citizens. This is problematic for honest TO work because most of the work identifies internal conflict in the context of long-standing external oppressions. With a mandate to deal mostly with the teens, individually, as agents of violence, we find ourselves challenged to do work of any integrity if we are not able to show sociopolitical contexts to violence (i.e., race, class, gender, nationality, income, etc.). This is a challenge, but not entirely insurmountable.

Peter: That raises many questions for me. What do we think about using the techniques divorced from the philosophy of the techniques, for example, using Forum in an English class? A teacher might use Forum in place of having the students write from a character's perspective. Instead of using a free-writing activity, the teacher could say, "Get this up on its feet and show the conflict. And let's show other alternatives that the protagonist could pursue in the coming chapters."

Warren: How is that different from what Forum does?

Peter: For me, it's about uncovering and naming oppression and having it be a vehicle to discuss the inherent oppression in the students' lives. It's a great technique, but I am wondering if there is a line we should be aware of when something is about uncovering the personal versus the inner-workings of a story removed from our own experience. That does not mean that you can't get to the personal this way, but it doesn't mean, necessarily, that you automatically do. If the protagonist is kept at an arm's length, we are only curious what happens to the protagonist in the context of that story and nothing else. And at that level, it ceases to be TO for me; it functions solely as in interesting and engaging pedagogical tool, because there isn't an interest in the oppression and the focus is on looking at a scene from a book in a creative writing sort of way.

Sonja: I wonder, too, what is the difference between using interactive theatre techniques, as you've mentioned, Peter, as a mode of active learning—or using sculptures in a theatre class as a way to generate ideas—and using TO as a specific practice? And is there a point in which TO—and especially Boal—get reified so that you're not looking at the genealogy of the practices that preexisted TO, that were being developed by a number of people prior to Boal's publications? At what point do we attach a name to something and then ask questions about whether it adheres to the name rather than looking at the roots of the practices that have not necessarily been codified under that name? That's a separate question from, at what point are you using the exercises without understanding the philosophy that is specifically associated with TO?

Elinor: I agree that it's a separate question really, but I also think another question needs to be addressed: does it matter? Do we always have to "name" what we do? I suppose I'm asking because I know that, as a teacher, I have used TO techniques as pedagogical approaches rather than as ways to fight open oppression. For example, I have used techniques within TO to give children the spaces to move away from what can be the oppressive physical act of writing. Instead, they have played with writing with their bodies, their voices, and their movements. They weren't fighting capital "O" oppression, but they were certainly freeing themselves up as individuals to think, act, and feel. So at what point does trying to name something actually take away its ability to liberate? Are we in danger of trying so hard to stick within boundaries in TO that we are actually limiting its possibilities?

Peter: It sounds like your work is done within the context of creating liberatory practices in the classroom. The techniques are not a means to get students to do what the teacher wants, but they are methods of engagement and critical analysis. I think it is exciting that the techniques are utilized in classrooms; I just hope that the residual benefits of the techniques are realized there as well.

Johnny: One "red flag" is current in-service theatre educators using Boal's "Games" as just that—theatre games for traditional classroom work or performance warm-ups, rather than exploring their metaphoric capacity and power to explore social inequity, dynamics, and so on. Boal himself acknowledges that his repertoire of Games has potential to assist directors with play production work, but I feel more in-service presence needs to be made by TO practitioners.

B. J.: Even Boal says that the techniques are out there, and you can't really brand them. I mean, if the English teacher wants to use it pedagogically and not go any deeper than that, it begs an extra question, right? *How does this connect to you?* Sometimes it's safe to do it fictionally by growing empathy first. I don't have a problem with it called by another name. I mean a rose is a rose is a rose is a rose.

Andrea: I think it's an interesting idea. Something that Sonja said about the idea of practitioners knowing what they're doing with the material— that's always more my concern than the name of it. If the practitioner delves too deeply into something with students who aren't prepared or the teacher isn't behind it, there can be things that come up there. It could fall into chaos if the facilitator doesn't know how to structure or facilitate a particular non-sitting-behind-your-desk sort of structure.

B. J.: Yes, exactly. The devil is in the connotation—what you're going to do with the word and its practice.

Andrea: This really is an interesting question. When you challenged us, Peter, to be sure that we used the language of TO in our chapters, we started thinking about the role of the oppressor with young children. Children are in a position of lesser power than the grown-ups in the room, and that's just a fact. And they understand that relationship really well. The head of something or the person in charge is usually an older person with the authority and therefore the oppressor, too, I guess, so talking back to that character or responding in some way was really difficult for them. Consequently, we had to make an adjustment. Did we start our own thing and completely leave the Boal connection? I don't think so. I think we came straight from that connection, but, given our audience, we had to make an adjustment consciously.

B. J.: You are giving the students a sort of dress rehearsal—they are practicing that sort of power. All they have to do is imagine it, even though it's really hard to do. You as the witness, you have your feet in both worlds. You understand what it's like to be them, and you understand what it's like to be an adult.

Diane: I have experienced both scenarios. It seems that more and more people are interested in TO techniques for the power of the techniques themselves rather than the underlying philosophy. I've seen appropriations of the techniques for very instrumentalist ends. In this case, I make a point of reminding facilitators about the philosophical commitments of TO. On the other hand, I've facilitated adaptations of what I consider TO techniques that don't really look like TO at all but where the philosophy is very much underneath the work we're doing.

Peter: For me, it comes down to intention. That's the litmus test for me. I think Boal is really clear that you can change TO techniques or adapt them because they are a living, breathing thing, not something that's set. So if you need to change the techniques, as long as it's for the specific situation, as long as it's for the unearthing of the oppression, then I think it's appropriate. So walking away from what's in the books is all but encouraged by Boal.

Johnny: It's not always the protagonist in Forum Theatre that needs to change his or her ways when confronting oppression; we also need to focus on the *problem* source: the antagonist him or herself. I recall a TV news item recently on a middle school principal who wanted the students to name the people in the school who most often bullied. When he got those names, the principal didn't intervene with punishment, but with counseling, social assistance, and TLC for the bullies. The news item noted how bullying from these targeted individuals dropped dramatically because they now felt "better" that someone was listening to their side of the story and helping them out. TO should also do the same thing with you. We have a responsibility to *both* the real-life protagonists and antagonists in the school setting.

Peter: What are our next steps for TO in schools? What are the things that we haven't thought to do in schools yet?

Elinor: I know this is controversial, but I'd like to see more work done on how to use TO practices safely in classrooms in relation to purely the techniques. The fact (for me, anyway!) is that teachers will use and have used TO techniques for helping children to access subject areas and so on, and I don't always think that's a bad thing. What I do think is difficult though is when the techniques aren't developed in a way that the teachers understand where they came from and how they can be used. I have seen teachers stepping into the role of Jokers in Forum Theatre performances, and they had no real idea what they were doing or how to facilitate the learning. I think that can be really dangerous; many of the latter techniques in Rainbow, for example, are therapeutic in nature. So rather than say people shouldn't work with these techniques outside the original frame of TO, it would be useful to say how can they be done appropriately.

Andrea: Maybe TO is there to facilitate conversations between adults and young people, so we continue to use TO as a form or construct to make sure that student voices are heard. I find there is often a disconnect. I think maybe something like TO could be a really good way to bring ideas out, act upon them, reevaluate and put them into action. That's what I would say could facilitate very possible steps toward that relationship in order to voice the frustrations from students and adults alike.

Diane: I agree. TO practices with youth have as much to teach adults about our social relations, structures, and how we might work to create more justice as they can help empower young people in relation to their life experiences.

Warren: I'm going to be working with a group of families and children. It's sort of complicated, but we're looking at the stories of children in schools and the alienation they feel in the schools as immigrant children and the alienation their parents feel from their kids. I am trying to figure out ways of working with the schools as families. We're using Forum Theatre to look at what are different relationships that we can create together and what kind of strategies we can use to get engaged with the schools in different ways where the children and their parents have no power. I don't know where this will go—we'll develop a technique together—but it's a strategic intervention we're doing using theatre.

Peter: One of the workshops I was involved with that I was proudest of was a family dynamics Forum we held at the school. We had about fifty parents and children that showed up for a few preprepared Forum pieces the students and I devised together about basic issues like curfew and clothing choices. We made sure that we had three family counselors there to provide support while we engaged in Image and Forum Theatre work together. By the end of the night, we had parents and teens practicing having difficult conversations together onstage. It became a powerful and moving night, and that some parents came out and took that sort of risk in front of their children was incredibly humanizing.

B. J.: In Southern California, we have option schools [called alternative schools elsewhere] and that sort of work would be developed with kids to deal with issues like homelessness, having to work two jobs, and dropping out due to the chaos. I just wish this sort of work was supported curricularly at the local level.

Sonja: I think the family context is a really useful framework to add to this conversation. Because the educational work with TO isn't only happening in the schoolroom space but also in finding ways to include parents into the conversation like you talked about, Peter and Warren. Something that several of you may have seen was Jan Mandel's students' work at the 2007 PTO conference from St. Paul Central High School. One of the things she did was to introduce a parents' breakfast because many parents were not available to meet after school because they were working or had other obligations. Just being conscious of the time that parents can be in conversation with their children has lead to some extraordinary exchanges that aren't quite TO but are working with the ideas of liberation, social justice, and celebration. Sometimes I feel like that part of the work can get submerged when the focus of the work is on power and oppression. The work is also about liberation and finding the spaces to create not only the opportunities for difficult conversations but also the spaces for communal connection and celebration through the embodied work of the theatre. This is a really vital part of the work that I've seen.

Elinor: I also think there is a need to understand that sometimes focusing on the oppression can actually put pressure on the young people themselves to "fix" things for themselves and their communities.

Warren: Yes, I was talking to a colleague about the work that we do in Native Canadian communities and the long-term issues that they face that you can't solve during a Forum workshop because they are bigger issues. The youth always say, "Why do you expect us to fix these problems if our parents haven't?" This is a difficult question that occurs frequently and it makes me wonder, how do we integrate this into an established long-term community development program that tried to address the bigger issues? We've developed a five-year project we're trying to get funding for that will culminate with the youth forming a youth advisory council that will then advise their tribal council around health issues and broader issues that affect young people. It has a Legislative Theatre aspect to it, and it involves more than the youth; it also involves the tribal elders and teachers. Our vision is to encourage the young people to become leaders through the theatre. Theatre has given them their voice. But the question is, how do they use their voice, and who hears them?

Andrea: It can become really frustrating when people unleash their new voice and have nowhere to go with it.

Peter: We're veering outside the school realm, which is useful. In this bigger context, what are your thoughts on TO practice with youth in general?

Brent: What I feel is a challenge rests in a few areas. I think that TO for youth practitioners may be confusing "morality" with "ethics." Morality heads people in a vectored direction—a "right" answer, a "better" choice. It's theatre with a "message" predetermined usually by funding sources and concretized. It's a sticky wicket, but it is surmountable if dialogue is clear and the process is *completely* transparent from the beginning—meaning the youth are aware and they have escape clauses built in should they need to opt out when they learn the lay of the land. Also, I think that TO for youth itself can be challenged by the need for acceptance of protagonist stories, on the one hand, versus the real advent of teens unconsciously "hosting the oppressor." TO practitioners may find themselves unwitting allies for oppression as a young teen identifies liberation in ways that serve to oppress others. This is not uncommon in TO, but may be even more prevalent in youth.

B. J.: Our earlier conversation really nailed it for me. We're not getting to the parents. For me, that's crucial. When you're a disenfranchised youth, you're part of a greater system and you have these different dependencies. So it feels like opening that up to the family and schools and not just to one's peers is so important.

Elinor: Perhaps opening it up to everyone is the way to go. Separating out youth from "everyone else" is not always a helpful construct, because, although young people have particular needs and issues, they are still part of a wider picture. I think Sanjoy hits on this really well in his chapter on Jana Sanskriti's work.

Sonja: I agree. I think that's where the work can be really powerful. It's going back to that part that is as much about community building as it is about examining oppression. That is not to take away the importance of that component of examining power and oppression but to look at all of the different stakeholders that could be included if the larger-term goal is to create a liberatory situation for everyone.

And if we look at Chen Alon's intervention, we see the importance of doing theatre of the oppressor. This work can be done to undo the structures that exist within the oppressor position; and not just to humanize like, "Oh, we're all just the same," and consequently ignore the power dynamics that exist but to acknowledge again what Freire acknowledges: that the oppressor wants to be humanized. It's not just about treating the oppressor as a human being but about deconstructing their role in the oppressor position.

Diane: I think TO is only possible if the oppressors have admitted their role and are looking for change. All too often those in positions of power (all of us, to some extent) are so invested in the status quo that, though we might give lip service to the idea of change, we're really not ready for the kind of change that is needed to make a difference.

Chen: One focus in this work for me that I think is crucial is about how we can work with TO without imposing politics on youth. Maybe for me that's because of the political context I work in [Israel and Palestine], but I feel that the main reason the young people I work with come for theatre is because they are trying to run away from politics. When they get to the work, they understand that the basis of the work is actually the indoctrination of a political view.

Peter: I have two questions about that. One, is anything "politics free"? I think that anytime we make a choice, it is couched in politics. Linked to that for me is a larger question: Why do we use TO with youth? Why don't we use drama therapy or something else? What is it about TO for all of us? Is it that we have certain topics that we want to cover with the populations with whom we work and so we use TO to go after that?

Elinor: I think politics in its widest term actually fits into a lot of what everyone does. But I'm also thinking about what Chen is saying; how do you *not* put your own spin on the situation at hand? How do you *not* put your own ideas, bias, or whatever forward when you're working with young people? I think all of us may have preconceived ideas about the way in which people, society, and so on should be, so how do we leave that aside, and what difficulty does it cause? I was also thinking it linked to something that Warren was saying about struggling with teachers not really understanding how this works.

Warren: You know, Boal talks about the small, personal stories and the structural issues being connected, and one of the things I am struck with is that in our work we have a real struggle working with youth to get beyond the personal stories and personal experiences that come out in the Forum plays and bringing in political analysis. They want to talk about the personal stories because stories are so strong for them. And then we bring it to the political arena and it gets lost. Maybe this is because of the context of the schools we work in, because they are not emancipatory schools.

Sonja: It's actually a major dynamic I found in working with Israeli and Palestinian youth. I've found that that's actually a dynamic about how people enter into the work. There are a lot of studies about people who work in groups with Israeli and Palestinian youth; Israeli youth tend to want to remain in the realm of the personal, they want to stay humans, they want to stay individuated. The Palestinians who are more impacted by the political situation, they see it everyday around them; the occupation is part of their everyday lives rather than an abstract condition that only affects them on occasion, really analyze things only much more through the political realm. TO in some ways allows for both entry points. You can't just remain only on a personal realm, because you're creating a situation that codes things. You use certain ways of adapting TO, then I find that you can offer opportunities for the young people to code the political situation and not only stay in the realm of personal story.

Johnny: I was looking at the excerpt from the chapter I submitted from the collection, and there was one passage in particular I wanted to share. Charles Banaszewski was a doctoral student here at ASU. This is where I quote him: "Banaszewski (2006) asserts that adult TO facilitators introduce and examine their personal yet hidden social agendas covertly and subtextually in the public school classroom." Now I go into my own work in TO deliberately with, as Chuck said, a personal agenda. It could be a pedagogical agenda, and, you know, if you want to call the pedagogical political, so be it. But I think that it is, for me, impossible to deny that I am definitely going into any kind of TO work, whether it be with children or adults, without some agenda, whether it be covert or overt, whether it be laid on the table, or whether it be subtextual.

Peter: I absolutely agree. When I used to live in Maine, I did a lot of work at the youth detention center there. I would do some TO work with them [the youth in residence] and just to help them find a way to communicate with the higher-ups about their life and circumstances there at the center. It was used as a communication tool back and forth. But even when you're dealing with specific things like the quality of food or only having a few choices about the clothing you can wear, that's a very practical or personal thing, and yet it is such a political idea. I don't know how we can do one without the other. We are such political beasts. Foucault talks a lot about that—where the personal and political can't be extricated.

Andrea: Can I jump in on that, Peter? Obviously we're working with very young children so we're aware of the power struggles and situations when you have adults and very small children; they are looking to us to be the guide. But I think it's very careful training that our Joker, called the outside facilitator, has to bring the children and their views really out and leave their agenda on the shelf, not put it away and not make it disappear. But interestingly enough, whether it's personal or political, asking children their ideas can become a political or pedagogical confrontation to teachers that is surprising to them. So the training of our facilitators or Joker is something that we have to work very carefully on because it's very easy to tell them what the right answer is, even if you don't mean to.

Elinor: There's an article that I read recently by Paul Dwyer about Forum Theatre and Jokers within Forum. The article highlighted the issue of Jokers leading the audience toward solutions that they have perhaps thought of or agree with. For me, it made me think about how you have to leave your own baggage at the door and think about how you work with that.

Sonja: It's a great point because I think there are a lot of assumptions that facilitation and jokering are so similar that you could just throw someone into a situation and easily facilitate a Forum Theatre. There hasn't been so much careful work about how to train Jokers rather than facilitators. Mady Schutzman writes about this as well in the latest *Boal Companion* book. In *Joker Runs Wild*, she talks about how the initial jokering system that came out of the arena was much more theoretically complex in some ways than what the position has become in terms of someone who can be more of a pattern recognizer, who makes everyone aware of the patterns that are surfacing in the room rather than just having a dialogue about what's happening onstage. It ties back to Peter's comment about Foucault, too, because it's a way of moving beyond positionality of saying a facilitator walks into a room with a certain set of assumptions and biases—which is always true—and more toward considering that what you're trying to do in jokering is to make visible all of the patterns that you see coming out of the dynamics of the situation.

Peter: I see my role as a Joker, whether working with youth or not, to heighten whatever the person's contribution is in order for it to be really clear what the idea behind it is so that we have a collision of ideas that the group collectively then gets to wrestle with. I use TO because it's the most effective way I know to have a communication of those ideas. I clearly have a bias going in there, but I feel that making the choice to use TO is in itself a political choice.

Chen: I want to jump in at this point because I raised the issue about the political dimension of the work. Because of the Viewpoints [Chen's theatre that does TO work with Israeli and Palestinian youth] projects that we do, we meet many audiences, especially Palestinians. We've always been accused by both sides of being manipulative in our scenarios, that we are trying to manipulate the audience. The Israelis often accuse us of manipulating the messages and of showing only the suffering of the Palestinians. This is a very crucial point for me because when we work with Palestinians, with mixed audiences, or in front of Israelis, I don't want them to feel that the reality is balanced; so our scenarios are not balanced. What we do try to do is create a balanced space in which each side can give voice to their concerns. But we are then accused of erasing the oppression dimension by doing this; by allowing both sides a voice. They also blame the Palestinian actors for creating reconciliation theatre too soon; they say it is too early, it is not the time to reconcile with the oppressor.

Sonja: I think this is the difference between Freire and Boal. When you create the Viewpoint scenario, Chen, you are working with a Freirian foundation, right? Because you are the intellectual that creates the scenarios. With Boal and TO, and that's the project I know you're working on now, the idea is that the scenario comes from the participants, so it's much harder. There are other things you can talk about in terms of what kinds of scenarios are available for people to be able to create, but the scenarios at least come from the participants, so it's harder to make an argument that you're manipulating them through the creation of what you're doing. And I think that's the difference between Viewpoints and the pilot project, as I understand it, that you're working on.

Warren: This rings true for me, too. We're working in schools with mixed populations, and we're also working, at the same time, on aboriginal reserves with aboriginal youth. They are completely different processes; they have to be completely different processes. In fact, the work with the aboriginal youth was about internalized oppression, and it's been sort of a struggle how to make that appropriate to the issues that they have. It demands a whole new method; it's a TO method, but it's something else as well. There are lots of power structures within the reserve that they can't really talk about but they can perform. On a reserve we worked on a month ago, reservists split politically—between those who have power and those who don't—and it was also present in the youth. If you come from a family that has power, your relationship with a family that doesn't have power is problematic. So how do we all work together? TO becomes a space to experiment with that. I don't know if that's the kind of experience you have in Israel, Chen. Have you worked with just Palestinian youth? And have you worked with mixed groups and seen a different method being more appropriate?

Chen: Yes, what we're trying to do in Viewpoints is that when we work with Palestinian homogeneous groups, [a Palestinian] is facilitating the Forum Theatre and the discussion. And when we work with the Israeli Arabs, [we have Israeli Arab] Jokers. But the method is the same. We had a discussion about whether we should mix the facilitators, and the decision was that each side would facilitate their own group. I didn't agree with this, as I don't think it's a good idea actually; I think it's better to work with mixed facilitators.

Peter: I remember, Chen, what you were saying this summer about trying to activate the oppressed and the oppressor and to use Forum Theatre to honor both sides of the problem. Are we asking too much of the form?

Elinor: It's kind of interesting because I have a feeling about this as well, and it links back to Sonja's and Diane's comments earlier. I don't think it's always as easy to separate oppressor and oppressed sometimes, because I think there are elements of both in everyone. The example I use in my chapter for this book shows how a supposedly renowned "oppressor" within a school context is also oppressed within that context, so I think, for me, it's contextual as well. Oppression and oppressors come in many different forms, and I think that oppressors watching a piece of Forum actually get a better understanding of how their behavior impacts other people. And by having that understanding, I think that helps them to change their ideas.

Sonja: I think that's a really amazing example of the power of bringing together groups of people who want to assume from the outside that people should be labeled in a particular way. And what Augusto and Julian keep bringing up is that you can't talk about oppressor and oppressed in terms of positionality, but only in terms of relationships. But it also makes it clear that you have to change your tactics depending on the politics of the situation. I think especially when you're working with Israelis, they don't see themselves as oppressors—never, especially the ones who participate in mixed groups. But the situation is one in which the power in the situation is held by Israelis as a group, for the most part. It's really hard, and I think that's the question that Chen was asking way back at the beginning: how do you bring the dynamics of a political situation into the analysis of the specific dimensions of an individual situation of oppression?

Chen: I just want to add a quick word on what Sonja just said and to name it under the term *political context*. For example, in Israel and Palestine, fifteen years ago you couldn't even find one political movement that was a joint movement. Even if there was a very large segment of the Israeli society against the occupation or struggling against the occupation, Israelis didn't cooperate with the Palestinians. Now the major groups are, and this is a shift in political activism in Israel—so you can't deny it when you go to work with TO; you can't say, "No, I don't care about the political situation."

*   *   *

At the end of our deliberations, we found ourselves with more questions than we started with! Maybe it's not just a "TO and youth" question but a bigger one about what we are all learning as a result of working with TO in our different contexts. How do we combine the many issues that we are dealing with, political versus personal, power versus relationships, youth versus adulthood?

We get the sense that this is not the end of the story but just the beginning of a very, very long journey.

Part I

Theatre of the Oppressed in Educational Settings

Puppet Intervention in the Early Childhood Classroom

Augusto Boal's Influences and Beyond

Andrea Dishy and Karina Naumer

A cry of "Stop!" rang out as the scene onstage started to heat up and become intensely charged with emotion. That "Stop!" was not from the performers but from an audience member exercising his right to do the unthinkable, to halt the performance and offer spontaneous alternatives to the situation onstage.

Such are the delightful and radical opportunities audience members, known as "spect-actors," are afforded in Augusto Boal's interactive theatrical convention called Forum Theatre. Unlike during a traditional theatre performance, audience members are encouraged to become active, vocal participants analyzing and offering new ideas for action and change, and then even stepping onto the stage to play out the new ideas themselves!

So when that "Stop!" was heard, that's exactly what happened. The performers—Luna, the soft, blue, flannel moon puppet with big eyes, and her supposed friend Sol, the plump, yellow, fuzzy sun puppet, his face twisted in a pain—froze in place until the teaching artist said, "Relax." The audience members, mostly age four, were very clear that the unfriendly behavior they were witnessing had to stop. Now they were ready to embark on the adventure of offering their ideas in action.

In this example, the "performers" are puppets and the "stage" is a kindergarten classroom in a public school, in Queens, New York. The children are taking part in a drama residency program with the Creative Arts Team/New York City Wolf Trap Program: Early Learning through the Arts (known as the Early Learning Program), one of the outreach programs of the Creative

Arts Team (CAT), an educational theatre company based at the City University of New York (CUNY).[1]

Since the early 1990s, Augusto Boal's theories and practice have influenced drama work being conducted with students of all ages and their teachers as part of CAT. This chapter will look at how this work developed within CAT's New York City Wolf Trap Program: Early Learning through the Arts, outline some of the tenets of the techniques, and examine how these strategies have been and are currently being used for children between ages three and seven.

The Early Learning Program's mission was, and still is, to provide drama work of the highest artistic and educational quality to young children and their teachers within the most underserved and at-risk communities within the five boroughs of New York City. Thus, we, the program directors of the Early Learning Program from 1992 to 2004, along with a very dedicated and talented core teaching staff, experimented with many drama methodologies. We also opened ourselves to other influences outside our field to tap into the imagination, innate intelligence, ethical insights, and problem-solving abilities of young children. Some of the issues explored by the program have been and continue to be inclusion or exclusion, violence prevention, separation from parents, accepting a new sibling, and being a part of a community.

Specifically, in 1995, the Early Learning Program within CAT began experimenting with Boal's Forum Theatre techniques as well as other strategies to develop what we have coined as "puppet intervention."

Defining Puppet Intervention

Intervention in a dramatic context is the convention of inviting a participant or, as Boal has termed, a "spect-actor" to step into a moment of unresolved conflict between characters. A facilitator leads the audience in a series of questions that invite audience members to reflect upon the conflicts, offer advice to the characters, and see their suggested strategies for change put into action either by the actors, themselves, or others. *The moment of intervention must, therefore, have potential for change.*

Puppet intervention is using puppet characters to engage in the process of intervention, as defined above, with modifications made appropriate to our target age group. The convention is enacted or facilitated by two teaching artists, known at CAT as actor-teachers, with support of the classroom teacher.

Why Puppets?

We capitalized on the fact that most young children have an instant attraction to puppets (just witness the *Sesame Street* and Elmo phenomenon), and thus we incorporated puppets early on. For example, within an early drama curriculum, *Children of Earth and Sky*, a puppet bird swooped in to deliver an important message to the child participants. In *The Queen's Tea Party*—an undersea adventure—an Octopus puppet actually played the main character that interacted with the children-in-role.

Using puppets for intervention work with this age group was a natural next step. Even though they saw adults manipulating them, young children related to the puppets on their own level as "peers" rather than as adult "authority figures." In puppet intervention sequences, the program staff found that the children would readily challenge, correct, and advise the puppets. Often, shy children who had difficulty relating to visiting or new adults willingly participated with the puppets.

Puppet Intervention Influences

We also began to look to a variety of influences—all of which informed the development of puppet intervention. Chris Vine, CAT's artistic and education director, had initially trained with Boal and was now teaching these techniques through the Paul A. Kaplan Center for Educational Drama[2] and had been expanding the use of Boal's work generally within CAT. Vine's theoretical insights and practical suggestions helped refine the puppet intervention work.

We observed CAT's high school program under the directorship of Gwendolen Hardwick for guidance in role replacement techniques that might be modified for early years. Members of the Early Learning Program staff added insights as well. Some had taken Vine's courses, worked directly with Boal, or both. New York City's Resolving Conflict Creatively Program led training for CAT staff and inspired the Early Learning Program to adapt some of their effective communication strategies for young audiences.

Trial and error also proved to be an important influence. As the program has been implemented in hundreds of classrooms over many years, best practices can be drawn from successful child interactions, classroom teacher comments, actor-teacher inspiration, and external observation by program directors.

Placing Puppet Intervention within the Curriculum

Puppet intervention, never a "stand-alone" strategy, has almost always been incorporated into a longer theatre-in-education (TIE) curriculum. Each year, the Early Learning Program continues to develop from one to three TIE curricula to be implemented within single classrooms in schools and Head Start centers throughout the five boroughs of New York City. These highly interactive curricula are composed of four or five episodes of a dramatic story, which are implemented in forty- to forty-five-minute classroom sessions, ideally held twice a week.

In these curricula, actor-teachers, the classroom teacher, and the children enter into the pretend world of the fiction and play roles. Actor-teachers wear lively costume pieces, employ puppets, and use props, musical instruments, and a great deal of pantomime and interactive narration to stimulate the children's natural sense of play as well as to bring the stories, the characters, and the world in which they inhabit to life in the classroom. Puppet intervention has become one of the Early Learning Program's most important strategies. These tangible, concrete, and experiential methods using drama help children understand the context of the fictional experience, which, in turn, enables them to engage in sophisticated thinking and problem solving.

Example TIE Curriculum: *Feria de Seveilla*

The following TIE curriculum, *Feria de Sevilla* (*The Seville Fair*), incorporates puppet intervention. Originally developed by Karina Naumer and senior teaching artist Steve Elm, this curriculum focuses on violence prevention and conflict resolution and was designed to unfold over a five-day sequence. The story is about world-famous performers who have come to the annual Seville Fair to perform their best acts and mingle with their friends. Colliding views about what makes a "good" show creates tensions between players. Before the final show can go on, these tensions must be resolved by all.

- *Human characters*: Sancho (story and joke teller) and Pepita (puppeteer)
- *Puppet characters*: Luna (moon puppet, female) and Sol (sun puppet, male)
- *Children's role/characters*: Various invited performers at the Seville fair
- *Teacher's role/characters*: Señor/a Cancione (a famous opera singer)

Day 1: Introduction Day

Story Content: Children view pictures of the city; performers, such as flamenco dancers in costume; fair decorations; a castle; and Spanish royalty. They also learn Spanish vocabulary words and prepare to take on the role of "performers" in the story.

Learning Focus: Children are introduced to the world of the story with pictures so that they will be able to imagine the place and build upon it once they enter the fiction on the following days.

Day 2: Inhabiting the Story World/Introduction to the Characters

Story Content: The children, as performers, enter into the world of the Seville Fair and meet up with a famous juggler/joke teller, Sancho, and his longtime friend, Pepita the Puppeteer (both played by the actor-teachers–in-role). They also meet Señora Cancione, the great opera singer (played by the classroom teacher). As the story begins, they have all met up in the "pretend" city square to practice their acts of flamenco dancing, juggling (in pantomime), and joke telling. They receive a surprise message that the queen has decided to attend their performances. Now they must really practice, practice, practice. Pepita agrees to practice her puppet show for them the following day.

Learning Focus: The children are engaged in creating the setting and establishing relationships in-role for future impetus to help "friends" in need. They are also building their expertise as show performers.

Day 3: Puppet Show

Story Content: Pepita presents a rehearsal of her puppet show, which is called, *Luna and Sol's Friendly Picnic*, to get feedback from the other performers. The show contains two mounting conflicts. These are the scenarios that will later be intervened on. The show even ends in a loud backstage puppet fight. While Pepita is pleased with the violence in the show—thinking it quite funny—Sancho raises concerns about the unfriendly nature of this so-called friendly picnic. The group discusses the impact on the audience, and Pepita feels compelled to redo some parts of the show but makes it clear that *she* gets to decide which version to perform for the queen.

Learning Focus: The children view and become familiar with the puppet show in order to intervene effectively on it later. They also discuss how the depiction of violence in the show may affect the audience, and thus the success of the show.

Day 4: Puppet Intervention

Story Content: Pepita enters forlorn. She has tried to change the show herself but has run out of ideas and realizes that she would do a better job with some help. So Pepita performs the show again, and this time the performers are invited to stop and intervene to help the puppets resolve their conflicts, thus making the show friendlier. Sancho facilitates the discussion and ultimate changes to the puppet show. (This is reflective of the Joker role in Forum Theatre.) Pepita likes the new show and decides to perform it for Queen Isabella.

Learning Focus: The children are given opportunities to intervene on the conflicts depicted within the puppet show in order to identify the causes of the conflicts, examine behaviors before and after the offense, and pose possible solutions.

Day 5: Human Intervention

Story Content: When the day begins, Sancho, who suddenly wants to become a puppeteer too, is playing with Pepita's puppets. He has taken them without asking and is so engrossed with them that he ignores Pepita's urgent request to return them. Pepita at first becomes frustrated, then angry, and then so angry that she raises her fist. However, before she can inflict any violence, Sancho realizes what is about to happen. He "freezes" the action and, somewhat clueless as to his part in the escalation, enlists help from the other performers to understand why the fist appeared. The other performers, better equipped to use some of the skills they have already practiced with the puppets, help Sancho and Pepita see their parts and work through this new conflict. Queen Isabella arrives, the performers perform for her, and all celebrate.

Learning Focus: The children reapply what they have learned with the puppets to conflicts between the "human" characters.

Puppet Intervention and Developmentally Appropriate Practice

The written puppet scenario and the step-by-step facilitation sequence of puppet intervention are purposefully and thoughtfully developed to take into consideration what young children understand, can do, and enjoy. The entire intervention may derail, if any one aspect of this process is not suitable to young children's interests or abilities. For example, if the puppet show is too long, they lose focus. If the story is too complex, they don't understand. If the intervention is not facilitated in a very clear and concise manner, they don't understand *and also* lose focus. Therefore, developmentally appropriate practice for young children has become a guiding influence. The following sections illustrate in further detail the nature of an appropriate puppet scenario and accompanying sequence for intervention for this population.

The Puppet Scenario

Puppet scenarios for intervention purposes are carefully crafted to meet the following criteria:

- The conflicts parallel those that young children have experienced.
- Each scenario contains several (at least two) "conflict points" for intervention.
- The scenario is of a length that will hold young children's interest.
- Each conflict contains more than one possible solution.
- There are a number of opportunities to engage the children both orally and physically.

Example Puppet Scenario from *Feria de Sevilla*

Pepita's puppet show: *Luna and Sol's Friendly Picnic*
Scenario originally devised by actor-teachers Maura Griffin and Alexandra Lopez

Luna and Sol, two good friends, have decided to go on a picnic. They think of all the yummy things that they would like to take with them. Then they travel to their favorite park, and when they arrive, they find the perfect spot to sit in. Unfortunately, they have different ideas of what makes the perfect spot. Luna wants to sit in the shade, and Sol wants to sit in the sun. After they disagree about this for a while, Luna gets very upset and aggressively yells, grabs, and drags Sol into the shade, hurting him with her tone and roughness. Sol shuts down and sits grumpily. Luna is oblivious to Sol's pain and just happy she has gotten her way so they can have the picnic, but then another problem soon arises when Luna and Sol realize that one of them forgot to pack the food in the picnic basket. They blame each other and come to blows, thus ending the picnic and the puppet show.

Intervention Facilitation

In the puppet intervention models developed with the Early Learning Program, it is important to note that both actor-teachers and the children stay in-role throughout the process. One actor-teacher, as Pepita, performs the puppet show, the children remain as 'the performers" watching and commenting on the puppet show, and the other actor-teacher, as Sancho, assumes the "unspoken" or unannounced role of the outside facilitator (OF), which is akin to the Joker in traditional Forum.

The Outside Facilitator

We began to use the term OF as part of the puppet intervention process, because not only was the actor-teacher playing a role, he or she was now employing additional skills—that of facilitator of a forum-like experience for young children. In the example of the story of the Seville Fair, Sancho, as the OF, is not only trying to help his friend Pepita, but he is orchestrating the intervention experience. This is done through the following stages: the setting of the forum guidelines, when and how to say "stop," the generating and gathering of students' ideas, as well as guiding the logistics of putting those ideas into action. The OF also guides the learning from *outside*—looking in on—the conflict occurring between the puppets in the show scenario. He is present to raise questions about the behavior of the puppets. In this sense, the OF is similar to Boal's concept that "the Joker must be Socratic—dialectically—and, by means of questions, by means of doubts (does this particular solution work or not, is it right or wrong?) must help the spectator or spect-actors gather their thoughts, to prepare their actions" (Boal 1992, 234). Generally, the OF is standing or sitting to the side of the performance area in order to keep and eye on all the action, especially the students' reactions, because like the Joker in Boal's work, he or she must always be present to maximize learning by gently interrogating, pausing, directing, or redirecting the situation without judging or swaying the ideas or thoughts of the audience. Different than the Joker, however, the OF here is always in role as the character in the larger story of the performers at the Seville Fair.

The Inside Facilitator

Another reason for coining the term OF was to distinguish from the inside facilitator (IF) who, as the puppet or puppeteer, is directly involved with reenacting the scenario while facilitating and challenging the ideas suggested by the children from *within* that scenario being played out. The IF's job is twofold: to reenact or replay certain scenario excerpts using children's ideas so the children can see their ideas as well as the ensuring consequence of their ideas comes to life. The IF also has the distinct task of encouraging children to think more deeply than they might do at first and to "invite" them to verbalize those thoughts through role.

Another attribute of the IF is that he or she has license to pause the performance in process and "turn out" to the onlooking children to ask for support or advice. For example, the puppet Luna suddenly becomes confused, and then Luna herself (with the adeptness of the IF) might turn out to the "performers" to ask for help or clarification. (This will be demonstrated in the script of a sample intervention sequence later in the chapter.) During the entire intervention process, the puppeteer usually sits "center stage" behind a waist-high puppet curtain (to create a useful boundary) but is always visible in order to witness the children's responses and to be readily able to respond to or connect with the OF. The interaction between the two is closely intertwined, as you'll see in the scripted examples to follow.

Both the OF and IF also have the dubious task of paying attention to solutions that might be considered "magical," as Boal would call it—like cheating to get the reward. However, magical for our population needs some consideration, as for them the line between magic and reality can be somewhat blurred. So with what might appear to be magical solution the IF must carefully maintain the scenario and challenge the child to present or verbalize his or her ideas more specifically. The OF may also challenge, but generally this happens before or after each scene is played.

Puppet Intervention: Sample Objectives with Possible Sequence

Intervention Objectives/Achievement Standards

Every puppet intervention scenario contains an overarching child-learning objective as well as specific achievement standards for each sequence (we had stated earlier that most of our scenarios contain two or three different intervention points).

In *Luna and Sol's Friendly Picnic*, the overarching objective is for Luna and Sol to both get what they want and still be good friends.

The specific child achievement standards for the following example intervention are as follows:

First Intervention Point, Part 1

- Children will identify feelings of the characters and be introduced to vocabulary accordingly.
- Children will identify the root of the conflict, who is being "aggressor," and why.
- Children will be introduced to ways in which one's aggressive behavior may impact another's feelings and examine options for change in this behavior.

First Intervention Point, Part 2

- Children will explore options for problem solving when the position of one person varies from the position of another.

Intervention Sequence Setup

First Point of Conflict (Parts 1 and 2) in Luna and Sol's Friendly Picnic

The following is a *possible* intervention sequence highlighting the first point of conflict, which has two parts, presented in *Luna and Sol's Friendly Picnic*. (Reminder: The Puppets can't decide where to sit for their picnic—Luna wants the shade and Sol wants the sun. Tensions mount, and Luna becomes very aggressive and pulls Sol very hard into the shade.)

Please note that this intervention sequence would change or adjust according to the age and responses of each group or class. We have added some possible child responses (based on what children have said in past interventions) in certain places to give an idea of how a facilitator engages young children (for our purposes, age four) in the process.

Possible Sequence

1. The OF Establishes the Forum Guidelines

After the initial puppet show has been played, the OF, as Sancho, raises a question about the unfriendly nature of the show and solicits thoughts from the children; they discern friendly from unfriendly behavior and examine the impact the various behaviors might have on the audience. They finally decide to help Pepita improve her show for Queen Isabella.

Before the children see the puppet scenario again, the OF asks the children to identify when to stop the action and gives them an opportunity to practice:

> OF: When you see either Luna or Sol not being friendly say, "Stop!" (with accompanying gesture). Let's practice saying that and making our gesture on a count of 3. Here we go. One, two, three, STOP!

2. Identifying the Aggressor and Naming His or Her Behavior
(You may also ID feelings here)

During the puppet show, once the children have identified unfriendly behavior and stopped the action, the OF asks the children to name the problem:

OF: Why did you stop the puppet show here?
Child: They were fighting
OF: Who was fighting?
Child: The puppets.

The OF asks the children to identify the aggressor:

OF: Who wasn't being a good friend?
Child: Luna.

The OF asks the children to identify the aggressor's behavior:

OF: What is Luna doing to make you think that she's not being a good friend?
Child: She pulled him hard.
OF: I saw that, too. How do you think Sol feels about that?
Child: Sad.
OF: And how was she using her voice when speaking to Sol?
Child: She was loud and rough.
OF: Is that a friendly or unfriendly way to speak to someone?
Child: Unfriendly.

3. Identifying and Trying on Feelings of Both Characters
The OF asks the children to identify and try on the feelings of both characters:

OF: My friend (name of child) said that Luna was feeling sad about being pulled like that. Let's show "sad" with our bodies and faces.
OF: Let's look at Luna for a minute. How do you think she is feeling right now?
Child: Mad. Bad.
OF: Another word for mad is "angry." Show me with your bodies and faces an angry feeling.
OF: Let's check in with our puppets. How are you feeling Luna? (Luna: Angry). How are you feeling Sol? (Sol: Sad). Wow. You all knew exactly what they were feeling.

4. Helping the Offended to Speak Up: Step One—Getting Ready to Speak
The OF identifies how communicating about the effect of actions and behavior may help the situation:

OF: Do you think Luna even knows that the way she is yelling and pulling on Sol is so unfriendly and is making him sad?
Child: No
OF: I bet that all of you could help Sol talk to Luna. Would you do that?
Child: Yes.

OF: *(to Sol)* Hey, Sol. We don't think Luna knows how you feel, and my friends here would like to help you talk to her.

Sol: Really? I'm not sure I want to get very close to her right now after the way she treated me.

OF: Well . . . you stand back, and we will help, OK?

Sol: OK.

OF: So, my friends, what can Sol say to Luna to let her know how Sol is feeling? *(At this point, children can talk directly to the puppet, coaching her through each step of the interaction.)*

Child: Sol feels sad.

OF: So Sol can say, "I feel sad"?

Child: Yeah.

Sol: *(practicing aloud)* "Luna, I feel sad"—like that?

Child: Yeah.

Sol: OK, I'll try it.

5. *Helping the Offended to Speak Up: Step Two—Speaking to the Aggressor*
Note: Sol speaks to the children and to Luna. Luna only speaks to Sol. The Sol and Luna voices are now operating as the IF, who can always pause and get help from the children to know what to say or how to say it. Or, if a puppet character "gets it wrong," the kids may "stop" the action to coach Sol or Luna into a friendlier outcome. The OF sets up the role-play and then takes a backseat as the IF takes over.

OF: Luna, Sol would like to talk to you.

Sol: *(to Luna)* Luna, I feel sad.

Luna: So?

Sol: *(to children)* See, I knew she wouldn't listen to me!

OF: I think you should try again.

Sol: But what can I say now?

OF: *(to children)* What do you think?

Child: Say, listen to me and don't yell at me.

Sol: Luna, listen to me and don't yell at me. *(to children)* Am I saying that right?

Child: Say, "Please."

Another Child: Speak louder, so she can hear you.

Sol: *(to Luna)* Luna, please listen to me and please don't yell at me. *(to children)* Was that better?

Child: Yeah.

Luna: OK, I'm listening.

Sol: *(to children)* Ohhhh . . . she's listening. What should I say now?

Child: Say, "I'm sad."

Sol: *(to Luna)* I'm sad.

Luna: Why are you sad?

Sol: *(to children)* What should I say now?

Child: Say, "You pulled me and you yelled at me—you are not a good friend, Luna. You should say sorry."

Sol: *(to Luna)* Luna, you pulled me and yelled at me—you are not a good friend, Luna. You should say sorry.

Luna: I guess I did pull you. I guess I did yell at you. I was so angry.

Sol: I was sad and even scared when you did that.

Children: Say sorry!

OF: Who should say sorry?

Child: *(points to Luna)* That one.

Luna: *(to Sol)* I'm sorry, Sol. I pulled you and yelled because I lost my temper. I want you to me my friend. Did I hurt you?

Sol: Mostly you scared me.

Luna: I didn't mean to scare you. You are my friend, and I want to have a nice picnic together.

Sol: I do too.

6. Naming the Reasons for the Changed Atmosphere between the Characters

The OF readdresses the feelings of the characters and the skills used that changed the dynamic between them.

OF: OK, let's pause there for a minute. How is Sol feeling right now?

Child: Better.

OF: How is Luna feeling right now?

Child: She isn't angry. She is better too.

OF: Did Sol say what you wanted him to say?

Child: Yes.

OF: How good of a job did Luna do at listening to Sol?

Child: Not good at first, but she got better.

OF: You really helped Sol stand up for himself and speak what he was feeling! Thank you. Let's find out what happens next.

7. Puppets Practice What They Have Learned

The puppet show continues with the now friendlier puppets until the sun and shade conflict emerges again, but this time Luna uses what she has learned from the group to handle the situation better so there is no yelling and pulling. Yet, the show comes to a standstill again because the *problem* of the sun and shade still exits.

8. Identifying the Problem

Once the children stop the show again, the OF identifies that Luna is taking their advice, but the practical problem remains. The OF helps the group to readdress the practical problem, asking for suggestions.

OF: They are getting along better. Luna isn't yelling or pulling. But they still have a problem. What does Luna want? *(To sit in the shade)* What does Sol want? *(To sit in the sun)* Why do you think Luna does not want to sit in the sun? Why do you think that Sol does not want to sit in the shade? Let's find out.

9. Solving the Problem

The OF first orchestrates asking the puppets about their preferences or reasons (answers may include Luna is afraid of sunburn, Sol will feel cold, etc.), then takes a variety of suggestions for either Luna or Sol and carefully chooses one to try "for now." Note: It is important at this point to take a variety of ideas up front and save a few to try out later. If only one idea is identified and tried out, the children think that the problem is solved and will offer no more ideas, even if the action is "rolled back" to try again.

OF: Luna, can you tell us why you *want* to sit in the shade and not the sun? Same for you, Sol. We had some ideas about why you don't want to sit in the shade and only the sun. Can you tell us your reasons? What can Luna or Sol do to solve their problem and still be friends?
Children: (Offer lots of ideas)
OF: I am hearing lots of ideas. Let's list them. I hear that Sol and Luna can take turns sitting in the sun and the shade. Luna can sit in the sun with an umbrella. They also can find a place near a tree where Sol is the sun and Luna is in the shade. Sol can wear a sweater so she won't get cold in the shade. Sol and Luna can say sorry.

Then, the OF chooses the idea and speaks it aloud so that the puppeteer (IF) knows which one to try out between both puppets (with coaching from the children, as appropriate). Sometimes the OF chooses an idea that may not work, such as "just say sorry" or "make them both sit in the sun," and then directs the puppeteer to try the idea so the group can see the consequences in action.

10. Children Stand In as the Voice of a Puppet

To show another idea, or at a later intervention point, the OF might "roll back the action" to try again. At this point, the OF might ask a child with an idea to volunteer and come up to become the voice of one of the puppets. The child, as one puppet, and the puppeteer (IF), as the other, try out the ideas with the support of the OF standing by. As mentioned before, the IF needs to challenge the children somewhat so that that the problem isn't too easy to solve or overly "magical."

OF: Let's try, the "Sol can wear a sweater" idea. Would you like to come up and speak for one of the puppets? *(The child who had the idea nods and comes up.)* Who should have the idea? Luna *(points to puppet)* or Sol *(points to puppet)*?

Child: Sol.

OF: So you put your hand on Sol. You will speak for the puppet. Let's try it. You say, "Hello," as Sol.

Child: Hello *(puppeteer moves the puppet's mouth as the child speaks)*.

OF: *(to child)* See how it works? Do you remember your idea? OK, so when we start, the other puppet will speak first, then your puppet. Are you ready, puppets? OK, everybody, let's give them a one, two, three, action! Here we go.

All: One, two, three, action!

Luna: But I want to sit in the shade! Do you have an idea, Sol?

Child: *(as Sol's voice with hand on puppet)* Wear a sweater.

Luna: Who should wear a sweater? Me or you?

Child: *(as Sol)* Me.

Luna: Oh, you will wear a sweater and sit in the shade with me?

Child: *(as Sol)* Yeah.

Luna: Well, that is very nice of you to do that. Do you have a sweater?

Child: *(as Sol)* Yeah.

Luna: Where is it? I don't see a sweater.

Child: *(as Sol)* It's here.

Luna: I didn't know that you were carrying a sweater. *(Sol pantomimes putting on a sweater)* I didn't even see it. Maybe I should get glasses. Oh, that looks very nice on you, Sol. How does it feel?

Child: *(as Sol)* It's soft.

Luna: See, isn't this nice in the shade?

Child: *(as Sol)* Yeah.

OF: Freeze *(to stop the show)*. Excellent. Let's give our friend here a hand, everybody.

11. Validating the Effort/Reflecting on the Solution

The OF validates the effort of the child who offered or role-played the suggestion.

OF: Did you try your idea? How did it go? Thanks for your idea!

The OF checks in with the group about the problem.

OF: Did that idea change something? What changed? Why do you think it changed *(if age appropriate)*?

An Alternate Pathway in the Sequence

The intervention process may take any number of given pathways given what the children seem interested in examining—or what the classroom teacher has determined is important. For example, we might focus on finding ways to help the aggressor, Luna, calm down so that she can communicate better, or we might "coach" the aggressor in effective communication styles (or do both if the children are fully engaged and can sit through the entire process). We have included an example of this second pathway so that you have an example of a different option. In this sequence, the action is "rolled back" to offer the children opportunities to further coach Luna. (This sequence would begin after the group has identified and tried on the feelings of both characters, as outlined above.)

Sequence for Managing Anger

The OF engages the group in identifying ideas that support helping the aggressor calm down.

> *OF*: *(to children)* My friends, Luna just said she is really angry. When we are really angry, sometimes we need to calm down before we can talk to anyone. What are some actions that Luna can do to calm down before she speaks to Sol?
> *Child*: She could count to ten.
> *Another Child*: She could eat ice cream.
> *OF*: OK. Let's talk directly to Luna and tell her these things. Luna?
> *Luna*: What?
> *OF*: The performers and I understand that you are really angry.
> *Luna*: I am angry.
> *OF*: We have some ideas to help you calm down. Would you be willing to try them out?
> *Luna*: I guess so.
> *OF*: *(to Luna)* OK. *(to child)* Would you tell Luna your idea to calm down?
> *Child*: Count to 10.
> *OF*: *(to Luna)* We will help you, Luna. *(to all)* Let's try it all together. Here we go . . .
> *All*: One, two, three, four, five, six, seven, eight, nine, ten!
> *OF*: How are you feeling now Luna?
> *Luna*: Maybe a little bit angry.
> *OF*: *(to child)* What was your idea to help Luna calm down?
> *Child*: Eat ice cream.
> *Luna*: I love ice cream
> *OF*: *(to child)* What is your favorite flavor?
> *Child*: Strawberry.

Luna: Mine too.

OF: Here you go. *(hands Luna pretend ice cream)* Let's all eat ice cream together. *(all pretend)*

Luna: That ice cream was delicious.

OF: How are you feeling now, Luna?

Luna: Better—hey, not so angry. Those ideas you had really worked. Thank you.

OF: Good. Are you ready to talk to Sol now?

This process continues until the character is communicating more effectively and the action—in this case, the puppet show—can continue.

Note: Obviously, time and the children's patience and abilities will be a factor in this process, and remember there is always another intervention point to be explored in the larger puppet scenario. That second point can be used to focus on the character that was less in the spotlight before, to touch on what was left out of the first, or to reinforce what was learned. Either way, the sequence has to remain energized, focused, clear, and fun or the children will lose interest.

Modes of Facilitation: A Closer Look

The program has identified three modes in which the OF and the IF gather and use the children's ideas within the intervention process. In ascending level of challenge, exposure, and complexity, they include the following:

- *Facilitation of children's ideas with puppet reenactment/enactment.* The OF gathers a number of suggestions from the children and identifies a suggestion for the puppets to act out. The OF communicates to the puppeteer the suggestion that will be enacted and at what point in the scenario the reenactment should begin. The puppeteer then enacts the suggestions without further input from the children.
- *Direct communication with the puppets (guiding/ facilitating).* The IF, as one of the puppets, turns out to the audience, asks them for advice, and then enacts their suggestions. The OF facilitates the puppets and the children through this interaction and questions the children about the effectiveness of their ideas. It is then up to the IF as a puppet to ask the children for guidance and advice
- *Replacement/role-play.* The OF gathers suggestions from the audience, identifies a suggestion to try out, and asks an individual child to use his or her own idea and speak for one of the puppets. The OF carefully directs the child to put a hand on the puppet in order to become the puppet's voice. They practice with "hello" first and then proceed. At

this point, the IF takes over to carefully improvise with students drawing out the most sophisticated thinking possible.

Taking Extra Care

Within the replacement/role-play process, the Early Learning Program has developed strategies for scaffolding child participation so even very shy and less verbal children are able to be successful. We have identified that sometimes shy or less verbal children need a quite structured experience in order to feel safe and become ready to offer their ideas.

These safety mechanisms entail slowing down the intervention process and adding one-on-one coaching by the OF (e.g., when inviting a child up, the OF invites the child to state his or her idea aloud just before role-playing with the other puppet and lets the child know that the other puppet will speak first so not to worry). If the child suddenly becomes very shy, the OF might coach the child to place his or her hand on the OF's shoulder and whisper the idea to him. Then the OF would place his or her hand on the puppet and say the idea (word for word) to the puppet. The OF would constantly check back with the child to make sure that he was passing on the accurate idea or information.

The following is an example of such an exchange:

OF: Would you like to try your idea?
Child: *(nods "yes")*
OF: Great. So step up here, next to the puppet. What is your idea again?
Child: *(whispers)* Taking turns.
OF: OK. Who do you want to have the idea? Luna *(pointing to puppet)* or Sol *(pointing to puppet)*?
Child: That one *(pointing to Luna)*.
OF: OK, you put your hand on Luna, and let's practice saying "hello" first—so say, "Hello."
Child: Hello *(puppet's mouth moves in unison)*.
OF: That works great. So when we start, Sol will speak first. Are you ready Sol? *(Sol nods)* Let's begin with a one, two, three, action from the class.
Children: One, two, three, action!
Sol: I don't know what to do! What is your idea, Luna?
Child: *(gets shy, takes hand off puppet, and moves away)*
OF: Do you want to put your hand on Luna and speak for him?
Child: *(hides head)*
OF: I have an idea. Why don't you whisper your idea to me, and then I will tell your idea as Luna? Would you like to try this? *(child nods)* Let's practice again with "hello."—First, you whisper "hello" to me, and we will see if it works.
Child: *(whispers)* Hello.

OF: *(as Luna)* Hello.

Sol: Luna, why are you telling me "hello"? We need some ideas here! *(Obviously, the IF has to be skilled enough to be on her toes to handle whatever the situation; here she must stay "true" to portraying the puppet character of Sol.)*

OF: *(to child)* Oh, it's working! Look. See? Sol heard us.

Sol: What is your idea, Luna?

OF: *(to child)* What is your idea again?

Child: *(whispering to OF)* Take turns.

OF: *(as Luna)* Sol, we should take turns.

Sol: Do you mean take turns sitting in the sun and the shade?

OF: *(to child)* Is this what you mean?

Child: Yes.

OF: *(as Luna)* Yes.

Sol: Hmm . . . that's a good idea. Luna, will you come and sit in the sun with me first?

OF: *(to child)* What do you think?

Child: Yes.

OF: *(as Luna)* Yes.

Sol: Good. You come sit over here with me for two hours, and then I will sit in the shade with you.

OF: *(to child)* Two hours. Does Luna like the sun?

Child: No.

OF: Do you think she would be willing to sit in the sun for two hours?

Child: No.

OF: *(to child)* How long?

Child: *(shrugs)*

OF: Lets look at the clock up there. How many minutes?

Child: Five.

OF: *(as Luna)* Five minutes, Sol.

Sol: Only five minutes? OK. Then I will sit in the shade with you for five minutes, too. Let's try it. Sit by me in the sun. *(pretends five minutes go by)* Now I'm going to sit by you in the shade. *(pretends five minutes go by)*

OF: Freeze *(to stop the show)*. *(to child)* Did we try your idea?

Child: Yes.

OF: How is it working?

Child: Good.

Scaffolding child participation in this manner supports pedagogy of classroom equality in that extra steps are taken to assure that children of differing verbal abilities and temperaments are able to participate. Also, by offering them extra care, shy children are able to be successful speaking aloud in a public forum, thereby building this important skill.

Problematizing

Even with these young students, Paolo Freire's concept of problematization was ever present within the intervention work. Freire, the celebrated author of the seminal work *Pedagogy of the Oppressed*, states that, "Problematization is a critical and pedagogical dialogue or process and may be considered 'demythicisation.' Rather than taking the common knowledge 'myth' of a situation for granted, problematization poses that knowledge as a problem allowing new viewpoints, consciousness, reflection, hope, and action to emerge." (Crotty 2004)

Speaking of *problematizing*, Chris Vine (2006) further clarifies that "for Freire the challenge was always to present reality in a way that makes us look at it anew. If this can be done, we might see that our problems, or perhaps the *causes* of our problems, are different than we first thought and therefore require different solutions than those we are traditionally encouraged to pursue. In this sense, Freire's concern that we should read the world—think critically to analyze the bigger picture—is very different than the usual utilitarian, *common sense* quick-fix orientated approach that looks at each problem—and its solution—mechanistically and in isolation."

For example, in a puppet intervention sequence, when the children offer, "Say sorry" to the characters as a pat response to the request for a possible solution, we challenge them to think more thoroughly about the situation in order to think beyond this often automatic, possibly "teacher-pleasing" response. When the children are able to look at the situation more completely, they come to understand that saying sorry, if said truthfully, may somewhat repair hurt feelings but won't ultimately solve the problem at hand. Most importantly, they are freed up to think of a host of imaginative ideas that may ultimately serve the situation better.

In order to put Freire's system of problematizing into action, generally the facilitators use a sequence of questions to clarify the issue for the young people and then challenge them. The trick is to gently push back and challenge a response in such a way that you are validating it at the same time. For example, the actor-teacher might ask, "Tell me why the puppet might say sorry right now," or "If the puppet says sorry, what will that do exactly? . . . And then what?" In this sense, students, while thinking more deeply, are engaged in meaningful discussion as they are prompted to explain and describe their point or idea.

Differences and Similarities between Classical
Boal Forum Theatre and Puppet Intervention

In classic Forum Theatre techniques, one character is *oppressed* by another. The objective of the intervention is to activate the oppressed character's options with the goal of changing the outcome of the scenario. This provides the spect-actors an opportunity to practice solutions they might try in "real life," to pre-view the possible consequences, and to evaluate the viability of solutions. This work is part of dismantling oppressive social and political structures.

Within puppet intervention work, the term oppressor has actually been changed to aggressor in order to de-emphasize the power relationship (such as parent–child, teacher–student, government official–citizen) conveyed by the terms oppressor and oppressed. The puppet or human characters depicted in intervention scenarios for young children are typically in peer relationships (friends, coworkers, teammates) rather than those defined by social power, as these are the relationships that they have the power to impact. Young children also rely heavily on the adults in their lives to be authority figures. Because young children need adults to have power over them, their intervention on these relationships would not be useful!

In each or either form of intervention, all spect-actors, whether adults or children, need to feel a sense of outrage at the oppression or aggression occurring "onstage" for them to stop the action and offer alternate possibilities. However, we have observed that young children are often more concerned with correcting "bad behavior" portrayed by the aggressor. To that end, it is sometimes more developmentally age appropriate to intervene for both the aggressor and the offended and, at other times, to intervene for only the aggressor. For example, often when young children intervene within the Luna and Sol scenario, at the first intervention point, they usually seek to modify Luna's aggressive behavior, rather than helping Sol speak up for himself. Nonetheless, they do become a kind of spokesperson for the "oppressed" Sol and have the opportunity to practice what they might say in Sol's position by revealing feelings or offering ideas to solve the problem of how or where to have a their picnic.

Also within the traditional Forum structures, scenarios are generally rewound to the action before the conflict and then replayed with suggested changes. In puppet intervention, we can either quickly assess the emotions of characters and then rewind to focus on the issue or dilemma that precipitated the emotional escalation, or we can stay in the moment and spend more time helping the characters handle their heightened emotions (i.e., identify them, speak them aloud with "I feel" phrases, and generally calm down). Once the characters have regained communication, *then* we can focus on the dilemma or issue at hand, by soliciting ideas to solve the dilemma or issue that caused the emotions to reel out of control in the first place.

What Are Young Children Learning?

Overall, the purpose of puppet intervention is to engage three- through seven-year-old children and their teachers in theatrical conventions designed to develop and reinforce children's skills such as meaningful talk, expressing and discussing feelings, projecting possible consequences, and problem solving.

A number of years ago, the Early Learning Program demonstrated a puppet intervention sequence that focused on conflict resolution for a group of colleagues in a TIE national preconference at New York University. We decided to bring in a group of kindergartners for the demonstration to offer conference-goers as authentic an experience as possible. In order to make the experience a success, actor-teachers worked with the children in their classrooms for three sessions before the preconference, and the children were primed to know that observers would be watching them participate in their final session of the drama.

Initially all went well. The children seemed focused and engaged. Then, seemingly out of nowhere, a boy turned and socked a girl in the stomach really hard. The girl wailed, then turned and hit him back. The actor-teachers stopped the intervention sequence, de-roled, and, once they and the classroom teacher assessed that the students were physically OK, tried to use the incident as a teaching moment. However, there were just too many variables and the stakes were too high for them to be successful. Some of the colleagues who were watching immediately jumped to the conclusion that this form of conflict resolution just didn't work with young children given evidence of what they had just witnessed.

Drama work of this nature, however, should not be considered a quick fix, nor can we expect such lofty goals. It is unrealistic to expect that children will internalize these strategies so quickly that they successfully navigate their own conflicts. In fact, we might say that this falls into Boal's realm of "magical solutions." Whatever was happening in that boy's real life had far more impact on him then two and a half drama sessions—as exciting and fun as they might have been.

Program objectives set for the children must be relevant and possible to accomplish within the scope of the experience being offered. Therefore, what we can and do expect is that children will *be introduced* to a host of conflict resolution strategies and principles and gain practice for life situations. For example, by watching for changes in body language and voice and then stopping the action of a puppet show, young children are learning how to "decode" the telltale signs of escalation so that they can become familiar with initial moments in conflict that have possibility for change.

By helping a character calm down so that he or she can talk more effectively, children are offering suggestions and practicing a skill that can be used in a variety of life situations. Identifying and discussing strong feelings of the puppets or human characters also brings to focus some of the ways these feelings affect one's ability to think clearly and solve problems effectively. Additionally, by witnessing the actions of a bully, students more prone to bullying are provided with opportunities to imagine consequences and hear what their fellow students think about this behavior.

In puppet intervention, children are given practice navigating problems and their emotional fallout. When young children are involved in concrete action, they are able to think about the problems posed and possible resulting consequences, and thus offer workable solutions. So when they put their ideas into action with the puppets, they are able to experience the consequences of their suggestions and make adjustments accordingly. Puppet intervention also allows them to witness the playing out of ideas that might not or don't work. For example, we return again to that often-universal idea of "say sorry." It doesn't always work when it is played out in action, so facilitators encourage children to think beyond this pat response to find more pertinent, actable solutions.

Children are also being introduced to new words to define emotions in order to stretch their vocabulary. Young children usually classify feelings as bad, sad, mad, and happy, though they actually have a richer understanding of emotional nuance. Words such as frustration or surprise are those they can understand and talk about when they are introduced to the children through expressive action.

Over the years, a number of teachers have expressed to the Early Learning Program staff that some children are using tools that they learned in puppet intervention to begin to mediate conflicts between their peers. For example, one teacher observed the following at recess on the playground. Two children were fighting, a third child, nearby turned to them and told them to, "Stop! You are being like the puppets. You need to learn like Luna and Sol did."

Actor-Teacher Training for Puppeteering and Facilitation

Working more deeply with puppets and intervention forced us, as program directors, to offer our actor-teachers additional training. We were fortunate that, each fall, the CAT staff hunkered down for five weeks of training and rehearsal to devise and refine curricula for the coming year. Comprehensive training for actor-teachers changed to include developing puppeteer skills as well as more sophisticated facilitation.

From 1995 to 2004, the number of program staff varied from year to year; usually there were between eight and twelve full-time actor-teachers training to implement the curricula. The program also employed one or two "swings" to work as substitutes for actor-teachers when needed. Each year, the mix of seasoned and new staff posed its own set of unique rewards and challenges.

After a lot of experimentation over the years, we decided that larger "Muppet-like" hand puppets with malleable faces and mouths that could show a whole array of emotions were the most effective for intervention purposes.

However, a Muppet-like puppet show requires specific artistry and a skill set to show that the puppets are neither inanimate, staid objects, nor are they overblown stereotypes. Puppets should be lively, engaging, yet "believable" characters. So we moved toward offering our staff opportunities to deepen their artistry. We employed a gifted and wonderfully inventive puppeteer, Spica Cheng, who designed the puppets and trained the actor-teachers in a variety of skills.

Cheng began by undoing bad habits. Initially, the actor-teachers tended to move the puppets around too much and were pronouncing every syllable of every word. Spica helped the actor-teachers choose essential movements and learn to manipulate the puppet's mouths in order to emphasize only certain syllables. Being specific with eye contact and focus was essential, too; the large dance mirrors in the rehearsal studio turned out to be very useful to this end. It was important that a puppet character be able to "look" at a specific student or to the group when addressing each respectively. Consequently, holding the puppets to achieve this took real effort. Spica even offered strengthening exercises to build arms, wrists, and fingers for better endurance and control. It was equally important that when the puppet was speaking, the puppeteer's focus be on the puppet, which signaled to children "this is where to look."

The puppeteers also had the difficult, albeit wonderful, acting challenge of playing *both* puppet characters of an intervention sequence. Consequently, they had to build their vocal abilities and ranges in order to develop clear, distinct, and sustainable puppet voices. Along with this, the puppeteers also needed to learn how to illustrate conflicts between the two puppets with physical clarity and good timing. Just as with good stage combat, the action had to slow down yet remain urgent, with distinct physical and vocal cues planted accurately to distinguish clearly what was happening between the characters.

Since the OF had the job of orchestrating every step of the process while trying to make educational meaning out of the fun, it was imperative that they understood or learned how to clarify and set up each step of the process. For example, the OFs must be able to do the following:

- Establish and practice clear audience guidelines of participation
- Effectively gather ideas from the twenty-five or more children
- Choose an idea to try out
- Decide where to roll the scene back to

- Establish clear cues such as deciding who will speak first and how to signal to the puppeteer that it is time to move on to the next beat of the puppet scenario
- Support shy children

Both the OF and the puppeteer (the IF) had to develop their questioning skills in order to challenge, deepen, and explore the children's responses. Though it may seem natural to ask these kinds of inquisitive questions, this did not come naturally to the actor-teachers who were new to the process. With new material, we actually scripted a series of questions so they would scaffold one another. As actor-teachers grew more skillful, these scripts became only guidelines to help them stay focused on the objectives in each intervention sequence.

Further Development at Creative Arts Team

Intent to keep experimenting with puppet intervention techniques, we continued to incorporate it as a key strategy. For example, another TIE curriculum, *Tobago Reef*, incorporated puppet characters into the *entire* curriculum, thus offering several opportunities for puppet intervention moments to occur. Unlike with *Feria de Sevilla*, the device of a separate puppet show wasn't used to frame the intervention sequences; puppet characters existed like human characters as part of the story. The OF continued to be played by an actor-teacher–in-role in order to orchestrate the intervention experiences. Also, in *Tobago Reef*, no puppet curtains were used; the actor-teacher was always in full view, and even as such, the children accepted the puppets-in-role and usually didn't try to interact with the actor-teacher playing the puppets.

Currently, under the new directorship of Helen Wheelock, a former actor-teacher with over ten years experience in the classroom, the Early Learning Program has begun to look at still other roles puppets can serve while offering opportunities for intervention.

Wheelock (2007) writes,

In "Coyote's Surprise," puppets were used to help the character of Coyote (teaching artist in-role) express her feelings of jealousy and anger when the arrival of a new baby bear disrupts her relationship with her best friend, Bear (teaching artist in-role), and the little bears (students-in-role).

Using a bear and coyote puppet, Coyote presents a show about the fun times Bear and she had together until, as the Coyote-puppet says, "things changed." Now, every time coyote-puppet invites Bear to go have fun, an increasingly dismissive bear-puppet says, "No! I've got to take care of the baby." This prompts coyote-puppet to say, "I guess Bear doesn't want to be my friend any more."

Incensed, the "real" Bear stops the show, and demands to speak to Coyote. Unwilling to confront Bear, she retreats behind the coyote-puppet, using it to "voice" her confusion and frustration. Bear turns to the little bears and asks if they can come up with different ways they can take care of baby bear and still have fun with Coyote. Somewhat unconvinced, Coyote uses the bear and coyote puppets to practice their suggestions, turning to the little bears for support and clarification whenever possible. Eventually, with the support of the bear family, Coyote herself actively tries out these solutions with the actual baby bear (a large teddy bear) and a measure of balance is restored.

Conclusions

Boal has internalized Freire's theories of problematizing and has incorporated these ideas into practical theatre techniques that have greatly influenced the work of CAT, at large, and puppet intervention within the Early Learning Program, in particular. Puppet intervention was one of the conventions developed at CAT to foster the company mission, which is, in part, to always place the young people—their ideas, reflections, feelings, and musings—at the center of the educational experience.

Augusto Boal's Forum Theatre work was originally developed for a particular population at a particular time and, consequently, had to be adapted and combined with other influences to be successful within an educational setting, particularly in New York City and specifically for ages three to seven. In the case of puppet intervention, developmentally appropriate practice guided the adaptation of Forum Theatre techniques to meet the abilities, needs, and interests of the target population.

In order to implement complex theatrical conventions such as puppet intervention effectively, theatre education professionals have to be trained adequately in theatre and facilitation skills. Within the Early Learning Program at CAT, we had to assess and identify specific training needs and provide actor-teacher staff with additional, ongoing training in both puppeteering and facilitation. As an outcome of this additional training, actor-teachers became more proficient in the work overall. Program challenges continued to revolve around how to find methods or systems to support successful training of new practitioners and yet allow seasoned staff to be able to experiment with possible future directions.

Puppet intervention, in the very best sense, is "learning by doing." It is a resourceful, educational method that, when implemented with care, may raise children's awareness regarding the roots of conflict and sensitize them to feelings as well possible choices in solving these dilemmas. If a child is able first to stop, breathe, and then think, his or her behavior has been impacted.

Trina Fischer, one of the program's former actor-teachers, wrote the following for a presentation on puppet intervention we made some time ago:

"These skills, we would argue, are initial, necessary stepping stones towards being assertive adults who will stand up for their rights and the rights of others. We are working on exploring the roots of oppression, and we enact situations with peers in conflict, as these are situations they as young children have the power to change" (Dishy et al. 2006).

Notes

Of important note: Some of the information included within this chapter has been taken from handouts that CAT created for training and conference presentation purposes. Andrea Dishy, Christina Fischer, Helen Wheelock, and Karina Naumer wrote these original handouts.

We gratefully acknowledge the past and present actor-teachers of the City University of New York/CAT/NYC Wolf Trap Program: Early Learning through the Arts for their contributions, commitment, and creativity in helping develop and refine puppet intervention. We especially acknowledge Chris Vine, CAT's artistic and education director, for his mentorship and suggestions regarding the final draft of this chapter. We also acknowledge the following actor-teachers for their long-term contributions: Steve Elm, Trina Fischer, Max Ryan, and Helen Wheelock (now program director), as well as the many other talented CAT actor-teachers whose skills and dedication contributed to this work.

1. The Creative Arts Team/New York City Wolf Trap Program: Early Learning Through the Arts is one of the Creative Arts Team's five residency programs. It is also one of the Wolf Trap Institute's fifteen regional sites. Founded in 1981, the institute provides arts-in-education services for children ages three to five and their teachers and families through the disciplines of drama, music, and movement.

2. *The Paul A. Kaplan Center for Educational Drama*, formally of New York University, is now housed with the City University of New York's School of Professional Studies. Chris Vine teaches several courses for the Kaplan Center.

References

Boal, Augusto. 1992. *Games for actors and non-actors*. London: Routledge.

Crotty, Michael J. 2004. Describing Freire. In *Foundations of social research: Meaning and perspective in the research process*, 155–56. London: Sage.

Dishy, Andrea, Trina Fischer, Karina Naumer, and Helen Wheelock. 2006. *Using puppetry as a means to cope with conflict in the early childhood classroom*. Handout for Theatre of the Oppressed Conference at the University of North Carolina, Chapel Hill, NC.

Vine, Chris. 2006. Quote from a private conversation with him at Creative Arts Team, New York City, NY.

Wheelock, Helen. 2007. *Description of puppet intervention in Coyote's Surprise*. Private collection, Creative Arts Team.

2

Exploring the Stigmatized Child through Theatre of the Oppressed Techniques

Johnny Saldaña

The purpose of this chapter is to profile a case study experience from a larger fieldwork project in Theatre of the Oppressed (TO) with fourth- and fifth-grade children (Saldaña 2005). One primary goal of the study was to explore how young people at the upper-elementary school levels responded to session content with Boal's Games, Image Theatre, and Forum Theatre—techniques often described in print for adult participants but rarely for youth. The most important goal of the project, however, was to provide children opportunities through TO to explore how their personal oppressions, such as victimization from bullying, could be recognized and dealt with in the classroom and on the playground.

A team of five adult facilitators from Arizona State University worked in a neighborhood elementary school's classrooms over an eight-week period in 2000 to facilitate and document their experiences and children's responses to selected Boalian theatrical forms. Before the study began, I interviewed participating fourth- and fifth-grade teachers to explain the goals of the project, to describe the nature and purposes of TO, and to gather ideas from them for session content. One story in particular from a fifth-grade teacher struck me, not just as an idea for a Forum Theatre event, but as a story hauntingly similar to my own childhood experiences with stigmatization from peers:

> *Teacher*: We've got a little girl in here—she looks different and she acts differ-
> ent, so they'll make up some name that they call her . . . It seems like every
> year there's one kid that gets picked on more than somebody else, because
> they're different, because they might look different, they might act differ-
> ent . . . Like with her *(pointing to a child's desk)*. I've watched them actually

walk by this little girl and purposely bump into her or something like that, but then, even though you're watching them, the kid'll turn around and say, "Well, I didn't do that," after you confront him.

Johnny: What kinds of differences do kids tend to target?

Teacher: With this one student, the kids seem to zero in because she did look different . . . You know, once they have this idea that something's wrong with them, or they don't like them, then when they start to interact with the kid . . . they're not accepting . . . But most of the other kids in this room have been together for years, so she's brand new . . . and so it's the [new] ones. They're kind of not fitting in because they weren't with this group as they moved on through school.

Johnny: Like a newcomer?

Teacher: Uh-huh, I think it *is* like a newcomer thing . . . It's basically the new ones.

I resonated with this story because, like the young girl, I too was a newcomer to one particular school during my childhood and felt lonely and isolated from brand-new classmates. I was also grossly overweight as a child and frequently teased and cruelly taunted by others for my physical appearance. Bullies intimidated and threatened me on the playground and in the classroom. There were many days I pretended to be sick so I would not have to go to school to face the humiliating verbal abuse from my peers.

Sarah's Stigmatization

In the teacher's account above, the young girl—whom I'll name Sarah (pseudonym)—had no distinguishing physical differences from others. She was of average height and weight for her grade level, wore glasses (as did a few others in her classroom), had long brown hair and plain facial features, and was, from my interactions with her, a pleasant young girl. The ostracizing Sarah received from peers was most likely due to her outsider status as a newcomer to the school and classroom cultures, her academic intelligence, and perhaps what might be attributed as, from children's perceptions, her mildly "nerdy" physical appearance.

A few weeks before the TO study began, I conducted ethnographic fieldwork at the school site to acquaint myself with its staff, students, and ways of working. I observed a schoolwide talent show assembly presented in the elementary school's cafeteria. The dancing, singing, and other acts performed by children varied in quality and most received enthusiastic applause. But one particularly poor presentation was a karate demonstration by three boys, choreographed to the Village People's *Macho Man*. Their work appeared as if it had been underrehearsed, and their discomfort, nervousness, and embarrassment performing in front of others led them to laugh and "goof around" onstage throughout the song. Their work received mild applause accompanied by "boos" from older child audience members, whom teachers quickly admonished.

Sarah was one of the few children at the talent show who performed solo with a new-age folk dance performance set to recorded music. I myself found her work to be of exceptional quality with good energy and presence. But despite the excellent work, she too received "boos" from her classmates. Again, teachers verbally admonished children for their inappropriate response. At the time, I was unable to rationalize why Sarah received disapproval until I later interviewed Sarah's teacher, who told me the story included at the beginning of this chapter. Even though Sarah exhibited what I perceived as natural talent, she received undeserved negative response from peers.

Young participants in this study frequently labeled their perceptions of nonaverage appearances and behaviors in others as "weird"—the childhood equivalent of stigmatization. The stigmas attributed to Sarah inspired a particular TO session with her fifth-grade class: to examine oppression toward the newcomer. Certainly I was not going to explore with these children in just one hour the sociological complexities and dynamics of stigma meticulously described by Erving Goffman in his classic text (1963), but instead I focused on one of his operational definitions: "the situation of the individual who is disqualified from full social acceptance . . . reduced in our minds from a whole and usual person to a tainted, discounted one" (i, 3).

The TO project received both the host school's permission and our university's approval through its Institutional Review Board to conduct the study. However, we approached our work and this particular session cautiously. I did not state in Sarah's classroom that the Image and Forum Theatre work was inspired by or exclusively about her own plight. Instead, we designed the session to explore *fictional others* who have been stigmatized to provide a sense of comfortable distance for child participants. Banaszewski (2006) asserts that adult TO facilitators introduce and examine their personal yet hidden social agendas covertly and subtextually in the public school classroom. This particular session would be no exception.

The Session Design

Session Preparation

I had already been working with Sarah's fifth-grade class once a week for approximately four weeks before the session on stigma was conducted. The TO curriculum thus far consisted of selected Boalian games and introductory Image Theatre work to acquaint students with basic terms and concepts such as *power* and *oppression*. Forum Theatre would be the next technique explored, but I wanted children to observe adults facilitate and participate in this relatively complex improvisational form before they attempted it themselves. *Demonstration*, *modeling*, and *example* are common pedagogical methods for instructing new learning. Therefore, I asked two of the other four university facilitators working on the TO project, Michelle White and Emily Petkewich, to participate and serve as a Forum Theatre protagonist and antagonist, respectively, with myself as the Joker.

Sarah's story as the stigmatized newcomer, recounted by her teacher, lent itself to Forum Theatre scenario construction—particularly the passage, "I've watched [students] actually walk by this little girl and purposely bump into her." I recalled Augusto Boal, at a Pedagogy and Theatre of the Oppressed plenary session, illustrate an elegant activating scene. He portrayed the antagonist who turned away from and folded his arms in indignation in response to the protagonist, who had approached him with a smile and an extended hand to greet him. Our Forum Theatre work would begin with the female adults portraying two elementary school students, one as the antagonist who would deliberately bump into the protagonist as they walked past each other. Emily was encouraged to portray the antagonist as "savvy" and slightly bullyish. Michelle was asked to portray the protagonist as a nice girl but reluctant to stand up for herself.

Midway through the study at the host elementary school, the university facilitators felt restricted adhering solely to Boalian theatrical techniques during our TO sessions. As drama educators, we were also acquainted with such dramatic structures (Neelands and Goode 2000) as "hot-seating," "teacher-in-role," "critical events," "role-reversal," and other improvisational forms that lent themselves readily to the praxis of TO. We modified our original charge to focus exclusively on Boal's techniques by integrating more developmentally appropriate dramatic methods for children. This was not perceived as "watering down" Boal, but rather enriching TO with a supplemental "arsenal" of tactics to employ when appropriate. For example, one of my own devices was a medium-sized cardboard cutout of a "thought balloon," commonly seen in print cartoons to reveal the inner monologue of a character. This visual aid had been used previously with Sarah's class to help children articulate the unspoken thoughts of people in sculpted images.

The activating scene, coupled with a variety of dramatic structures described above for more detailed examination of the issue, would eventually evolve into a one-hour session reminiscent of theatre-in-education, a hybrid form of performative content by adults, interspersed with child audience improvisational participation. The protagonist and antagonist actors were informed beforehand of the session's basic content and goals but knew that their in-class contributions would be truly improvisational as the children and I explored the issues surrounding stigma. As you'll read below in the "Instant Forum Theatre" section, there were several opportunities (or, in educational parlance, "teachable moments") in which new Forum Theatre scenarios were spontaneously constructed, based on ideas contributed by children.

It is difficult to prescribe or recommend to others "how" TO with youth gets designed. The predetermined plotting of this lesson, coupled with the spontaneous, in-class choices from the instructor's "mental rolodex" of dramatic structures, were the heuristics employed before and during the case study session described later in this chapter. In one sense, elementary school classroom drama educators already possess, by the nature of their training, the requisite facilitation skills of Boalian Jokers. Like a Forum Theatre event, we enter the space with a prepared script or scenario but must keep ourselves open to the unexpected and sometimes creative directions our class of young spect-actors takes us.

Documentation of the Session

Selected sessions of the TO project were videotaped to gather more detailed qualitative data for analysis. This particular session was recorded, since it would be the children's first experience with Forum Theatre. The single-camera placement provided an excellent visual record of the events, but children's soft voices were not always captured audibly on tape. Nevertheless, the recording enabled me to transcribe and thus quote most children's comments and to identify Sarah's specific contributions as a participant and spect-actor during the Forum Theatre scenes inspired by her classmates' oppression.

Narratives of TO with children are rare (and even rarer on video), so the extended description of our work in this chapter, written in the present tense, provides artists and educators a case study with selected details to vicariously experience this session on stigmatization.

Term Review and Warm-Up

Since I had not worked with Sarah's class for two weeks, I begin the session with a review of terms we previously explored, and I ask children for definitions or examples:

- *Oppression*: "Like, when someone gives you a hard time, does something bad"; "put-downs"
- *Power*: "Like, you're the ruler of something"; "You have control"; "You act like you're the best"
- *Images*: "Pictures of us sculpting"

We then review our sculpting techniques such as asking the person for permission first to touch and sculpt her, moving the person's body gently, mirroring an image for her to copy (especially for facial expressions), verbally telling her how to shape herself, and not pulling on a person's clothing to sculpt.

Afterward, I facilitate a physical warm-up with a grouping game from "The Space Series" (Boal 2002, 128). I tell children I do not want to explain why they will play the game but that they simply play as I observe. I direct them to group together by twos, then by threes, then fours, fives, and sixes. For the most part, they assemble and reassemble fairly quickly, but there is noticeable gender division since boys cluster primarily with boys and girls with girls. Sarah does not appear to have any difficulties participating in the game or finding a group. Afterward, I ask them to describe what went through their minds that influenced and affected their choices for who would be in which group: "Why did you decide to go with some people and not with others?" Children offer the following responses:

> *Boy*: Some people that were being mean to me and stuff.
> *Girl*: They're our friends.

I remark that factors such as these play an important role in deciding whom we choose to work and be friends with.

I then introduce them to the terms and their modified definitions that will serve as the focus for our session:

- *stigma*: "Something about the person that other people have decided isn't right" *(I use the example of my own overweight childhood)*; "But a stigma might also be for other reasons; maybe a stigma is something you *do* that other people may not like, and have decided 'You're not going to be a part of us anymore.'"
- *stigmatized*: "Someone who has a stigma"

Michelle and Emily, the adults who will portray the protagonist and antagonist, respectively, are introduced to the class as actors and teachers who will work with us today. (Michelle was asked beforehand to wear her reading glasses to the session since eyewear is sometimes a stigma among youth. Coincidentally, Michelle's clothing choices are light and soft textures, appropriate for the protagonist's character, while Emily, as the antagonist, wears a dark-colored wardrobe.)

Images of the Newcomer's Oppression

I ask for three volunteers to sculpt Michelle into someone who looks as if it is her first day in class at a new school in the middle of the academic year. Three girls are chosen, one of them Sarah, who not only raises her hand to volunteer but also waves it energetically for selection. I ask whether Michelle should stand or sit; Sarah says she should sit and gets a chair for her. Then, three other volunteers (all girls) are chosen to sculpt Emily as if she is a "regular" in this school who has attended it from the beginning. They, too, seat Emily, but sitting next to her is one of the volunteer girls as a classmate/friend.

Now that Michelle has been sculpted to look as if it is her first day at a new school (slouched, looking downward and downcast, with one arm crossed in front of her), the thought balloon is placed over her head, and I ask children to voice what she might be thinking or feeling. One example from a girl is "I don't have any friends, and I'm sad."

I read just Emily and her classmate friend's heads to look toward Michelle. The cardboard thought balloon cutout is placed over Michelle, and children contribute the following as her thoughts:

> *Girl*: I wonder what they're thinking about?
> *Girl*: They're looking at me weird.
> *Boy*: Maybe I should get to know them.
> *Girl*: Why are they staring at me?

Sarah offers, "I wonder if they're thinking about being my friend?"

I place the thought balloon over Emily, who is staring at Michelle, and I ask children a series of questions:

> *Johnny*: What if Emily looked at Michelle and wanted to stigmatize her? What if Emily got an immediate dislike of Michelle because of something? What might Emily say about Michelle that says, "I don't like her"? What *about* Michelle does Emily not like?

Children respond with the following:

> *Boy*: I don't like your hair.
> *Girl*: I don't like your glasses.
> *Girl*: She looks very quiet; she might not be an interesting person.
> *Boy*: I think she has "four eyes."

Sarah does not raise her hand to offer any ideas for Emily's image.

Emily and Michelle are prompted by me to stand and face each other approximately ten feet apart. Both are asked to voice a brief, inner monologue:

> *Michelle*: I'm so nervous, it's hard to be new and not have any friends and kinda scary.
> *Emily*: I don't think I wanna be friends with her; she has "four eyes."

The Activating Scene

I then ask the two women to dynamize their images by walking toward each other to see what will happen. Emily passes by Michelle and deliberately bumps into her, which draws gasps and giggles from the child spect-actors. I instinctively call out "Freeze," place the thought balloon over Michelle, and ask, "What is Michelle thinking or feeling?" Sarah is the first to raise her hand, and I call on her to respond: "Why in the world did she do that?" The thought balloon is then placed over Emily, and children are asked to voice her thoughts:

> *Girl*: That was funny.
> *Girl*: That was fun, let's do it again.
> *Girl*: She looked very funny.

As before, Sarah does not raise her hand to volunteer any ideas about Emily's thoughts.

> *Johnny*: Emily has stigmatized Michelle. But was there any good reason, I wonder?
> *A few children*: No.
> *Johnny*: Not to me. I don't know about you . . . Emily, in character, why did you stigmatize Michelle?
> *Emily*: 'Cause she's new, and she wears glasses, and I don't like her clothes.

The two actors then sit apart from each other yet stay in character for a brief "hot-seating" exchange. Children are invited to ask questions of the two characters, and Sarah raises her hand to ask Emily, with a slight tone of admonishment:

> *Sarah*: Why in the world are you judging someone like that? You should judge them by their attitude and not how they look—that wasn't right.
> *Emily*: I know, but I already have friends, and I don't need any more, so I really don't care.

Examples of questions for Michelle include the following:

> *Girl*: Were you thinking, "Why did she do that?"
> *Michelle*: Yeah, I smiled at her and she bumped into me. I don't know why.
> *Girl*: Is this someone you think you should avoid?
> *Michelle*: Um, maybe, I don't know. We're in the same class, but I don't know how much I can avoid her.
> *Boy*: Why didn't you stand up for yourself?
> *Michelle*: I was afraid. I don't know. She looks mean. She's kind of tough.

Sarah raises her hand periodically throughout the exchange above. I call on her to speak. Rather than ask a question of Michelle, though, she makes a statement:

> *Sarah:* You really shouldn't really mind much about how people think you look, as long you feel good about yourself.
> *Johnny (to Michelle):* But do you think you'd have the courage to do it?
> *Michelle:* Not right now. I move around a lot, so, I don't know . . .

The class and I briefly discuss the problems encountered by someone who moves frequently, such as readjustment to a new climate and the inability to make long-term friendships. I then walk toward Emily and ask the following:

> *Johnny:* Emily, do you care about Michelle?
> *Emily:* I don't even know her.
> *Johnny:* So I guess it's kind of hard to care about somebody if you don't know them. I guess I still don't understand why you hate her.
> *Emily:* Well, I don't "hate her," I just don't wanna be friends with her.
> *Johnny:* But you bumped into her. What was the reason for that?
> *Emily:* It was fun; it was funny. It made my other friends laugh.
> *Johnny (to the class):* We're going to have to find some ways to help Michelle. One of the things when we face oppression is that we can't always change the person who's giving us a hard time. We have to work sometimes, when we feel oppressed, on overcoming it and try to make *ourselves* feel better.

Simultaneous Dramaturgy

We replay the activating scene—Emily deliberately bumps into Michelle as they walk past each other. I solicit ideas from children to explore through Boal's simultaneous dramaturgy technique, which will later segue into Forum Theatre scenarios: "We're going to take the ideas that you've got and play them out and see if they work." A noticeable surge of excited talk and energy emerges from children with this proposal. One child recommends that Michelle push Emily back when Emily deliberately bumps into her. The idea is played out, but it escalates into a shoving match and verbal confrontation between the two women. I stop the fight saying, "Pushing back might not be the best idea."

Sarah has been waving her hand energetically before I ask if there is another idea to try out. When I call on her, she offers, "What if Michelle had somebody with her? After that happened, she would have someone to help her." Since an additional "character" for the activating scene is suggested by this idea, and since my way of working in Forum Theatre is to encourage the contributor to enact her own suggestion, I ask Sarah, "Can you volunteer to be that person?" Sarah nods then moves to take her place in the action. The activating scene is replayed. Emily deliberately bumps into Michelle, and Michelle walks toward Sarah:

> *Michelle*: Uh, hi. *(pointing to Emily)* See that girl over there? She's kind of unfriendly, and I really don't know how to handle it myself. Could you help me?
> *Sarah*: Sure!
> *Michelle*: OK, what do we do? *(they walk toward Emily)*
> *Sarah*: You just tell her you didn't like it; that's all.
> *Michelle*: And you'll come with me?
> *Sarah*: Uh-huh.

(There was a visually stunning moment on videotape when both Michelle and Sarah simultaneously brushed their hair back behind their ears as they dialogued. It was as if, for one fleeting moment, they were mirror images of each other.) The two reach Emily. Michelle looks at Sarah for help. Sarah smiles at Michelle and nods as if to encourage her to speak:

> *Michelle (to Emily)*: Um, why did you push me? I didn't like it.
> *Emily*: I don't know. I just thought it was funny.
> *Sarah*: It wasn't very funny, 'cause if you do it a lot harder, you could really hurt her.
> *Emily*: But I didn't push very hard.
> *Michelle*: You could have.
> *Emily*: It was an accident.

I stop the action at this point (in retrospect, a bit too early; I should have let the scene continue) and ask the group, "How did that idea work?" Children collectively respond with "Good," yet one girl rightly observes, "But there's still some problems," since Emily denied that her bumping was deliberate. I offer that Sarah's idea was a start to reconciling the problem and one possible solution to Michelle's oppression. When I ask children if there are any other ideas to try out, children now take the problem to other settings in their school milieu: the cafeteria and the playground.

Instant Forum Theatre

A girl suggests that Michelle join Emily at lunch and try to start a conversation. My original plan was to forum only the activating scene, but the new idea and its setting sound inspiring so I accept the scenario. Chairs are arranged to suggest a lunch table, and the suggestion is played out. Emily and a child cast as her friend chat with each other about boys during lunch. Michelle asks if she can sit at the table with them. The friends half-heartedly say, "Yes," but both ignore Michelle afterward. Emily offers to her friend that they play four-square after school. Michelle asks if she can join the game— she was quite good at it at her previous school—but Emily coolly remarks that they already have enough people.

I stop the scene noting that Michelle made a concerted effort to become friends with Emily, but I ask the children what else happened. The children observe that the rejection continued. One girl suggests that Michelle get contact lenses so she won't be a "four eyes," but I counter with, "I wonder if her family can afford that?" Michelle, in-role, says that her family just moved here and her father got a new job, so there is probably not enough money to make that happen. Then, the following dialogue occurs:

> *Girl*: She should maybe look for someone else to be friends with.
> *Johnny*: So just avoid Emily altogether?
> *Girl*: Well, not avoid her, but you know, if it's not working out, then she should find someone that it does work out with. She shouldn't be mean to her; she should just be friendly still.

Another girl suggests, "Maybe, when they're playing four-square, she can just go up and play or ask different people if they want to play."

A new Forum Theatre scenario has been proposed. I seek two volunteers to set up the space with Emily and her friend to play four-square. Several children, including Sarah, eagerly wave their hands and call out "Me, me!" I select two boys closest to the presentation space. When the area is established, the four friends play as Michelle comes by to ask if she can join. Emily replies that they already have four players. Michelle then asks if she can play with them tomorrow, but Emily seems reluctant to commit to her request. Michelle acknowledges the rejection and ends the scene by saying meekly that she will find others to play with.

After a brief discussion of the oppression, children are asked to replace Michelle and try out their ideas in this scenario. Sarah raises her hand for selection, but I feel the need to call on others to maximize participation. I ask a girl to replace Michelle and select three other girls to join Emily as her fellow four-square players:

> *Protagonist girl*: Hi, can I play ball?
> *Emily*: Well, we're in the middle of a game. *(to her four-square friends)* This girl wants to play with us.
> *Antagonist Girl 1*: I don't know. She's funny looking.
> *Antagonist Girl 2*: I don't know if she can play.
> *Johnny*: Why? Let me stop you.

The interruption is an instinctive act on my part to examine the rejection from the antagonist's perspective through "hot-seating":

Johnny: Why can't she play? Why won't you let her play?
Antagonist Girl 2: I don't know her or anything. She shouldn't be playing this game. We don't know her.
Johnny: Aren't you supposed to be working together, to help people make friends? Why all of a sudden are you stigmatizing her?
Antagonist Girl 2: I don't know.
Johnny: If you don't know, then why are you doing it? *(silence)* You don't have an answer for me, do you? If you don't know why you're doing it, then why are you doing it?
Antagonist Girl 1: What if she's different?
Johnny: *So what* if she's different?

A boy is then selected to replace the protagonist's role (and the gender of the character is changed to "Mike"):

Mike: Do you think I could join in your game?
Emily: No, I don't know, we're right in the middle of the game right now. But maybe you could have a turn.
Antagonist Girl 1: When somebody gets out.
Emily: Yeah, after somebody gets out.
Mike: OK.
(The girls look at each other and wickedly smile, suggesting that it's not going to happen.)

We examine the outcome and infer from the female antagonists' nonverbal communication that the acceptance was insincere. Sarah is then chosen to explore her idea, and three different girls are selected to join Emily as antagonists:

Sarah: Can I play?
Emily: No, this is our court. Go find another one.
Sarah: What's your favorite game?
Emily: This *is* our favorite game.
Sarah: Do you have any others you like?
Emily: *(pause)* I like basketball.
Sarah: Hmm.

I ask Sarah, "What did you try to do?" Sarah explains that her next idea is to see if Emily will join her and her friends in a game of basketball. Though Sarah, in one way, veers into a "that's magic" direction from Forum Theatre (in which the solution proposed is improbable because the circumstances are radically altered by the spect-actor), I nevertheless accept Sarah's proposal. I inquire if she needs additional people to complete her scene. Sarah says, "Yes," so I ask her to choose her teammates. Many children raise their hands asking Sarah to select them. She assembles six others to join her and gives them directions before the scene begins:

> *Sarah*: OK, we've been playing a basketball game, but we're short some people, so we're gonna go ask them if they wanna play with us.
> *(Sarah and her group approach the four-square players)*
> *Sarah*: You guys wanna play basketball with us?
> *Antagonist Girl 1*: No, we're playing.
> *Sarah*: Are you sure?
> *Antagonist Girl 2*: Yeah, we're kind of busy right now.
> *Sarah*: How long do you think you're gonna be? *(pause)* You guys wanna play after you're finished?
> *Emily*: How many people do you need?
> *Sarah*: We only need four. 'Cause, everybody else is playing soccer and all those other sorts of things.
> *Emily (to the antagonists)*: You guys wanna play after we're done with our game? *(they reply "Yeah," "Sure")* OK, we'll come when our game is over.
> *Sarah*: OK. Do you know how long it's gonna be?
> *Emily*: *(shrugging her shoulders, asking her friends)* How long? *(brief pause; to Sarah)* Just a few minutes, OK?

I bring the scene to a close, and we gather for whole group discussion. When I ask what just happened in the forum, one girl remarks, "They created conversation." I also observe how Emily seemed different: "She was willing to listen this time."

Attitude Adjustment

The original activating scene—Emily deliberately bumping into Michelle— is replayed. I then ask children to recommend solutions to Michelle on what she can do this time to overcome this particular oppressive action. After Michelle hears their ideas, she employs several of them. Emily deliberately bumps into Michelle, yet Michelle responds politely with, "Excuse me," and initiates a friendly conversation, noting that she saw Emily playing four-square and offers to teach Emily a special four-square maneuver she learned at her previous school. Emily says that would be nice. I interpret that Michelle had opened the door to a new friendship, but some children infer that Emily's acceptance was a trick to learn the new maneuver then shut Michelle out of the game. I suggest the following to the children:

Johnny: There are times you can do some things to help you overcome your oppressions . . .

Boy: Maybe Michelle should invite Emily to do something.

Johnny: But you know what? Michelle can do all of those things, and Emily still won't be her friend. Isn't that kind of realistic? *(children agree)* So, we can do our best to try to stop being stigmatized, but ultimately we also gotta work on it ourselves. It seems as if we've been spending so much time on trying to change Michelle and what she could do, that we really haven't been putting enough focus on where the problem really is: the person who stigmatizes. This is what we need to work on. *(to Emily)* You need to adjust your attitude.

The next portion of our work incorporates an Image Theatre technique demonstrated by Chris Vine of New York City's Creative Arts Team at a Pedagogy and Theatre of the Oppressed conference session. I borrowed but relabeled the technique "Attitude Adjustment."

Emily sculpts herself into a position that shows she accepts Michelle as a friend by sitting next to her, smiling, with her hand around Michelle's shoulder (the ideal image), then creates an antagonistic image by sitting away from, pointing at, and defiantly giggling at Michelle (the realistic image). I encourage children to stand behind Emily and say things that might persuade her to transform herself incrementally out of the realistic image and move closer toward the accepting and ideal image. I prompt children to "Change the way she thinks and feels." I also caution them that there might be statements they make that will have no effect on Emily and statements that could even motivate her to retreat back toward the realistic or stigmatizing image. As I give these directions, Sarah raises and waves her hand briskly throughout, but I select two other children to go first.

One girl's initial idea stimulates a subtle change in one of Emily's gestures: "What you like about her. Look for something that you like about her." A second statement from a boy initiates no change in Emily's image: "Just be her friend." Sarah is then chosen to speak to Emily:

Sarah: I think you need another friend. Michelle, she's really very nice. You should get to know her; she's really nice.

Sarah's idea motivates Emily to drop her taunting gestures and to move her chair three feet closer to Michelle.

The following sample ideas bring Emily incrementally closer to Michelle and the ideal image:

Boy: Maybe you should think about how you felt when you first came.

Girl: She's very smart. She could help you with your homework.

Girl: When you're learning Spanish, she could help you learn Spanish.

Emily makes no change when a girl says, "She could keep your secrets," and even retreats back slightly toward the realistic image when another girl offers, "She can help you find a boyfriend."

Lightning Forum

Due to limited remaining time for the session, I initiate Boal's "Lightning Forum" technique. I ask children to line up directly behind Emily, who by this time has moved two-thirds the distance toward the accepting image, and speak their ideas quickly to get Emily to the final ideal image. Nine children assemble themselves behind her, and Sarah moves quickly to be first in line. (Due to the distance of the camera's microphone from the final unit of action, I was unable to document what children said exactly.) With less than a minute remaining for the session because the class has to leave for lunch, I ask the nine children (Sarah among them) clustered around Emily to simultaneously whisper their ideas to get Emily to move. Several mention that there would be access to a car if they were friends. Their ideas eventually work, and Emily shifts into the final ideal image and places her arm around Michelle's shoulder. I enthusiastically praise the class with "You did it!" The children applaud and shout, "Yay!" but Sarah is the only child who raises both arms in triumph and jumps up and down enthusiastically. Time does not remain for us to process the climax of the unit, but I close our work with, "Thanks for helping Emily realize there's no reason to stigmatize, that it's just stupid to begin with."

Reflections on the Session

Sarah, whose real-life oppression generated the day's TO work, contributed the most ideas, initiated the Forum Theatre scenes that required additional casting, and played the role of spect-actor protagonist with fairly fluent dialogue. After the session, she came up to Emily and Michelle and confessed that she had experienced the same problems we explored today. As TO sessions progressed with this group, Sarah became one of the most engaged and active participants in the fifth-grade class.

Self-esteem is one of the most critical psychological foundations for human beings. How we each feel about ourselves impacts our identity and shapes our functioning and ability at daily living, particularly with interpersonal relationships. When we think less of ourselves, when we feel we have a "spoiled identity," as Erving Goffman phrases it, our social interactions with others become ineffective. We assume a subordinate role and make ourselves vulnerable to oppression. We become easy prey and the target of a dominant individual's or group's stigmatization. Sarah's perceived similarities with the protagonist made the session "high stakes" for her. There was resonance, investment, and ownership because Michelle's problems, their stigmas, were identical.

During "Attitude Adjustment," Sarah said to Emily—who represented the classroom antagonists in her own life—"I think you need another friend. Michelle, she's really very nice. "You should get to know her; she's really nice." Sarah now had a public forum, situated in a simulated dramatic context, to express her inner desire to peers. "Attitude Adjustment" suggests that the goal of the spect-actor is to change the attitude, value, and/or belief systems of the antagonist (or protagonist). But Sarah was not only trying to persuade Emily to stop stigmatizing Michelle. *Sarah was also searching for acceptance from Emily.* The triumphant moment for her, when Emily accepted Michelle as a friend, fulfilled her own need to belong to the classroom community, to no longer be ostracized as an outsider, to no longer be stigmatized for misperceived differences.

There was also acceptance of Sarah in other ways during the session. By dramatizing the daily reality of her life, there was acceptance of her problem as a legitimate concern and worthy of examination. By selecting her—accepting her—to shape Michelle's image, there was transference of her unspoken feelings into Michelle's own body, which Michelle accepted. And when her suggestions were played out in the role of spect-actor, not just once but several times, there was acceptance of her ideas because they generally "worked" to stop the oppression. Sarah's status was elevated from stigmatized student to expert player and problem solver.

One fourth-grade girl in the TO study poignantly told me, "Sometimes, you can't be nice to deal with oppression," after I expressed concern that the children's Forum Theatre solutions were mostly combative. But Sarah took the high road in this session. When needed, she admonished Emily gently but confidently. Her Forum Theatre tactics were neither deceptive nor diversionary—they were sincere attempts to communicate, sincere attempts to create community, sincere attempts to make friends with those who unfairly stigmatized her. Goffman (1963) speaks primarily of individuals with physical disabilities when he offers the following advice, but it so readily applies to Sarah's peacemaking efforts: "The nondisabled, when they stigmatize, should be tactfully helped to act nicely. Slights, snubs, and untactful remarks should not be answered in kind. Either no notice should be taken or the stigmatized individual should make an effort at sympathetic re-education of the normal [*sic*], showing him, point for point, quietly, and with delicacy, that in spite of appearances the stigmatized individual is, underneath it all, a fully-human being" (116).

Children who label peers "weird" have stigmatized them. Jokers have the opportunity to examine stigma through Boal's theatrical forms with young people. Not only can we explore how the protagonist might respond to oppression or stigmatization, but we also can examine the antagonist's often-irrational reasons for labeling and thus oppressing. TO facilitators have the potential to become supportive allies for the stigmatized. Goffman further reminds us that "the first set of sympathetic others is of course those who share [her] stigma. Knowing from their own experience what it is like to have this particular stigma, some of them can provide the individual with instruction in the tricks of the trade and with a circle of lament to which [she] can withdraw for moral support and for the comfort of feeling at home, at ease, accepted as a person who really is like any other normal [*sic*] person" (20).

I admit to having a soft spot in my heart for those mistreated unfairly by others. Given my own stigmatized past (and by some, my own stigmatized present), I can't help but empathize. When I see that one of my students, regardless of age level, has been oppressed and needs a mentor—or an ally, a friend, a rescuer, and so on—I take him or her under my wing, as the cliché goes. Most times the relationship strengthens the stigmatized student—and me. Only on rare occasions have I been disappointed or burned from trusting too much or too easily.

I cited earlier that adult TO facilitators introduce and examine their personal yet hidden social agendas covertly and subtextually in the public school classroom. So, could this session have been designed and driven by my subconscious need to exorcise my own personal demons? Did I step onto precarious shaky ground or venture into some ethical conundrum by dramatizing and scrutinizing a real person's story in front of her peers? Was Sarah's engaged participation and dramatic victory some form of emotional catharsis for my own troubled childhood memories? I would prefer that readers themselves reflect on those questions and develop their own answers. As for me, I was simply trying to do my best as an elementary educator to "change the world"—one child at a time.

Closure

At the time of this writing—fall 2009—Sarah should already have graduated from high school and may now be a junior in college.

I have heard from my adult female university students how adolescent girls can sometimes act "viciously" toward each other during their young adult years. Popular media stereotypically portray high school girls as cliquish rivals, vying for popularity, and insulting of each other's appearance if it does not conform to current fashion trends and standards of beauty. I wonder if Sarah was still taunted by her peers, still stigmatized, and whether those TO sessions during fifth grade empowered her to stand up to oppression as she grew. School privacy acts and my originally approved research protocol do not permit me to track down Sarah's whereabouts, yet I really do want to know how she's fared with her adolescent life course. I hope she has not experienced the same type of peer abuse I encountered in junior and senior high school.

The TO project with children produced observable but sporadic outcomes from teachers' perspectives, due primarily to the relatively short amount of time we spent in their classrooms. One teacher both quantified and qualified the results by suggesting we had influenced and affected perhaps only one-third of the children and that there were some—mostly boys—whom we would "never be able to reach." Nevertheless, seeds of social consciousness and strategies for dealing with oppression were planted back then through TO. I can only hope that they fell on good soil in Sarah, took root, and grew deep within her.

Acknowledgments

Funding for the Theatre of the Oppressed with Children project was provided by a grant from the Research Council of the Katherine K. Herberger College of the Arts at Arizona State University. The research team included Emily Petkewich, Gordon Hensley, Doyle Ott, Johnny Saldaña, and Michelle White. Thanks are extended to Sally Dorothy Bailey, RDT, who introduced me to Erving Goffman's *Stigma*, and to Jim Simpson, psychotherapist, for analytic consultation.

References

Banaszewski, C. 2006. *Adult theatre of the oppressed facilitators' questions, roles, and rules when using theatre of the oppressed with adolescent participants.* Unpublished doctoral dissertation, Arizona State University.

Boal, A. 2002. *Games for actors and non-actors.* 2nd ed. Trans. A. Jackson. New York: Routledge.

Goffman, E. 1963. *Stigma: Notes on the management of spoiled identity.* Englewood Cliffs, NJ: Prentice Hall.

Neelands, J., and T. Goode. 2000. *Structuring drama work: A handbook of available forms in theatre and drama.* 2nd ed. New York: Cambridge University Press.

Saldaña, J. 2005. Theatre of the oppressed with children: A field experiment. *Youth Theatre Journal* 19: 117–33.

3

Silent Screaming and the Power of Stillness

Theatre of the Oppressed within Mainstream Elementary Education

Elinor Vettraino

Although I can't remember the exact date or time, or even where I was particularly, that I saw Francis Bacon's infamous *Study after Velazquez's Portrait of Pope Innocent X 1953* for the first time, I do remember what I felt. All that power, all that energy, all that rage trapped in silence, unmoving. It had quite a remarkable impact on me. As I gazed at it, I had one of those *raised hairs on the back of your neck* moments. I had a similar feeling when I looked at Dana (nine years old and part of a group of children working through an Image technique from Rainbow of Desire), placing herself as the protagonist in her image of oppression, surrounded by the tall and powerful structures of antagonism that she had positioned around her. Watching her sitting on the floor, hugging her knees to her chest, reminded me of all the times that I had felt squashed as a child, unable to move, trapped by my own fears, and without my own voice. And yet here she was, aged nine, more eloquent about her pain in her stillness and silence than I am in the writing of this. If I needed another example of the power of Theatre of the Oppressed (TO), then here it was, in Technicolor.

The power of TO work with youths, and my journey with it *so far*, is what this chapter is all about. I say "so far" because I don't think I could ever truly stop learning about the ways in which TO has impacted the "I" that is Joker, participant, spect-actor, and human being and the ways in which I have impacted others through this pedagogy. So yes, I am definitely only *so far* along.

In the Beginning Was the Word, and the Word Was "Curriculum"

My journey with TO really began when I was involved in the field of human resources. But it wasn't until I became simultaneously a youth worker and an elementary school teacher that I really began to understand what oppression was and how theatre connected to it. In my capacity as an elementary school teacher, I felt the paradox of wanting to be an enabler of children's dreams and hopes while simultaneously being employed in a system that, for much of the time, felt more like a lead weight of expectation. I felt I was suffocated by the need to conform to guidelines and frameworks, to meet national targets that didn't (and still don't) reflect external influences on the school and community, and to ensure that the children *produced* at the end of the learning conveyor belt could think and act appropriately in society. It was all about image and yet not Image.

When I "found" TO though, I had a bit of an epiphany: "When you show [your oppression], it sort of makes it real doesn't it? And if it's real and it's wrong and shouldn't happen then showing it means that someone's got to do something about it . . . I've got to do something about it" (Lisa, twelve years old).

Over the years since my engagement with TO began, I have collected stories from the many children who I have had the joy (and often heartache) to work with. The statement above was made by a child in one of my classes after an afternoon of Image Theatre work where we were using shared stories to explore the fears and hopes associated with moving to secondary (high) school. Lisa's words stuck with me because it spoke to a human truth: we are the masters of our own fate. And therein lies the power behind TO and the "Aha!'" moment I referred to earlier.

I don't need to *enable* liberation, I just need to open the space up and let the children find their own freedom to breathe. Sounds easy? It isn't.

The term *space* conjures up a number of different mental images: physical space, mind space, spaces in dialogue (or monologue?), canyon spaces, crevice spaces, intentional space, fabricated space. Boal (1995) discusses *space* as being something that moves outside of time and physicality, a separate reality to the one that we inhabit daily. This is an important distinction because in this separate, aesthetic space, movement, sound, image, and music all take on new meanings, as our imaginations are fired and we connect with our previous experiences and those of the individuals around us to create a shared understanding. So, when I ask participants to *make a space*, I am speaking physically (*make sure you can move around*), emotionally, and psychologically (*make sure you clear space in your head for what we're about to do*), because they have to want to be part of the process, too, not coerced, but cojoined collaborators in the journey. The setting up of this kind of free space with children requires teachers to feel open enough themselves to take risks, particularly because from a teacher's perspective it is sometimes very difficult to find the courage and ability to allow children to find anything for themselves, let alone freedom.

At this point, however, cognizance needs to be taken of the context within which I offer this chapter and discussion, because "times they are a-changing" here in Scotland, and there are opportunities for TO to become an embedded, pedagogical approach to educating all about what it is to be human, what it is to be alive in *this* world at *this* time.

TO and Scottish Education: Yin and Yang?

As I write this, Scotland's newly devised Curriculum for Excellence 3-18 (CfE) is being implemented in many schools across the nation, from kindergarten to high school (preschool, primary and secondary), with a view to rolling out the new framework across Scotland in 2009 to 2010. This curriculum has been termed as a radical cultural and pedagogical shift in the nation's conscious understanding of education (Hyslop 2008). And a shift has certainly been needed, according to the new framework's proponents who believe that cultural, social, economic, and technological paradigm changes have led to a need for a more dynamic and responsive style of education system. This system also needs to embrace creativity and innovation in order to ensure that the next generation is equipped with the skills necessary to work in the world of the twenty-first century. By stating this need openly, there is a tacit understanding that creativity does not currently exist (or is evident enough) in our current education system. Indeed, Robinson (2006) stated, "We don't grow into creativity we grow out of it . . . or rather we are educated out of it." As such, there are huge expectations put on CfE's ability to deliver its promise to create a future workforce generation of successful learners, effective contributors, responsible citizens, and confident individuals (the four capacities of the CfE).

CfE replaces a previous framework that many thought was restrictive in its approach to education. Although not requiring a prescriptive approach to what was taught and when (unlike its sister curriculum in England), the previous framework, known colloquially as *the national guidelines*, placed subjects within silos where making connections became difficult to achieve given that assessment of learning was driving the curriculum content and delivery.

So, the new curriculum has been formed at a time when it has been recognized that Scotland's economic future lies not in its tradition of manufacturing and engineering but in softer skills and technologies. Young people are being prepared for jobs, the nature of which may not even have been invented yet. Maureen Watt (Minister for Schools and Skills in Scotland, at the time of writing this) believes that CfE will be "more coherent, more flexible and more enriching, focusing on the needs of each and every child" (cited in Murtagh 2008) and, in doing so, allowing each and every child to develop their interests in line with their skills and aptitudes. Debates are still raging between teachers, politicians, and educationalists about whether CfE will improve the abilities of a future workforce. Interesting to note is that although these *children of our future* have been given spaces in which to voice their views on the proposed changes, they are generally a focus group that is seldom heard from in the wider educational arena.

A colleague of mine told me a story once about a school where the children were asked to design a job description for an ideal teacher. Not only does the school currently employ this job description when they embark on the hunt for a new teacher, but the children also interview prospective candidates along with the school staff team. Though not directly connected to CfE or to TO, this example indicates what is possible when it comes to giving children the freedom and responsibility to take control of their own (academic) lives. This is the kind of experience where I see TO and education fitting together. So when I ask the question, "Can TO and education ever comfortably share the same airspace?" my first thought is *yes*.

I recently reread hooks's (1994) and Felman's (2001) thoughts on the power of education as a truly transformative act. As always, they brought a smile to my face because that is what education *should* be: it should be both empowering and transformational for students and teachers alike. Education as the practice of freedom (hooks 1994) is an ideology I believe in wholeheartedly. Throughout all of his work, Freire argues for this when he talks about freedom from the oppression of lack of knowledge.

As my own practice as a teacher (and now teacher-educator) has developed, I have linked Freire's concept of praxis with Boal's *metaxis*,[1] gaining a sort of four-dimensional view of how I, in my attempts to facilitate children's learning, would sometimes also be an oppressor of their innate freedoms and ideas. Part of the reason for this was my belief, as a new teacher, that children's knowledge was a thing, an object in the world that could be compartmentalized and boundaried without always connecting (an attitude that has been encouraged through the categorization of subjects within the primary and secondary school curricula in Scotland). The very nature of spect-acting in TO actually underlines the very organic and fluid nature of knowledge, the interconnectedness that is so important because it is the construct of how we live our lives—not in boxes but in spaces (Davis, Sumara, and Luce-Kaplar 2008). When I interrelate these two, I begin to truly interact with myself in all of my incarnations—Joker, participant, and so on—and the incarnations of all the young people with which I work.

Joining Both Ends of the Circle

As a teacher, my focus in drama has been on using it as an enabler for children, to help them express their "voice" in a classroom setting where many voices are competing for the same airspace. Educational drama not only is about making use of techniques and skills within dramatic processes to learn about a range of issues, stories, ideas, and events; but it is also about linking to educational objectives, to levels of ability, to assessment and attainment, because arguably, in this context, it has to be. Culturally, we require *proof* of children's ability to "do." The debate over the requirement of proof is an argument for another chapter or book! TO is almost the polar opposite of this. For me, TO has always been about the freedom to challenge, fight, laugh, share, experience, and live.

The difference between the two can therefore truly be seen in the intention of the action. An example of this came about during a very difficult experience working with teachers during an in-service day. The head teacher of a school in a challenging area asked myself and a colleague of mine, Martin,[2] to showcase some of our work on children's oppression in the hopes that the teaching staff would be interested and willing to take part in training that would help their work within their own classes. The hostility and challenge we encountered while attempting to carry out this in-service request would fill another chapter alone! Suffice it to say, we met resistance—resistance against the evolution of revolution!

Resistance, however, can be useful. It can focus your thoughts and ideas; it can make you really think hard about why you are doing what you are doing. In fact, resistance deserves respect (Salverson 1994) because often resistance comes from fear; I believe that this was certainly the case with this staff team. The following is an indicator of the type of conversation that was repeated throughout the day with the teaching team:

Teacher: I can't believe you got that from [the children] . . . How did you get
    them to be like that?
Me: I'm sorry, I'm not sure what you mean . . . like what?
Teacher: Like that . . . to do the work . . . How did that happen?
Me: Well, the children were passionate about their lives and the things that
    prevented them from being free to being who they needed to be in their
    classroom space. Getting them involved wasn't really an issue. They had the
    freedom to show us and each other what they truly felt about being in their
    classroom, and I suppose the fact that they were all working together to
    think about ways of liberating that experience meant that they had a vested
    interest; it was their own lives.
Teacher: Yes, but how did you get them to be like that?

Me: I'm sorry, but I still don't understand the question. Get them to be like what?

Teacher: How did you get them to *behave*?

For this teaching team, the subject of children's oppression was an irrelevance when held up against the need to behave, the need to conform, and the need to fit in. Don't get me wrong—I am fully respectful of the straitjacket that teachers often find themselves in, tied up between the red tape of bureaucracy and the assessment-driven weighted chain. But the question should not be "How can the children behave?" but rather "Why do they not want to?" In fact, that should be one of many questions that ask what education is truly about. Is it driven by grading and attainment targets, or is it about empowerment of youth and growing through knowledge?

Perhaps not surprisingly, my belief is that education should be about the latter, and I have had many experiences working with TO that have continued to reinforce this view. Among the many pivotal moments, a brief and voluntary pilot project myself and the aforementioned colleague, Martin, carried out with Dana's class of nine-year-olds in a local elementary (primary) school stands out. To say that this particular class had developed some form of a *reputation* for all the wrong reasons would be to put it mildly! The class in question consisted of approximately twenty-four children—the figure was flexible depending on who had been excluded and who turned up—and was staffed permanently by two teachers. It appeared from discussion with the staff that the *big problem* with the class was a lack of ability to gel. There was no sense of community spirit, and behavior was becoming increasingly challenging. The school itself was based in an area of social and economic deprivation, not quite a black hole when it came to getting the appropriate resources and funding required to support the community, but pretty close. As a result, situations from outside the school often spilled over into clashes on the playground and angry words in the classroom.

Before developing a program with the children, we wanted to talk with them about their experiences of being in their class. We felt it was crucial not only to building a sense of mutual trust and understanding but also, very importantly, to ensuring that the work we engaged with was not something *done to* the children without their support or invitation. This was an aspect that we had stressed to the senior management and teaching team so that they would understand that whatever we did would be a coconstruct with the children. So we spent time with them on their playground during recess, very much in their territory with their permission. We learned that they often felt restricted by the classroom setting; again, that term *space* arose—not only in relation to the class's physical space but also to the context of that space, in particular, the behaviors of both peers and of the teaching staff. We learned that the reward-sanction schemes in place (of which there were several) did not really provide any sense of purpose for the class and, in fact, only confused the children. Having spent some time in the classroom space with the children, we witnessed some genuine moments while they played where we could see the frustration pour out of them, like a river bursting its banks. Thinking back to Bacon's image, I saw all that trapped, silent energy that sat unmoving in the classroom needing a place to go; outward or upward, it didn't matter.

In short, then, our conversations and time with the children indicated that they felt that their class didn't work well together. This journeying into their territory proved to be a useful first step into talking with the children about their understanding of two very important concepts on which we would be working with them: oppression and liberation. One of our concerns in naming the terminology was that we wanted to ensure that the children's understanding of oppression and liberation really came from them and was not imposed by us and our adult understanding, which would be wrapped up in the baggage of our own youth.

Having said that, we explored this in the first session with them as we asked them what they understood the terms to be and found that we needed to give them some indication of what we meant by both words. So we offered an explanation that we hoped would be wide enough not to restrict the children's ideas and yet specific enough to help them connect with their own experiences. The explanation of oppression was to *think of it as something that makes it difficult for you to play a real part in the life of the classroom or to feel as though you really get something useful out of being in the classroom.* The explanation of liberation was to think *of it as being something that would help you to feel really free to be who you want to be and do what you need to do to feel like a valued member of this class.*

This then opened up a floodgate of discussion about thoughts, feelings, and behaviors that the children associated with both terms. We accepted all of their ideas and comments because we wanted them to feel genuinely connected with their own understanding of both terms. However, even as I write this, I still wonder about the ways in which our own understanding of the terms impacted the children's choice of themes, particularly given that many of them in their later image work drew upon experiences of being bullied and stigmatized to represent their own oppressions.

Once we had defined oppression and liberation with the children, we continued our foray into their class community by asking them to draw themselves and others in the class as animals and then to show dialogues between them. This Gestalt technique allowed us to understand a little more about the communication that existed in the classroom space. People, places, and things were never named in the images (neither during these art experiences or the TO work that followed), but it was possible to see their projected selves manifested in the difficult conversations their animals had.

We carried on employing a therapeutic art approach, linking the concepts of oppression and liberation by asking the children to consider experiences that they found oppressive and to imagine these as shapes, colors, textures, lines, and so on. In constructing abstract images, the children were able to offer iconic and effective responses where the representation was symbolic, having true meaning only to the artist. Rather than name the stories emerging from the aesthetics of the images, the children were asked to comment on shared aspects of the images (e.g., where similarities existed in terms of colors used or lines drawn). They also offered thoughts on what was different (e.g., shapes drawn or areas of containment). The possibility of moving from oppression to liberation was then invited through repeating the process but focusing this time on what it would look like if it were transformed, and again, shared elements were discussed.

Although employing therapeutic art techniques was not adhering to pure TO, I believe it was an important first step in freeing the children's desire to express and also share commonalties and build community. Paper, crayons, and pencils are extensions of the self; they are by "me" but not "me," and therefore I am not on show here. It could also be argued that these materials are extensions of the (oppressive) school system and, for that reason, could have negative connotations for the children. I have had many conversations in my time as a teacher-educator with individuals whose fear of art has stemmed from being told that their creativity and imagination are "wrong" and not good enough. However, the use of mark-making materials in this work was deliberately developed in a nonrestrictive way in order to offer a conduit for expressing in one visual form the children's concepts of oppression and liberation.

These images proved vital in laying the foundation discussions with the children in the following Image Theatre work. The artwork became a transitional object for moving into the images they created individually and as a group; this initial experience of sharing commonalties (the depth of line, color, shading, and shape) formed the groundwork for sharing common experiences through movement and the physicality of Image.

Following the therapeutic art techniques, the children were introduced to Image work through games and exercises, many of which were taken directly from *Games for Actors and Non-Actors* (Boal 2003). The immediacy and positivity of the response from the children to the freedom of movement took the class teachers by surprise. One of the teachers confessed to me that she was sure they were just going to "run riot" and instead had been stunned to discover the concentration and energy focused into keeping each other safe in the games work. The other surprise for the teachers was the way in which the class bonded together as a whole unit in both the art and drama work. This was the first time that the teachers had experienced the class as a cohesive, positive, communal unit, as they rarely brought the whole class together for any form of practical activity due to their concerns over behavior. This revelation continued to grow as the project unfolded and the teachers were able to see the care and attention individuals paid to each other's silent stories.

Although we had been asked to help the children work more cohesively as a whole class unit, Martin and I wanted to focus more on what the *children* needed and wanted out of the process. In order to do that, we needed to give them (all of) the space required to freely explore their individual *voice*. To do this, we worked with single-sex groups of five or six children over a period of four weeks. The class had a reasonably even split of boys and girls, and yet, as we observed their interactions, it was obvious that it was a very male-dominated arena. Single-sex groups gave both sexes the chance to explore their own sometimes very gender-specific oppressions. Both the girls and the boys commented positively on the experience of engaging with the process surrounded by peers of the same gender.

During those group sessions, we developed drama based almost entirely on a prospective technique employed by Boal called Image of the Images (for a full description of the technique, see Boal 1995, 77–80). Each week, the children within their group shaped an image of their oppression using their peers as the clay and placing themselves as the protagonist at the (often literal) heart of their image—transforming their thoughts into corporeal form. Each week, every child would honor their colleagues' stories by holding the shapes they had been placed in, allowing themselves to be directed by those with whom they had played, argued, laughed, cried, intimidated, fought over, loved, and hated. In this space, all were equal, all were vital, and, I believe, all were transformed in some way through the silence of their storytelling and the power of their stillness in these held images.

Boal (1995, 45) crucially says, "We do not interpret, we explain nothing, we only offer multiple points of reference." I had to keep this in mind constantly when working with this class because the images formed in stillness and silence in that physical space screamed at me, and there were times when the children's *physical* voices were deafening. Dana was one example. Another would be Michael. Described by the class teachers as "rough," "a bully," and "you can't miss him!" (he was physically quite large), Michael directed the individuals in his group, gently and very precisely, to create his image of oppression: two separate lines of children, one in front of the other, staggered, with arms linked in a symbol of solidarity, facing forward with Michael standing at least five feet behind them on his own, facing their backs, uninvited and unable to fit in.

On the face of it, he did not appear to share a common understanding with his peers of what it was to be oppressed. When he was invited along with the rest of the group to offer objective and subjective feedback on the curled up, fetal images of protagonists created by his peers, he professed to not identifying, recognizing, or resonating with them. He had no experience of being pushed to the floor or trodden on. But he absolutely understood what it was to be alone.

During each session, once the children had created individual images of oppression, they then set to work on creating a shared image that drew on shapes and positions they had been placed in (by themselves or others) with which they identified, recognized, or resonated (related to Boal's three levels of connection). They each were then given a wish to transform their image of oppression into one of liberation, moving themselves or one other person. This process proved to be extremely hard work with no group managing to achieve anything resembling a consensus on an image of liberation in fewer than six attempts. It was during this process that I believe another transformative moment occurred with Michael.

Once Michael's group had managed to achieve some agreement on an image of liberation, I invited them to dynamize the image: bring it to life in slow motion so that they could experience the transformation from oppression to liberation as a physical act. The group had a central protagonist, Craig, who Martin and I understood to have been at the receiving end of Michael's violence in the very recent past. Craig had chosen his own protagonist image to offer the group image, curled up and half lying on the floor, surrounded by large, imposing antagonists in various quasiviolent poses. As he assumed the protagonist's position in preparation for the process, Michael pointed at Craig and said, "Can I do that?" to which I replied, "You'd like to take Craig's place?" "No," he replied. "I'd like to join him."

A quick check-in with the group indicated that no one had a problem with this (I paid particular attention to Craig's reaction); however, it was still with some trepidation that I said, "Sure." My understanding from the class teachers was that Michael's aggression could engage at the flick of a switch; was I taking an unnecessary risk here? Michael lay down next to Craig, mirroring his pose, taking time to get it right. The antagonists took shape around them. When they were ready, I gave the signal to begin. Craig immediately started moving slowly to escape the antagonists. Michael, on the other hand, began slowly rolling from side to side, apparently enjoying the experience of being on the floor; he appeared very relaxed. As the antagonists became more intent on keeping Craig in his place, Michael began to move upward and out, always slowly but methodically and with real intent. Within a short space of time, Michael had extracted himself from the group, but Craig was still "trapped" inside, still moving slowly but now with more effort and less focus as the antagonists now only had one person to aim at. At this point, Michael did something I won't forget. He turned around to face the group and bent down to reach in. I confess that my immediate thought was *he's going to join the antagonists!* What he actually did was reached his hand out to Craig and said, "Come on, Craig. Take my hand. Take my hand!" Michael pulled Craig to safety.

Each individual's journey became a shared group journey that, in turn, became a whole class experience. At the end of the four weeks, we brought all of the groups back together for a merry-go-round of images, inviting protagonists and antagonists from each image to move around the groups offering solutions to the challenges posed. A true community in praxis and definitely an opportunity for me to observe myself as facilitator of the process, battling with my own desire to leap in and rescue when I really needed to be the Joker, Jack of all Trades, the Every(wo)man. Not only did the children engage in the physical "discussion" of what they had created, but they also verbally unpacked the experiences for them as a class, taking great joy in working together for a common goal.

What was created at the end of the project encompassed the journey that all of us had made. The children, determined to share their experiences with the rest of their school, asked to put together an interactive assembly where they could invite their schoolmates to *try liberation on for size*. As a result, they "performed" their group images of oppression and, with individuals from the class acting as facilitators of the experience, all the children from the ages of five to twelve were invited to step up to the challenge of changing the picture to one that, in their words, *felt better*. The number of first and second graders that stepped up to the plate easily matched the ten-, eleven-, and twelve-year-olds, and all ages participated, roaring with delight when an image suggested freedom and togetherness.

Evaluations with the class were carried out in both image and word. The children were invited to show their experience of the process through individual images and also through a round-the-circle discussion. The images and words moved from excitement and anxiety prior to the TO intervention to enjoyment and freedom at the end. Given that this project was extremely brief in its contact and development with the children (in total, there were nine sessions spread out over seven weeks), hearing the children's own narratives about the discoveries they had made about each other and themselves was an indication of the power that this work had. The main outcome for them seemed to be that they had been given the chance to show, tell, and hear about what it was like to be in the spaces of their classroom and, through that knowledge, begin to think about how they impact their own and other's experiences of school.

For me, this particular project was a glimpse of the possibilities of TO working from the inside of the education system in a way that did not compromise the integrity of the process. Starting from the children's own needs and desires ensured that we were building on individual and shared oppression. We were not doing anything *to* the children, but instead we were working with them. Casdagli (1999, 31) states that "just as teaching is not about what is but what could be, expectations are crucial." For us, it was vital that any program we developed was done in collaboration with the children, to offer them the time and a space to show themselves and each other how they felt about sharing all these spaces together and through that showing, a chance to transform their experiences through shared understanding. Had the children at the outset said to us "We don't want to do this," the project would not have been put in place, and this is where there can be issues about embedding TO in the processes and procedures of education.

When connecting so concretely with the education system, the idea of developing programs or projects that truly stem from the children's own concerns or ideas can be a tricky "ask." I was aware from discussions with the two-teacher team and the head teacher that their desire was really to change the children's behavior; in fact, at one point we were told that they were hoping this work would *fix* the children. Throughout the project, we did not engage in any discussion around behavior or behavior management. Instead, we worked with whatever the children brought to the table that related to our initial discussions with them about how their class community actually functioned. The result was that the children implicitly and explicitly identified, explored, and challenged a range of behaviors that they (and the teaching team) engaged in that were constructive or destructive for them as friends, learners, peers, and human beings in school. That this exploration originated from the children made the process much more meaningful for them than if we had come into the work with that agenda.

I also had the desire to show the teaching staff that TO could work alongside educational outcomes and objectives. Because of this, I linked the components of the work to the relevant guidelines.[3] In doing so, I had to keep asking myself if tying into the national framework was going to restrict content and experience of the work for the children. We were able to address this by going back to the question, "What is the intention of this work?"

For the children, engaging with Image Theatre and TO was like holding up a mirror in front of their life experiences but with the ability to change the outcome of that experience. By working through the processes involved in the Image of the Images techniques, they were able to engage with themselves as individuals, as part of a community and as characters within a play process. They were in that wonderful space in between reality and real: metaxis. Linds (2006) talks about embodiment in this space, about learning becoming meaningful and open to further discovery, and this was very true for the children who would return to their sculpts and images to tell more stories and share more possible solutions. They were directing others in enacting their own stories, and truly wondrous things were happening for them.

The Place of TO in Teacher Education

More important than procreation is the child—more important than the evolution of the creation is the evolution of the creator.

—Jacob Moreno, cited in Hoey 1997, 3

The assembly the children carried out marked the end point of the project for them, and us. In a very short space of time, the children had shown their teachers and senior management how being given the physical and emotional space to identify and examine their experiences as a whole group could have a transformative effect on their desire to engage with life in the classroom. But (and this is a large but!) the observable transformations appeared to only occur during the times they were with us, either in groups or as a whole class. Evaluations from the teaching team indicated that the class we worked with "just wasn't the same class" as the one they dealt with day in day out. Lack of funding and the remit of our project meant that we were not in a position to investigate the long-term effect of the TO work or to consider how the children's daily experience of classroom life was altered by the project. However, I believe that if we had the ability to continue working with both the children and the school staff, the journey of discovery that the school as a community would have engaged in would have enabled all those sharing the physical and emotional spaces in that building to understand each other better and, through that understanding, begin to work together on liberating the education experience for all.

The teachers working with that class were embedded in an education system that, despite all of its incarnations, has not altered fundamentally since its original conception back in the postindustrial age. At the end of the day, teachers teach and children are supposed to learn, the argument being that behaving appropriately enables that learning to take place. What this philosophy fails to take into account is that children are also teachers and that teachers also learn. We give lip service to that but to what extent do we truly allow all players in the game of education to give voice to their concerns, fears, ideas, and freedoms? And this is where, perhaps controversially, I would like to make a pronouncement: TO in education should be about giving the spaces to *all* who come to the table wanting to learn from themselves and each other in order to create a better world in which we can all live. When I say *all*, I mean all, regardless of age, role, or experience, because teachers are not *the* antagonists. That they *can be* antagonists I think is a given, but they can also be protagonists in the same way that the children they teach can be both. While I recognize that manipulating TO for corporate gain strikes against the very heart of the philosophy grounding TO work, I do not believe that using TO to work with individuals or groups who find themselves in "oppressor" roles on a daily basis fits this profile.

As a teacher-educator, I have used TO techniques to help student teachers unpack their own practice. This has been fundamentally beneficial to their understanding of themselves in their many roles: student, teacher, facilitator, challenger, and, most importantly, human being. By addressing the antagonist within, these beginning teachers are identifying behaviors that frustrate and restrict their ability to do their job but, more importantly, that are unkind, unnecessary, and oppressive. This was no more eloquently demonstrated than through a discussion I had recently with a teacher education student in the third year of his Bachelor of Education Honors degree. He told me that the most powerful experience he had to date in relation to teaching happened in one of my classes. We were using TO techniques to construct Lightning Forum Theatre pieces to consider how our teachers' behavior choices often oppress those they work with in classroom settings and how that can lead to a range of challenges, many of which are manifested in the children's behavior. With his colleagues, he constructed a story that we "Forumed." In this story, based on the real experiences of himself and his colleagues, he, as the teacher-actor, made behavior choices that were pivotal in determining the way in which the experience fell apart for him as a teacher (e.g., his management of the physical space the children-actors were working in, his physical interaction with the children-actors and their learning).

However, the most crucial aspect of this scenario lay not in the physical choices that the student as teacher-actor made but rather in the attitudes he demonstrated toward the children-actors in this fictional class. Through his eyes, we were able to see his frustration and anxiety build as the scene played out. We could also see the anger and boredom of the children-actors in the scene, and, very importantly, we were also able to see with our own "dramatic eye" how key ways of relating to the characters in the scene and behavior choices he made were leading to a breakdown of communication between himself and the learners in his care.

At the end of the scene, when the interventions came, they were directed at the teacher-actor. All of us bore witness to the desire to change this oppressor's behavior, and as the changes manifested themselves in the student teacher-actor's actions, we could see how they came to enable and empower the children-actors as oppressed, freeing them to engage with the learning that the teacher was striving to develop and also freeing them to voice their needs and experiences without fear of being shut down, shut out, or shut up.

Embedding TO in initial teacher education would open a powerful and important door to understanding the way in which the education system can be a deeply oppressive place to be. In Scotland, the time to embed this could be now.

Watt argues that Scotland's new curriculum is about "giving teachers back their professionalism" (cited in Murtagh 2008). Words like "empowerment," "freedom," "creativity," and "innovation" are used almost as the thesaurus of CfE "speak," so perhaps we are heading along the right route. Certainly, enacting these concepts as education would link to Freire's desire for *conscientization*, which hooks (1994) defines as engagement and critical awareness in learning. However, the kind of radical transformation of ideology that is required for the education system to truly embrace the philosophy behind CfE is not something that comes easily or quickly, if at all. Change is a difficult act that can enlighten as well as destroy. Moving from something that is comfortable into something that is unknown can be a painful experience; I have seen this myself in my own teaching when I ask my students to jump out of their comfort zones and into an area that they have no expertise in. With TO however, we are all alive (even if we are not truly alive), and we all therefore have expertise.

Where to Next?

Caminante el camino no existe . . .
[Wanderer, there is no road . . .]

—Antonio Machado, quoted in Augusto Boal's *The Rainbow of Desire*

I have a passionate belief that through TO, all people—young, old, and in between—are enabled in their own minds, bodies, and spirits. In an education-structural context, TO frees us from the restraints and constraints that national testing and levels of ability and curriculum time allowances all put on educational practice. Education is tied up so tightly in its own web of red tape and bureaucracy that real learning, the rich and deep learning that needs to be there often, struggles hard to escape.

However, my hope is that all over the world a revolution is taking place in the classroom. It may not be a loud revolution or a particularly big one, but it is happening, spurred on perhaps by an unspoken understanding among the people of the world that education is the practice of freedom. TO has a place in this revolution because it is not theatre of the *one* oppressed; it is a communal event, a shared understanding, a meeting of minds and hearts. If we are to avoid education, strip mining the minds of future generations as though hunting for a particular commodity (Robinson 2006), then we need to rethink not just the structures of education but the purpose. Incorporating TO into the rigidity of educational structures and systems may feel like a strange thing to want to do, but I believe that if we did, we would be embarking on a vital revisioning of the reason we learn. TO and education can sit together and share the same aesthetic space because at the end of the day, the search for knowledge is really a search for self.

Notes

1. Metaxis is the term Boal uses to explain the way in which theatre enables the participant (actor-character) to be in two realities at once; that of the real world that they inhabit and in which they are themselves, and that of the character that they are portraying.
2. Martin Williams, formerly senior lecturer in education at the University of Dundee, now runs his own consultancy, Ultimate People Empowerment, and can be contacted at martin.swilliams@tiscali.co.uk.
3. From 1992 until recent developments in Scottish education, primary schools have been working with a set of national guidelines known as the 5-14 documents. These guidelines cover a range of subject areas such as mathematics, social subjects, and expressive arts. The latter covers four creative arts areas: drama, music, art and design, and physical education. The 5-14 are used by teachers to determine what areas within each subject need to be taught at any given stage of the child's primary education. They also indicate the level of ability a child should be at by a particular age or stage of schooling. These guidelines are in the process of being replaced by a new curriculum, Curriculum for Excellence (CfE). This curriculum purports to be different because it is aiming at the development of softer skills such as creative thinking and confidence building. However, it also has outcomes and levels of attainment against which children's progress will be measured.

References

Boal, Augusto. 1995. *The Rainbow of Desire: The Boal method of theatre and therapy*. Trans. Adrian Jackson. New York: Routledge.

Casdagli, Penny. 1991. *Trust and power: Taking care of ourselves through drama*. London: Jessica Kingsley.

Davis, Brent, Dennis Sumara, and Rebecca Luce-Kapler. 2008. *Engaging minds changing teaching in complex times*. 2nd ed. London: Routledge.

Felman, Jil Lyn. 2001. *Never a dull moment: Teaching and the art of performance*. New York: Routledge.

Hoey, Bernadette. 1997. Spontaneity—the linchpin of psychodrama. In *Who calls the tune?: A psychodramatic approach to child therapy*, ed. B. Hoey, 10–19. London: Routledge.

hooks, bell. 1994. *Teaching to transgress education as the practice of freedom*. New York: Routledge.

Hyslop, Fiona. 2008, September. Keynote speech at the Scottish Learning Festival, Glasgow.

Linds, Warren. 2006. Metaxis dancing (in) the in-between. In *A Boal companion: Dialogues on theatre and cultural politics*, ed. Jan Cohen-Cruz and Mady Schutzman, 114–24. London: Routledge.

Murtagh, Cera. 2008. The business of politics: A curriculum for excellence. *Holyrood Magazine*, October 2, http://www.holyrood.com/content/view/2970/10524/ (accessed October 3, 2008; site now discontinued).

Robinson, Ken. 2006. Do schools kill creativity? TED Conference, Monterey, California, http://www.ted.com/index.php/talks/ken_robinson_says_schools_kill_creativity.html (accessed October 27, 2008).

Salverson, Julie. 1994. *The mask of solidarity*. In *Playing Boal theatre, therapy, activism*, ed. Mady Schutzman and Jan Cohen-Cruz, 157–70. London: Routledge.

Part II

The Political Life of Youth

4

Viewpoints on Israeli-Palestinian Theatrical Encounters

Chen Alon and Sonja Arsham Kuftinec, with Ihsan Turkiyye

Operating from distinct geographical and experiential locations, the authors of this chapter have, over several years, exchanged ideas about adopting Theatre of the Oppressed (TO) techniques with youth in conflict regions. Having identified dialogue as the fundamental principle of TO, they deploy a conversational format to propose how interactive theatre can productively work with both occupied (Palestinian) and threatened (Jewish Israeli) youth. This dialogue illuminates how adaptations of TO generate situations of identification with the Other and raise consciousness about the operations of power and oppression in the region while modeling political alliance within the facilitation context. In Viewpoints Theatre and follow-up programming, the medium promotes the message of creative collaboration while also prompting reflection and transformation from the youth spect-actors. The young people come to understand the political situation of the Other, particularly the dynamics of occupation, through direct and indirect encounter. These theatrical encounters reflect an expansion of Boal's TO model. While Boal mainly focuses on homogenous groups of the oppressed, the authors work with encounter, believing that both groups of Palestinian and Israeli youth gain a fuller humanity through this process that acknowledges and transforms power relationships.

The scene takes place in an Israeli high school classroom. Leather-bound books, cheerful plants, and colorful construction-paper collages line the walls. The students gather, chatting in Hebrew. One young girl leaps into the room, her hair flying wildly, before she plunks down beside a quiet, freckle-faced boy. They are there to witness Viewpoints, an Israeli-Palestinian interactive theatre group that will present a variety of scenarios generated by members of the company—two Palestinians, two Jewish Israelis, and one Arab citizen of Israel, who translates between Hebrew and Arabic. As a project of the Israeli-based Peres Center for Peace, the actors gathered in 2002 outside of the contested territories in which they lived, working long, difficult days on the island of Malta with director Igal Izraty. Over the next several years, new actors added their own scenarios, developed from moments of transition, trauma, and questioning. Chen Alon, a reserve Major in the Israeli Defense Force, decided in 2002 that he could no longer serve in the Occupied Palestinian Territories. He depicts the moment of his transformation in a condensed theatrical manner, adopting and adapting Augusto Boal's Image Theatre techniques, blended with commedia-style physicality. *Alon will later introduces a Forum Theatre scenario to the project and cofacilitate TO workshops with Israeli and Palestinian youth. In this opening scenario for the Israeli students, he recounts his political awakening.*

Three actors clad in black, wearing leather character masks, hunch together as Alon, in a half-mask, with hands clasped sternly behind his back, calls out in a commanding tone, "Soldier, get ready!" He alters his posture and confides to the students, "I want to be a combatant. I want to be an officer in the Israeli Defense Force." Again, he shifts his stance. "Day. Today I saw a three-year-old child looking at me with hatred." The students watch with rapt attention. "Night. My platoon and I are sieging a Palestinian house. The family is probably sleeping." We see the other characters standing in an image of sleep. Alon continues, "We don't ask questions. The goal: to arrest the wanted man. To prevent the next terror attack. Is he there?" The masked Palestinian characters awake, startled, and raise their hands into the air. "No, he's not there. The instructions were very clear: if the wanted person is not at home, we should arrest another family member to put pressure on the wanted man to surrender. The mother held her son very closely"—we see one actor pulled between the masked soldiers and a Palestinian actress playing his mother—"and refused to let him go. We had to separate them." Another half-masked Israeli actor enters, one hand held up in the shape of a gun, and she tugs at the mother's arm. "The mother didn't free her arms. A big sheltering and protecting body. A brave woman. A mother." The other actors are tensely extended, pulling on each other's arms. "The guys raised their guns. I did the same." The actors stretch even farther. "And then I felt it happen." The impact of his actions exceeded the intent of Israeli security. Alon reaches behind his head. "My mask came off." He pauses, looks searchingly at the mask in his hand, at the mother, and again at the mask, the persona of a soldier.

> Chen Alon: As an actor, the turn to TO from normative theatre parallels my turn from being a "normative citizen" of Israel, and serving in the army reserves, to a Refuse Soldier. I realized that I can't live any longer with the contradiction of wanting peace and serving as an officer in the Occupied Territories. It was the same conclusion in my artistic life: I can't commit

to my values and be willing to sit in jail for them but stay nonpolitical as a theatre artist. I was curious to learn how to use theatre for activism, which I realized is the most important part of being a citizen in a democratic state.

Sonja Kuftinec: So in your scenario, the dropping of the mask reflects your transformation to a more politically aware actor, in both senses of the term.

Chen: Yes. I discovered how Boal uses theatre as a tool for liberation. This experience informs all of my work with youth in Israel and Palestine, and the expansion and adaptation of Boal's TO techniques in the Palestinian-Israeli context. Basically, this is the heart of the work: I don't believe in the liberation of the oppressed alone, or that they must liberate the oppressors. As a former oppressor, I believe passionately in the need for the oppressors to release themselves from their role. In my personal liberation from this role, I experienced no less than gaining my life back. This mutual liberation process, of both the oppressed and the oppressors, is a kind of democratization. It produces a more genuine dialogue on power relations that ultimately moves toward equalizing those relationships. The various phases of the Viewpoints project—from actors generating scenarios, to performing an interactive forum scene with separate groups of Israeli and Palestinian students, to developing longer-term projects with these youth—moves from witnessing, to intervention, to direct encounter. The theatrical process generates situations that allow for redefinition and identification with the Other, raising consciousness about the power relations in the region while activating political alliance.

Generating Scenarios, Concretizing Traumas

Sonja: Boal proposes that theatre concretizes problems. I know that Viewpoints initially developed scenarios within the group, designing performances for as well as interactive scenarios with Palestinian and Israeli youth.

Chen: The generation of theatrical scenarios from personal trauma transforms a therapeutic moment into a political action. It humanizes the Other.

Ihsan Turkiyye: It opens the eyes of the other about the reality that we have to find a way to coexist together, but in justice. Once when we were doing the show, a conservative Israeli kid watching Chen's scene said to me, "I'm changed." He saw the soldier lifting up his mask and saw that he is a human being. "I say it's a good show, and I think it will change a lot. Keep doing it."

Chen: When you don't demonstrate your ideology but you structure it into the medium of the theatre, it also allows the other side to identify and to feel the emotions that the medium provokes. The fuel for acting is feeling.

Sonja: It seems like this refers to the emotional force required for the creation of theatre as well as for taking political action. Within the Viewpoints group, encountering each other's trauma exposed the humanity of both the oppressor and oppressed while providing a concrete experience of that humanization for youth audiences.

Chen: Yes, the encounter work started within the group of actors. Then we developed interactive scenarios.

Ihsan: When we first developed the piece, we brought tough scenes. We have sometimes a misunderstanding between the actors. It's difficult when it's competing groups. Everyone wants to show that his people are nice and full of morals. But the reality is not like that.

Sonja: You've talked about developing the scenarios from your individual moments of oppression or trauma that are not only about the Israeli-Palestinian dynamic but also introduce other sets of power relations. You offered a scene that focused on gender.

Ihsan: I made a scene from when I returned to Palestine after living in Lebanon. It was in 1994, and I took a taxi from East Jerusalem to Gaza. Really, you could do this then! But I have a Lebanese accent, so I was like a tourist. The driver, he is touching me, putting his hand on my knee, and the Israeli police stop the taxi because it's swerving—the driver has his hand on me and not the wheel. So we make the scene, and in it I say everything is OK to the police, not to betray the Palestinian. Then in the theatre, I ask the children directly, "Should I have told the police about him?" Even the Palestinian kids say, "Tell him, tell him. You have to tell the police, even though he is your enemy." So you see, we make scenes that show more complications within our societies, scenes that show there are other types of oppressions We also open the scene for the kids to think what they would do in this situation. This prepares them for the Forum Theatre.

Chen: In the Forum, the kids experience for themselves what it feels like to represent the Other within a more interactive scenario. The scene takes place at a checkpoint in the West Bank where two Israeli soldiers must determine whether to allow a pregnant Palestinian woman and her husband to cross from their village to a hospital in Ramallah, another West Bank city. The scene provides some details that are not well known among Jewish Israelis, such as the fact that most checkpoints are between Palestinian cities and villages and not between Israel and Occupied Palestinian Territories. Separate audiences of Palestinian and Israeli youth see the scene play out, and they can stop and intervene in the action. First, they replace their group—the Israelis act as soldiers, the Palestinians as the couple—then we invite them to take the place of the Other.

From Spectator to Spect-actor

Sonja: In this second stage of the Viewpoints presentation, it seems that audiences of Israeli and Palestinian youth move from spectators to spect-actors, from empathy to sympathy, and from awareness to a state of Frierian *conscientizacao*. Freire describes this kind of consciousness as one that comes from a dilemma, recognizing contradictions between, for example, state rhetoric and action.

Chen: Yes, it's true, this idea of a dilemma. After intervening in the checkpoint scenario as a soldier, one Israeli girl reflected, "It's a no-win situation." She recognized the responsibility of the soldiers for both the security of Israeli citizens—the Palestinian woman may really be carrying a bomb—and for the health of the pregnant woman. The forum scenario allows the Israelis to experience that there's no way to be a "good" occupier. In my opinion, this is part of the Forum Theatre strategy, to introduce a "no-win" moral situation that the youth may act on later as a resistance against the oppressive system.

Sonja: Political theorist Zygmunt Bauman suggests that the idea of "resolving" conflict, either internal individual or external social conflict, is a modernist thought—the idea that the force of rationality applied to a particular situation will lead to solution. But the majority of moral choices are made between contradictory impulses. Some moral impulses, if acted upon in full, can actually lead to immoral consequences. "It's a no-win situation." But I also think that it's only when confronted with a dilemma, with a contradiction, that individuals can change even if—or especially when—they cannot immediately change the contradictory situation. They confront the difference between their sense of self—their code of ethics—and their actions.

Chen: This is the first military tactic that I learned as a soldier: put someone in a dilemma where both choices are bad. Now I use it more positively in the theatre work. We create scenarios that "unhouse" the youth from their habits of thinking and being. It's an idea of Foucault. Ignorance is active. To learn is isolating and painful. It is a movement from "tolerating" an idea or a person to integrating that idea, that being of the Other.

Sonja: Participating in the scenario heightens the conflict within the young people. In the video I watched of one Viewpoints performance, an Israeli boy who intervened to play the pregnant Palestinian woman in the checkpoint scenario reflected afterward, "As a spectator, I thought, 'It seems so easy,' and onstage I realized that they should let her through. She suffers. They have to let her pass." As a spectator, the student empathized with the woman in a way that naturalized her passivity. From his viewpoint as a (Israeli) spectator, the Palestinians at the checkpoint had "nothing to do." Placing himself within the situation, taking action and feeling onstage in sympathy with the dilemma of the Palestinian woman, shifted the student's consciousness.

Chen: He felt intuitively on his flesh and blood how frustrating it is to be onstage without being able to take an action, a feeling made stronger by his stage partners' expectations for action. He felt the frustrating gap between witnessing and experiencing. He felt for the first time the lack of ability to take an action in this specific violent situation.

Sonja: The kinds of feelings evoked within the Israeli students seem to resonate with Boal's critique of Aristotelian empathy.[1] According to Boal, when we feel *for* a character (em-pathy) rather than *with* that character (sym-pathy), we remove ourselves from the necessity of investigating causality and from taking action to transform the conditions that lead to suffering.

Chen: But Boal's critique of Aristotle's concept of empathy is based in an understanding of catharsis as containment rather than purification—for Boal, experiencing suffering at a distance erases the need for action. The Israeli students do not all follow up with direct action, but their reflections show a movement in understanding. You remember the boy with the freckles. He makes a breakthrough in recognizing the Other: "I think it's very hard for the Palestinians. The checkpoints. The permits. And we come and go so easy everywhere." Often for the first time, the kids on both sides face the fact that they don't know anything about the situation, that the "facts" provided by their media are, under an optimistic interpretation, lacking a lot of information and, under the worst interpretation, full of lies and manipulated.

Sonja: The encounter with the Palestinian and Israeli actors and their situations seems to break stereotypes and inspires the sympathetic identification on both sides.

Chen: You know, at the beginning, we were surprised that in the discussion after the Forum that on both sides the children reacted the same. They have the same fears, the same anxieties, the same stereotypes of the other, and what we are trying to do is to break these stereotypes to create a more accurate image of the Other.

Sonja: But I still see a difference in response to the Forum scenario between the Israeli and Palestinian youth.

El Khader, West Bank

It is late November 2007. I [Sonja] *sit in the passenger seat of a van that is waved through a checkpoint with barely a lift of the heavily armed soldier's head to glance at our Israeli license plates. We leave the smooth, paved roads built for Israeli settlers—roads that often pass through Palestinian farmland and swerve onto bumpy tar toward El Khader, a town in the West Bank. There is tension in the air. This is Chen's first time in the village since he demolished a house here six years ago. It was the moment of his unmasking, the decision not to serve anymore in the Territories. It is also the first time that Viewpoints has performed in the West Bank. The other encounters with Palestinians were with Arab citizens of Israel and Palestinians from the Occupied Territories who were brought to east Jerusalem. For most of the kids in El Khader, it is also their first encounter with Israelis who are not soldiers.*

We enter an open room on the ground floor of the town hall. I am taken aback by the bareness of the space. Stamped onto the cracked plaster walls are signs indicating that cell phones, cigarettes, and guns are prohibited. A few staff members lean against the walls smoking and chatting on their cell phones. The actors rehearse. A group of children shuffle quietly into the room. The girls giggle beneath their hijabs as they file into the front-row seats. A group of boys, their hair slicked back or gelled straight up from their scalps, sits in back, their faces eager and open. Just before the show is scheduled to begin, the Mayor of El Khader calls the actors to his office.

Ihsan: The mayor wanted to make sure that this is not "normalization" with the Israelis. He said it's a great opportunity to have Palestinians and Israeli groups to perform for us. We are living the occupation every day and it makes our life difficult, but we are willing to open a new vision for peace and education for peace. I tell him that we wrote our script from our agony. We wanted Israelis to recognize the pain of the occupation. So, the show is within the Palestinian pro-peace policy.

Sonja: I saw that the kids loved the show, and they willingly participated in the intervention scenario facilitated by Ismael, a Palestinian actor.

Chen: It's worth mentioning that in front of Palestinians the joker of the forum is Palestinian and in front of Jewish Israelis, I do it.

Sonja: But the kids in El Khader didn't try to intervene in a way to "improve" the situation. In fact, when playing Israeli soldiers, they put more pressure on the pregnant couple.

Chen: This is their reality. It is a structural dilemma.

Sonja: When I asked Ismael later to translate for me what the youth felt in the scene, he told me one boy said, "Watching is nice, but it is difficult to go into the scene. That's how the Israeli soldiers behave with us."

Chen: They also said, "The solution is not with us, it's to end the occupation. It doesn't matter how I behave. We are not the people to find the solutions." This is a dilemma of using TO with this scenario. In fact, what is needed is to create a new reality rather than only to transform the present situation.

Ihsan: They don't try to resolve the situation; they repeat what they experience. They feel inside themselves that the checkpoints are staying. They don't have hope.

Chen: I know that Viewpoints is not miraculous, but the replacement of the antagonist is another brick in the humanization wall.

Sonja: I also think some hopefulness appears when the Palestinian kids see Israelis who are not soldiers, when they witness the group of actors modeling alliance, working together. Chen, what did you say to the kids after the performance? When they took you outside to see another demolished house?

Chen: I wanted them to know how I felt when I was demolishing the house in El Khader. I said that my feelings, beliefs, and actions have transformed. Now I'm not willing to participate; I refuse to serve in the Occupied Territories, and I think what the Israeli Defense Force is doing here are crimes. When I was their age, I was taught that they—the Palestinians—are my enemies. But now I have a new way of seeing them. I'm now interested in understanding what causes transformation in beliefs and thoughts through theatre. But what is most important is that we would later work with these kids directly, that they will work with each other and not through our group as a mediator.

Chen: Last year we developed a pilot project where Israeli and Palestinian high school students met separately in a parallel process, followed by a daylong binational workshop. This year we initiated a four-month project between the youth in El Khader and in Yeroham, a town in the Negev Desert. The youth first developed their own group, meeting uninationally, then we planned that every three to four weeks, they would meet together. The long-term project of direct encounter with these groups showed us something different than the one-time Forum Theatre. It also shows how the external conflict is mirrored in and sets the limits for what we do with the groups.

The Intergroup Encounter

Another road trip through Israel in the fall of 2007. Chen and I [Sonja] drive three hours south from Tel Aviv through the Negev, passing mainly Bedouin villages and army training posts. Chen points to where he trained as an officer, Military Base Number 1. It is hardcore, the West Point of Israel. As we drive, Chen sets the scene. A few weeks prior to our journey, Chen had asked the Yeroham Community Center director if a youth group might want to participate in the encounter theatre project. "To tell you the truth," the director had admitted, "I don't trust the Palestinians. But I'll put the project to the kids and see if they want to do it." Chen had convinced the director to allow him to share some theatre activities and talk with the kids directly. This evening was his "audition" for the project with the youth and staff from the center.

We reach the center, an old warehouse transformed by the municipality with vibrant murals, a café, music, and theatre rooms. Chen leads an hour of gentle theatre activities, after which a small group of youth, aged fourteen to seventeen, sit down and burst into anxious Hebrew. After several minutes, they gesture toward me; I sense that they are indicating that I don't understand the discussion. But I think I do. "You had a great time tonight and you want to do more theatre, but not with the Palestinians," I propose, and they nod in agreement. I hesitate about how to share the feeling I get from them, beneath their words. "You are taking a long time to say this. So I think that there is fear of the Other. But underneath that fear there is also curiosity." As this comment is translated, the youth nod more reflectively. Chen adds that they will be changed by the process—not necessarily in any political direction, but the encounter will change them. The tone of the discussion shifts as it models Chen's promise; there is no attempt to debate, convince, or discipline the youth. They stay in dialogue, and eventually they change. They say yes, they will encounter the Other, but only once. They commit to meet with the Palestinians only once.

> Ihsan: When I began my process, it was also with this sense of curiosity to know the Other. So this was the first thing—it wasn't about peace.
> Chen: I suspected the same feelings were happening with the kids. So, in the early uninational sessions, we worked with separate teams of Israeli and

Palestinian facilitators to build the group. We also explored the imagination of the Other. The kids in Yeroham had a fantasy of the Palestinians as primitive and even monstrous. One of the girls said she was afraid that if she went to the bathroom during a binational meeting, one of the Palestinian boys would knife her or rape her. But in the first encounter, they have the experience of more genuine humanistic encounter. They were completely surprised by this, by even small details like that the Palestinians are wearing jeans and T-shirts, not like the Bedouin Arabs that they know from the desert. One girl admitted, "Some of them are even cute." She is indicating through this that they can play together.

Sonja: Besides reproducing "normal" teenage flirtations and resultant adult anxieties, how do you think that this kind of encounter work extends TO?

Chen: From my experience with Boal, he tends to avoid dealing with group dynamics, and this is a main part of our focus. Within the workshop room, the Israeli and Palestinian youth experience what I would call critical equal participation. For example, in the second binational encounter, we used Boal's Columbian Hypnosis exercise (*Games for Actors and Non-Actors*). Partners of Palestinian and Israeli youth took turns leading the other with their hand. Through the exercise, we reflected on the role and the responsibility of the leaders outside the room, in this seemingly eternal state of conflict, and also for the youth as citizens in a hierarchical structure. It was obvious to all the kids that the leaders have no interest to finish the conflict, and they, as citizens, have to take this responsibility.

Sonja: But don't power relations still exist in the room, in the situation, outside of the "decisions of leaders"?

Chen: Yes, of course. I am talking about experiencing this together through TO as equal participants; it is very powerful and, in my opinion, transformative. They experience power relations in the room and they know it is echoing relations outside. They have the insight they might transform their relations in the room, then in the state, and then in the world. But, first, they reflect on those relationships. The Israelis want to keep things on a personal level, but the Palestinians introduce the occupation. One Palestinian girl asked in the first session, "Are you aware of the fact that my father didn't want me to come here because he didn't want me to pass three checkpoints? He didn't want me to be harassed by soldiers."

Sonja: I think what you're saying is that within the room, the young people can experience equal participation in pointing out the group differences around, for example, mobility.

Chen: Yes, and the situation outside is also reflected in the room in other ways. In the first encounter session, the Israelis said that they didn't want to talk directly about politics, that as kids they had no impact. But before the second session, there was a suicide bombing in Dimona, a town near Yeroham. Many of the Israelis chose not to come to the next binational meeting, but they said it was because they had other responsibilities—a few of the girls said they had a manicure class. One of the two Israelis who did attend the binational session at first tried to make excuses for the others, but at the end of the session, he asked if he could say something. He shifted from excuse to acknowledgment and apologized to the Palestinians that not all the Israelis were there.

Sonja: Was there any mention of Dimona?

Chen: Not directly. But he hinted that the Palestinians in the group did not "take revenge" in response to attacks in Gaza by staying away from the binational meeting. In their uninational encounter the next week, the Israeli participants admitted that the Palestinians' perception of the Gaza attacks parallels their own response to the bombing in Dimona, but that the Palestinians had still made the choice to attend the encounter with the Other.

Sonja: You mentioned that even the Israeli youth who did not attend the binational sessions experienced indirect transformation.

Chen: Yes, and this is why we were insisting on uninational and binational processes. To encounter the Other—even an imaginary Other—through theatre is still transformative. In the Yeroham meetings, we dismantled the monstrous Other, separated stereotypes and opinions from needs. We combined this work on needs and opinions, which are used in the Israeli-based Adam Institute for dialogue, with Boal. We developed conflict scenarios in which the youth had to think about what is behind the actions of the antagonist—the one who is blocking the desires of the protagonist. What are the antagonist's opinions and actions, how are they shaped by needs, and why are these needs shaped into an oppressive response? These scenarios were not about the conflict, but they introduced a way of analyzing and dismantling the demonized Other. We developed Forum Theatre that tested solutions asking two important questions: Are the proposed solutions realistic? Are they fair? The goal is not to defeat the antagonist, but to satisfy the needs of both sides in the conflict by acknowledging the oppressive outcome of the antagonist and to transform his or her actions without ignoring their legitimate needs.

Sonja: In the final binational encounter that I attended, there were only three kids from Yeroham. But I felt that those three really went through a process. One girl at first wouldn't even shake the hand of the Palestinians, but toward the end of the session, she was in dialogue with a group of Palestinians, speaking directly to one in English.

Chen: At the end of the session, the teacher of the Palestinian girls from Hebron addressed one of the Israeli boys as being "like her son."

Sonja: And one of the Israelis, a settler who, as part of her military duty, works with the teenagers in Yeroham, noted that "something had penetrated" her about the process.

Chen: She did not change all of what she thinks, but she felt a transformation she couldn't explain.

Sonja: How did you feel about the fact that most of the Israeli youth didn't attend the last binational encounter?

Chen: Of course I was disappointed and frustrated, but I feel that even the ones who didn't attend that last session went through a real process. For example, one of the girls who attended almost all of the uninational encounters and not a single binational one mentioned she had gained knowledge and information about the Palestinians that wasn't in the media or in her education. I reflected their earlier texts about the Palestinians, their fears and anxieties, and shared that it is powerful to be able to contain these complexities and ambivalences.

Sonja: It's a different point of view than you had initially. You felt the project was a failure.

Chen: I guess I am in a process, too. Is that what you're saying?

Sonja: You mentioned that in the final session, the Yeroham youth also talked about the tools they were learning.

Chen: They were referring to how theatre is not what they thought; it is not about them being on the stage as "stars," but it is a medium where they can learn about the society and the place they live in and to change them.

Sonja: It seems that they came to see themselves as social beings in a way that expands rather than reduces their sense of self. To me it is similar to how Martin Buber talks about "genuine dialogue," the need to regard the other as is. This acceptance allows for disagreement, but the other is always affirmed as a person. They struggle as partners rather than as enemies.

Chen: It is a step in the process toward alliance that we feel more strongly as facilitators and as actors in Viewpoints. This partnership is quite different from "collaboration," which has a negative connotation for the Palestinians. Many feel that it is not the time to reconcile with the oppressor. But Israeli audiences have also accused us of creating unbalanced scenarios showing only Palestinian suffering. I think we don't show only this, but, in fact, Palestinians *do* generally suffer more—on a daily basis—than the Israelis.

Sonja: What about those Israelis who live near Gaza, who are being attacked by rocket fire?

Chen: My responsibility is for my society. As Brecht said, "I will speak for my disgracefulness and let others speak about theirs." I do feel responsibility for my people's suffering, but I know that the occupation is a major cause for all our mutual suffering, and I feel responsible for that.

The Challenges of Building Alliance

Chen: Ultimately, the theatre is not only a medium to transform these feelings but also a model for partnership. Fifteen years ago, you couldn't find one political movement that was a joint movement. But the most influential movements these days are joint projects like Combatants for Peace, a nonviolent alliance group of ex-combatants from both sides that I belong to. This is the political activism conduct that I think has to merge into TO work.

Ihsan: In Viewpoints, we work as a group, really as a group, as a family, as Israeli and Palestinian actors. But it is not easy working together. The situation doesn't help us. We are living under siege, occupation, and roadblocks every day. And Israelis, they are not living in Switzerland. Their neighbors are not French, Danish, or Germans. They are the Lebanese, the Syrians, the Palestinians, the Jordanians, the Egyptians. And you will not believe it, but these kids, they understand. The leaders cannot make peace, so this is our mission as people, as actors, and as citizens to work with our people, to create a place that we can start to have a solution, to live together.

Chen: This is very important that our activity is actually against both our administrations. The essence of theatre is action, and we are saying to the people don't wait for the leaders to make peace, don't wait for the leaders to change the situation. As citizens, we are responsible to change the situation, and the best way to rehearse change is in theatre.

Ihsan: It's not so easy to make a change. It has to be a process; that's what I believe. I don't believe anybody who comes and says, "Hey, I want to make peace with you!" No. I think he is a cheater, in one way or another. We are human beings, and we have to go through a process, and in this process, you will cry, you will curse yourself, you will curse everybody. You will curse that you were born in this world, that you were born in this country. But in the end of this process, you will see the change.

Sonja: It's optimistic. But I know that there are also some important problems with the work, especially in regard to who has access to TO and facilitation trainings. Do you think that, in general, the Israeli and Palestinian facilitators experience "critical equal participation"?

Chen: Within our process as facilitators, yes. Within the process with the kids, no. The experience was the opposite of empowering sometimes for Nina and Ahmad, the Palestinian facilitators. But the dynamics within our group also reflected the outside situation. We were dealing with the fact that the Israelis have more experience and training, more access to education resources. More access to publishing on the work, as you see here.

Sonja: So how was the "critical equality" manifested in the project with the youth?

Chen: We were dealing directly with the fact of inequality. We faced many imbalances: the facilitators always met in Tel Aviv and not in the Occupied Territories for preparations, and, of course, the funding of the project is from an Israeli institute, the Peres Center for Peace.

Sonja: So you were dealing in "critical equality" with the fact of inequality?

Chen: We were practicing many kinds of alliances, breaking and building new ways of working together.

Sonja: There's also the factor of inequality of how an alliance project is viewed within the societies: not only that you are funded by an Israeli institute but also that the Palestinians are, in contrast, under suspicion and threat by participating. Do you think the process allows you to confront this threat directly?

Chen: This was discussed a lot in the facilitation unit. I can say that the topic you've mentioned was a main issue among the facilitators and a stumbling block for genuine dialogue. Ahmad said that we cannot really understand him, because we don't know what it means to work with Israelis without a permit from the Palestinian authorities. I was thinking of Boal's quote of Che Guevara: "Solidarity is running the same risks." I don't know where to go with this problem. Sometimes, I think to work with youth only is to give fish and not fishing rods. And we are in danger of maintaining the facilitation inequality.

Sonja: I know it's a struggle for you, and I know that Ahmad and Ihsan have different struggles—of how much to work for change within Palestine, and how and whether to continue working in alliance with Israelis. I know that it is draining for all of you to continue to try to deal with all the dilemmas of the occupation.

Chen: I read recently something from Sanjoy Ganguly, the director of an Indian forum theatre group Jana Sanskriti. It really inspired me. "In the dialectic between insoluble problems on the one hand and the attempt to surmount them on the other lies the key to human development."[2]

Sonja: So what is next in the development of the work and of the humanity of its participants?

Chen: To find ways to support more opportunities for Palestinian facilitators, to build a stronger alliance. This is the key to end the political oppression and to develop the humanity of both sides, as partners in an ongoing process rather than as enemies in an ongoing conflict.

Notes

1. See Paul Dwyer, "Theoria Negativa: Making Sense of Boal's Reading of Aristotle," *Modern Drama* 48, no. 4 (2005): 635–58, for a particularly astute critique. Frances Babbage also provides a more general critical reading of *Theatre of the Oppressed* in *Augusto Boal*, part of Routledge's Performance Practitioners Series (New York: Routledge, 2004).

2. See Sanjoy Ganguly, "Theatre—a Space for Empowerment: Celebrating Jana Sanskriti's Experience in India," in *Theater and Empowerment: Community Drama on the World Stage*, ed. Richard Boon and Jane Plastow (New York: Cambridge University Press, 2004), 221.

5

TELAvision

Weaving Connections for Teen Theatre of the Oppressed

Brent Blair

Thus I, gone forth as spiders do
In spider's web a truth discerning,
Attach one silken thread to you
For my returning.

—E. B. White, "Spider's Web"

The world is made of spider webs
The threads are stuck to me and you . . .

—Joan Osborne, "Spider Web"

Teen Education in Liberation Arts (TELA) is a multidimensional youth theatre training program that hosts a diverse assembly of teens, mentors, and facilitators from Los Angeles and Santa Monica in annual twelve-week training workshops, which end with a series of public Forum Theatre events on the themes of relationship and dating violence. Founded on Boal-based theatre training, this chapter recounts the past experiences, present challenges, and future desires surrounding the phenomena of building and maintaining a youth Theatre of the Oppressed (TO) program in an urban setting. Participants and facilitators alike contribute their thoughts on negotiating the space between discipline and disorder, aesthetics and accessibility, spirituality and political awareness, and cultural identity and consensus.

Response to Rupture: An Academy of Healing Arts Moment

During the summer of 2006, I had a conversation with my longtime friend and colleague Jennifer Freed about the idea of creating a new teen theatre arts and leadership training program in the Los Angeles area. The project would be based primarily on the philosophical principles of her own Academy of Healing Arts (AHA), the enormously successful teen leadership training program in Santa Barbara, which would which would also foot the inaugural bill for the venture. Freed and her partner, Rendy Freedman, had created AHA in 2000 to respond to "kids on the margins who have often felt that they were left out of dominant narrative" (Freed 2008). AHA brings these teens together through a series of workshops and Native American Counsel sessions and, in turn, offers them the tools to see themselves in situ (Boal 2003, 26) and engage in embodied experiences of healing as coparticipants, rather than clients, of the healing process.

Freed and Freedman were keen to work with TO techniques, as Jennifer Freed stated, "The reason that we wanted to work with Theatre of the Oppressed . . . is that our entire philosophy of AHA is a communitarian model instead of an authoritarian model, and . . . Theatre of the Oppressed is really the only type of theatre that was fundamentally about inclusiveness and wasn't oriented towards stars and side players . . . we were looking for something that would go right to the core of each person feeling that they had an important part to play in the drama of their lives and in the community as it was unfolding" (Freed 2008).

Why was I so profoundly drawn into working with teens? I know there is a palpable vitality about adolescence—all things are possible, everything is on the edge, yet there is a palpable shadow to this dynamism. It seemed as if our own culture was itself stuck in adolescence, perhaps never more clearly illustrated than after 9/11 when Americans found themselves at once fully terrified and fiercely terrifying, armed and alarmed, more *reactive* than responsive, and highly skilled in the genius of their technology but showing little wisdom for its responsible use: what good are "smart bombs" in a dehumanized command? Finally, Americans seemed a culture more bent on fantasy (i.e., engagement with external images) than imagination—a conscious engagement with and cocreation of these same images.

For years I had been surrounded by a cultural field supremely interested in youth, particularly in the population rather loosely defined as "urban teens" (but is not a young person from Beverly Hills an "urban teen" also?), and had learned to view patterns of suffering and dis-ease as ruptures rather than problems, the latter inviting a "solution" or fix, the former really asking for little more than investigation and a curious heart. If I saw the surrounding symptoms typically associated with "at-risk teens" (who has created this risk?) as the "problem," I would have to seek objective solutions to crime, violence, school dropout rates, and early pregnancy, for example. The teenagers with whom I worked, however, weren't the *problem*, nor was their "at-risk" behavior; on the contrary, they were seeking solutions with only reactive, but not responsible, tools to guide them. We had healing to do, but the client was the country as opposed to the individual teen. The teens, it would turn out, were to be the healers.

The Birth of TELA: Choosing Liberation

As I put my attention on the topic of liberation arts, I encountered myriad philosophers, artists, poets, activists, and indigenous feminists who were writing about experiences where spiritual practice and activist integrity were not mutually exclusive: Gloria Anzaldúa identifies the liberatory path as an abandonment of the battle across opposing river banks "so that we are on both shores at once" (1999, 100); Aurora Levins Morales speaks of the work of liberation artists as "cultural activism," which insists that the political *is* the personal (1998, 4) and invokes a "new theory that can explain why we mustn't abandon anyone" (ibid., 123). My mentor and friend Mary Watkins reflects on the intentional use of the word "liberation" in conjunction with the field of psychology: "Liberation was chosen as a better term for the goal of cultural change, for it is relational, based on a paradigm of interdependence. The liberation of one is inextricably tied to the liberation of all" (Watkins, in Slattery and Corbett 2000, 213).

The more I encountered writings on liberation theology and liberation psychology, the more curious I became about implementing this model with teenagers. In consultation with some of my students, colleagues, and friends in the Los Angeles TO community, I decided on a new acronym that seemed more suited not only to our Los Angeles community but also to the underlying philosophy that would turn out to inform our entire body of work. Thus, TELA was born in the fall of 2006, and we recruited ten teens from fourteen to eighteen years of age who built a successful assembly of some eight Forum Theatre scenes, which they performed for an audience of several hundred peers to rave reviews. Much was gained by the lessons learned during this important partnership that would force TELA to deeply reinvest in a philosophical interrogation before it reconvened. Crucial to this interrogation were the numerous conversations with TELA-continuing participants, student volunteers, associates, and the AHA sponsoring partners. Though TELA had been in practice for one year, it felt like the praxis of TELA was just beginning.

The Thing about Webs: The Philosophy of the *TELAraña*

TELA not only invited the language of liberation theology and the pedagogy of the oppressed into the name, but it crossed borders too. Its acronym represented English-language terms but the program title itself, *habló en español*, reminded us of the Spanish word for cloth—*tela*—also shorthand for a spider's web—*telaraña*. It was polyvalent and multilingual, a philosophical mandate to investigate a new paradigm to traditional "normative" patterns for working with teens that had disturbed me in the past twenty years. Gloria Anzaldúa, Aurora Levins Morales, Mary Watkins, Helene Lorenz, and others had spoken constantly of the need of cultural field-workers to imagine the world as *interconnected* rather than *oppositional*. In my years of exposure to other teen theatre programs stuck in the "right or wrong," "healthy or unhealthy" binaries, I witnessed firsthand the damage caused by simplistic behavior modification theatre programs driven by adult "experts" intent on instructing, correcting, and healing troubled or "at-risk" teens without questioning the sociocultural surround that contributed to their challenges or pathologized experiences in the first place.

The name and the metaphor also linked us to mythologies of the art of arachnids. It connected us to the trickster figures like Anansi of Ghana, the Tsuchigumo people of Japan, and Iktomi of the Lakota people and the creative forces like Neith from Egypt and—perhaps most familiar to us Westerners—the transgressive and subversive actions of Arachne of Greek mythology. There is something creative and resistant about them all, perhaps elusive or mysterious, but definitively connective and occasionally healing. In her book, *Weaving the Word*, Kathryn Sullivan Kruger marks the significance of the spider's web in the language of the Navajo (Diné) people of the Southwestern United States, who note that Spider Woman "weaves all human activity and relationships into a living tapestry. Hers is the first and last song" (2001, 25).

In addition, these representations reminded me of Carol Gilligan's interrogation of dominant patriarchal psychological norms, which formed the core of her book, *In a Different Voice*: "Illuminating life as a web rather than a succession of relationships, women portray autonomy rather than attachment as the illusory and dangerous quest" (1993, 48). Somehow I resonated with this. I had been raised in such a culture of independence and self-propulsion that I hardly detected the subtle damage being done to the inner workings of my own psyche. Painfully lonely and alone, I felt a failure if I were to reach out, to consult, to share with my friends, or to seek help. Perhaps the greatest pathology I recognized in the teens was an amplified version of this neurosis—problems were to be handled autonomously; to seek help was to admit defeat.

Not only was the web model useful for reframing the way of the psyche, adolescent or otherwise, it was also useful for making links and connections from the personal to the political, from the individual to the collective. To view "their" pain as "my" pain was not only empathic but also radical in today's individualistic economy. Seeing the pain of others is costly and implies a certain coresponsibility for suffering: it removes the veiled myth of isolated incidence, the "no-fault" clause. It destroys colonialism, and I realized that if I wanted to work with teens in a radically different way, I had to be willing to throw out older models that threatened to colonize the apparently rebellious, nonconformist, or transgressive language of adolescence, no matter how well intentioned they may seem.

Furthermore, as a young man initiated primarily by women teachers, I strongly identified with Gilligan's notion of the interrelationship of the web as a response to the more linear comprehension of relationships I had been taught growing up. I realized during my own adolescence that men, too, were ruptured by the patriarchal psychology of our forefathers. Gilligan offered a new paradigm in which I was able to replace "the hierarchy of rights with a web of relationships." Through this replacement, our theatre group could challenge "the premise of separation underlying the notion of rights" and articulate a "guiding principle of connection" (Gilligan 1993, 57). It is what Chela Sandoval frequently referred to as the expanded capacity to "sustain the complexities"—quite a far cry from the black-and-white world of my father's generation (Sandoval 2007).

Finally, the act of spinning the web is mythologically a creative act, weaving new language and creating new domains of thought. Through TELA, then, our teens would weave new narratives that would investigate classic notions of oppression from an ever-increasing web of complex relationships. At the very least, our interconnected web would insist that we eschew traditional rules and regulations that usually are the first order of business for teen theatre programs.

Therefore, for our group leaders to impose any written or formulaic syllabus or agenda would break the very fragile filaments of the *tela*. The teens, in dialogue with the adult facilitators and some of my university student volunteers, would have to codesign our meetings, cofacilitate the sessions eventually, and create a peer-led, peer-written, peer-performed theatre event for other teens who would, in classic TO style, bear witness to the rupture without having it "solved" for them.[1] We would inevitably create a rather classic Forum Theatre event based on the rupture of teen dating and relationship violence (this was the mandate of our partners at both Violence Intervention Program (VIP; affiliated with Los Angeles County and the USC Medical Center in East Los Angeles) with Sojourn, a project of OPCC[2] (Ocean Park Community Center's program offering services for battered women and their children in Santa Monica, California), but beyond that we would have to proceed with the complexity that TELA required.

The Structure of the Work: TELA Praxis

TELA follows a model familiar to practitioners of TO. Participants are first identified from word of mouth through peer recruitment, typically inspired by their participation in an actual TO workshop that may have visited their school. There is decidedly no audition process. Through funding from an affiliated organization of AHA in Santa Barbara, the teens receive a nominal stipend for three-hour weekly meetings over the course of twelve weeks that roughly rivals standard California minimum wage in the form of a cash payment at the end of their opening public performance. Their time is valuable, and our commitment to reimbursement is essential to the program's success. From the guidelines of our particular grant, this stipend is contingent on their completion of some standard pre- and postsession psychological evaluative measures and their timely attendance at the great majority of all of the working sessions.

True to the structure of the paradigmatic "web" of the title, the work is a multifaceted tapestry consisting of *most* of the following ten stages each week:

1. *Opening*: The official welcome and call for *physical greetings*, then an invitation for teens and adults to *mix up* the circular seating arrangements in order to *dis-invite clique configurations*.
2. *Meditation*: A different teen serves as the "leader" each week. This is followed by a circle "check-in" relevant to the events of the week, such as the highs and lows.
3. *Agenda*: The whole group *codesigns* and endorses by *consensus* the working agenda for the evening.[3]
4. *Games*: TO and ATA[4] games *relevant to the work* expected to be done that evening.[5]
5. *Group process*: Known as "council" work[6] on a theme, dedicated by a teen in the circle.
6. *Nutrition*: Food! After all, they are *teens*, so this is vital. Typically, there are "dyad-processing" assignments to encourage informal dialogue around certain topics.
7. *Educational dialogue*: Dialogue that centers around a topic relevant to the needs of the working group.
8. *TO technique*: Usually toward building the antimodel, writing the scenes.[7]

9. *Evaluation*: Feedback and process. Reflective resonance over the content and the delivery of the material. Spect-actor engagement is welcome and encouraged; none of the material is precious or off-limits in this regard, yet immense care is given to the protagonist's material and the delicate nature of the narrative.
10. *Closing circle*: A round of appreciations and three "ritual breaths."[8]

It is a tall order to cover all ten items each week, and in the spirit of our willingness to be flexible and alter the best plans of the group and its members, we have readily surrendered many items each week as occasion demands; however, the structure of the workshop stems from a core philosophical perspective that never alters, though the format may change from week to week. *Why* we do our work remains the same, even as *what* we do, and, in the next section, *how* we do it may alter significantly.

The Strategies of the Work: How We Do It, in Five Strands

In understanding the need for connectivity, conscientization, and interdependent engagement in order to heal our culture (very realistic goals, we feel!), the facilitators agreed that each group may have different methods or strategies for traveling along the same journey. What follows is a model of some of our own identifiable strategies for engaging in the web and making connections. We have found each strand to have a significant influence on the overall efficacy of our journey together.

1. The Rituals of the TELAesthetic Space

The format in our weekly meeting is quite obviously pretty packed solid with events and activities so, as a result, our meetings seldom end early, neither do they end very late; however, what is as important to us about beginning on time is the promise of ending on time.

Ritual beginnings and endings form the crucial bookends of our group and are adhered to almost religiously. If for whatever reason the facilitators omit any part of the opening or closing structure, one or more teens will make mention of it and insist that we hold to the order. This yearning for rituals seemed curious to me in my early days of this type of work, until I recognized the significance of meaningful ritual in everyday life and its notorious absence in modern society.

Most rituals today are unconscious and accidental with markers that serve as little more than announcements of events rather than preparations for transformation. Daily rituals familiar to the teens of our program include the ritual of school bells followed, in no time at all, by mass exodus with little care for what topic was being taught or who was in the middle of an important sentence; the ritual of breakfast marked by low grumblings in the long line at the donut shop or, on rare occasions, the high price of a simple, blended drink at Starbucks; or the ritual gesture of sitting *facing* the window in a restaurant to stay alert to drive-by shooters. These "rituals" may be significant, but their relative importance is perhaps better evaluated against the backdrop of the low level of human witness or mindful intentionality of each ritual. Most notably, these events seem *ritualistic* rather than truly *ritual*— a distinction, for example, like Victor Turner's classification of liminal versus liminoid in *From Ritual to Theatre*.[9] These ritualisms of daily life do not deepen our human interactive capacity or offer much more than temporary comfort, a "holding together" that reminds us of entertainment.

Rarer, though, are the "true rituals" of shared family or community experiences. These rituals are embedded in the kinds of important greetings at arrivals and departures that go beyond the obligatory "hey" and the colloquial, if now somewhat antiquated, "whassup," which neither invite responses nor require much attention. Rituals communicate intention in much the same way that TO invites a clear and *aesthetic* delineation of the playing space from the spect-actor space. Boal reminds us that the theatre is both a *physical* and an *aesthetic* space: physical because it has boundaries and aesthetic because it is co-created imaginatively by our distant witnessing of what transpires in the empty space. By allegory, the rituals of TELA invite an aesthetic engagement insofar as they attract a mindful, if momentary, space for conscientization.[10]

2. TELA Games

Games play multiple purposes in the TO world. As Boal notes in his seminal work *Games for Actors and Non-Actors*, games "deal with the expressivity of the body as emitter and receiver of messages" (1992, 60) and acknowledge the notion that "one's physical and psychic apparatuses are completely inseparable" (ibid., 61). Games do more than bring mind and body together; they allow for spontaneity and free play, essential elements for inviting personal and then political transformation.

There is perhaps nothing terribly revolutionary about what games we play, but what seems most important from a TO perspective is the underlying philosophy of our play time. For us, in preparation for our work in connectivity and liberatory praxis, it seems clear that we needed games to move us, as Boal notes, from a position in culture as passive objects toward that of more active subjects (1985, 91). This movement is accompanied by a series of paradoxes inherent, perhaps, to the TELA population. Firstly, working with teens at the margins of power during the last twenty years has taught me that there is certainly a compelling hunger for freedom, even as they may project an early timidity of expression or a dependence on old modalities of thinking and being, which may seem stifling and indeed psychologically imprisoning. Secondly, or perhaps concurrently, there is a powerful craving for structure, even while they may project a resistance to any rules or regulations. The key to understanding this set of twin paradoxes may rest in the third great paradox—a profound cry for independence and autonomy, even while it is manifest in the most dependent behaviors.

Imagine the combined paradoxes, then a group of youth who, at the same time, seem to hunger for freedom but prefer the imprisoned safety of their habitual thinking, desire structure but manifest chaotic behavior, and declare autonomy even while they may occasionally collapse in perceived incapability of doing something on their own. Make no mistake about it, these multiple paradoxes are not teenage *problems*; they are teenage *symptoms*. The common rupture in all three areas exists ubiquitously throughout contemporary society.

Just look at our neurotic response to the 9/11 attacks: we proclaimed ourselves promoters of freedom by hosting some of the most oppressive laws that imprisoned thousands, often with no legal recourse, and fomented an unjustified war in the name of world peace on a perceived enemy that in fact bore no threat nor had any part in the attacks. We culturally yearn for order and structure, while our politicians routinely break laws, our government does not participate in global legal treaties, and our most affluent tycoons of industry cry foul over perceived government regulations, new taxes, or any laws that remove their myth of autonomy. Finally, our cry for independence and autonomy is perhaps never louder than from the heads of our larger financial institutions and the barons of Wall Street itself, until the economy collapses under the weight of its own gluttony, at which point the same barons heave out a new cry and "we the people" open our wallets to bail them out.

In every way, the surrounding culture is steeped in the pathology of its own uninitiated adolescence, and the true adolescents in our teen theatre programs are simply mired in reaction to the world they see, but lacking any articulate response. Theatre games under these circumstances and in this specific context, therefore, are uniquely designed to invite duality and engage the teens in a mindful state of paradox. This is and has always been the unique domain of game players and, historically, the job of tricksters, fools, and jokers. This capacity to sustain complexity informs every game we play, whether it toys with the dualities of freedom and confinement, structure and chaotic disorder, or competitive autonomy and complete interdependence.

Quite simply, game playing celebrates paradox, and this is ultimately a very healing notion for these paradoxical times.

3. Group Dialogue

Under the connective web philosophy, we understood from the beginning that group dialogue would be a crucial component of the TELA experience, yet dialogue in the Freirean sense carries with it some rather strict rules of engagement. First, dialogue exists between and among humans "in order to name the world" (Freire 2001, 88). Freire acknowledges that this can't happen when one party wants this and the other doesn't—that is, between oppressor and oppressed (ibid., 88). Though on the surface this seems exclusionary, we understood dialogue within a group of liberatory practice such as ours to carry with it a certain responsibility that implies a baseline desire to speak. For us, this is cannot be a mandate to speak or, on the other hand, can it be a place for speech that denies others their own words. First and foremost, then, our circle was a place for speaking our own truths, completely uncensored, but truth that was the synthesis of action *and* reflection, for without either, it is reduced to mere activism or verbiage (ibid., 87), which were not liberatory. The minimal requirement for speaking in our circle had to be a sense of reflective ownership of our own voice and a mindfulness of the *action* of our own words within the group. It was not to be a circle of blame or shame. Essentially, it needed to be a circle of love: "Dialogue cannot exist . . . in the absence of a profound love for the world and for people. The naming of the world, which is an act of creation and re-creation, is not possible if it is not infused with love" (ibid., 89).

The late physicist David Bohm identified dialogue by its etymological roots—a mix of *dia-*, meaning not "two" but rather "through," and *logos* indicating the meaningfulness of the word (Bohm 1990, 1). Here Bohm almost conjures up the image of our own spider's web of connectivity. For indigenous and Native American communities, this group "glue" often comes in the shape of a leaderless circle with a talking stick and some patience.

For TELA, dialogue with the talking stick is at once political and personal, activist and reflexive, and an extremely patient practice. It is a circle of learning as much about how to listen as it was a process of naming things and speaking from the heart. In his essay *"La treceava estela,"* Subcomandante Marcos of the Zapatista movement imagines the process of dialogue to be like a *caracol*, a conch shell where the community enter from the outer rim and "consider words such as 'globalization,' 'war of domination,' 'resistance,' 'economy,' 'city,' 'country,' 'political situation,' and others that the eraser goes around eliminating after the rigorous question 'Is it clear or is there a question?'" (Marcos 2003). In this way, then, the journey of group dialogue is not simply an "encounter group" of shared and reflective emotions, witnessed in respectful resonance and left for the confines of our minds at the end, but rather a trip to the center, from the political and social big-picture outer world toward the internal heart of the group, "'The Votán. The guardian and heart of the people,' the Zapatista people" (ibid.), whereupon we have to weave our way back out once again toward the place where the personal and political once again collide. For Marcos, it is a place of proposals and thoughts—the community word that is only made real as it becomes spoken out loud.

For our TELA talking circle, the "decision" is less a conscious agenda item as it is an implicit contract to bear the heart and the political soul of what was shared into the education and training, and eventually the TO practice, of our public forum and our world's work.

4. Education, Not Indoctrination

The organizing principal of TELA is a philosophy of liberation and transformation. The theme around which our group is constellated has been primarily a focus on dating or relationship violence. To this end, there are experiences from the reactive domains of the lives of our participants, and then there is context and knowledge—a critical reflection that involves a gathering of information and a negotiated dialogue with what is not known. This constitutes the responsibility of the group: a critical education, or what Paulo Freire may have called a formation of ethical responsibility. For our group, this was placed in radical contrast with any sort of "pharisaical moralism" (Freire 1998, 25) or any notion of message-based, "motionless, static, compartmentalized and predictable" youth training (Freire 2001, 71).

Before we could embark on any practice of education that would avoid the pitfalls of concretized training of "the known" (i.e., information planting—in short, before we could engage the teens in a critical dialogue about dating violence), we had to negotiate some thorny contradictions. In an interview with Ada Palotai, one of our OPCC TELA cofacilitating partners, we noted the complexity of working with young male teens of color, for example, who, on the one hand, may have experiential understanding of racism and socioeconomic oppression but, on the other hand, "make jokes about skin color, they make jokes about weight, there's a lot of fat jokes . . . and that's a little hard, you know, to sit through, and tolerate, and not to impose a message of tolerance, of acceptance" (Palotai 2008). What is perhaps worse, particularly for this group and its assigned focus on dating violence, was the paradoxical coexistence in the young male teens of color with a sensitivity to racial oppression, on the one hand, and an apparent lack of sensitivity to gender oppression leading to violence against women, on the other. Again, Palotai (2008) states, "The other more distinctive thing that happened was last week where we were doing the 'two circles' exercise,[11] and when the men were in their circles, one of the comments was made was—and the topic was, 'What do you wish women knew about you?' and one of the comments made by one of the men was about how women dress in these certain ways and certain 'slutty, really tight short skirts, and what do they expect? What do they expect but to get cat-called?' and that really pushed a button" (Palotai 2008). What she describes here is what happens when, as Freire notes, the oppressed "discover themselves to be 'hosts' of the oppressor" (1970, 48). Similar to this experience just a few years earlier, when one of our teens struggled with misogyny at the Department of Mental Health facility during the first year of TELA, the leadership's response was disapproval of the statements and the attitude that made its way into the performance text and, in the words of the teen himself, "They had me censor almost everything, they almost demoralized my character." ("D." 2008). What is to be done? It is clearly unacceptable to have uncritical statements that promote attitudes of objectivity toward women in a teen performance purportedly addressing issues of dating violence! Yet correcting this young man caused him to ultimately leave that program, and a potential for understanding and awareness was lost.

Freire says that when you are dealing with oppressed who themselves host the oppressor and place other oppressed communities in jeopardy of further marginalization, what is called for is an educational arena that will serve as "an instrument for their critical discovery that both they and their oppressors are manifestations of dehumanization" (1970, 48) Another teen reminiscing on "the "demoralized" experience of "D." comments on the failure of adults who understand the role of education as "correction" of false ideas: "When you try to tell a seventeen-year-old [that he's wrong] and you try and treat him like a *five*-year-old, he's gonna get pissed off even more" ("O." 2008). It is easy to understand where adult parents and teachers learn this failed response. Palotai notes that it may be a question of empathy, where adults and teachers do well when children are young, but as soon as they enter adolescence,

we go into this blackout phase where all of a sudden we don't talk about things; all of a sudden when kids and teens and youth are at the point of their most conflicting emotions, the hormones, the personality development, developing your own sense of identity, there's all of these—there's such turmoil going on during these years, and I think what happens is parents sort of shut off. Adults shut off. Educators shut off, and all of a sudden we can no longer see the person or the struggles they're going through or the conflicts they're experiencing and now teens are just left to their own devices to figure it out, and then they turn to each other." (Palotai 2008)

The question of empathy is central to the problem of education. Jennifer Freed notes that this plays a central role in the spiritual, psychological, and educational component of the AHA, where the facilitators "really try to instil in the teenagers empathy as a core spiritual practice—empathy—to feel and to be with somebody else's journey is the first step to becoming realized" (Freed 2008). Does empathy mean agreement? Of course not. But the misinformation—in this case, the misogynistic statements—are themselves by-products of a dehumanized culture. These bits of misinformation reflect our culture's imperial history and not only invite curiosity but also, at times, quite simply need to be contradicted. Historian and cultural critic Aurora Levins Morales likens this type of work to the traditional healer or *curandera* of Central and South American cultures: "Part of the task of a curandera historian is diagnosis. We need to ask ourselves what aspects of imperial history do the most harm, which lies are at the foundations of our colonized sense of ourselves" (Levins Morales 1998, 27). In short, the response to misogynistic statements in a teen group firstly is the development of a relationship to these same statements and the teens who make them, and then a subsequent curiosity about the context of the misinformation and the domain of the speaker. In counseling psychology, this is known as cognitive reframing—a particular curiosity about the framework of the speaker that, to others in the group, appears so narrow, oppressive, or damaging. Perhaps the most eloquent spokesperson for negotiating this tension is a past teen member of TELA with whom I had a recent conversation about this very topic:

> *Brent*: So . . . people are working with teenagers and they want to do something . . . on dating violence. You have a kid who says misogynist or ignorant things about women, like "Women who dress in tight clothes deserve what they get" . . . what is the role of TO organizer or Joker [in terms of education]?
>
> *O.*: I kind of like to be the Joker when something like that happens. I love to ask questions. "Why?" *Why*? 'Cause then you know, *really*, [that] they *don't know* why. They just *say* things because for some reason, they don't *really* have a good reason *why* they believe that. And I don't get tired. I mean, I will just ask them until they *do*. And once that point comes, they kind of figure out! I mean, "She has a good *point* . . . why the hell . . . ?" (TELA teens 2008)

Teen perspectives based on the advent of hosting the oppressor may not change overnight, but changes indeed happen in their overall perceptions and attitudes over time. Our system of education in TELA is dialogic and inquisitive, based on mutual curiosity and respect, born of empathy and our courage to sustain complexities. We will surely have disagreements and concerns, but teens seldom drop out of the program for fear that it is an unsafe place or that it is a place of censorship or indoctrination.

5. TO Practice for TELA: Of Trees and Worlds

It is impossible to imagine our work together without the central defining component of our TO training. Despite the therapeutic and humanizing effects of our council dialogues, educational sessions, and the opening and closing rituals, TELA was founded primarily as a TO long-term workshop for teens. The work we do follows a rather classic model of TO training familiar to those who have seen the Tree of TO sketch in *Aesthetics of the Oppressed* (Boal 2006, 3). The fruits of our laboring tree come in the form of a series of shared Forum Theatre events in local high schools at the end of our period of training. We hope these events will promote further dialogue in each school and the development of a new conscience around the teen dating violence and the surrounding sociopolitical framework in which this violence takes place.

The Tree of TO is a teleological system constructed sequentially that leads rather neatly to a fruitful end. In the spirit of the chaotic, nonlinear complicated matrix of the spider web, however, and perhaps more important to our own work, we recognize teen rupture less by linearity or *telos* than by the complex *ontology* of location—less "What's wrong?" "Why?" and "What can we do?" but more "Where does it hurt?" The latter does not replace the former but perhaps informs it somehow.

Accompanying our model of the classic Tree of TO, we identified a *geography of TO*, a schematic offering a responsive mechanism for applying the techniques on the basis of the location of the culture of oppression. Where exactly does this rupture live? Informed through my personal work many years ago with Jungian analyst Marvin Speigelman, we similarly identify four "realms" or worlds of the culture of rupture: the world within, between, among, and around.

As the reader will begin to observe, these realms are not concrete domains of disease but rather constellations of experience. A protagonist may experience a rupture that appears to the Joker and other spect-actors to have its origin clearly in the *world among*: a case of racism, poverty, sexism, or gender discrimination; however, the teen may experience it entirely as an internal, *world within* difficulty. Respecting the protagonist's reality, we do not disagree with the teen and will begin our work accordingly as if the unrest is almost exclusively internal. Through the implementation of multiple "within" techniques—namely Cop in the Head which Boal (2003, 8) gives examples of as being: "'loneliness', the 'impossibility of communicating with others', 'fear of emptiness'"—the teen may discover an external living and very concrete antagonist with whom he or she now needs to engage using a technique from the *world between*, perhaps classic Rainbow of Desire using the "kaleidoscope of images" technique. Another week we revisit the external "between" dialogue as a narrative of race, class, and culture, and we are inviting classic Forum Theatre work employing auxiliaries from the culture of sociopolitics, gender, race, and sexual identity. The collective issues and themes uncovered in TELA will likely migrate many times from world to world as the exploration expands and the antimodels are refined. By the end of our workshop, we will arrive more or less at a scripted performative public Forum Theatre event ripe with fruit (to use Boal's metaphor) from all worlds, touching the teen spect-actors' lives wherever they may live.

What follows is a rather simple list of our specific TO or TO-inspired preparations and techniques that we use, offered to give an inside view of our overall process, divided by these four realms. For seasoned practitioners, these may appear to be rather rudimentary examples of the most standard forms of TO, and, as they are widely available, only the most cursory descriptions appear in this chapter. Those newer to the work are advised to seek more in-depth explanations at the source by exploring the core texts of Boal and by investigating schedules of offered TO workshops in their local area.[12]

The World Within: Rupture in the Intrapsychic Domain

- *Image Theatre*: *Tableaux vivants* of internalized forces of oppression, aesthetic arrangements of iconic oppressors (i.e., "shame," "guilt," etc.).
- *Image of the Unspoken Word*: Protagonist-created *tableaux vivants* of projected perceptions of their world, not only what's "ordinary" and what's "missing" but also *perceived*.

The World Between: Rupture in the Interpsychic Domain

- *Complete the Image*: Creating images that complete or respond to a previous image on theme of relationship conflicts.
- *Rainbow of Desire*: The "kaleidoscope of images" in which the protagonist and antagonist work around the theme of present-tense interpersonal relationship difficulty, where hidden and overt strategies are investigated and analyzed by the spect-actors.
- *Boxing Ring*: Interpersonal conflict where protagonist and antagonist struggle, then are "counseled" by their own "boxing coaches" to develop stronger strategies
- *Carousel of Antagonists*:[13] Pairs of protagonists and antagonists assembled opposite each other in concentric circles, engaged in dialogue, then rotating to engage with other pairings of new partners until the circle is complete and they have returned to their original partners. This enhances the skill of strategic engagement.

The World Among: Rupture in the Sociopolitical Domain

- *Image Theatre*: *Tableaux vivants* of a variety of different oppressive scenarios, including the first date, the peer pressure, the family dinner table, and so on.
- *Rainbow of Desire*: "Parade of images" in which rotating protagonists among diverse *tableaux vivants* of oppressive scenes, identifying strategies of resistance, and clarifying desire.
- *Forum Theatre*: Classic antimodel development of situations touching on the collective political and cultural realm of oppressions. Protagonist and antagonist, but touching on the iconic realm of the *every person* or politically archetypal domain, the epic experiences.

The World Around: Rupture in the Archetypal and Numinous Surround

- *Museum of the Unspeakable*: Creating collections of human "statues" in response to a particular rupture that feels unspeakable or generally vague yet powerfully oppressive, nonetheless.[14]
- *Dream Theatre*: Inspired by my years of exposure to Jungian analysis and depth psychology, I have shared interest in this technique through my friendships with Jon Lipsky of Boston University, Jungian analyst Robert Bosnak, Mary Watkins of Pacifica Graduate Institute, and more. In TELA, we have on occasion used dream images in the context of classic Image Theatre exercises to interrogate the "Other."[15]

Freire and Macedo wrote, "Reading the world always precedes reading the word, and reading the word implies continually reading the world" (1987, 35). Perhaps in our paradigm of spiders' webs, trees, and worlds, "reading the world" carries a geographic and psychological dimension. If we could develop a literacy of location as cultural field-workers, we might better identify the approach or technique that best responds to the rupture. Reading the "worlds" of suffering also may help participants migrate from world to world, to transgress imposed societal boundaries that would otherwise separate the personal from the political. In our TELA experience, the work itself invites an immigration in and out of the worlds within, between, among, and around until, we hope, they are all in communicative dialogue with each other.

The Telos of TELA: Arachne's Forum: The Case of "O."

Freire is more often seen as refusing political and religious teleology rather than promoting it. For the teenagers and for our TELA community, we prefer to look at the final stages of our workshop not in terms of the "purposefulness" of traditional theological traditions or the goal-oriented ideology or demagoguery of politics, but rather the *function of purpose*—an *intention* of the twelve weeks' work together—directed toward the youth spect-actors toward a mutual investigation of a common rupture.

Forum Theatre is a mutual labor of love, not an artistic performance. It is creative in the most basic sense—creating dialogue together. In the mythology of the web, Arachne's crime of transgression was the weaving of a tapestry that called into question the very actions of the gods. She was condemned not for jealousy but for heresy.

If our workshops celebrate a certain ontology of humanization, investigating the process of human beings without prescriptive manipulation, then our performances face to shift the landscape a bit and introduce trajectory into the world, a process of humans becoming and a heretical transgression of the way things are. Indeed, we were heading out with a purpose—a mindful intention—even while we rejected opinions or concrete assuredness. We were teens, assembled in front of teens, purveyors of the collective nightmare, presenters of the rupture, and open to altering or amending our narratives as the spect-actors willed. Forum Theatre is an invitation for mutual transgression. It is, in our terminology, an act of *telos*.

In the first year of Forum Theatre, TELA teens created eight antimodels based on personal narratives adapted for the sociopolitics of dating violence. "O." recounts her experience as a playwright, and the labor of working through the personal narrative of surviving attempted suicide as a young lesbian in a religious and homophobic household, to the process of sharing this unresolved narrative in the public forum. She talks specifically about the unusual experience of writing an unfinished scene:

> Once I got the hang of it, I kind of started really enjoying it because when you stop there [before the conclusion], you really engage the audience, because all these people . . . start coming up with resolutions of their own. They start saying, "Oh you know what? You could have done this!" or they might just have statements like, "This guy's an asshole!" or something like that. You kind of start seeing how it works, it's like, you know, by not having one resolution, you could go so many different directions. It's not obsolete anymore. It's not like, "Okay, that's the end, you can't change it, nothing!" but [rather] once you . . . get other ideas from other people, you really can completely change the *story* and take it somewhere different, [a place] that you didn't even *know* about as a writer. ("O." 2008)

Here, the *telos* of the work is not directed at changing the audience but inviting change from the spect-actors, not only as a human being in a traumatic rupture, but also as an artist seeking a fresh perspective on an impossible narrative. This kind of *telos* would likely be called *poesis*—poetry (literally, "making")—by the Greeks.

For "O.," creating her narrative invited transformation in three arenas: as experiential creator of the piece, as an artistic writer of this narrative, and as a performer for many other teens. She spoke of the internal changes that occurred during the TO workshop:

> I completely changed—I became more social . . . that was always difficult for me . . . I *changed* . . . [Before, there] was always that fear that if I showed my *true* self . . . and [people didn't] like that—how messed up would *that* make me? . . . But [now] if that person doesn't like me, it's their loss. I'm not gonna beat myself up for one person . . . I'm gonna be me. And the people that actually do like me, they're my real friends . . . Now it's like I come in . . . [and] I'm *talking* to them. I would have never done that. I would have *never* done that. ("O." 2008)

Next, I asked about the *telos* of writing her scene:

> *Brent*: What happened to you in writing that scene? Was it traumatizing to write that scene? Was it liberating? What was your experience?
>
> *O.*: It was more on the liberating side—just kind of getting that fear out, because my whole problem . . . was keeping things in. You know, never—I mean everyone thought I was OK. Because that was just me. I wanted to keep people as far away from me letting them know that I was OK, that nothing was wrong, because I wanted them to see that nothing was wrong. It was like . . . I've been depressed for so many years that it just came a point where . . . it was kind of an ambush for my mother, too, because "why would she do that? Why would she try to kill herself?"

Lastly, the *telos* of the performance:

> *Brent*: Had you ever . . . performed in public about your circumstance? Because you had a lot of people watching you [during the Forum]—we had about 500 kids in the audience watching you. Can you describe what the experience was like for you to "come out" in that way, through a story?
>
> *O.*: It was funny—it *was* kind of "through a story," which kind of gave me more courage . . . It was a lot easier just to *play the character* than to be actually standing there, "———" [her name], you know, "coming out." It was kind of easier doing it through a *story*, whether they thought it was actually me or not. It was just—it was just much easier in my mind, you know?
>
> *Brent*: Would you have said that before you performed the piece?
>
> *O.*: Before I performed the piece? Um, probably not.

Forum Theatre when conducted over time in a long series of perfor-mances can invite a malleability and ongoing adaptation and reconfigura-tion of the scenes. As "O." suggests, the spect-actor interventions helped her as a playwright to rewrite or alter her scenes without ever "solving" them. The hope for TELA is that the *telos* of the publicly shared event will evolve our somewhat complex struggles into much more complicated situations. As the tour progresses, so too does the work. By the last Forum Theatre event, the actors will have created antimodels that are more challenging than ever. Not only is there dialogue between actors and audience members, there is also a running dialogue from the previous performance to the present one. The narrative itself evolves and grows through to the construction of nearly impossible antimodels, at which point few options remain but to adopt a Legislative Theatre model, shifting from experience to action. In Forum, we have shifted from an ontology to a *teleology*, from being to doing. To be clear, we understand this as a "stage" but not a final stage; it is a point along the spiraling journey, continuously called back to stillness and being once again, when we may reinvestigate our state, analyze the influencing factors of oppression, theorize about them, develop new performative narratives, and share in new teen Forums over and over.

Evaluating TELA: Untangling the Web

The First Lesson: Dismantling the Mantle of the "Serious Expert"

Central to the dissolution of the department of mental health (DMH) part-nership was the tacit distinction between the notions of expertise, education, and authentic experience. TELA teens and some staff struggled to negoti-ate the precarious tension between our role as facilitators of the authentic voices of the teen participants versus our role as "carriers of a message" to other teens, a message that was fairly concrete even as there was ample room for creativity of its delivery. One teen, "D.," now a nineteen-year-old Afri-can American male, perceived the differences between TELA and the partner organization's style of management in the following way: "One of my charac-ters [the host organization staff said] was too strong, it could not be beaten in an antagonist–protagonist battle . . . so they told me either to censor my char-acter or leave, so they kicked me out of the group because they told me that my character was too strong" ("D." 2008). As archetypal psychologist James Hillman notes, often the narratives of what actually transpire may be less important than the perception of what has happened (Hillman 1983). The result—good intentions notwithstanding—was that "D." *felt* shut down by the partners, and distinctly did *not* feel shut down by TELA: "It doesn't hap-pen [in TELA]—here I can be as frank—I can make my character as strong as

I want it to be. I can say what I want to say. There they had me censor almost everything [that] they almost demoralized my character. Here, you got the freedom to do whatever you want" ("D." 2008). Through the narrative of this teen's rupture, we devised a new philosophy for our group process that distinguished our work from other teen therapy programs.

The Second Lesson: Avoiding the Trap of "Message Theatre"

Chela Sandoval notes that the oppressor culture—by virtue of its own paralyzing lack of a "metanarrative" that might otherwise encourage critical self-reflection and bring change when needed—actually contributes to a culture of silence by those who fall under this simple "right or wrong" binary. In theatre programs for teens, it is most prominently displayed by "message theatre"—organizations in prisons, youth programs, anti-gang, antiviolence, antidrugs, in fact, so many "anti's" that the very theatre itself seems to resemble an "antimodel."

Ignacio Martín-Baró, slain El Salvadoran Jesuit and pioneering liberation psychologist, argued that the failure of Western psychology was its insistence on a problem–solution paradigm that proffered a "one-size-fits-all" approach to healing. Included were symptoms of suffering that matched a diagnostic and statistical manual's often flawed classification system. Excluded were the subtle complexities informed by popular experience. What was at stake, he argued, was the domain of *epistemologies*. Industries with vast profits lay claim to "ways of knowing" that solidify their stake in the disease model and create an illusion of expertise from which public policy is made, funds are invested, and programs are implemented. This imposition of a hierarchical will at the exclusion of the common people's experience frequently clears *symptoms* temporarily but does not address core sociopolitical sources of the deeper rupture.

"Message theatre" is largely funded by such "antimodel" systems. Theatre was initially the dominion of creative artists imagining utopic worlds in the midst of great cultural decline. Community-based theatre in indigenous culture regularly *subverts* and overturns the systemic oppressions that have defied other forms of resistance. "Message theatre," on the other hand, packages the voice of the hegemony in often brightly colored festivals with abundant money, resources, volunteers, and a *creativistic*, if not a terribly *creative*, *mode d'emploi* for the construction of the theatrical project.

Boal, of course, speaks eloquently on this phenomena. It is the cornerstone of TO to radically reimagine Aristotle's "coercive system of tragedy" and identify whose voices are actually being represented and whose are being left out. What is perhaps less clear in TO models for youth is the "line in the sand" relative to the relationship between instruction and invitation. At what point do teen cultural field-workers invite the unfettered, uncensored voices of youth to speak on their own behalf, and at what point do the facilitators have an obligation to contest these same voices when they bespeak a new oppression against another marginalized group even while telling the narrative of their own oppression? Ada Palotai notes that in traditional teen theatre, "there's a problem that's posed and then there's a solution to the problem that's also posed," whereas "in Theatre of the Oppressed, what's different is, the solution is not presented. There is no solution" (Palotai 2008). For the teens, this may have been initially confusing. "O." mused,

> I mean at first I was like, there's no resolution? What? What do you mean? It's like a cliff-hanger! It's like . . . you got to know what happens afterwards! It's like cutting a good book . . . like . . . what if you read *To Kill a Mockingbird* and then you get to the trial and it stops there? What the hell happens to Atticus? . . . but once I got the hang of it, I kind of started really enjoying it, because when you stop there, you really engage the audience, because all these people, they start coming up with resolutions of their own . . . they start saying, "Oh, you know what? You could have done *this!*" (2008)

Not only did it seem to open up access for the protagonists and spect-actors, but as a budding young writer, "O." found this interrupted narrative artistically invigorating: "Once you get other ideas from other people, you really can completely change the story and take it somewhere different that you didn't even know about as a writer" ("O." 2008).

The Third Lesson: Beyond the Binary of Antagonist–Protagonist

Sandoval speaks eloquently about the need for cultural field-workers to "expand their capacity to sustain complexities" (Sandoval 2007). This notion challenges TO practitioners around the world to start thinking outside of the realm of classic protagonist–antagonist models, and the original Freirean 1970s model poses some challenges for postcolonial, indigenous feminist theorists: "Since it is a concrete situation that the oppressor–oppressed contradiction is established, the resolution of this contradiction must be *objectively* verifiable. Hence, the radical requirement—both for the individual who discovers himself or herself to be an oppressor and for the oppressed—that the concrete situation which begets oppression must be transformed" (Freire 2001, 50). M. Jacqui Alexander gently complicates this duality in her text *Pedagogies of Crossing* by challenging what she terms "oppositional practices" even from marginalized groups: "If hegemony works as spectacle, but more importantly as a set of practices that come to assume meaning in people's everyday lives . . . then all spaces carry the potential for corruptibility . . . oppositional consciousness is a process rather than a given before the fact of political practice. And further, we cannot afford to be continually, one-sidedly oppositional" (2005, 6).

Jennifer Freed of AHA contextualizes the aspect of simple binaries in the history of resistance movements and the methodologies of the patriarchy in response to a question about the importance of spirituality in the AHA–TELA process. Was this training important? "Oh, definitely—that's part of it, because frankly I come from a whole history and family of social activists who were emotionally and psychologically arrested. They were still—even in their zealous liberal progressive attitudes—as incredibly splitting and oppressive of the people as they were trying to change, so first and foremost change has to be within, and eradicating those places in each of us that have *dominant* and *submissive* narratives, and then, once that's *conscientized*, then we need to move that out into the community" (Freed 2008). On the other hand, we cannot afford to romanticize oppression either. Boal is most eloquent in his recent castigations and thorough rejection of quasispiritual workshops offering to address the phenomenon of "theatre of the oppressor"! Complicating the struggle and moving beyond the binary cannot also mean enabling the oppressor by offering TO workshops for corporate moguls whose use of the techniques may improve their capacity to solidify their power and manifest more suffering in the world.[16]

The middle road, third space, or borderlands arena at the forefront of TO today is beginning to be investigated by none other than Boal himself. In a workshop in 2006 in Rio de Janeiro, Boal's Jokers were investigating two protagonist scenes in what he was loosely calling "psychological forum" at the time (Boal 2006). In this process, we acknowledge two protagonists in the same room, each exerting antagonistic influences that are diminishing the desire of the other yet neither wielding any institutionalized or hierarchical power over the other: they are on more or less equal footing. For our own community of urban teens, this frequently invites a dialogue between male teens experiencing racism and female teens experiencing the misogyny of their male counterparts in the room. These dialogues are complicated and important, and our focus returns to an appreciative inquiry about the strategies each side employs that may interfere with their own best interests.

TELAvisions: Imagining the Future

"Where do we go from here?" That seems to be the classic, if cliché, obligatory next step. In a spider web model, perhaps we are invited to surrender thinking in linear terms of past or future, and rather obliged to reinvestigate where we are relative to where we have been and what seems to be in development. Where we are as a community is in our third year of twelve-week workshops. We have twelve teens from fourteen to eighteen years of age and a diverse mix of backgrounds. We are investigating the challenges of our present and preparing ourselves to work on a new Forum Theatre piece for the spring of 2009. Even as we problematize current dating violence scenarios, we celebrate the continuation of at least three teens who enter their third consecutive year and three who enter their second. Fully half of our group are veterans who are better at creating TO than ever.

What this invites is a new challenge that, typically, we embrace even as we find it daunting. There is a difference in abilities and capacities, a need for peer leadership and peer TO training and education, and a restlessness with material that may lead to a need for moving on to yet another level. Perhaps the greatest fear that poses the most pressing challenge for future work is the advent of complacency, ironically born out of a simple love of the work. Jennifer Freed discusses the future trend of AHA and TELA:

> *Jennifer:* I think that sometimes youth are still under the impression that this is a *game*, this isn't real life, like they can't take this out in the world and do something impactful with what they've learned. It's still like a classroom activity. I think . . . that we want to take this learning that we're all finding in the Theatre of the Oppressed and AHA, and actually start doing Theatre of the Oppressed *actions* and social *actions* so that it becomes like, "In the room we do *this*, and now we go to the city council and do *this*" . . . that there has to be some real-time *delivery* of this experience into the world and the locations where they live.
>
> *Brent:* Are you saying that our next phase should be AHA and TELA legislative theatre?
>
> *Jennifer:* I'd say the goal of mine is to see this become much more embedded in the social structures that oppress youth and therefore you should be more a part of. So, school board, legislation, articles, Web—you know, that the voice has to be taken out of the classroom and into their actual system. (Freed 2008)

I am left with a sense that our work in TELA has been a powerful connective experiment that continues to enlighten, challenge, and reinvent our notions of working with adolescents using the modality of TO. While we keep exploring and creating circles of relationship, we acknowledge the ancestors at the end of every session. It is fitting, then, to acknowledge a teen participant from a theatre program I led in Boston in 1991 whose recent passing[17] calls to mind that no matter what we write or how much we cite from participants, scholars, and mentors, we are always at the mercy of the unknown.

Love, endurance, and witness to the human journey—these are ultimately the only "outcome measures" that will determine the future vision of any such teen theatre program: "No matter how hard or terrible our lot in life, to choose against lovelessness—to choose love—we can listen to the voices of hope that speak to us, that speak to our hearts—the voices of angels. When angels speak of love they tell us it is only by loving that we enter an earthly paradise. They tell us paradise is our home and love our true destiny" (hooks 2000, 237). To know we are not "in charge" of the paths of our participants but at the very least "responsible"—quite literally, *able to respond*—to their untold or undertold stories, this is the greatest lesson we have made in TELA. What emerges is a pedagogy of the heart, a philosophy of love, a strategy of connection that is not measured by quantitative measures or counted in grade point advancements or psychological measures but is marked by relationship and recorded in the echoed voices of the teens.

Acknowledgments

This chapter was written with the voices of Jennifer Freed and Rendy Freedman of the Academy of Healing Arts, Ada Palotai of OPCC, and past and present teen participants of TELA.

Notes

1. It begs mention here that TELA was itself conscripted around the host organization's mandated theme of dating violence, and the workshops are organized around the principles and techniques of TO, a process which these teens were cognizant of but about which they had no voice in creating. The transparency may lie in the creative engagement of cowriting and performing, which may mitigate the apparent hierarchy of the preselection of thematic material and theatrical form, but only time will tell.
2. OPCC was formerly the Ocean Park Community Center but is now simply referred to as OPCC.
3. This process typically becomes more interactive and participatory the more the teens know each other.
4. TO refers to games in the tradition of Theatre of the Oppressed; ATA refers to applied theatre arts.
5. Depending on where we are in the twelve-week journey, the group may opt to spend more time processing a particular issue or topic (i.e., "love" or "the elections") or simply build and rehearse the TO scenes.
6. A tradition of some Native American communities, this is a practice of resonant reflection and group dialogue that emphasizes heartfelt connection and intentional listening. Typically done in a circle with a talking piece, the TELA council contains a liberatory praxis explained in the "Group Dialogue" section of this chapter.
7. The term "anti-model," coined by Boal, refers to a constructed scene demonstrating oppression, typically between a protagonist with desire and an antagonist who thwarts this desire. It is the model of how things should *not* be.

8. First breath is for the ancestors to remember the past, the second breath is for the group and our work that evening, and the third breath is for ourselves—"may our days be productive and our nights be peaceful." The closing is a call and response from the Igbo tradition of Nigeria—*ise* (literally, "it has been spoken").

9. In this anthropologist's treatise on the nature of group ritual in indigenous theatre events, Turner noted that rituals typically had a *liminal* quality representing a community-wide *threshold* experience, which marked a noticeable transgression of the status quo and a shift in perspective or power from before to after the event. Community gatherings that mimicked these rituals in *form* but did not denote any subversion or noticeable change from before to after the event were deemed *liminoid* by Turner.

10. *Conscientization* is a word coined by Paulo Freire to describe the humanizing experience of moving from mere consciousness to *conscience*, and from stagnation to *mobilization*, hence the hybrid *conscientization*. Boal sums it up as the movement from passive *object* to active *subject*.

11. The "two circles" exercise came from a Pacifica Graduate Institute workshop where two communities form concentric circles in order to bear witness to each other's experience. In this instance, the circles were between teen women and men, each describing what they "wish the other" knew about their experiences.

12. Of the many books by Boal, *Games for Actors and Non-Actors* (1992) is a nice starting point. It offers simply constructed exercises preceded by a brief history of TO, a parable about the origins of theatre, and an explanation of some of the most basic terminologies. *Theatre of the Oppressed* (1985) is, of course, the seminal text, a more complex articulation of the work and a must-read for TO practitioners and cultural field-workers alike who seek to understand the philosophical underpinnings of this work. Drama therapy techniques are in *The Rainbow of Desire* (2003) with an in-depth introduction on the development of these and other techniques throughout the history of TO. *Legislative Theatre* (1998) reveals Boal's model of political theatre that uses classic "Forum Theatre" for invited legislators to respond legislatively to political rupture. There are numerous collections that outline other TO experiences around the world. Top among these are *Playing Boal* and *A Boal Companion* by authors and senior TO practitioners Mady Schutzman and Jan Cohen-Cruz. More resources and groups are found at http://www.theatreoftheoppressed.org.

13. I first saw B. J. Dodge operating this exercise at a Center for Theatre of the Oppressed and Applied Theatre Arts, Los Angeles (CTO/ATA/LA) workshop in 2004.

14. This technique was first inspired when CTO Rio member and TO Joker Geo Britto invited me to visit the Museum of Images of the Unconscious in Rio de Janeiro. There we saw the extraordinary artwork depicting unspeakable ruptures from mental patients. My subsequent trips to Rwanda in 2007 and 2008 required a technique to address collective trauma in such a way as not to reproduce the trauma. Our technique developed slowly, and we use this in TELA with the teens for particularly sensitive topics. At the time of this writing, there was an article under submission titled "We cry on the Inside," which expands on the entire technique as experienced in Rwanda.

15. During the same trip to Rio in 2004, I led a Dream Theatre workshop for the CTO/Rio Joker community. When I began to invite the dreamer (protagonist) to engage with the dream images, I fell into treating these images as antagonists until members from the community protested. We needn't necessarily identify them in such simple binaries. I learned a lot from this experience.

16. In a recent TO training workshop in August 2008 with thirty-five cultural field-workers, several council practitioners expressed interest in working with oppressors. A vibrant discussion left us concluding that though I am opposed to this work, there may be room for TO relationships with oppressors if it invites humanization within and among the ruling class; however, perhaps this calls for yet another book to identify how to distinguish between healing and enabling oppressors.

17. Struggling for the majority of his life, Al took his own life on September 19, 2008, at thirty-four years of age. He had been a participant in "New Land/'scapes," a teen theatre program I started in partnership with the Strand Theatre in Boston from 1991 to 1995. The text work was Shakespeare, and Al played many roles during our time together. His first role was Horatio in *Hamlet* in the summer of 1991. He and I had maintained a spider's web of contact from 1991 to 2008, just weeks before he passed.

References

Alexander, M. J. 2005. *Pedagogies of crossing: Meditations on feminism, sexual politics, memory, and the sacred.* Durham, NC: Duke University Press.

Anzaldúa, G. 1999. *Borderlands/La frontera: The new mestiza.* San Francisco: Aunt Lute Books. (Orig. pub. 1987.)

Boal, Augusto. 1985. *Theatre of the oppressed.* New York: Theatre Communications Group. (Orig. pub. 1979.)

———. 1992. *Games for actors and non-actors.* London: Routledge.

———. 1998. *Legislative theatre: Using performance to make politics.* Trans. A. Jackson. New York: Routledge.

———. 2003. *The rainbow of desire: The Boal method of theatre and therapy.* Trans. Adrian Jackson. New York: Routledge. (Orig. pub. 1995.)

———. 2006. *The aesthetics of the oppressed.* Oxon, UK: Routledge.

Bohm, D. 1990. *On dialogue.* David Bohm Seminars, Ojai, California.

Freed, Jennifer, 2008. Conversations with the author. November 10. Santa Barbara, California.

Freire, Paulo. 1998. *Pedagogy of freedom: Ethics, democracy and civic courage.* New York: Rowman & Littlefield.

———. 2001. *Pedagogy of the oppressed.* New York: Continuum. (Orig. pub. 1970.)

Freire, Paulo, and Donald Macedo. 1987. *Literacy: Reading the word and the world.* London: Bergin & Garvey.

Gilligan, Carol. 1993. *In a different voice.* Cambridge: Harvard University Press.

Hillman, J. 1983. *Healing fiction.* Spring Publications; Woodstock, CT.

hooks, bell. 2000. *All about love: New visions.* New York: William Morrow.

Kruger, K. S. 2001. *Weaving the word: The metaphorics of weaving and female textual production*. Selinsgrove, PA: Susquehanna University Press.

Levins Morales, A. 1998. *Medicine stories: History, culture and the politics of integrity*. Cambridge: South End.

Marcos, S. 2003, July 24. Chiapas: La Treceava Estela. Primera parte: Un caracol (Chiapas: The Thirteenth Wave. First part: Conch shell) La Jornada. D.F., Mexico.

"O" and "D." (former TELA teen participants). 2008. Conversations with the author. November 14. Los Angeles, CA.

Palotai, Ada. 2008. Conversations with the author. November 12. Santa Monica, CA.

Postman, Niel. 1995. *The end of education: Redefining the value of school*. New York: Vintage.

Sandovol, C. 2007. Frontiers of depth psychology, DP 963. Class lecture, Spring quarter. Pacifica Graduate Institute.

Slattery, P. and L. Corbett, eds. 2000. *Depth Psychology: Meditations in the Field*. Daimon Verlag, Einseideln and Pacifica Graduate Institute; Santa Barbara, CA. (Reprinted 2004.)

TELA teens. 2008. Conversations with the author. November 14. Santa Monica, California.

6

In Search of the Radical in Performance

Theatre of the Oppressed with Incarcerated Youth

Diane Conrad

The Radical in Performance

In Baz Kershaw's *The Radical in Performance* (1999), he develops his thesis that the radical in performance can scarcely exist in mainstream theatre today, which is so highly commodified and market-driven, but that if the radical can exist in performance, it is in alternative sites, such as street theatre, protest events, heritage sites, cultural festivals, reminiscence theatre, and in prison contexts. It was my search for "the radical in performance" that took me from working with so-called at-risk youth in schools—also highly market-driven in today's society—to working with incarcerated youth. My hope was that the radical in performance might provide opportunities for these youth and me to rethink or think differently about ourselves, our life experiences, the structures and institutions that construct us all, and construct them as "criminals"—with the aim of positive change in the lives of individuals toward greater social transformation.

As Kershaw describes, "The freedom that 'radical performance' invokes is not just freedom *from* oppression, repression, exploitation—the resistant sense of the radical, but also freedom *to reach beyond* existing systems of formalized power, freedom to create currently unimaginable forms of association and action—the transgressive and transcendent sense of the radical" (1999, 18). It is this sense of the radical in performance that I sought in working with youth in the context of incarceration through participatory drama inspired by Boal's Theatre of the Oppressed (TO; 1979)—a kind of performance that I hoped ultimately had the potential to open up possibilities that might radically alter social relations including public attitudes toward youth crime, toward greater justice for the youth and for us all.

Performing TO-based Research

The TO-based work with youth in a provincial youth jail (Young Offender Centre, as it was called) in Alberta, Canada, that I facilitated from 2005 to 2008 was framed as my scholarly research as a faculty member in drama and theatre education at the University of Alberta, under the title "The Transformative Potential of Drama in the Education of Incarcerated Youth" and funded by the Social Sciences and Humanities Research Council of Canada. The project passed rigorous ethical reviews by both the university and the Alberta Office of the Solicitor General. The question that guided my study, articulated for the academy and for the funding body, was *How can participatory drama contribute to the education of incarcerated youth to avoid future negative outcomes of their "at-risk" behaviors*? I was interested in exploring the following:

- The educational needs of incarcerated youth to help them make positive change in their lives
- What drama practices could best contribute to meeting those needs
- How spaces could be created within institutions such as prisons and schools for transformative processes to occur
- How we could assess the benefits of drama intervention in that context

The research was arts-based (Barone and Eisner 1997) using the arts, specifically applied theatre processes (Prentki and Preston 2009), as ways of collectively making meaning—in a qualitative research sense, to generate, interpret, and present (or, in our case, perform) understanding. The research was performative in the sense that performance studies or performance ethnographic (Denzin 2003) approaches explore the performative qualities of our identities, social interactions, and structures and in that it aims to do something in the world. The research was also participatory, valuing participants as coresearchers in the process of creating knowledge (Freire 1998; Park et al., 1993), to the extent that the institutional context permitted, by allowing the youths' needs and perspectives to guide the process. The popular or applied theatre process (Prentki and Selman 2000; Prentki and Preston 2009), conceptualized as research, involved a series of TO-inspired projects with youth in jail to inform new understandings of the youths' experiences, their crime, and incarceration.

Performing Incarceration

In *Discipline and Punish*, Foucault's (1979) historical study of prisons, Foucault reveals incarceration as an apparatus of power and punishment (and describes schools as analogous in that both were founded as disciplinary bodies). He claims it has long been known that prison environments serve more effectively to reinscribe a criminal mentality rather than deter crime or reform offenders. Foucault's notion of *governmentality* in relation to criminal justice (Dean 1999; Foucault 1979; Pasquino 1991) offers a way of understanding why this might be so. He analyzes the mentality of governance, the taken-for-granted ways of thinking behind institutionalized practices that attempt to normalize individuals' behaviors. He suggests that the wielding of institutionalized power is accompanied by an attitude toward those over whom power is exerted, constituting individuals as objects of power, to which individuals often respond with resistance. Such unbalanced distribution of power engendering resistance in institutional settings, particularly acute in prison environments, is antithetical to the project of education for individual development and social change.

My experiences working at the youth jail confirmed Foucault's assessment of the prison context. While the Youth Criminal Justice Act (Doob and Cesaroni 2004) declares "rehabilitation," not punishment, as the primary goal of youth incarceration, rather than personal development for the youth, I saw priority given to security—justified as being for the protection of youth from themselves, from other youth, and for the protection of society from them. Security was accomplished through containment and control—close surveillance and segregation; a fixed schedule and set of strictly defined rules and procedures; a daily point system for behavior that awarded or revoked privileges; regular pat downs; the risk of punishment, dorm confinement, or isolation for bad behavior; and the ever-present threat of strip search. The jail accommodated an education program and offered some recreational activities and some well-intentioned, but tokenistic, "rehabilitative" programming. The only exception to the dearth of appropriate programming for the youth was the Native program, the coordinator of which invited my research, in the form of a drama program for the youth, to be a part. The Native program coordinator, a Métis woman and corrections officer, facilitated arts activities and Native cultural activities for the youth and developed relationships with them that were mutually caring and respectful. Her extraordinary example inspired hope for me that alternatives are possible.

The fact that a Native program was offered at the center raises a significant issue for my research. Upon arriving in Alberta, after teaching in two Dene communities in Canada's Northwest Territories, my interest in researching with youth deemed "at risk" brought me to the innercity, to a rural community, and to jail. In each of these locations, I found a disproportionate number of aboriginal youth deemed to be "at risk." In fact, aboriginal youth as well as adults are disproportionately overrepresented in provincial jails and federal prisons across Canada (Silver 2007)—clear evidence of systemic racism in our criminal justice system.

In response to the injustice, which I have witnessed, my research has compelled my own radical performance on various occasions. In letters to the editor, in radio and newspaper interviews, in academic presentations and articles, in speeches at awards galas, in classes I teach, in the ethnodramatic play I am writing, I performed my role as public intellectual in bringing the issue to attention—in particular to advocate for youth caught by our unjust social structures not of their making.

Since the current legislation—the Youth Criminal Justice Act—was instituted in 2003, with recommendations for alternative measures, only the most serious offenses or repeat offenses have received jail time. The incarcerated youth with whom I worked were charged with or faced some serious charges. Over the three years of the study, more than fifty different youth between the ages of fourteen and nineteen participated in the drama program. There was anywhere from there to fifteen youth in any given week, mostly boys, but also a handful of girls when mixed-gender programming was allowed. The youth could sign up to participate in the program given they were on "good behavior," as determined by staff. While the program experienced considerable turnover of youth from week to week and month to month, as youth were dorm confined, released, or sent elsewhere, or as new youth arrived, we also had some consistency with a number of youth attending regularly while they were at the center, and even a few youth who were with the program for a year or more. While the constant turnover presented challenges for the development of a real sense community so vital for TO work, the majority of youth who attended the program were First Nations youth from Alberta, so there was some shared culture and geography within the group, if not prior to their arrival in jail. They certainly all shared the culture, geography, and lived experience of their immediate reality on the inside.

I found that the great irony of working within the context of incarceration was that while the environment was not at all receptive or conducive to TO-based practice with radical intent, its very constraints created the potential for moments of radical performance, which I explore in this chapter.

TO with Incarcerated Youth

Alternative to the restrictive agenda of the youth jail, Freire's popular education methods, which informed not only Boal but also my TO practice, focus on reading the world, the development of critical consciousness to examine and transform society (Friere 1970; Boal 1979). For Boal, theatre was a rehearsal for revolution.

Our TO-inspired projects engendered moments of radical performance—performance that occurred both inside the theatre work (during games, devising activities or formal performances) as well as outside it. In the discussion that follows, I identify moments that were distinctly performative, with radical potential, which occurred during our TO work, in discussions about our work, and during casual conversations and activities surrounding the work. As an example of the latter, in our passing interactions with the youth, if ever we facilitators commented on the way many of the youth wore their standard issue faded and stretched-out, navy-blue sweat pants low on their hips almost to the point of falling down, a young person might spontaneously pull his pants all the way up to his chest, tight around the crotch, in mocking imitation of some despised authority figure. Like this moment, the ones I examine below hint at the potential for a kind of freedom that Kershaw describes—moments that transgressed and transcended the system of formalized power in which we were caught.

From the outset, the conditions imposed by the center's administrative body, in order for my research to proceed, restricted what we could do. Concerns over security precluded us doing any work that was perceived as too risky for the setting. We were instructed not to raise any issues related to criminal activity or gang activity. This edict, as a critical pedagogue, I found counterintuitive—believing rather that we need to dialogue about experiences and issues in order to understand them better and make change. I expect, however, that for those working within the institution, whose prime directive was short-term containment, these young inmates and radical TO work likely posed a threat. As such, our TO work tread a fine line, always testing the boundaries between what was allowed, yet still relevant and meaningful for the youth, and the outlawed, forbidden terrain. This challenge was itself an opportunity for radical performance as the youth, the Native program coordinator, and I conspired to work meaningfully within the constraints. On one occasion we overstepped the bounds, were censored and reprimanded, putting the entire drama program at risk.

The projects described below, if not radical in a fully active sense given the constraints of the setting, at least offer glimpses into the potential for the radical in performance with youth within the context of incarceration (and outside)—showing that where oppression is most acute, its limits are most clearly revealed (Kershaw 1999).

The first three projects described below, while perhaps not immediately recognizable as TO activities, were certainly inspired by my background, training, and experience facilitating TO. The philosophy that underpins TO—including the identification of issues by participants, theatre work based on their stories, development of critical consciousness, critical analysis of the social contexts of our lived experiences, the search for alternatives, and the notion of rehearsal for future action—frames all of my work. There was never a prescribed agenda to which we adhered; rather, we allowed the youth determine the content and direction that we took.

Much of our work, as it turned out, relied on digital technology. This was a medium that was of interest to the young people. They always thoroughly enjoyed having their photos taken, seeing and working with pictures of themselves. The digital technology also became a sort of audience for our work, a record of our drama-based endeavors in the absence of the more usual kind of audience. For each of these projects, I worked with graduate students as research assistants whose interests and areas of expertise also helped to shape the work. As part of our agreement with the center, our plans and resources for each project had to be submitted to and vetted by the administration before our work could commence.

Symbolic Escape through Digital Storytelling

This project began with the group choosing one of the "Cree teachings" represented on posters that the program coordinator had hung around the unit. From among "love," "courage," "honor," and so on, the group chose "respect" as the theme for a story. The story involved a young man, Bobby, learning respect from his grandmother and then enacting the teaching within his community. We collectively wrote the story—the youth drawing on their cultural backgrounds and experiences. We storyboarded it in stick-figure drawings on a flip chart, and then took digital photos of the youth posed in positions to represent each image of the story. We took the digital photos to the school's computer lab where we Photoshopped them onto various backgrounds appropriate to the events of the story. When the editing was complete, we stitched the photos together using a free downloadable program designed specifically to create stories using only still images and sound in a simplified and accessible environment. The youth enjoyed customizing the movement of images and playing and experimenting with transitions and other visual effects to enhance the story. We then recorded their voices narrating the story and added background music of their selection.

The result was a five-minute video with which the youth were delighted. We collectively created a story that helped them express their understandings of respect and that showed how learning and change are ongoing processes involving us all. What most delighted the youth, and where the real radical potential lay, was how the doctored photos showed the youth in various new contexts—walking together down a dirt road, at grandma's house playing video games, on a backyard patio enjoying burgers and soda, with friends in a pickup truck, at a community round dance. The digital medium became a way for the youth to imagine themselves on the "outs"—to symbolically escape the constraints of the prison, to move into another time and place, and to imagine themselves in situations and relationships other than the ones in which they currently found themselves.

Re-storying Self through Transformed Magazine Images

This project, which began from an interest in visual literacy and gender identity, involved a group of boys in meaning making from images and storytelling around values and life choices. We brought in a wide selection of images cut from popular magazines of males of various ages and racial-cultural backgrounds engaged in a range of activities. We asked each boy to choose an image of a man whom he thought he might like to be and another of a man whom he would not like to be. We asked the boys to identify the characters in the images they chose and provide a sentence or two of explanation for each of their choices. Discussion among the group regarding their choices elicited a lively exchange of ideas regarding the portrayals of men in the images.

With the images of the men that the boys wanted to be, at one of the boys' suggestion, we cut out the faces of the men in the magazine pictures and replaced them with the boys' faces cut and pasted from digital photos we took, for which the boys astutely posed in positions that exactly matched the positions of the men in the images. The boys were thrilled to see their faces on the bodies of the men in the images—again giving them a chance to see themselves differently. This visual activity greatly enhanced the drama that followed.

We engaged in various drama activities to help them bring the characters to life, including an activity that had them walking in their characters' shoes. We had them interview one another in character, enact conversations with persons close to them, tell stories of key events in their characters' lives, and identify significant life choices their characters made. Finally, we had them devise three alternative endings for their characters' life stories.

The work was insightful in the choices made, in the contrast between the images selected and in the language used to describe or explain them. The work provided new understandings of the life worlds of the youth, presenting their perspectives as both quite ordinary—what we might expect from boys of their age—and also quite distinctive in the specific cultural referents.

Selecting images, creating characters, and telling stories involved a process of examining and articulating one's ways of being and becoming aware of the nuances of one's values and choices. The images spoke to the viewers in unique and varied ways. Through character development and storytelling, the boys had opportunities to speak through their characters' voices, using "I" sentences and internalizing and making connections to their own lives. The storytelling and multiple endings to the stories explored choices, actions, and consequences. We moved from the stereotypical to a more relational level through developing life histories and exploring key life events and possibilities for the characters' futures. We examined how a life story can unfold in different ways. The boys made choices regarding how their stories could end. Through the drama, through enacting the characters, through imaginative interactions between self and other, they had opportunities, in the reconstruction of their own identities, to imagine themselves as otherwise—as other than "offender" or "criminal"—to help them make sense of their life experiences and look for alternatives.

The moments that resulted from this project, which I would identify as the most radical, were statements by the youth outside of the drama work during a discussion in the presence of journalists (a radio producer and a newspaper reporter/cameraman) who visited us at the jail to report on our work. In our discussion to draw conclusions from the magazine images activity, one young person said, "It's all about decisions. One little measly decision will change your life totally, completely turn it right around, turn it upside down" (MacQuarrie 2007). Another young person said that the drama process "helps me to come out of my shoes, so I can look at myself" (Gerein 2007). The comments implied that the youth had gained insights from the activity that they could apply to their lives, but more significant were their comments that showed how the youth understood precisely what the public wanted to hear from them (indeed their comments made it on radio and in print) in order to validate the work, which they valued for their own reasons, whatever those might have been.

Reimagining Relationships with Animals through Traditional Storytelling

This project developed from an interest in exploring aspects of environmental education through drama. We began by sharing stories of our experiences with nature—outdoor adventures, sports, hunting, and encounters with animals. Many of the young people's stories involved cultural activities and, we noted, revolved around conflict with animals—hunting animals, animal attacks, fighting animals for sport, and the like. We decided that relationships with animals might be a fruitful area for further exploration and chose to do so through traditional storytelling. We found a traditional Cree story online, which, it happened that one of the boy's grandfather's had also told him. The story, titled "Ghost Stallion" (First People n.d.), was about a Cree chief who was cruel to animals if they were weak and sick. In retribution, he was visited by a supernatural power, the Ghost Stallion, who took away his prized horses and sentenced him to spend the rest of his days traveling the land searching for them.

We decided to devise an alternate ending to the story in which the chief, in relation to animals, would have an opportunity to redeem himself. As the alternate ending unfolded, two opportunities for the chief's redemption arose, but both times he failed to change his offending behavior. When asked about this, the youth explained that the man ought to be given at least three opportunities to fail before he could be expected to make a meaningful change in his life. This was a performative reversal of the popular "three strikes and you're out" policy so common now in criminal justice and in school discipline procedures. The youths' understandings of human nature and the challenges involved in making life changes proved much more realistic, charitable, and compassionate than the intolerant "three strikes" policy.

The conclusion to the story had the chief make an arrangement with the Ghost Stallion to transform him into a coyote in order to learn to empathize with animals. As a coyote, the chief fell in love with a female coyote and had pups. When his new family came under attack by a bear, he fought to protect them. His bravery in the face of danger and his loyalty to the coyote community earned him his redemption, but when the Ghost Stallion offered him to return to his life as a man, the chief chose to remain a coyote in order to look after his vulnerable pups.

The episodic alternate ending to the story that was collectively devised took twists and turns that I never could have imagined. It revealed insights into the youths' understandings of offending behavior, discipline, and punishment that are instructive to our society, which is so quick and decisive in meeting out punishment to offending individuals without adequate opportunities for them to make meaningful change. The heart-wrenching ending demonstrated the youths' understanding that what is needed to truly know the Other is to become Other and displayed the extraordinary human capacity for empathy, given the chance.

The final two projects I describe are more recognizably TO-based. The first was an adaptation of TO practitioner David Diamond's adapted Image Theatre activity, which he calls *Your Wildest Dream*. The second was intended as Newspaper Theatre (Boal 1998) into a Forum Theatre hybrid; but the creation of a "problem" scene based on a newspaper article was, however, due to circumstances, never taken to Forum.

Envisioning Our Wildest Dreams through
Image Theatre and Digital Photography

This project was an adaptation of David Diamond's *Your Wildest Dream*, which employs Boal's Image Theatre techniques (Diamond 2007; Boal 1998). We integrated Image Theatre and digital photography with the aim of exploring possible future goals for assisting the youth in developing self-understandings to make positive change in their lives possible. As Freire says, "You never get there by starting from there, you get there by starting from some here" (1998, 47). The process helps participants envision a path from "here" to "there." The activity involved creating a series of "now" or "real" images depicting how the youth perceived their then-present realities. For each "real" image, we created a number of different "ideal" future images. All the images were digitally photographed. For each sequence of "real" to "ideal," we created a series of images tracing the steps needed to achieve the "ideal." The photos were all printed and laid out on the floor. Participants negotiated placement of each image on a continuum within each scenario, representing the choices and decisions the characters needed to make to go from the present to the desired future. We gave images titles and articulated characters' thoughts and wishes. Participants then had opportunities to present their versions of the story for any of the sequences of photos and, in the process, elucidated their narrations of self, relationships, community, culture, values, beliefs, and desires. The activity provided a structured space for the youth to make sense of their lives and their circumstances and to generate new meanings about their futures through interacting with peers, images, and a creative process. The youth thoroughly enjoyed making images and telling stories.

Two image series are worthy of mentioning in relation to the potential for radical performance. The first series began with a "now" image, which they titled "Single File," of a number of youth walking in single file formation as they are required to do in the halls of the jail. One corresponding "ideal" image, which they titled "Jail Role Models," showed a group of youth proudly posing and flexing their muscles for a photo. This series elicited stories and discussion around what is a role model and how does one become a role model. The responses, seriously considered and sincere, involved the need for giving and receiving respect, good decision making and care for self in terms of eating well, working out, and not smoking weed.

Among several retellings of this story, one young person's retelling, which he titled "Teen Problems," came to me as a surprise. The story was about a group of young men in a "bisexual club." It involved the young men negotiating understandings about their sexuality with friends and girlfriends and concluded with them posing together for a swimsuit calendar. For us as facilitators, the story and the youths' reactions were pleasantly surprising in that the story was taken up quite seriously, without the mocking of alternative sexual identities that we had often experienced from youth (particularly young men) of this age. In fact, the youth were perfectly at ease being implicated in the story, which was, after all, based on images of them, and were quite willing to engage in an open discussion about the matter. Comments like "In here, everyone's a little gay," or "We have no closets," and expressions of appreciation for "having a friend to give a hand," revealed alternative ways of thinking about sexuality that they had developed through the shared experience of incarceration. That they were able to discuss this freely with us and with peers, including some girls in the group, within the context of the drama activity, was intensely liberating. The story certainly helped me think anew about changing attitudes among young people toward alternative sexual identities.

Another interesting image sequence began with a "real" image of a group of youth sitting in a circle around a drum—an image of a traditional Cree drumming group, which they titled "Spiritual Gathering." The corresponding "ideal" image showed the youth in a pose of celebration, which they titled "Aboriginal Champions." The various retellings of this story all, more or less, involved the group entering a competition and having to overcome a series of challenges to ultimately emerge as winners. This story can be read as a positive metaphor for the youths' lives—the need to overcome challenges in order to succeed.

Recurring themes that we identified throughout the images, both "real" and "ideal," included aspects of aboriginal culture, friendship, competition, sports, food, sexuality, as well as aspects of street life including drugs, gangs, and crime. Not surprisingly, the images and the stories elicited related closely to the youths' lived experiences. We noted that the images and stories, in fact, never ventured very far from reality (e.g., into the fantastical, which was a possibility). Even the "ideal" images were still quite realistic, set in the not too distant future. The "Aboriginal Champions" image was a bit more distant, with a more challenging goal, but still set within the realm of their experiences. The "Jail Role Models" image, still set in the jail, was not a far stretch from their present "now" but was clearly very relevant to them. We also noticed that the overall work on this project displayed very positive relationships and much support for one another, a sense of community—in itself expressing a hopeful future.

Diamond has witnessed communities, he says, who have extreme difficulty imagining a "there," because they are so entrenched in their present "here." De Castell and Jenson, working with street-involved, queer, and otherwise marginalized youth, also note that youth in difficult circumstances are challenged to set realistic goals. Dominant or mainstream "discourses of power," they claim, "of 'self-realization' and 'careers,' of education and lifestyles and 'planning for one's future'—are superimposed on, but too often discontinuous with, the identities, positions and conditions of these and many other marginalized youth" (2006, 239). Rather, they suggest, we need to offer youth discourses that make sense for them. Our project was an opportunity for the youth to reflect on their "real" situations and choices and to imagine possible futures in their own terms.

Exploring Issues of "Citizenship" through Newspaper Theatre

This project took an approach that was a Newspaper Theatre into Forum Theatre hybrid. Beginning from the youths' response to a newspaper article, the aim was to create a Forum Theatre scene, which we hoped to perform for other inmates at the center.

To work within the center's demand that we not talk about criminal activity, I looked for material that would raise challenging issues and be relevant to the life experiences of the youth, without addressing crime or criminality directly. The *Edmonton Journal* (Kent 2007) newspaper article we drew upon discussed the mayor's suggestion to adopt a bylaw that threatened fines up to $10,000 for coercive panhandling. (In 2008, such a bylaw was passed in Edmonton with fines up to $250.) The issue of panhandling in Edmonton as raised in the article met the criteria. It pushed the limits of what is and is not considered "criminal" and engaged with a meaningful, local current event with broad social implications.

When I first read this article, I was struck by its absurdity, which, I suspected, would not be lost on the youth. I was particularly incensed by the article's claim that "[the mayor] isn't concerned about someone quietly seeking a handout." I reflected that perhaps if our mayor *were* more concerned over the need for citizens of our city to seek handouts, there would be no need for concern over coercive panhandling.

To justify the project to the administration, I drew on Alberta Education's rationale and philosophy for the K–12 social studies program: "Social studies provides opportunities for students to develop the attitudes, skills and knowledge that will enable them to become engaged, active, informed and responsible citizens . . . Social studies helps students develop their sense of self and community, encouraging them to affirm their place as citizens in an inclusive, democratic society . . . It promotes a sense of belonging and acceptance in students as they engage in active and responsible citizenship at the local, community, provincial, national and global level." (2005, 1). The language of the social studies curriculum around responsible citizenship and benign neoliberalism, full of vague platitudes and empty rhetoric, was easily reinterpreted by us in more radical terms.

Newspaper Theatre, one of Boal's earliest TO forms, allows topics raised by newspaper articles to be reexamined from multiple alternative perspectives through theatre (Boal 1998). Newspaper Theatre's aims, as outlined by Boal, are to popularize the means of making theatre, demonstrate that theatre can be practiced by anyone to show and defend their ideas, and demystify the pretended objectivity of journalism, allowing people to read newspapers differently.

Like me, the youth responded to the article with fervor. We began our process with discussion of the article and the issues it raised. As I anticipated, the youth perceived the proposed bylaw as absurd. They wondered how someone who needed to panhandle could be expected to pay a $10,000 dollar fine. They saw the tactic for what it was—the criminalization of the poor, a way for the municipal government to control undesirable behaviors. They saw panhandling as a measure of desperation, and all agreed they would never want to be in a position to have to panhandle to survive. They identified poverty and addictions as factors that led to panhandling and described a vicious cycle that, once caught in, was difficult to escape. They felt that rather than create bylaws, the government had a responsibility to address the needs of the poor, homeless, and citizens with addictions. They linked the criminalization of the poor with the similar criminalization of youth by police and "citizens," claiming that in their experiences any group of two or more youth were treated as a threat. They spoke at length about their experiences of police harassment and, in fact, wanted to create a scene about police harassment of youth. When I responded that the administration would never allow such a scene, they were incensed that they were not allowed to say what they wanted. This led to a lengthy discussion about censorship and how to get around it. In devising our scene, we explored ways of saying what the youth wanted to say without overstepping the boundaries of what was permitted.

To elucidate our discussion, we created images and scenarios about panhandling, addictions, loitering, conflict between "citizens," and police harassment that built toward our scene. We titled the scene we created "Need Change?" The setting for the scene was a store owned by a local businessman—a good "citizen." We see the storekeeper and employee inside the store. The storekeeper's character is established as he complains about his employee's laziness. Next, a group of three youths arrive outside the store, their prearranged meeting place, to plan what they need to buy for one of their cousin's eighteenth birthday party that evening. A panhandler approaches the friends asking them for money or food. They give him five dollars and send him away. A customer approaches the store. The panhandler asks the customer for money and gets a bit pushy. The customer becomes angry, shooing the panhandler away. He proceeds into the store, where he immediately complains to the storekeeper about being "harassed" at the door. Meanwhile, the panhandler returns to the friends asking for a cigarette, which they give him. Just then, the storekeeper steps outside and immediately accuses the group of friends of loitering and harassing his customers. The friends try to explain that they are customers, but the storekeeper refuses to listen. A heated argument ensues with the young people trying to defend themselves, all the while sheltering the panhandler from the wrath of the storekeeper, while the storekeeper threatens to call the police. Frustrated, the friends leave saying they will go elsewhere. After the friends have left, the storekeeper notices the panhandler, still standing where the young people had been. Angry, the storekeeper knocks money from the panhandler's hands and goes into the store to call the police. The scene ends with the panhandler picking up his money from the ground.

While we never did get to present our scene in Forum to an audience of other inmates as we had hoped to, we talked about the intentions behind Forum Theatre. The group was very aware that we had created a "problem" scene, and we practiced a few interventions looking for solutions. We did perform the scene once for an audience of staff and administrators to vet. The youth were very excited to perform—nervous beforehand, but very willing, and afterward elated by the performance rush, their achievement, and the opportunity to have spoken out. The audience was thoroughly impressed at the youths' performance skills and the emotional reality they were able to portray. The level of emotional reality achieved was, of course, precisely because the content was based on the youths' actual lived experiences. The audience also commented on the compassion the youth's characters showed toward the panhandler. While we were granted permission to show the scene to other inmates, logistical constraints ultimately prevented us from doing so. Just at that time, two of our actors were released. We had prepared a bit, recast, and rehearsed the scene again, but we could not achieve the same level of performance. By then, the youth became tired of the scene, so we let it go. Unfortunately, an excellent opportunity for further radical performance around the issues with peers was missed.

This opportunity for engaging the youth in expressing their perceptions and critically analyzing issues to contextualize their experiences within a larger social reality had the potential to help them better understand their experiences, thereby awakening the potential for making positive change in their lives and contributing to working toward greater social transformation.

Incarcerated Youth and the Power of Performance

Kershaw claims, and my experience confirms, that the prison setting is "inherently *dramatic*, because it is built on a context between a supposed immutable rigour of rule and the infinite suppleness of the human soul . . . [and] also quintessentially *theatrical* because it stages the absolute separation that society seeks to impose between good and evil" (1999, 131). As such, my drama-based, TO-inspired research study with incarcerated youth was wrought with potential for radical performance.

Diamond believes that individual and community health is vitally dependent on people's capacity to imagine. If the moments I have described in this chapter are moments of radical performance, they are so because they have offered possibilities to radically imagine and reimagine current realities. Both within our drama work and in relation to it, through comic strategies—reversals of status, unexpected responses, surprises, and other moments of honesty—disclosures, insights into the human condition, or telling it like it is, the youth found the "freedom to create currently unimaginable forms of association and action" (Kershaw 1999, 18).

The critical pedagogical strategies that emerged through the work, including open dialogue about issues relevant to the youth, storytelling, and interpretation from the youths' perspectives; the examination of choices and consequences; and the devising of alternative endings, opportunities to reimagine themselves, and various possible futures, proved powerful for opening up moments of radical possibility. As we found, through performance, the "mechanisms of discipline can sometimes be turned inside out to produce resistant and transcendent empowerment" (Kershaw 1999, 139).

Although our work did not always directly address the politics of the context in which our work was set, it was "actively engaged in widening the bounds of political processes" (Kershaw 1999, 84), whether through subtly destabilizing the structures of authority, opening up new ways of thinking or acting, or through performative playfulness.

The potential for radical freedom through performance was apparent in our TO-based work. Kershaw's postmodern concept of the radical in performance has further potential, I believe—particularly for youth at odds with the dominant structures of our society, through acknowledging the performative nature of society, and their role in its performance, suggesting performative alternatives. I also believe there is potential for the freedom achieved through TO practice to leak out into performance of social relations in everyday life—a rehearsal for future action. This offers hope for the creation of autonomy, agency, and the possibility of radical freedom.

Engaging youth through TO-inspired theatre in expressing their perceptions and critically analyzing issues to contextualize their experiences within a larger social reality has the potential to help them, and to help us all, to better understand their experiences, thereby awakening the potential for making positive change in our lives and contributing to a greater social transformation. As Kershaw proclaims, "If radicalism can flourish through performance as part of *those* social processes, then it may potentially prosper in many others" (1999, 20). Boal writes, "We know that s/he who transforms reality [through the creation of art] is transformed by the very action of transforming" (2004). In this sense, our art had and has the potential to radically transform reality.

References

Alberta Education. 2005. *Social studies kindergarten to grade 12—Program rationale and philosophy.* Edmonton, AB: Alberta Education.

Barone, T., and E. Eisner. 1997. Arts-based educational research. In *Complementary Methods for Research in Education*, ed. R. M. Jaeger, 2nd ed., 72–116. Washington, DC: American Educational Research Association.

Boal, A. 1979. *Theatre of the Oppressed.* Trans. C. McBride and M. McBride. London: Pluto.

———. 1998. *Legislative theatre: Using performance to make politics.* Trans. A. Jackson. New York: Routledge.

———. 2004. Aesthetic education of the oppressed. International Theatre of the Oppressed Organisation, http://www.theatreoftheoppressed.org/en/index.php?nodeID=83 (accessed February 15, 2009).

Dean, M. 1999. *Governmentality: Power and rule in modern society.* Thousand Oaks, CA: Sage.

De Castell, S., and J. Jenson. 2006. No place like home: Sexuality, community, and identity among street-involved "queer and questioning" youth. *McGill Journal of Education* 41(3): 227–47.

Denzin, N. K. 2003. *Performance ethnography: Critical pedagogy and the politics of culture.* Thousand Oaks, CA: Sage.

Diamond, D. 2007. *Theatre for living: The art and science of community-based dialogue.* Victoria, British Columbia: Trafford.

Doob, A., and C. Cesaroni. 2004. *Responding to youth crime in Canada.* Toronto: University of Toronto Press.

First People of America and Canada. n.d. "Ghost Stallion: A Yinnuwok Legend." Native American Legends. http://www.firstpeople.us/FP-Html-Legends/Ghost_Stallion-Yinnuwok.html (accessed December 10, 2008).

Foucault, M. 1979. *Discipline and punish: The birth of the prison.* Trans. A. Sheridan. New York: Pantheon.

Freire, P. 1970. *Pedagogy of the oppressed.* Trans. M. B. Ramos. New York: Continuum.

———. 1998. *Pedagogy of hope.* New York: Continuum.

Gerein, K. 2007, April. Researcher uses drama to motivate offenders to plot new life stories. *Edmonton Journal* 24, http://www2.canada.com/edmontonjournal/news/cityplus/story.html?id=c84ad4df-c55c-4e04-bd0e-0232f1f4b8a7 (accessed November 23, 2007).

Kent, G. 2007, June. Mayor says Saskatoon's approach worth exploring: Saskatchewan city's bylaw calls for fines of up to $10,000 for coercive begging. *Edmonton Journal* 20, http://www2.canada.com/edmontonjournal/news/story.html?id=0518f170-45a6-40aa-a0a6-22718c35bcc3 (accessed February 12, 2009).

Kershaw, B. 1999. *The radical in performance: Between Brecht and Baudrillard.* London: Routledge.

MacQuarrie, J. 2007. *Sounds Like Canada.* Vancouver: CBC Radio.

Park, P., M. Brydon-Miller, B. Hall, and T. Jackson, eds. 1993. *Voices of change: Participatory research in the United States and Canada.* Westport, CT: Bergin.

Pasquino, P. 1991. Criminology: The birth of a special knowledge. In *The Foucault effect*: *Studies in governmentality*, ed. G. Burchell, C. Gordon, and P. Miller, 235–50. Chicago: University of Chicago Press.

Prentki, T., and S. Preston, eds. 2009. *The applied theatre reader*. London: Routledge.

Prentki, T., and J. Selman, eds. 2000. *Popular theatre in political culture*: *Britain and Canada in focus*. Portland, OR: Intellect.

Silver, W. 2007. Crime statistics in Canada, 2006. *Juristat*: *Canadian Centre for Justice Statistics* 27(5), http://www.statcan.gc.ca/pub/85-002-x/85-002-x2007005-eng .pdf (accessed November 23, 2007).

7

Rethinking Interaction On and Off the Stage

Jana Sanskriti's Experience

Sanjoy Ganguly

Introduction

While addressing the question of using Theatre of the Oppressed (TO) with youth, I find myself questioning the category of youth. As I hope to make clear in the next section on Jana Sanskriti's place of work, the idea of youth does not translate easily in our context. This is not to say that there is no specificity with regard to age but that the idea of being young problematically slips into the notion of having youth. Observing the experiences of people in rural India, it is hard to identify youth as having an experience that is somehow distinguished as experiences of the youth. In other words, the continuity they bear to more general experiences stands out.

In this chapter, I will first focus on the context of our work where I elaborate on the lack of nutrition, health, and education for young children in India and what I see as the most basic stages of growth that are denied to the youngest members of our society. Then, I discuss how these oppressions are reproduced in the political culture of West Bengal, which further denies the possibility of intellectual development among rural citizens. I then describe Jana Sanskriti's methodology of TO to highlight its specificities and variations from the TO cannon. In this chapter, I show our focus on providing a space for collective and reflective action. I present a couple of examples from plays on patriarchal domination to highlight the nature of interaction and spect-actor formation that foregrounds the distinguishing characteristic of Jana Sanskriti's work. Finally, I argue that our specificity rests on a particular theoretical or philosophical conception of interaction that has emerged from Jana Sanskriti's practice.

Context

The holistic development of any population can be measured first and foremost by the health, nutrition, and education of its children and women. The significance this has received in modern societies is inversely related to the degree to which this has faced neglect in India. This deprivation has resulted in malnutrition among India's children that is worse than children in sub-Saharan Africa. According to the National Family Health Survey, the percentage of children who suffered from malnutrition in 2005 to 2006 was 46 percent. The ratio of child mortality was fifty-seven per one thousand people. Among women between the ages of fourteen and forty-nine years old, the percentage of those with anaemia was 63 percent. It is also clear that a similar survey conducted in 1998 and 1999 shows little progress in terms of family health terms in the past seven years.

Does the deprivation and health situation of youth and women solely affect them? In reality, this affects the entire population and this has long-term consequences. Adequate health, nutrition, and education for children play a role in determining adult health, capacity to work, and intellect. In the same way, the health and nutrition of women determine the health and future of their children. Research has demonstrated that those societies that have high human development indices have higher average heights and weights and better health. In Japan, where people were stereotyped for being short, their average height has now exceeded the United States. This fact is not unknown to policy makers in India.

In 2002, Pratichi Trust released its report on the state of primary education in West Bengal that clearly pointed to a nearly collapsed condition of the primary school system.[1] The entire primary education system of West Bengal was marked with several deficiencies and implementation failures. A different sort of privatization in the form of private tuition almost replaced the public primary education. Children learned so little in the schools that they could not even write their names without having the external support of private tutors. The preprimary facilities, crucially important for making the primary schooling effective, were almost absent. While the lackluster delivery of primary education in the state had its roots in the paucities of the school's education department (that dealt with the children above five years of age), what came along, in addition with it was the extremely poor delivery of services that was called the Integrated Child Development Services (ICDS), meant for the children under six years of age.[2]

Taking holistic child development into account, the central government instituted the ICDS in 1975, the largest program for the Indian child in which a major component was preschool education (PSE). The coverage of this major and centrally important program for the children below six years of age was very poor; in addition, the functioning of the existing centers was awful.[3] It is regrettable that the way in which children have faced indifference and neglect from their cradle onward, this program too has faced similar neglect. Yet, after thirty-three years in existence, no more than 50 percent of Indian children receive coverage by this program. As a result of various social movements, the Indian Supreme Court directed that ICDS become universalized on November 28, 2001. Despite this, the intervention has hardly expanded its range. Moreover, there are numerous problems in its implementation; for example, the food supplied for nutrition is of terrible quality and other important aspects, such as preprimary education, are hardly even implemented.

In other words, the context in which we have to work with youth is very complex. Is there a "childhood" for those children who suffer from malnutrition and grow up as malnourished youth? Their childhood is lost in the murky waters of reality. You can see children of four to five years of age working with their fathers. Girls of similar ages are working with their mothers. These are the children who grow to be the youth spectators of our performances. Jana Sanskriti, the Center for Theatre of the Oppressed, works mainly in villages. In some cities, we also work among slum dwellers. It is questionable whether India is progressing. First, who is progressing? Which class? Is the meaning of progress the ability to consume more? There is no room to elaborate on these questions in this chapter. However, it must be said that in a country that has been independent for sixty years, where the question of universalizing preprimary and primary education has been recently raised, and where the index of human development relies on people's capacity to sign their names, it is true that tiny steps of progress may seem like massive occasions for celebration. Actually, development is relative.

In other words, the youth we work with in villages and towns neither had a childhood nor an adolescence. They didn't have nutrition or quality education. Even now, a number of children drop out of middle school because of the poor foundations established in primary education. Even in the case of our actors, they were mostly dropouts as well as engaged in child labor. They have worked as domestic workers to menial jobs in small shops. As they grow up a little bit, they start working in the unorganized sector. Even now, those who work as daily laborers need to migrate to the city in search of work. Along with this is caste discrimination, although caste has been politicized in a way that the external manifestations of it are not as aggressive as they are outside of West Bengal. The reform movements in nineteenth-century Bengal and in the mid-twentieth-century land struggles and trade union movements had relied on class unity to affect caste hierarchy in some undoubtable ways. However, caste discrimination still exists in pernicious forms.

Now market fundamentalism has become an added factor. Everyone wants to participate in the market even though the market excludes. As a result, people's wants are increasing. To satisfy these wants, people are working harder and searching for more work. Earlier the search for work was aimed at meeting subsistence needs, and now it satisfies wants. This difference is apparent in a number of places, although it is not true everywhere. In Indian villages, a lot of people do not eat well for even one meal a day. Wherever middle-class aspirations have increased, individualism has increased too. Civil society is weakening. As a result, the collective initiatives that used to be taken up by civil society no longer seem possible today. People are increasingly dependent on nongovernmental organizations (NGOs) and parties that sometimes bring the government closer to people. In this kind of context, when we work with youth in these villages, we can hardly see their situation as somehow distinguished as a "youth" issue. After all, here the youth can see the origins of all kinds of exploitation and oppression in political and economic social relations. The content of our theatre becomes political where youth, aged men and women, everyone, searches for the relations of oppression. With this they are enthused to debate and think about oppression and exploitation and to look for a path toward transformation. I now turn to the description of our methodology.

Methodology Adopted by Jana Sanskriti

Forum Theatre is our main arsenal. But for us, Forum Theatre is a production of a play as well as the process of creating a play. It is also the process of a total transformation. Process is as important as the product here. We do not determine the aspect of oppression to be addressed in a play beforehand. Actors in the workshop identify various forms of oppression and then choose one among them to focus on in the play. Play making is part of our political methodology. Here, we script plays before we play the script. While scripting the play, actors find their reality in a critical way. Actors not only engage in social critique but also embody social critique, as they study characters to be scripted and played as social constructions rather than as individuals. For example, the process of scripting a play requires them to analyze the ideology of oppressors, beliefs that oppressed characters have in mind, the practices and rationalizations through which these ideologies are apparent in behavioral norms, and so on. The whole playmaking exercise becomes an intellectual journey for the actors who we view as empowering. Together, actors explore the social root of the problems and characters in the story. These stories are always based on facts and not fictions, on a multiplicity of perspectives on characters, rather than a singular interpretation of their characteristics.

In the next stage of this methodology, the play is taken to the audience to invite engagement between actors and spectators. A dialogue between actors and "spect-actors" takes place during a performance. They discuss, debate, and become argumentative. In this debate, actors and spectators engage themselves in the intellectual journey I mentioned previously. This is how the actors and spectators travel together from particular to general, from experience to theory, and this is the intellectual journey. This intellectual journey is at once an affective journey that I characterize as internal transformation. The internal transformation develops desire within people to go toward creating social transformation offstage. Performance is not enough. Acting takes place in real life in the form of social action. The meaning of acting becomes apparent in its dual sense. When actors and spectators act onstage, they are actors and spect-actors, and while they act outside the stage to bring change in their reality, they become activists. Our method here brings acting and activism, acting onstage and offstage, into relation and confrontation with each other.

The scripted play is taken to the same group of spectators at least three times over the course of a month. When actors perform a Forum Theatre play in front of spect-actors, we call that collective action. In Forum Theatre, the spect-actors and actors debate and discuss the oppression depicted in the play. Often, the oppression remains unresolved, revealed in its complexity and multiple challenges and dilemmas. The collective witnessing of such complex oppression leaves spect-actors reflecting on how to resolve, complete, or reconcile the problem depicted in the Forum play. They start reflecting during and after the Forum performance. Every such collective witnessing and action leads to reflective action. So we create a space for an ongoing engagement in collective and reflective action. Actors and spect-actors travel that path in order to rationalize the situation depicted in the play.

The Forum play is performed in a particular region for at least six months to a year. In other words, audience members see the same play at least three times. At this time, a large group of audience members and actors continue to discuss the issue at hand. This discussion relies on the collective witnessing, debate, and reflective action that comes out of Forum Theatre. At a particular point in this process, the discussants begin to contemplate how they might translate the solutions debated onstage in their offstage lives. Bringing the audience members together is the initiative and mobilizing agenda of the local theatre teams.

So Forum Theatre is a process that starts from the workshop and continues as performance and then goes beyond performance. After rationalizing, spectators feel like acting toward changing their immediate reality. In this way, theatre continues as offstage politics, and the offstage politics then informs the next cycle of playmaking. It never ends.

In the last two decades, we have addressed a wide range of issues. For example, corruption in the public distribution system that affects nutrition and health in households, liquor production that drains household income from schooling toward liquor consumption, corruption in the local government, the existing relationship between party and people, superstitions, caste discrimination, lack of quality in rural primary education, and forms of violence experienced in particular by women. In fact, patriarchy in the home and in public institutions is a common thread of Jana Sanskriti's work across regional contexts within India. In most cases, we have succeeded reasonably in addressing these issues. And I would argue that part of our success has been a result of refusing to see a youth issue as simply a youth issue, a women's issue as simply a domestic issue, or a party issue simply as an adult issue.

In our work, theatre is always theatre for change. Change can come through a rational participation of the spectators—the people. This constitutes an alternative for people. After all, the dominant political culture expects blind following, which is not something that sits particularly well with people. Theatre creates debate among people, and that is its primary contribution to the formation of collective political action. In addition to the form of oppression being discussed in the play, we also distribute information to the public in the form of pamphlets and meetings. This is also part of the democratizing process.

Membership and Examples: The Outcomes of Our Method

Jana Sanskriti membership is striking. The ratio of men and women in Jana Sanskriti theatre teams is almost 50:50. Similarly, its spectators are equally divided among men and women. Further, our actors range from the ages of sixteen to early thirties.

In this section, I will bring out some examples from plays that center on the experience of patriarchy. Through this, I hope to communicate with readers a common experience of power relations everywhere.

The first example comes from our theatre unit in New Delhi. We work there through an organization called Delhi Sramik Sanghathan (Delhi Workers' Organisation). They are active with workers in an unorganized sector. The team we have developed is made up of youth ranging from ages sixteen to twenty-three. Most of them work as domestic workers, and some of them work in various unorganized sectors like construction work, vegetable selling, and so on.

The play they were performing was called *Stop! Don't Go!* It was about a young woman married at an early age. This young woman wants to act in a play staged by a social activist group, but her twenty-four-year-old husband is not willing to see his wife acting in public. To him, women should not engage in theatre. He was a patriarch in the play. The actor Kailash plays a very tricky husband in the play. He can justify his actions very well. Jaya plays his wife, one who is not ready to be the victim of patriarchal oppression. She is trying to resist his control but not succeeding. This is very important in any Forum play. We try not to portray total victims without hope in our plays; rather, we portray an oppressed person engaged in combating the oppressor but not succeeding for various external and internal reasons. Let's talk about the play.

> *Husband*: You can't go to perform in a play that takes place on the street.
> *Wife*: Why? What's wrong in doing that?
> *Husband*: My friends will laugh at me. You should obey me. Don't go.
> *Wife*: This is not an ordinary theatre; it is a kind of social work. I feel dignified while acting in the play.
> *Husband*: Get lost! Don't talk big. After all, you are a domestic worker; dignity is not something you can ask for.

This is how the dialogue proceeds in the play. We called spect-actors to come onstage. They were coming one by one and the Forum was advancing. Suddenly, a young girl shouted "Stop! I want to come." The Joker was a bit conscious. I saw this girl acting as a spect-actor previously in one of our plays. She is a very intelligent young woman and works as a housemaid in a middle-class household. Her name was Anju. She came and replaced the protagonist in the play. The interaction between the oppressive husband and the oppressed wife started again.

> *Husband*: You can't go to act in theatre.
> *Anju (the spect-actor)*: I love to do that, so I will.
> *Husband*: My friends are laughing at me and telling me that I am not a strong husband.
> *Anju*: What makes a strong husband?
> *Husband*: Don't argue.
> *Anju*: My friends are also laughing at me.
> *Husband*: Why?
> *Anju*: You play cards on the street and they think you are gambling without letting me know.
> *Husband*: You think men will have to let their wives know about what they are doing with their friends? We men can play cards. That is acceptable in society. But women acting in street theatre is not acceptable.

The interaction between the oppressor character and the spect-actor was reflecting a patriarchal society. The character of the husband was looking at his wife's will from the perspective of society. It was hardly a problem between two individuals. The genesis of the problem to them lies in the society.

The Joker was about to stop the interaction. Anju preempted the conclusion of the intervention and said to the joker—"Let me say something before you stop us." In this way, she prolonged a debate that the Joker might have concluded prematurely. The intervention continued.

Anju: Do you watch Bollywood movies?
Husband: Yes, very much. You can also see some with my kind permission.
Anju: Don't you see women dancing with men, sometimes very scantily clad women?
Husband: *(with laugh)* Yes, so what?
Anju: Are they not women in public? Are they not wives or sisters of some one? If you don't see any problem in watching women dancing with men as in the movie, why do you see me acting in the play as objectionable? In fact, the play I want to act in raises social consciousness among citizens.

The husband's character became silent. He had no response. Spectators, and even the actors, started clapping.

After the play was over, I found Kailash, the oppressor character in our play, standing quietly in the corner of the temporarily made green room. I put my hands on his shoulder and asked, "How did you feel about the intervention of Anju?" He said, "Sanjoyda,[4] the intervention made me stand in front of myself and I realize that I had a patriarch in me even though I act in the play that addresses patriarchy." I was amazed. This is how a collective action leads to an introspective action.

I would like to offer one more example that comes from rural West Bengal. This is from a play called *Sonar Meye.*[5] For the past eighteen years, Jana Sanskriti's twenty-five theatre teams have performed this play a few thousand times in rural areas. In this play, a young girl who is not yet eighteen is being forced to get married. In this play, a girl's experience of life before, during, and after marriage is depicted. I will illuminate a particular scene from *Sonar Meye.* In the play, the family of the girl is very poor. There is also a young son in the family in addition to the protagonist, the daughter. In one of the scenes, we see that the girl is about to be inspected by a prospective groom and father-in-law. This practice of the groom's family inspecting the girl is a common practice. This inspection supports two sets of related norms. First, the family wants to inspect the girl to see if she meets expectations. Here she is reduced to a commodity. The groom and his family study the girl's body and person—from skin complexion to any disabilities she might have—to ensure that they know what they are getting. If they like her, then the second step of negotiating dowry begins. In modern times, the demand for dowry has increased as a result of consumerism and commercialism. Dowry is an integral part of marriage even though it is an agonizing institution. The girl's father is among the most oppressed with this institution even though he perpetuates the problem of getting his daughter married early and for a price. On the one hand, he has to get his daughter married and cannot let her choose her own companion. On the other hand, the socially sanctioned requirement that he give dowry for her marriage throws him into severe debt. No doubt the troubles of individuals are apparent in social relations. Individuals and society are related in this way.

In the next scene, we can see that a young girl sits on a chair. We can see a young man and an elderly gentleman inspecting the young girl. They are likely the prospective groom and father-in-law. The parents of the girl are extremely tense, as they are anxious that the inspectors like their daughter. As the girl is inspected, the prospective groom measures her hair by his arm's length, he looks at her eyes closely, and he asks her to walk to ensure that her mobility is normal. In this scene, not only is this woman oppressed, but also the idea that she can desire dignity is not even recognized. In this scene, we invite interventions to see how people respond to the norms depicted in this play and how the girl can be liberated from the inhuman disregard for this woman. In the place of the woman, spect-actors intervene with various forms of action. Acting as the protagonist woman, a number of spect-actors resist the measure of their hair, refuse to walk, insist on pursuing their education, and refuse to get married. Moreover, almost all the spect-actors destroy the dowry system in their interventions. When the spect-actor as the woman protagonist says that she wants to study and not get married, the father in the play says that he cannot educate his son and daughter because he does not have the financial means to support both. The audience is pushed to consider this norm as well. Why is the daughter not entitled to a right to education? Why is the father's financial means dedicated to the son? In other words, this Forum play is holistic because, along with the daily oppressions of patriarchal norms, it addresses various forms of discrimination and exclusion in society.

One day there was a performance of *Sonar Meye* in a village. Forum Theatre engagement began on the scene described above. A number of men and women began to show a number of solutions to the particular experience of the woman. On one occasion, a woman stepped onstage to act as spect-actor. The spect-actor has visible markers of her poverty. In her lap she holds a malnourished child, and there is a veil over her head. She comes onstage to replace the girl onstage. In the play, when the prospective groom wants to inspect the girl's hair, the spect-actor resists.

> *Female spect-actor*: You cannot measure my hair in this way. But my question is it is not my concern what you as an individual are doing. In fact, as an individual, I too can resist your actions. But the question is, why should social norms be such as to give men the authority to inspect women in this way. If women similarly inspected men before marriage, would it be any good?

As the woman uttered these words, the women in the audience clapped to register their applause. For this woman, the problem depicted in the play is not the problem of some individuals and families; rather, in this play about one family, she saw the problem of a patriarchal society. This is an interaction when a person is led to articulate not just an event but the social forces producing an event. They can see the origins of a local problem in the broader forces of society. In this way, the audience grow together intellectually. In the world of intellectual thought, they begin to feel a sense of comfort and confidence. This is an aesthetic experience. This makes life meaningful. This is what I am calling an internal revolution—one that breaks human passivity and makes them transformative agents of the external social world. They crave transformation of the external world. TO becomes a rehearsal of total transformation.

My Conception of Theatre of the Oppressed

Based on the examples previously described, I will now highlight what I view to be the kernel of Jana Sanskriti's conception of TO. I often think that theatre is a tool for constructing relations. It works as a connecting thread, sometimes between the actors and the audience, sometimes among actors, and sometimes among the audience. And sometimes, it enables the actors and the audience members to connect their internal lives with their external worlds. The most important thing in TO is this construction of relationships. That is why, while the performance is on, the center of the gravity onstage cannot be perceived as somehow limited to the stage. It moves amid and among the spectators. Just as this universe is subject to centrifugal and centripetal forces, in that way, in Augusto Boal's theatre, as well the relationship between actors and audience members, is characterized by these forces. The actors and audience have come together on the basis of these two forces. As a result of this connection, progress becomes possible. Collective action is constructed as a result of actors and audience coming together. And then, thought constructs the ways ahead, the ways for change. This is progress. Actually, unity and collectivity are the causes of progress.

Besides, what is aesthetics, anyway? Aesthetics is also a collective expression, a mixture, a sign of unity. When we look at a forest, we see not only a collection of trees but also a collective characteristic in the relation among the trees. If in this forest we did not experience the trees in their relationship with each other, then we would hardly have a conception of a forest. The genesis of aesthetics and even truth is the relationship between one and another.

In the audience of TO, particularly in Forum Theatre, the audience member steps onstage and shows how he or she wants to depict the characteristic of the oppressed. This makes people think that the structure of the play is being destroyed. Besides, the audience is not used to seeing the magic of acting. Typically, they see characters as action figures rather than acting. In this form of collective action, the actors act and the spect-actors engage in action. But the meeting of the two result in the formation of beauty. It is true that this beauty is much more a matter of affective realization. The beauty of the play is not its external colors and structure, but the relationships that emerge through Forum Theatre.

Whether it is conducted with youth or any other designated group, what's important is the way in which we understand TO. The weakness in understanding TO adequately has caused much of the crisis characterizing the practice of TO in the world today. This is not just a bunch of theatre techniques; it is a method and concept for politics. In that politics, multiple dimensions and ways of thinking come together. Each person observes this method in different ways. Nobody will identify a special philosophy or philosopher among them. After all, a number of ways of thinking and contexts of practice have come together. To forget this is to give TO a dogmatic character. This is a troubling trend because it will turn TO into doctrine and take it away from philosophy. At any rate, let me get back to how I see TO.

Theatre or any other art is a means of constructing relations. But it is very important to understand how these relations are constructed. Often, the relation between actors and audience members is based on hierarchy. But the actor is not always aware of this hierarchy. In some kinds of theatre, this is obvious, because the actor is a star. In TO, star culture is anathema. Still, on the question of constructing relations with the spectators, a number of issues come up. The Joker is often tense. This is because the Joker is busy measuring success by the number of spect-actors who come onstage to intervene. This is not the appropriate form of this work. First, whether spect-actors come onstage and how and why they come onstage depend on how the actors and Jokers look upon the audience members, with what attitude. This determines how the spect-actors come onstage and in what numbers. Second, it is not a matter of how many people intervene during a Forum but what exactly this interaction means in Forum Theatre. Actors will assume that in front of them are various intellectuals in the audience who are each keen to think and reflect. They want a democratic space where they can articulate their thoughts. The moment the actors and the Jokers realize this, they will be able to construct a relationship. The hierarchy between actors and audience members will break. At this stage, dialogue is hardly a technique; it is a practice with which both are comfortable. Collective thinking and intellectual contemplation has been a foundational sphere of human society. When hands became free, the human could see an endless horizon and much more information than was previously available. The question "Why?" was born as humans had to explain the endless horizon on the basis of the information available thus far. Already, the differences and contradictions between the information in their heads and the vast sources of information around them create the conditions for asking "Why?" Overcoming this conflict leads to the formation of human society. There was no centralization at the time, no institutions, and hence no institutional head. People's collective thinking has led to various forms of progress. The conflict I was talking about is, in one sense, art—an art of existence. And at the same time, the conflict is a source of intellectual debate expanding people's engagement in the world of intellectual thought. In other words, art and intellectual debate are constitutive and habitual to humans. And yet, modern life has removed most people from the world of intellectual debate and art. In their place, an elite class has established control over intellectual debate and art.

Artistic creation is born from society. It is not surprising then that art is social metaphor. Artistic debate makes people social critics. When I began work with agricultural workers in villages, I noticed two important features in people's art form. First, in rural folk culture, the relationship between art and audience is extremely democratic. This is because they understood that any form of collective learning democracy has to play a significant role. Second, I have witnessed the use of classical tales in rural folk culture and never found characters that lack complexity. The characters are present onstage replete with the qualities and flaws. As a result, it is hardly possible to fully empathize with them. Alienation is the norm. The artists wanted the audience to be alienated from the characters and be able to examine them. Brecht may have been born in India before Germany—one would not be mistaken in thinking this. That's why in the recent past, the rural artists in villages have taken a pioneer role in critically reflecting on social relations and events. Perhaps this is why the colonial governments and independent Indian government has made little effort to keep these folk arts alive. Indeed, in some cases, they have actively worked to destroy and repress them. Like these folk forms of art, TO too believes in democracy between actors and spectators and the importance of democracy for collective learning. Besides, the making of spectators into spect-actors was a thoughtful plan to democratize political action.

Democracy is the principle element in artistic and intellectual life—indeed, in social life itself. Moreover, making an ideological commitment to a world where artistic and intellectual learning is part of the comfort zone for every person brings revolutionary change in the practice of art and theatre.

For this reason, TO is for us a rehearsal for change. In particular, Forum Theatre, the formation of a relationship between actors and audience members, is constructed in the journey from "I" to "We" and from "We" to "Them." This is extremely important. In order to elaborate on this, it is imperative for me to resort to a story. In Boal's theatre, fact is primary. But I am taking recourse in fiction. Many years ago, in Turkey, there was a scholar named Mullah Naseeruddin. Naseeruddin was a great storyteller. One day, a layperson asked Naseeruddin a question: "Respected Mullah, what is my relationship to you?" In response, Naseeruddin told him a story.

> One day, I decided that I would go and see my murshid. [In the Sufi tradition, the intellectual guide and priest is known as murshid.] After walking for three days I reached the guide's home. When the murshid heard the knock on the door, he asked, "Who calls?" In response, I said, "It's me, Naseeruddin, sir." When the door did not open, I knocked again. Again, without opening the door, the murshid asked, "Who is it out there?" I said, "It's me. Me, Naseeruddin." Again the door did not open. Disappointed without an option, I walked on without any direction. I had a deep anguish in my heart. At one time, I felt that this pain allowed me to reflect on myself. I was a spectator of myself. Who am I? I asked myself. A number of hours went by as I contemplated this question. In the end, I would return to the murshid's home. I went, and as I reached, I knocked on the door. From inside, the murshid asked, "Who are you out there?" This time I said, "You." Amazingly, the door opened. I saw the murshid standing in front of me.

The story demonstrates with great clarity the fact that the journey from "I" to "You," from "We" to "Them," lies at the heart of interaction. In this, there is the experience of oneness. This is the philosophy being the politics of relation and politics of spirituality. Spirituality is oneness. It has got nothing to do with institutional religion.

In Forum Theatre, there is a journey from audience to actors—that, is from actors to spect-actors. We are all spect-actors. The audience in Forum Theatre are actors, and the actors are audience members. Everyone is a spectator of society and themselves. Let me reiterate these fundamental principles: that spectators are basically intellectual, that democratic relationship between actors and spectators is the principle element in theatre, and that the journey from "I" to "We," from "We" to "Them" is imperative. Is it enough for us to consider these fundamental principles simply as theoretical positions? Probably not. In any such position, there must be two dimensions: theory and logical emotion. Catharsis is an expression of a negative emotion, whereas positive emotion does lead the person to be rational. I am talking about that emotion that lives in our heart and generates complementary feeling for the theory that lives in our brain.

Conclusion

In this chapter, I have described the context in which we work where the distinction between working with youth and working with adults does not emerge as a defining characteristic of the issues at hand. Yet the characters, actors, and spect-actors often reflect on the structural exclusions and domination young girls face in the process of being pushed toward early marriages. Moreover, the neglect of school as an institution for poorer citizens, in general, and for girls, in particular, is commonly discussed onstage as a problem tied equally to state neglect and patriarchal norms.

In this context, TO provides some tools with which to publicly and collectively reflect critically on the social forces and individual consent through which domination and discrimination rules people's lives. Forum Theatre provides an opportunity to not only recognize the individual problem as a social one, but it also highlights, practices, and publicizes an alternative mode of social interaction itself. That is, it reveals the possibility of a form of democratic and reflective interaction among human beings in ways that accord dignity and respect in action. This is not accomplished overnight but through long-term engagement, repeated performances of the same plays in the same places, and ongoing offstage political action that reinforces the commitment to the possibility of interacting beyond the scripts of patriarchal norms, histories of hierarchy, and state exclusion.

Notes

1. *The Pratichi Education Report I, with an introduction by Amartya Sen*, TLM Books, in association with Pratichi Trust, Delhi, 2002. Some other reports also, like, *The Report of the Education Commission* (headed by Ashok Mitra) (1992) Government of West Bengal, popularly known as the Ashok Mitra [Commission's] Report; Chattopadhyay, Raghabendra et al. (1998): *Status of Primary Education in West Bengal* (A project sponsored by UNICEF, Kolkata), Government of West Bengal, Kolkata.

2. The Integrated Child Development Services (ICDS) is one of the largest child intervention programs in the world. The program came into existence in 1975 following the recognition of the vitality of an all-around child development by the national policy for children in 1974. The physical and mental development that takes place in early childhood is crucial not only for the child but also for the society as a whole, without any doubt. It has also been realized that there is a very strong case for simultaneously providing all the basic services for the proper development of the child—nutrition, health, and education—through supporting the children and their mothers in their own habitations. The policy to be developed was, thus, an integrated delivery of services for total child development. Though the policy was launched in 1975, it needed more than a quarter century and a wider public grumbling to attract the Supreme Court to make a substantial reach among the children. The Supreme Court in its order (the *Peoples' Union of Civil Liberties v. the Union of India and Others*, Civil Writ Petition 196 of 2001) dated November 28, 2001, directed the Union government, all the state governments, and the Union territories to bring all children under six years of age into the fold of this program. Not only this, the Court also had to

pass several interim orders to make the Union and state governments comply with the orders. For details, see FOCUS 2006.
3. *Pratichi Education Report I.* See also NCAER 2000.
4. The suffix "da" is placed after names to address older brothers.
5. *Sonar Meye* literally means "the Golden Girl." It references the gold paid in dowry by the woman's family to the bridegroom's family to seal a marriage. The term *sona meye*, however, is a commonly used term of endearment to describe a precious daughter. The play satirizes her precious value to natal and marital families.

References

Chattopadhyay, Raghabendra, and others. 1998. *Status of primary education in West Bengal (A project sponsored by UNICEF, Kolkata).* Kolkata: Government of West Bengal.

Focus on Children Under Six (FOCUS). 2006. *Citizens' initiative for the rights of children under six.* New Delhi: FOCUS.

Majumdar, Tapas. 1993. An Education Commission report. *Economic and Political Weekly* 28 (19): 919–20.

National Council of Applied Economic Research (NCAER). 2000. *Integrated Child Development Services (ICDS): Overall performance of ICDS Programme in West Bengal.* New Delhi: NCAER.

Rana, Kumar. Abdur Rafique, and Amrita Sengupta. 2002. *A study in West Bengal (The Pratichi Education report I).* New Delhi: TLM Books.

Rana, Kumar, Samantak Das, Amrita Sengupta, and Abdur Rafique. 2003. State of primary education in West Bengal. *Economic and Political Weekly* 38 (22): 2159–64.

8

Acting Outside the Box

Integrating Theatre of the Oppressed within an Antiracism Schools Program

Warren Linds and Linda Goulet

I think a positive thing happens when you dramatize everything; you get to play someone else, feel what they feel, not just be yourself . . . You can see secondhand knowledge. You see how it might feel to be discriminated against . . . You can never know how someone feels, but you get a sense of it.

—Student, interview

This chapter will critically examine issues emerging from the incorpo-ration of Theatre of the Oppressed (TO) in an antiracism program in schools. We will explore an adaptation of Theatre of the Oppressed that not only de-normalizes acts of discrimination but also provides a space to develop an "as if" world, where antiracism is practiced and transformation is possible.

The Context

In 2005, a Canada-wide survey (Ipsos-Reid 2005) found that one in six Canadians (17 percent) report they have been the victims of racism. More specifically, the residents of the Prairie Provinces of Saskatchewan/Manitoba (27 percent) report they have been the victims of racism. Residents of the same provinces (76 percent) say that Aboriginal people are the most likely to be the victims of racism. In the report, Rudyard Griffiths, executive direc-tor of the Dominion Institute, stated, "These poll results unfortunately indi-cate that racism and discrimination are a fact of everyday life for millions of Canadians. Despite the advances we have made as a country to eliminate intolerance, we cannot become complacent about the need to challenge racism and discrimination at their every occurrence" (ibid., 2).

The survey showed approximately 30 percent of Canadians feel schools and families would be the most effective in promoting racial tolerance. At the same time, other studies have documented that schools are sites of racist incidents and practices and part of the reason for the lack of engagement of minority students in schools (Huff 1997; Schissel and Wotherspoon 2003; Silver and Mallett 2002; Wilson 1991). In order to facilitate antiracism education, we strive to use this contradiction to an advantage, as we examine, through experiential activities, racism as it occurs in the lives of students at school.

In this chapter we describe a public school board program in Canada. The school division has ten high schools and close to fifty elementary schools. The student body is primarily Euro-Canadians with a cultural and racial mix. The Indigenous students, who make up 30 percent of the student body, are the largest group of racialized students in the schools. Within this group is where the greatest amount of racial tension in the community exists.

The Antiracism Program

The antiracism program works toward building school communities where individuals are safe from discrimination, prejudice, stereotyping, and racism. A 1986 report to the school board identified the need to improve the multicultural climate within the schools and for antiracism training for all educators. In 1996, funding was obtained to implement a school-wide antiracism program.

The main goal of the program is to develop the capacity of twelve- to eighteen- year-old youth for leadership in antiracism and cross-cultural education in their schools. The program motto—"Together We Will Make a Difference!"—reflects a belief that it is everyone's responsibility to work toward building communities where individuals are safe from discrimination, prejudice, stereotyping, and racism. Such a safe space is created and modeled in one of the program components—an intensive three-day training retreat that brings teachers, students, and facilitators together in a setting away from the city and schools. In these three days, Power Plays have been adapted to the particular needs of the program, which include community- and trust-building activities around issues of identity and power. At the end of the retreat, school teams get together to design an antiracism plan for their school. In this way, school teams take responsibility for adapting the program to suit the strengths of their teams and address the issues of racism and discrimination particular to the situation in their school.

The students who attend the retreat are a heterogeneous group. Each of the ten high schools in the city selects six to eight students to participate. Selection procedure varies from school to school; some schools have students write essays. At other schools, students simply volunteer, while in others, teachers approach students who they think would benefit from attending the retreat. Therefore, there is a wide range in age, ethnicity, race, and those who have taken part in bullying or racist acts, those who have been subject to those acts, and those who have witnessed acts of bullying or racism.

Antiracism Education

Often, schools in Canada teach about cultural differences by providing information about ethnic groups through cultural practices such as food, festivals, and folklore. Dei (1996) believes cultural programming is an aspect of antiracism education, but romanticized notions of cultural difference have served to mask the underlying power relations that maintain inequity. A cultural approach alone is problematic in addressing racism for both "majority" and "minority" students. St. Denis (2002) argues that education about culture fails to assist minority students to deal with the material and social conditions of their lives as members of marginalized groups. The focus on culture alone does not give students the tools to overcome the systemic barriers that face them. Nor does it equip them with the language to name what is happening to them or discuss strategies to respond to discriminatory treatment.

Both Henry and Tator (2005) and Kumashiro (2000) also critique the cultural approach as the only lens through which "majority" students learn to combat racism in their lives. Cultural programming that "teaches about the other" is problematic because it stresses how individuals "think about, feel towards, and treat one another" (Kumashiro 2000, 35) or "stipulates what differences are tolerable" (Henry and Tator 2005, 30) by the mainstream culture to the exclusion of structural causes of racism. In other words, the cultural approach's emphasis on difference means majority students are not required to look at their own privilege and power relationships with those on the margins or examine their participation in school cultures and practices that marginalize those who are different.

Ng (1995) believes there is an individual, as well as a collective, responsibility for learning and teaching in antiracism education. Effective interactions point to the need to develop meaningful partnerships with all involved in antiracism initiatives.

Theoretical Foundation of the Antiracism Program

Any good theatre will itself be educational—that is, when it initiates or extends a questioning process in its audience; when it makes us look afresh at the world, its institutions, and conventions and at our own place in that world; when it expands our notion of who we are, of the feelings and thoughts of which we are capable, and of our connection to the lives of others (Jackson 1993, 35).

Research that investigated antiracism theatre projects for youth found "theatre is a powerful way to address the issue of racism, and that it is effective in educating youth about racism and other forms of oppression" (Seebaran and Johnston 1998, iii). As Donoho comments in reference to a performance project involving people from different communities, the development of a shared language through theatre engenders a "commitment to each other and to the common project" (2005, 71), creating "interest in rather than fear of individual differences" (ibid.). Sanders notes the goal of using theatre[1] to address racism is not to show that racism is bad and acceptance is good. Rather, it is to "bring to the forefront of our consciousness the idea that transitivity, changing our communities in relation to intolerance, is preferable to intransitivity or no action" (1999, 226). Sheared's (1999) concept of "polyrhythmic realities" adds to this, highlighting the complexity of bridging cultural differences as there are complicated perceptions rooted in lived experiences based on "race," gender, class, sexual orientation, or simply the geographical origin of participants. This complexity necessitates adaptation of the method we use to the particular lived identities of the participants.

We draw on the work of both Boal and Freire. Freire analyzed banking education, where the teacher's relationship to the student involves pouring knowledge into the "empty" student, where "knowledge is a gift bestowed by those who consider themselves knowledgeable upon those whom they consider to know nothing" (Freire 1970, 58). Freire's approach is a transitive praxis where learner is both subject and object. He addresses the teacher-student relationship by challenging the one-way dynamic to create a critical pedagogy that (among other influences) inspired Boal to rework the monologic structure of traditional theatre and its spect-actor segregation.

Boal proposed dialogue, the belief that the marginalized are not outside but central to the structure of society, that social existence is dialectical and interdependent in nature, and that pedagogy is situated in an ever-changing, not motionless and memorized, reality. "Boal shared with Freire an understanding of the praxis—the inseparability of reflection and action, theory and practice—in pursuit of social change" (Schutzman 2006, 133).

The Program Retreat

Risks are inherent in discussing what we want to de-normalize. Racism and discrimination are risky subjects, partly because they are not talked about in school and partly because the issues are a complex interweaving of power, identity, attitudes, behaviors, and institutional and cultural structures. Nicholson asserts that drama education involves the "enactment of trust" (2002, 84). Accepting or taking risks in drama often makes people vulnerable. Trust is both an attitude and a process through which people allow themselves to enter situations of risk. Trust is performed and is "dependent on context, continually negotiated and re-negotiated according to the specific context and circumstances" (ibid., 88), enabling people to share their lived experiences of discrimination. We use many experiential activities involving themes of exclusion and inclusion and link them, through debriefing, to life in school. Our goal is that all participants (including adults) become familiar with the language of discrimination and racism, to enable trust to be developed and for stories to begin to emerge that help both facilitators and participants understand the racialized reality of students.

Experiential Activities and Theatre Games

Experiential activities include warm-up games and trust exercises that inform different levels of the creative process, provide experiences of issues of power (i.e., exercises embodying leaders and followers), and enable a safe space to emerge. We begin with "Who Is Here?"—an exercise that introduces concepts of multiple identity and group membership. "Responding to Difference" explores how difference is constructed and dealt with both individually and societally. We engage in activities and debriefing on important aspects of racism. One game, "Discriminadot" (Selby 1988), introduces the notion of exclusion through the random placement of dots on participants' foreheads and asking participants to group themselves. "Sticky Labels" explores how we are "labeled" by others in terms of negative and positive qualities that affect social interaction and status. "Power Flower" (Arnold et al. 1991) looks at identity and which forms of identity have power in society.

The theatre games used contribute to a sense of community through Boal's "Knowing the Body" (1992), as we work in small groups developing our sensory consciousness of the world and share the storied lives of the participants. The games, small group work, and theatre activities build trusting relationships among participants that allow a deep level of sharing. A powerful sense of community is developed that extends beyond the retreat setting.

Storytelling

Renk writes, "Drama teachers have inadvertently found a method of communicating that is much better adapted to the human process of understanding and orientating than the abstract and denotative teaching prevalent in schools" (1993, 198). Wright (2000) asserts that drama has two interrelated aspects: embodied experience and reflective explanation of experience. In this process, drama becomes an alternative space where potential becomes possibility.

Students begin to represent their world by nonverbally sharing stories through Image. Stories are central to the learning process, as they mediate between self and others. As students recall an incident or experience, they create a body shape or image to represent that experience. As students develop different sets of images, they develop the capacity to give expression to experience. Imaging enables the participant to fill the body shapes with feelings and thoughts that come from the interplay between the physical shape and experience. Thoughts and words initially emerge from the individual's awareness of the static body in the Image and the world around the Image. Images can be activated into further motion, movements that arise out of the interplaying of the physical shapes of bodies and their interpretation in words and action.

Image as narrative is introduced through "Complete the Image" (Boal 1992, 130), which is first done by two people shaking hands in a frozen image in front of the whole group. Anyone who has an idea can replace one of the pair in a new body shape in relation to the other, adding a new element, creating a different Image—a new story. After a few Image pairs, more characters are added to one of the Images until there are six or seven people making a story out of the original paired Image. We then decode the image by asking the group what they see as the story, emphasizing that one image can be interpreted in many ways, from many perspectives. When it seems the group has understood the method, we begin again. This time, we ask the group to think of a particular theme, like life or racism in school, while completing the Image. We ask the group to identify who has power in the Image story, who doesn't, and why.

Using Image to Analyze Racism

At the retreat, the students create Images that tell the story of their experiences of power, oppression, and racism in their lives. The Images they create most often deal with stories of oppression in their lives at school but sometimes include experiences in families, with peers, or in the community. As we examine each individual Image to identify commonalties and differences, students recognize they are not alone in their experiences of exclusion and powerlessness. Termed "analogical induction" by Boal (1995, 45), this recognition of self in the experience of others illustrates the commonalties shared by students, forging bonds among them. While thinking about their own stories, they explore the interconnectedness of stories and alternatives to the actions. Building on this, a composite image is then created that incorporates the most powerful aspects of each of the individual images. We call this the Image of Oppression (IO). Students reflect on the IO to identify the characters and their role in the Image. We discuss with the participants who has power over, who is under power, and where the central conflict is in the Image. This exploration helps students deconstruct the power relationships inherent in racism and oppression, leading to an examination of how that power is developed and maintained.

The IO is followed by an adaptation of "Your Wildest Dream," an exercise developed by David Diamond (1991) as an extension of Boal's *Image of transition* (1992, 173–74). "Your Wildest Dream" takes the IO and asks the participants to make an Image that is not a reaction to the IO but one that takes us into our imaginations to explore what our dreams might be for an ideal that would represent, for example, "a world without racism." Images are then made to represent the intermediary steps that could transform the IO (which is of a concrete situation) into the Image of the "Your Wildest Dream," which is much more imaginative and abstract. As students develop the intermediary steps between the Images, they discuss the possibilities for change and examine the consequences of the attempts to change. We begin to see the little, albeit necessary, changes. Who is able to change first? How might other characters respond? What changes does this cause? Students start to see where hope lies and the significant moments of change, creating an "as-if" world or, more accurately, a "what-if" world that is about "what if we could change things" or "what if we acted to change things."

Doing so gives student voice so their issues lead the program within the structure set by the adult leaders. Sharing helps students overcome isolation, breaking the silence of oppression. Discrimination starts to be denormalized. On numerous occasions we have heard students comment that they thought bullying and discrimination were just the way things were, but hearing others' stories enabled them to understand these acts were wrong and they could do something about it. In the representation of a common incident of oppression, they discover the features of domination and how it is enacted. Students come to understand how power is achieved through numerical strength, different forms of power, and coercion and fear. They see how power is exercised in speech and in their body. In working through the stages from the incident of oppression to the wildest dream, students identify who the players are and the roles they play and gain some insight into the possibilities for change, for personal or societal intervention.

Forum Theatre: Exploring Possibilities for Action

In demystifying the theatrical process, Boal points toward the astonishing ability of non-actors, when given a decent workshop process and capable facilitation, to grasp this work with the whole body and come up with pieces of theatre that put in front of us an important problem. We find the TO approach is suited to the discussion of racism as it is interactive, it names and deals with power, and it integrates well with a pedagogy that involves political action. Creel et al. point out that "Theatre of the Oppressed must be responsive and reflexive; it must be situated in the moment. Even to bring TO into the classroom is to distort it, to bend it to a purpose and a set of power relations for which it was not initially constructed" (2000, 150). Therefore, because the program must respond to the particular context of schools and the issues of racism (and other "isms" interconnected with questions of identity) students are facing, we have made adaptations to the approach.

For example, Boal (1992) explores the interplay between the oppressor (those who have and exercise power over others) and the oppressed (those who are subjected to power). These roles correspond to Adams et al.'s idea of agents (members of dominant groups who unknowingly or knowingly exploit unfair advantage over members of target groups) and targets (members of social identity groups that are victimized in many ways).

Green sees TO theory and techniques moving away from "the dynamic of one oppressor and one oppressed" (2001, 53) to exploring a plurality of contexts, perspectives, and forces where oppressive conditions are being addressed through transformative practice. In developing *Power Plays,* David Diamond (1991) added a third important role in the development and interactive performance of plays: the "powerless observer," a bystander who does not intervene in the situation, either by confronting the oppressor or assisting the oppressed to take action, but has the potential to become an ally[2] to the target. (Through their stories, many of the students identify themselves as often being bystanders.) For example, we could have a bystander who, for any number of reasons, such as peer pressure and fear of being a target themselves, does not attempt to assist the person being oppressed, although they know the situation is unjust. We have found in our workshops that including the powerless observers' experiences has enabled an exposure of oppression in an often silenced atmosphere where no one wants to name the homophobia or racism that is occurring because that would make people uncomfortable. We "open up" this question of how a bystander might become an ally (Linds 1998), "a member of the agent social group who takes a stand against social injustice directed at target groups" (Adams, Bell, and Griffin 1997, 108). Ironically, though the term used is "powerless" observer, through Forum we discovered that often this is where "power" to change lies.

These characters have the possibility to become more than mere witnesses: they have the potential to take action in the moment, to explore and disrupt the simplicity of good and bad, powerful and powerless. This opens up the process to more complexity and uncertainty as we explore the obstacles to becoming an ally and examine various actions used to address them.

In the program retreat, we have a student leadership team, composed of more senior students and past participants of the program, who have experience in representing their reality through theatre. We work with this team[3] to develop a Forum play that incorporates their common experiences of exclusion, discrimination, prejudice, and racism. Each play includes the various characters of oppressors, victims, and bystanders, or potential allies of the antagonist and protagonist. The first time we perform the play for the participants in the retreat setting, we use it for discussion of the issues faced by the characters. The students in the audience ascertain the character with whom they most identify. After the play, we ask the audience to help us create a Status Lineup, so we can physically place the characters in the play according to the power they have in the scene. This leads to discussions about who can potentially use their power, who will refuse, who will never have power, and what the potential for certain characters is to take action.

Later in the retreat we perform the play again in front of the retreat participants. After the play reaches its problematic climax the play is repeated several times with students invited to become spect-actors. Students can and do intervene on behalf of a character they identify with, whom they see having a struggle to overcome power. We encourage students to try out their ideas for action, that they can learn from each intervention, not just those that produce a more "satisfactory" result in the play. "The keener the desire to take action, the more the spect-actors hurry on to the stage. They enact thoughts, rather than just speaking them" (Dwyer 2004, 199). We find that as students see their peers go on the stage, everyone is likely to be more engaged and critically conscious. "There is a kind of knowledge—or perhaps, better a will to knowledge and power—which is apprehended in similar circumstances and which is qualitatively different from knowledge sitting in your seat as silent witness" (Dwyer 2004, 200).

We debrief each intervention by asking both the actors as characters and the spect-actors who intervened what has happened and how the intervention affected their character. We also explore the barriers to action, because usually, each new action carries with it some kind of risk. Students identify the need for courage to act in order to challenge oppressive situations.

Following the retreat, students return to school to join with their teachers and other students to form the antiracism group at their school. A few of the groups go on to create and perform Forum plays about racism and discrimination for their school or other student groups including elementary schools (who, themselves, develop antiracism teams). Other school groups do activities such as assemblies, multicultural events, or antiracism days to raise awareness regarding the issues. Some invite guest speakers, create bulletin boards, or organize interactive activities such as poster contests or antiracism art projects.

Exploring the Efficacy of the Program

In the spring and summer of 2006, the sponsoring school board asked us to document the impact of the program and make recommendations for possible changes. We used focus groups, student interviews, teacher interviews, and a drama workshop (where Image exercises explored the reactions of the student leadership team) to ask students and teachers to reflect on the program's impact, both at the retreat and back in their schools. From this data, we identified the effect of the program on the students, the teachers, and the schools.

Impact of the Program

The findings revealed the program had a profound impact on students. Most students talked about going through a personal transformation as a result of their involvement in the program. The retreat was reported to be a powerful experience that created an awareness of racism and empowered students to take action. The students were enthusiastic about the use of theatre for learning about racism as it engaged them and was useful as an analytical tool. Students gained empathy through the use of theatre and got useful ideas for educating others about racism and how they could change their actions when confronted by situations of racism and discrimination. Where school teams were active, the program impacted the group, the students in the school, and the school environment and educated others beyond the school including families, younger students, and community groups.

The teachers interviewed were strong believers in the program and the potential it could achieve with more support. They agreed the program developed students' understanding about racism and discrimination. They believed students gained awareness and insights and saw them develop leadership skills through the different program components. One teacher, who was part of the program before Forum Theatre was incorporated, saw the use of theatre as one of the more effective methods for addressing the issues. Other teachers agreed on the effectiveness of theatre at the retreat; however, most were not comfortable using theatre in the in-school component of the program and wanted a wider variety of methods used.

Forum Theatre Opens Space for Emotion and Bonding

[The retreat was] intense. Absolutely intense. When we did the candlelight ceremony, that was the craziest thing. My friend had told me, "I guarantee you're going to cry." I knew it was going to be sad, and yeah, everyone within five minutes was balling. That's probably something that I would never remove from the retreat—because it's so deep.

—Student, focus group

Through the trust-building exercises and the sharing of personal stories, students formed emotionally close relationships. They were not afraid to share their fears, frustrations, disappointments, and negative emotions. Many students appreciated what they felt was a safe environment, feeling they could open up and be themselves—some for the first time in their lives. Possibilities for action emerged as students exposed their thoughts, feelings, and fears. Students thought this happened when they saw others "step out of the box," "then more people are brave" (Student, drama workshop) and people start shedding their facades. As one student leader put it, "We did not have to be somebody we were not. We did not have to keep up a facade" (Student, drama workshop) or continue to keep their guard up as they did in school. "When we realized that people did not care who we were on the outside, we opened up" (Student, focus group). The experience of being able to show who they truly were was an emotional experience for the students. "I was crying after the retreat, cause you feel so secure about your feelings—that no one would judge you" (Student, focus group). The bonds of friendship developed at the retreat built an important support system for many students. They developed personal strength in making connections with others who shared the same values of social justice: "[The retreat] strengthened me—to see others that have the same values because I don't see many people who have my ideals. People tend to discriminate, thinking others are inferior and they're better. I don't have that. I hadn't seen people who didn't have that attitude. But when I came to the [antiracism program], I actually found people who can relate to me" (Student, interview). Many teachers often see their role as imparting knowledge and content, so they are not prepared to respond to the expression of strong emotion in their classroom. This view was illustrated at a meeting of high school teachers where, at the coffee break, one teacher was sharing with others how distraught she was when the topic of discussion caused one of her students to cry when describing her escape from a repressive regime in coming to Canada. The concerned teacher was seeking advice from others about how to prevent such a thing as a student crying from happening in the future. On the other hand, students in the program valued the norm of emotional expression that accompanies personal stories of oppression and discrimination.

Developing Consciousness and Facilitation of Internalized Learning

I do notice [racism] more. I didn't really know what it was. People used to pick on me. I didn't really know how to deal with it. Now I know how. I can deal with some of it

—Student, focus group

The program lays the foundation for an analysis of the pervasive nature of racism. Forum theatre supported the analysis of the different aspects of racism in situations of discrimination in the student's life. It provides students with the freedom of self-expression. Student's stories of their own experiences give the description of racism and discrimination an authentic voice that reflects the truth as experienced by students in school. Problem-posing education (Freire 1970) is an inactive and cognitive praxis that continuously inquires into the oppressed relationships with the world. Rather than learning specific responses or techniques to deal with a problem, images and forum plays promote generative learning, and therefore encourage the actor to explore different behaviors within particular circumstances and context.

As students reflect on their own and others' experiences, commonalties become evident. They begin to analyze the structures and processes and see the interconnected social relationships in instances of oppression that allows them to reflect upon their role and involvement in discrimination. When the analysis comes from the student, they make sense of their experiences using their words and their ways of interpretation. Because they are using their own cognitive frame of interpretation, authentic meaning is brought to bear on their experiences: This is clear from student comments, such as the following: "[The antiracism program] changed my perspective of people and how I treat them. I treat them better than I used to. I'm not as mean to them, just because of their color or race or something. I've learned to respect other cultures more and not make fun of people because they look different. If I see other people making fun of somebody because they're different, I'll tell them to stop" (Student, focus group).

Boal has written that TO is a form of maieutics: "the Socratic process of assisting a person to bring out into clear consciousness conceptions previously latent in his mind" (2001, 354), enabling "the student to discover what he [*sic*] already knows, without knowing he [*sic*] knows it, by means of questions which provoke reflection, thus opening up the path to discovery" (Freire 1998, 147). One way this is done is to explore our senses through warm-up exercises. Boal calls this seeing what we look at, feeling what we touch, and listening to what we hear. We feel this also extends to the mind as a sense—becoming mindfully aware of all that is happening around us. Within the safety of the aesthetic space, the group is able to ask themselves the following: What feelings are emerging? What are the issues that concern me? What do I see as potentially threatening to my physical or emotional well-being? Does anyone else here share my fears and concerns? This exploration helps students connect the social and the personal. As expressed by one student,

> I've been a victim of racism for a long time. I'm African Canadian. Even back in kindergarten other students would ask me why my skin was dirty, why I didn't bathe. Even back then it hurt. As I go older, stuff like that kept happening . . . [The antiracism program] changed a lot of the way I look at things. It has changed my perspective on the world, on different people. It gave me a place to come and be myself and not have to put on any type of a front. Everybody is themselves . . . [The program] changed me a lot. It helped me get over a time in my life when, honestly, I wanted to end everything. (Student, interview)

Students become aware of the racism in their lives. They can name situations where they experience or witness acts of racism. They have ideas of how they can respond to situations differently. At the same time, they begin to develop an awareness of how widespread the problem of racism is: "At the end of the retreat, you're there, and it hits you—like everything you've talked about—like it just gives you like a total bigger picture of it all. I'm more conscious of our society, people within it, [and] about the issues in our society. I became more aware of how common [racism and discrimination] is. It made me want to teach people that everyone is equal" (Students, focus group).

Effectiveness of Forum Theatre in the Antiracism Program

> [Forum theatre] is effective in antiracism education because it actually shows you what happens in some situations. You can see how people, like, react to it. The plays can be harsh, and the students know that's real, and then when they know that something isn't right or something is wrong. They know what it is when they see it [happening in their school]. I think there should be more theatre.
>
> Yeah, because, it [theatre] gets to most people because it actually shows you what happens in situations like that.
>
> —Students, focus group

Students and teachers both believed in the power of Forum Theatre in antiracism education. The students embraced theatre as a way to explore the issues and their role in acts of discrimination. Forum Theatre gave them the insight and confidence to challenge, often in new ways, the discrimination they encountered in their schools.

We remember one intervention from a few years ago. A student came up to the stage and, rather than continuing to confront the student with power, turned to the person he was helping and said, "Let's go. There's no need to keep talking to her." In this Forum performance, all the interventions had been direct confrontation through arguments, insults, or threats. The spect-actor in this case had shown another alternative, one that transformed the relationships between the characters in the play and robbed the person with power of their influence. This action illustrates a change from acceptance of oppression accompanied by anger as the only solution. Rather, the interven-tion the student suggested indicated a move toward solidarity as a viable response: One student described that movement this way: "[Forum theatre] is really effective [in antiracism] because [students] get to see it in life, and you know that kind of thing is going to happen. You think, what if I was in this situation? You see life changing situations. It gives [the students] the power to change it" (Student, interview).

Student Leadership in the Antiracism Program

No one lives democracy fully, nor do they help it to grow, if, first of all, they are interrupted in their right to speak, to have a voice, to say their critical discourse, or, second, if they are not engaged, in one form or another, in the fight to defend this right, which, after all, is also the right to act.

—Paulo Freire, *Teachers as Cultural Workers*

Youth as leaders repositions youth from passive subjects of inquiry to deci-sion makers about what topics or questions are to be studied and what is to be done with the knowledge that emerges. Meaningful youth participa-tion in leadership seeks to generate knowledge that is useful for their own well-being.

Youth simultaneously exercise and develop their leadership capacities in the program. There is a process of youth leadership development through the theatre work, and there is a production of material through the theatre. Both elements are integrated in a healthy way. As London points out, "These elements exist in a state of dynamism, sometimes supportive and comple-mentary, sometimes contradictory and divisive, always seeking balance, but always shifting" (2002, 4).

We have focused on how the Forum Theatre process helps us achieve the goals articulated for a social justice and antiracism program. This has required us to look at the key elements of the program (i.e., antiracism edu-cation and action, youth leadership development) and the use of theatre in these processes of transformation. Such a program provides opportuni-ties for interaction with caring adults, peer group support, and meaningful engagement in community and civic life, developing the capacity of youth to become engaged citizens. Youth leadership can "strengthen a community's capacity to respond to its problems and build its future" (Innovation Center for Community and Youth Development 2001). Young people's energy and ideas can contribute meaningfully as they participate in community building and address social problems, work toward social change, and apply leadership skills while gaining access to supports that facilitate their own development: "[The program] has developed leadership skills. These students have no fear of public speaking now, doing presentations, organizing events, fundraising. They're developing skills for adulthood, a lot of real life stuff" (Teacher, interview).

The use of theatre in the program develops student voice, confidence in action, and skills in dialogical learning while keeping the focus on the issues that have brought us together—racism and discrimination. Theatre enables students to become connected to the issue and, through shared leadership with adults, come to recognize the use of theatre to represent reality and not just be seen as "play." As one student stated, "The antiracism program made me aware of the problems, but it also instilled a sense of self-capacity, a sort of pride in participating in something that's helping. Like not just looking past differences, but being able to celebrate the difference in events like Multicultural Day and Aboriginal Day, which we organized. So I really feel a sense of being able to do something instead of just being aware of it—more than that, doing something about it" (Student, focus group).

Potential for Transformation

As facilitators who helped design the program, we wonder about the effectiveness of theatre to transform students and schools. It has been difficult to measure this, but there are examples.

A Site of Transformation: The School Dance

For most young people, adolescence is a time of conditional citizenship, with rights and responsibilities tightly administered by teachers, parents or guardians, and the police and other figures of authority. As young people struggle to learn the rules of the game, they jockey for position with one another and new oppressions are born (Pye 2002, 3).

The retreat was a place to explore, through experience, the "what-if" world and any contradictions we notice between theories and implementation of antiracism work. One of the areas investigated was around an important event in school life—the school dance.

In the program, we strive to have the student leaders lead by example. At our early retreats, we had a dance where students could release some tension, express themselves as youth, and get to know one another in an informal setting. However, we noticed the dance operated in a traditional manner, with the older student leaders being the "in group" who made no effort to involve students who were uncomfortable at the dances. We confronted the student leaders with our observations in our debriefing. They were somewhat resistant to our message, saying, "That is how dances are." Dances at further retreats were changed and eventually eliminated, as they seemed to create an atmosphere of popularity, stratification, and exclusion, with participants separated into different subcultural groups.

Following one retreat, one of the elementary schools combined the student council of the school with the student antiracism team and called it the Student Leadership Team. These students decided their first project would be to address the issue of students not feeling welcome at school dances, so they began by trying to make dances more inclusive.

Another example was provided in a recent retreat. Several students returned to their school for a dance that took place during the retreat. At the school dance, their learning from the retreat gave them a new awareness of the exclusion of certain students and groups happening there. When they expressed their insights to friends at the dance, their friends rationalized what was happening and told the students they were being brainwashed at the program's retreat. Back at the retreat the next day, these students expressed dismay at their friends' responses, noting that they themselves had not noticed these friends being so insensitive before.

As these examples show, the theatre work in the program helps students make connections between their learning about racism and their life at school. To Dei, the purpose of antiracism education is to forge a connection between "the mind, body, and soul" (1996, 31) that brings about an understanding of the self, situated in relation to others. The program develops student responsibility and student voice that engenders self-knowledge forged in connection with others. Students develop the confidence and strength of spirit to face the challenges of discrimination in their schools and in their lives.

Beyond the Individual: Broader Program Impact

Just as there was variation in the antiracism school teams, there was variation in how students saw the impact of their activities on racism in the wider student body in their schools. Some felt they were successful in raising awareness of the issues, while others believed they had impact on the school climate. They saw the changes in how students treated each other in their school: "The play we did was a real positive [one]. It raised awareness as to the issue of the inclusion of special needs student at [our school]. Before that, special needs students were not considered for welcome-week activities or clubs, committees, teams, nothing, and since then [these groups] have opened up to them—they're more integrated" (Student focus group).

Students responded positively to theatre as part of the antiracism program. Students felt empowered when they created and performed Forum Theatre. At the same time, they recognized its limitations with all students: "Some students think that all we do is drama. I don't think they like the idea of [the program] being drama . . . All they see is that you'll be acting and a lot of students aren't comfortable with that" (Student, interview).

Challenges for the Future: The Transition from Retreat to School

Many students experience profound personal transformation that impacts how they see and interpret their world. Students are prepared to act differently. But when they go back into the school, others around them may not share their views or know how to respond to the student's new perspective. This is illustrated by a story told by one of the student leaders: "During the weekend following the retreat, students were calling me, telling me how they felt in their schools after the program. Suddenly, they kept seeing instances of exclusion and were having trouble coping with their new consciousness. It was as if they started seeing their school communities and the interactions within it with new eyes, that they were "becoming conscious" and found it overwhelming and hard to deal with. And they were asking me what they could do with these new feelings and thoughts" (Student leader).

One of the critiques we have is that we haven't yet found a way to prepare students for such awareness that emerges when students return to their schools from the training program. The safe space and the "as-if" world created at the retreat do not necessarily transfer to the school group, which, more often than not, includes many students who were not present at this particular retreat. This is illustrated by a comment of one of the teachers: "When they get back from the retreat, the big thing students hit is they get back to the real world, which is not as supportive and not as open and caring. They're back in high school and it's not necessarily a real friendly place, particularly if you're trying to get out a message of tolerance" (Teacher, interview).

Students (and, to a lesser extent, their accompanying teachers) are thus living in the space of *metaxis* ("belonging to two worlds at the same time" [Boal 1992, 201]), in the borderlands between the retreat and school, between what they were before the retreat and what they are afterward. It is hard to deal with this beforehand, because this space is one in which "the hidden power assumptions about the kinds of selves" (Turnbull 2000, 228), relationships, and contradictions are allowed to become visible.

Forum Theatre and the Enactment of Shared Leadership in Schools

> To engage in dialogue and joint decision making means to be willing to change the adult ways and experiment with new solutions . . . Youth participation is not a technique; it is a way of conceptualizing youth development, a willingness to engage in an intergenerational dialogue.
>
> —G. G. Noam, "The Meaning of Youth Participation"

In Forum Theatre, dialogue replaces the monologue. The space for student expression also develops shared leadership. In schools, when the teacher voice is dominant in the analysis of experience, learning is imposed externally. Deciding and defining what terms are important to the discussion of racism externalizes learning in the abstract so it is no longer situated in the lives of students. If a teacher imposes their interpretation of students' experiences, students don't have the opportunity both to make sense of and learn to describe their own lives. When students are given the freedom to analyze their own experiences with the guidance of a democratic leader, the process is situated within the student and not externalized. Students develop the confidence to recognize and interpret the oppression in their own lives, building leadership capacity to solve their own problems, to address issues in their schools, and the power to make changes. Collective empowerment occurs when people are able to take up their roles in relation to each other, fully with a sense of purpose, confidence, and authority. This happens best when there is mutual respect and recognition of the validity of all their roles, however large or small (Kirk and Shutte 2004, 247). In some school teams, where the teachers have embraced Forum Theatre, we see the enactment of shared leadership where teachers follow the lead of the students and act as facilitators in bringing students ideas for action into being: "[Our high school students] organized [an event for elementary schools] that included their Forum Theatre play. The students planned it. They ran it. I was in the background, to provide support. I helped facilitate some of the activities to deal with some of the Forum Theatre situations, but other than that, my students ran the whole thing" (Teacher, interview).

A difficulty with this approach is that the transformation of teacher into facilitator challenges the traditional educational system for both teachers and students. In schools, teachers often exercise authority in a way that does not develop the autonomy of the learners. Likewise, students emerging from this system are conditioned to learn in ways that do not develop their autonomy or democratic practice. "In a special sense they need leading into freedom and integration, when they enter another more liberated educational culture where these values are affirmed" (Heron 1999, 24).

Forum Theatre in Schools

Since Forum Theatre arose from a theatre base, often the emphasis is on the production of a Forum play, joking the play, and facilitating the interventions, which does require knowledge and skills. At the same time, the emphasis at the retreat is not on the product of Forum Theatre but on the process and the participants. Time is devoted to theatre games, creating and sharing stories, and analysis work through images. We have found Image work to be an especially powerful tool to use with students. Often, when students are unable to clearly articulate difficult experiences or concepts, they can represent and then clarify experiences in Image to communicate meaning.

Teachers believed in the effectiveness of theatre in the retreat setting, but many didn't feel prepared to use it with their school groups. These teachers felt they lacked the necessary training and skills to use Forum Theatre on their own: "The theatre part of it is powerful. I saw it with the kids, with the student leaders. It is. It's very good. The truth of the matter is, though, [that] I'm not equipped to do that. I'm not saying the school couldn't do it, but with me, that's just beyond something that I would be able to do" (Teacher, interview).

Teachers in our program who are interested and who avail themselves of training have become skilled as Forum Theatre directors and Jokers. They work with their student groups to create Forum Theatre plays. They have become part of the leadership team and facilitate at the program's retreat and other program events. But these teachers are few in numbers.

Although the teachers see the impact of theatre on the students and the power of theatre at the retreat, many teachers remain reluctant to use Forum Theatre in antiracism work. Forum Theatre is not scripted, and its process involves a pedagogy of exploration, of uncertainty. "A pedagogy will be that much more critical and radical the more investigative and less certain of 'certainties' it is. The more 'unquiet' a pedagogy, the more critical it will become. A pedagogy preoccupied with the uncertainties rooted in the issues . . . is . . . a pedagogy that requires investigation. This pedagogy is much more a pedagogy of question than a pedagogy of answers" (Freire and Macedo 1987, 54). In Forum Theatre, many teachers find the space for student expression too uncontrolled, especially the open-ended nature of student-initiated interventions.

I think it would be helpful if [the retreat] was more directed towards something the kids could come back and do here in the school . . . They do the drama, which is great. It's really liberating for them. But they really can't make the transfer back into the school . . . There isn't support by the student body for [antiracism and Forum Theatre]. You'd have kids saying really stupid things and doing crazy interventions . . . Like I don't know if you could weed out the kids who are going to cause grief . . . I think [drama] is useful at the retreat. It helps students assume the other—a role they normally wouldn't, so they understand it from different angles, the whole idea of difference and being other, so it's good for that, but as a tool for the wider school audience, I'm not sure that it would work. (Teacher, interview)

With another teacher, it appears the reluctance to use Forum Theatre was influenced by the representation of the reality of discrimination and racism in the students' lives in the Forum plays:

You're dealing with pretty intense issues. I wouldn't want to get up and deal with those intense issues; those are dangerous topics at times. If you're going to be touching those topics, you'd better know what you're doing. That hits home and that's what they hear in the hall, but you're using some pretty intense language, and some pretty intense emotions and feelings. There's a lot going on there. I think if I was going to facilitate that, I would need to feel 100 percent comfortable and know what I'm supposed to be doing, and what the objectives are, and what's safe and what's not safe . . . I can see it getting out of hand fast and causing problems, if you didn't know what you were doing. I'm not a drama teacher . . . There are other ways to explore issues besides drama. We have been successful in a lot of multicultural issues, like when we did diversity day. (Teacher, interview)

This teacher is supportive of the program but reticent to have the reality of the destructive nature of racism and discrimination explored as part of a school program. When students reflect on the power of Forum Theatre, they appreciate the representation of the reality of their lives. They appreciate the space to discuss issues that profoundly affect their lives in school. This teacher appears reluctant to take the risks that are inherent in Forum Theatre, to move beyond the bounds of the safety of knowing the outcomes and being able to control them. In this way, our use of TO around an emotional and political issue brings to the fore and challenges what Giroux calls the "hidden curriculum" of schooling: "those unstated norms, values and beliefs embedded in and transmitted to students through the underlying rules that structure the routines and social relationships in school and classroom life" (1984, 47).

Conclusion

Anti-oppressive education works against commonsense views of what it means to teach. Teachers must move beyond their preconceived notions of what it means to teach, and students must move beyond their current conceptions of what it means to learn . . . [It] involves constantly re-examining and troubling the forms of repetition that play out in one's practices and that hinder attempts to challenge oppressions, desiring and working through crisis rather than avoiding and masking it . . . [and] imagining new possibilities for who we are and can be.

—K. Kumashiro, "Toward a Theory of Anti-Oppressive Education"

Ginwright and James have proposed Principles, practices, and outcomes of social justice youth development to examine "how urban youth contest, challenge, respond to, and negotiate the use and misuse of power in their lives" (2002, 35). They propose that youth and adult allies work together toward a common vision of social justice, which means adults should also be engaged as part of a community committed to working against racism and oppression. This means capacity building should not only focus on youths but also the capacity to develop collaborative relationships between adults and youth. This is not a simple matter. The participants we are working with are also teachers and students who are embedded in a hierarchical educational system where leadership is often vested in the authority of one individual. Consequently, adult and youth leadership is often envisioned as an individual action or quality. Leadership in confronting oppression and racism requires the development of notions of collaborative leadership because systemic change most often requires the development of collective action. We can begin by having adult leaders and teachers enact leadership that recognizes the students as knowers, modeling the practice of shared and collaborative leadership.

In any system designed by some to control others, there almost always will be a space for resistance, a fissure in which to forge at least a little freedom. Such spaces are not best seen as openings into which drama can be inserted. Rather, we should see them as crucially constituting the dramaturgies of freedom because they present an absence that creativity seeks to grasp, like the word or action. These spaces, these absences, are inherently dramatic, because they can not be perceived without the oppressive systems that seek always to eliminate them. Creative work is a challenge to authority, an unpredictable disruption of norms, a kind of playing with fire (Kershaw 1998, 68).

Forum Theatre disrupts the "normality" of racism and oppression that students experience on a daily basis in schools. It is because of its creative and disruptive nature that we believe the students, and we as facilitators, embrace it. There are powerful truths represented in the students' creative theatre work.

Freire writes, "It is truly difficult to make a democracy . . . It is not what I say that says I am a democrat, that I am not racist or machista, but what I do" (1998, 67). To Freire, it is in the contradiction between saying and doing that we learn that we are in a challenging and ambiguous state that asks us to find a way out. Becoming consistent between saying and doing is a challenge that we feel theatre helps us to overcome as it identifies contradictions and, at the same time, enables us to address them. It is this challenge that continues to inform our work in theatre, youth leadership, and antiracism education.

Epilogue

Following the submission of the report of our research to the school board in the summer of 2006, changes were made to the program based on the recommendations that were made. School teams and high school teachers are now given more support in the use of Forum Theatre with their students. High school students are taking leadership in putting on workshops for elementary students in antiracism education. The program continues to grow and flourish. The importance of continuing to insert Forum Theatre as a mechanism for the development of student leadership in social justice is illustrated by a story shared by one of the students in the program: "[The antiracism program] basically changed my life, in the way I view things, the way I do things . . . in the direction that I'm going with my life now . . . I want to do something with human and social justice . . . with community development. I think [the program] was a start to help me [get] into the direction that I want to go" (Student, focus group).

Notes

1. In an e-mail debate around the terms *applied theatre* and *applied drama*, Helen Nicholson states that making a distinction between theatre and drama isn't always useful: "A small number of practitioners make a distinction between applied drama and applied theatre—applied theatre as having an element of theatrical product, and applied drama as entirely participatory. Most radical practitioners, however, recognise that there is a more fluid and productive consonance between performance and participation in many practices and interpret performance more flexibly than the work of professional actors" (2002, 91). While the literature often separates drama from theatre, we, too, find the distinction problematic, and so we use either term, *drama* or *theatre*, where appropriate to the context. The work within the program involves transformational aesthetics through both interpreting participants' stories through Image, for example, and the development and

presentation of Forum Theatre. Often, Image work involves performance, and the development of Forum theatre plays includes a participatory process. We recognize that Boal's work is *Theatre* of the Oppressed and not *Drama* of the Oppressed, and this links the approach to a history of theatre. Still, short of a new term, both drama and theatre are the best way to describe our work.

2. "A member of an oppressor group who works to end a form of oppression which gives him or her privilege" (Bishop 1994, 126). In our Forum theatre plays, this is not always the case. Sometimes the ally is someone from the oppressed group or a member of a group oppressed for other reasons (e.g., homophobia or sexism) who was a bystander and afraid to intervene.

3. We conducted a separate theatre workshop to evaluate the impact of the role in the program of student leaders who were also Forum actors. Our analysis of the interviews of, and the image work involving, these leaders leads us to concur with Peter Duffy that Forum Theatre is an "attitude-altering tool for the actors in the student troupe presenting the work" (2006, 5). More research is needed on this aspect of TO.

References

Adams, M., L. A. Bell, and P. Griffin, eds. 1997. *Teaching for diversity and social justice: A sourcebook*. New York: Routledge.

Arnold, R., B. Burke, C. James, D. Martin, and B. Thomas. 1991. *Educating for a change*. Toronto: Between the Lines.

Bishop, A. 1994. *Becoming an ally: Breaking the cycle of oppression*. Halifax: Fernwood.

Boal, A. 1992. *Games for actors and non-actors*. Trans. Adrian Jackson. New York: Routledge.

———. 1995. *The Rainbow of Desire: The Boal method of theatre and therapy*. Trans. Adrian Jackson. New York: Routledge.

———. 2001. *Hamlet and the baker's son: My life in theatre and politics*. Trans. Adrian Jackson. New York: Routledge.

Creel, G., M. Kuhne, and M. Riggle. 2000. See the Boal, be the Boal: Theatre of the Oppressed and composition courses. *Teaching English in the Two Year College* 28 (2): 141–56.

Dei, G. S. 1996. *Anti-racism education: Theory and practice*. Halifax, Nova Scotia: Fernwood.

Donoho. B. H. 2005. Scrap mettle SOUL: Learning to create social change at the intersection of differences through community performance theater. *New Directions for Adult and Continuing Education* 107 (Fall): 65–73.

Duffy, P. 2006. I didn't know I had anything to say about racism. *Stage of the Art* 17(3): 5–6.

Dwyer, P. 2004. Making bodies talk in Forum Theatre. *Research in Drama Education* 9(2): 199–210.

Freire, P. 1970. *Pedagogy of the oppressed*. Trans. Maria Ramos. New York: Seabury.

———. 1998. *Teachers as cultural workers: Letters to those who dare teach*. Trans. Donaldo Macedo, D. Koike, and A. Olivira. Boulder, CO: Westview.

Freire, P., and D. Macedo. 1987. *Literacy: Reading the word and the world.* South Hadley: Bergin.

Ginwright, S., and T. James. 2002. Assets to agents of change: Social justice, organizing, and youth development. *New Directions for Youth Development* 2002 (96): 27–46.

Giroux, H. 1984. *Theory and resistance in education: A pedagogy for the opposition.* New York: Bergin.

Green, S. 2001. Boal and beyond: Strategies for creating community dialogue. *Theater—New Haven* 31(3): 46–61.

Henry, F., and C. Tator. 2005. *The colour of democracy: Racism in Canadian society.* 3rd ed. Toronto: Thomson Nelson.

Heron, J. 1999. *The complete facilitator's handbook.* London: Kogan Page.

Huff, D. J. 1997. *To live historically: Institutional racism and American Indian education.* New York: SUNY Press.

Innovation Center for Community and Youth Development. 2001. *Broadening the bounds of youth development: Youth as engaged citizens.* Takoma Park, MD: Innovation Center for Community and Youth Development.

IPSOS-Reid and the Dominion Institute. 2005. March 21st International Day for the Elimination of Racial Discrimination—survey highlights. http://www.dominion.ca/Downloads/IRracismSurvey.pdf (accessed May 13, 2008).

Jackson, T., ed. 1993. *Learning through theatre: New perspectives on theatre and education.* London: Routledge.

Kershaw, B. 1998. Pathologies of hope in drama and theatre. *Research in Drama Education* 3(1): 67–83.

Kirk, P., and A. Schutte. 2004. Community leadership development. *Community Development Journal* 39(3): 234–51.

Kumashiro, K. 2000. Toward a theory of antioppressive education. *Review of Educational Research* 70(1): 25–53.

———. 2001. "Posts" perspectives on anti-oppressive education in social studies, English, mathematics, and science classrooms. *Educational Researcher* 30 (3): 3–12.

Linds, W. 1998. Theatre of the Oppressed: Developing a pedagogy of solidarity? *Theatre Research in Canada* 19 (2): 177–92.

London, J. 2002. Youth involvement in community research and evaluation: Mapping the field. http://www.youthinfocus.net/pdf/London_YouthResEval.pdf (accessed June 1, 2007).

Ng, R. 1995. Teaching against the grain: Contradictions and possibilities. In *Critical Studies in Education and Culture Series: Anti-Racism, Feminism, and Approaches to Education,* ed. H. A. Giroux and P. Friere (series editors) and R. Ng, P. Staton, and J. Scane (volume editors), 129–68. Westport: Bergin and Garvey.

Nicholson, H. 2002. The politics of trust: Drama education and the ethic of care. *Research in Drama Education* 7(1): 81–91.

Noam, G. G. 2002. The meaning of youth participation. *New Directions in Youth Development* 96 (Winter): 1–3.

Pye, C. 2002. *Community theatre, cultural expression. Using Forum Theatre to name and change our world.* Unpublished manuscript.

Renk, H. E. 1993. The art form of drama and the new paradigm of constructivism. In *Arts Education; Beliefs, Practices and Possibilities*, ed. E. Errington and Ed. Geelong, 193–200. Geelong, Australia: Deakin University Press.

St. Denis V. 2002. Exploring the socio-cultural production of aboriginal identities: Implications for education. PhD diss., University of Saskatchewan.

Sanders, M. 2004. Urban odyssey: Theatre of the oppressed and talented minority youth. *Journal for the Education of the Gifted* 28(2): 218–41.

Sheared, V. 1999. Giving voice: Inclusion of African American students' polyrhythmic realities in adult basic education. In *Providing culturally relevant adult education: A challenge for the twenty-first century: New directions for adult and continuing education*, ed. T. C. Guy. Vol. 82, 33–48. San Francisco: Jossey-Bass.

Schissel, B., and T. Wotherspoon. 2003. *The legacy of school for aboriginal people: Education, oppression, and emancipation*. Toronto: Oxford University Press.

Schutzman, M. 2006. The Joker runs wild. In *A Boal companion: Dialogues in theatre and cultural politics*, ed. M. Schutzman and J. Cohen-Cruz, 133–45. London: Routledge.

Seebaran, R. B., and S. P. Johnston. 1998. *Anti-racism theatre projects for youth*. Victoria: Community Liaison Division, Ministry Responsible for Multiculturalism and Immigrant, Government of British Columbia.

Selby, D., with G. Pike. 1988. *Human rights: An activity file*. London: Stanley Thornes.

Silver, J., and K. Mallett, with J. Greene and S. Freeman. 2002. *Aboriginal education in Winnipeg inner city high schools*. Winnipeg: Winnipeg Inner-City Research Alliance, Canadian Centre for Policy Alternatives–Manitoba.

Turnbull, D. 2000. *Masons, tricksters and cartographers: Comparative studies in the sociology of scientific and indigenous knowledge*. Amsterdam: Harwood Academic.

Wilson, P. 1991. Trauma of Sioux Indian high school students. *Anthropology and Education Quarterly* 22(3): 267–383.

Wright, D. 2000. Drama education: A self-organising system in pursuit of learning. *Research in Drama Education* 5(1): 23–31.

Part III

Theatre of the Oppressed Practice with Youth

9

Staying Alert

A Conversation with Chris Vine

Peter Duffy

The following conversation was conducted between Peter Duffy and Chris Vine.

Chris Vine is the Artistic and Education Director for the Creative Arts Team (CAT), one of America's premiere theatre-in-education (TIE) organizations, housed at the City University of New York (CUNY). He is also a Distinguished Lecturer and the Academic Program Director of the MA in Applied Theatre at the CUNY School of Professional Studies.

Peter: You have had the opportunity to conduct Theatre of the Oppressed (TO workshops with youth all around the world. Are there things that you've learned about TO or any moments of clarity that you've had about the practice of TO because of the work that you've done with youth?

Chris: What I've learned is that you need to start by being very clear about your goals and objectives, being more focused and specific than the phrase "breaking the oppression" suggests. TO can be used to do a range of different things. But it can't do everything we want. Terms need to be defined very clearly. So we have to be very clear about what is the project in hand and what are the objectives. What are the strategies, techniques, and methods that can be applied to try to address those objectives and reach those goals?

Oftentimes, for me, TO is not the first thing to spring to mind. I've often talked to people who have said, "Oh, I've got to do such-and-such, and I think I'll use TO. But how should I do that? How would *you* do that?" My response is frequently, "I wouldn't use TO methodology. Have you thought about *other* drama methods to do what you say you want to do?" I think there is a danger that because TO has become so popular and prominent in our sphere of work, and that more and more people know *something* about Boal's methods, that they don't really think about or take the time to explore a range of other related interactive drama and theatre approaches from other sources that are also at our disposal.

Peter: When do you think about using TO instead of something else? There are lots of TIE models. When do you think TO is most appropriate?

Chris: If you are looking at situations in which individuals are in some way being manipulated and/or silenced, that their voice is being taken away or they are being made to do things that they don't want to do, and in which there is a clear power dynamic at play between those with power and those who apparently have little or none, then those are obviously appropriate situations to explore using TO. And situations in which you can use adaptations of TO would, by extension, include those where negotiations are necessary, negotiations that will often involve . . . will *always* involve . . . a power dynamic of some sort. I'm thinking, for example, of young people interacting with adults who are not necessarily oppressors in the sense that they are seeking some obvious social or economic gain by exploiting the other person, but nonetheless are using their adult status to get their way. These include social situations in which the biggest problem may be a lack of communication and mutual understanding (e.g., between parent and child or teacher and student). So we are not necessarily always examining polarized situations between oppressor and oppressed. Oftentimes, in such situations, the larger oppression may be in the background. The parents may have a lot of things going on in their lives. They may be the subjects of all kinds of oppressions in their world, trying to manage alone or to handle difficult adult relationships or to make ends meet in the face of economic and social inequalities. So, for understandable reasons, they are not able to negotiate conflicting needs, and they are not listening to the child, who therefore *experiences* oppression, although it might not be intended or recognized as such. Neither party is communicating. They are not listening to each other. They've lost the sense of how to connect with each other. These are "good" situations in which to use TO strategies, even though you might now be somewhat changing the original oppositional oppressor-oppressed dynamic of the work, as Augusto Boal originally conceived it.

In response to your original question about having moments of clarity with respect to how young people respond, I am not sure that those responses are necessarily so different from the responses of adults. Of course it's difficult to generalize because all groups are different. Even if you're talking solely about work with adults, responses will still vary from group to group, according to the kind of group you're working with and the kind of situation or context in which you are working.

Peter: This is very true. It could be said that a Forum Theatre piece needs a protagonist, antagonist, and context. The oppression that unifies a group plays a significant role in how the TO experience will play out, and therefore what strategies you employ with that group. When I was working with a group of parents on issues surrounding family dynamics, the parents were all too willing to show how their children could be oppressive forces in their lives. They were absorbed in our work together that evening. They laughed, played the games enthusiastically, jumped into the Image and Forum work; the atmosphere was fun and full of the relief that comes with collectively naming the challenges in our lives.

As soon as the work took a turn toward the parents' shared culpability in the relationship they had with their children, the mood shifted and members of the group were not willing to participate and explore the very same activities they were enjoying ten minutes earlier.

The same is true in working in schools. If we were to produce an anti-model of a teacher oppressing a student, it is very likely that the level of participation among the students would be very high. However, one of the things that I am constantly struck by in my work in schools is how oppressions are stratified. Rarely is there one clear antagonist. Some adults in the building can obviously be an oppressive force. The institution itself can be oppressive, and in response to this and other factors, peers can become oppressors of their peers. Working in a school is not working with a homogeneous group of people who share the same oppression like factory employees or prisoners. It is much more nuanced and reflective of the general population.

I think that has very much to do with the young people's hunger and a thirst not just for knowledge but also for a means by which to reflect on and alter their own situation, driven by a need to change those immediate things they don't like, that are rooted in their everyday existence. In other words, young spect-actors are not distanced from their needs by other social barriers that you sometimes find among adults. But again, I say it depends on the groupings—the groups of people and the context in which you are working. Often in our society people are constrained and hesitant because of cultural mores, because of a fear of looking foolish, a fear of being "wrong." Because of fear.

It takes a long time to work through these feelings and fears with a group, doesn't it? You really have to work together for some time before you can plumb the group's experiences for the core of their shared oppressions.

Chris: And this is why time is important. If you're going to build Forum with young people, I don't think you do it in one session. I don't think that's responsible. I know this from working with youth theatre groups in other contexts—nothing to do with TO, per se. The first things they give you are what's at the top of their head, top of their brain at that moment. When you've got a little bit of time to explore these ideas, you suddenly find that actually they represent the tip of the iceberg of their concerns and that there are other things that they're much, much more interested in. So when you have the freedom to let them use early sessions to work out the obvious sex and violence scenarios, they often, very quickly, translate those into something else that is of a much deeper—or more specific—concern to them. It is not that they are *not* concerned with those earlier issues, but rather that, given time, they are able to take them somewhere else and look at them differently, often from surprising perspectives.

And of course there is then the question of our own agendas [as facilitators and adults]. Where do they come into relationship with the group's agenda? You have to ensure that you're using strategies that will open up a lot of possibilities before you narrow back down and select—and we have to select together if we're genuinely honoring the co-intentional process. But it's important to explore the potential richness of the suggestions before you make that final choice. If you go too quickly to the final choice, you might find it's not as rich, not as resonant as you first thought, and then in a week or two's time, everyone's very bored with it and the young people want to change again. But now you've got less time to do so.

Peter: There is so much to consider when setting out to do this work. What are some of the considerations you wrestle with when working with a new group of students?

Chris: Let me talk first about the actors—the professional actors who are to present and facilitate the work *for* the students. (I am not here talking about a process where you create the Forum with the students—that is a luxury few TIE/educational theatre groups enjoy.) First of all, you have to consider the artistic demands on the actors, how to play the scenes, the clarity of motivation, and the pursuit of the theatrical and dramatic objectives, which need to be particularly sharp and well focused. That would be true anyway: if we want good theatre then those things are always important. What are the objectives being played? What is the status of the characters? In TO, the status relationships are particularly important in respect of the power that each and every character has and how and why they use it. But then as you're rehearsing the playing of the scenes, of course, you also need to be thinking ahead—particularly as you start moving toward the stage where the spect-actor interventions begin—about how you *reveal to the audience* those character motivations and objectives.

In Forum Theatre, you are going to be asking the spect-actors to analyze, unpack, and work with or against what the characters are trying to do and how they're trying to manipulate each other. Indeed, you ask them to come onstage and jump into role to change those manipulations, to oppose them. To attempt, in their own ways, different, counter-forms of manipulation, working against the *oppressor* characters. So, in preparation with the actors, you need to help them clarify, in the playing, what is *really* going on. This, of course, includes subtext, but it also includes the momentary transitions, the tactics and strategies that people use with each other in the communication, imposition, and reinforcement of status in relationships. The subtle revelation of objectives, plus the power that the characters hold—and the means of exercising that power as social beings—are all part of what you must help the actors to find concrete ways to bring out through their performances.

There are different ways in which power is both made manifest in individual behavior and supported by the social structures—which, in turn, may be more or less oppressive to certain individuals and groups. A Forum actor must try to make the audience aware of this somehow, without the Forum model becoming a threadbare, didactic piece of theatre that is entirely word driven by "talking heads." So we have to think about the presentation of the characters as social beings revealing the power they hold and the social means they have of exercising that power. For example, these might include the ways in which the law will support an employer against employees wanting to take strike action or the way that minors are restricted in what they can do in face of the demands of adults seeking to control their lives. Or perhaps the Forum is more about the ways in which we are constrained by social mores and cultural expectations. In this case, these should be exposed to scrutiny, made available for analysis *in action*.

But we haven't finished with the poor actor yet. Beyond all this you must also develop and build into your model strategies to support your spect-actors, to encourage them to find their voice, and to give them opportunities and time to develop their arguments and actions. By the way, I'm distinguishing this from the *pedagogical* processes of challenging and problematizing; I'm talking about preparing the actor for *performance*, in terms of how you modulate and modify your characterization, particularly as the oppressor, in order to give the spect-actors the time, space, confidence, and motivation to express themselves. This will support the pedagogical objectives, blend with them, but is not identical to them.

As you get more adept at this process, you think about it in the early preparation of the Forum at the point when you begin selecting or "shaping" your characters. You learn to make choices for the scenario that will support you to do this better. And then you extend it to the character development with the actors. It is important, both dramatically and pedagogically, for example, to find the sympathetic and supportive tendencies within the oppressor's character, however obnoxious his or her objectives may be, and not just to portray those characteristics that demonize the oppressor as a one-dimensional, mean, aggressive person. I don't think this makes an interesting or effective Forum piece in any case—or interesting theatre of any kind. The same principle is true for the characters that inhabit the penumbra between the possibilities of acting as allies or reinforcing the oppression: they should not be selfless good Samaritans or fair-weather friends. They should have their own contradictions, strengths, weaknesses, and vested interests. In other words, they should be human but always, *functionally*, for the Forum, approachable and accessible to the spect-actors. This does not mean that interventions need be made easy, but they should not be impossibly intimidating.

I believe this more holistic view of the function of the actor in the Forum process helps us to find *theatrically* richer and more multidimensional interpretations of the characters *and* suggests ways in which we can theatricalize the whole *event*, using space, voice, body, movement—all of the actor's tools—both when presenting the antimodel and then translating that into the encounters with the spect-actors, theatricalizing those encounters *as they happen*. We have to remember that we have the tools of the theatre at our disposal. By utilizing them, we can enrich the audience's experience. Often times in a Forum, spect-actors will make a suggestion but will be turned upstage or will speak so quietly that they cannot be heard. We can manipulate where the spect-actor stands on stage in order to help the spect-actor be more clearly seen and heard by the audience. As an actor, if you move yourself downstage so the spect-actor has to turn to face you and the audience, you are helping the idea be heard by the entire group. If she faces upstage, she turns her back on the audience, and no one will hear her suggestion. An actor can aid in making status more visually explicit by using the space and levels—standing, sitting, advancing, retreating—to adjust physical relationships. Doing all this as you pursue your pedagogical goals is indeed *part of* pursuing a clearer and more theatricalized Forum.

Peter: I worked with a TO troupe of high school students in Maine for about six years as a public school teacher. One of the ideas we were experimenting with was how do you introduce some kind of pretheatrical performance before the Forum to inform or expand the themes of the scene. So, for example, when we were doing a Forum with middle school students exploring how insults fester and really take a toll on a person, we employed a simple pre-Forum performance. We played a song that was popular at the time that dealt with a kid being bullied, and the actors ran out into the audience and had quick altercations with each other. Every time one actor insulted another, a balloon would pop. The highly stylized pre-Forum piece lasted about twenty seconds, and it was just long enough to jar the audience into thinking abstractly and to prepare them for the form of Forum Theatre.

I think finding those ways in so that the spect-actors have an immediate connection with the material to get them thinking about the general theme before the Forum begins helps a great deal—especially if you're dealing with more concrete thinkers.

Chris: And by doing those things, by using a more physical form of theatre, by using dance, for example, you are implanting physical images within the work, be it in the antimodel or in some kind of prework. Oftentimes, this moves us away from realism but actually helps us meet the challenge of revealing the character relationships, the power relations, more clearly in their fundamental state. You can show the power structures very clearly through images, through movement patterns and spatial relationships that don't rely on words. On the one hand, you abstract them, and, on the other, you look much more concretely at their essence.

I think this is particularly useful today given the way young people read images—which is certainly much faster than I do. I'm not of that generation, you know—not of the computer age! I didn't grow up with computer games and wall-to-wall music videos: things that move so fast and change so frequently. Young people can register these images, but they seldom think about their meanings. It doesn't occur to them to deconstruct them until you ask them to do so. Then you find, and they find, that they have quite an extraordinary vocabulary for doing so. If you have the opportunity to do some sort of theatrical prework as you're suggesting, before you begin working with the model itself, it helps to acclimatize them, loosen them up. It can be lots of fun, but it also introduces them to the language of theatre—which *we* know is different than TV and the movies—and ultimately it supports the serious work of the Forum Theatre.

One of the things over the years I've had the fortune to experiment with is form. In the early days, this was certainly aided by working long term with more permanent ensembles, having the chance to develop skills and approaches with actors over a period of time as they became more confident and adept in the Forum process. For example, I've created dance-based Forum—working with choreographers—where the whole dynamic of oppression is revealed without any words at all. Of course, when moving into the spect-actor intervention phase with young people, we did not expect them to dance, but if they had been reading the imagery and symbols provided by the form, it was easy to change the rules and say, "OK, you've seen what is happening to these people. If you don't like it, you can now step into it and disrupt it; stop what is happening! You can use words if you want." Looked at in one way, there is something restrictive about the patterns and rhythms of dance—useful for reinforcing a Forum model—that it becomes quite liberating to break apart. Drawing on other forms in this way has helped to enrich the vocabulary of Forum and open it up in a way that makes it more accessible and fun for young audiences.

Peter: I want to know your thoughts on the role of the Joker. He or she is so much more than a facilitator or conductor of experiences. I am particularly interested in how you have developed the Joker role when engaging spect-actors from an audience of young people?

Chris: There's a range of challenges when you have to bring the artistic and the pedagogical functions together and essentially distort the reality you are presenting in order to reveal its features more truthfully. You have to find ways of building hypotheses when you're talking to a young spect-actor. For example, as the Forum actor playing the overbearing parent, you might challenge the spect-actor, in role as the daughter: "So, if you were in my position, what would you say if *your* daughter came to you and said she wanted to go here and stay out this late and be with this boy? What would be some of the thoughts that would start going through your head? What might happen? What would you worry about? What's your responsibility?"

You look for dialogical and dramatic ways of saying, pedagogically, that you, the spect-actor, need to be thinking from the other person's point of view in order to be able to counter it with your own arguments. Another example from oppressor boss to oppressed employee might run as follows: "If you were running this business, what, as the boss, would be your main aim? Why are you in business? What is it you want to do?" You start by posing these questions to the spect-actor, to try to get them to think beyond "character," to develop hypotheses about power and vested interest, to help them see that actually this situation is not being driven by the fact that this is an unpleasant boss—he might be very personable—but that it's driven by the fact that he's in it for profit. He needs to make money. Seen in this light, you need to understand that in certain circumstances, you might be expendable. It's not personal! But of course your oppression is!

So all of this means you're asking your actors to understand and work as part of a dialectical process that is full of artistic and pedagogical contradictions. Some actors, encountering TO work for the first time, are soon arguing that their character wouldn't do that or say this: they cannot find the psychological truth. Such is the grip of Stanislavski and the vice of realism! As director, you have to find ways of asking what the actors understand by "dramatic truth." Is that the same as psychological truth? Is there an objective truth that transcends the personal? How far does the dramatic medium permit us—impel us—to distort our conception of reality in order to reveal it *more* truthfully? So we posit some more "What ifs?" and "Why nots?" and then find out how far we can extend these and translate these speculations into action, into being, into becoming, that does not trap us in the literal, everyday minutiae but enables us to uncover and understand universal tendencies, motions, and laws:

undergoing the process of "ascesis," or the interplay between tendencies and the laws that govern those tendencies, as Boal calls it.

I think this makes for a very rich kind of exploration, but it's also very testing because you are dealing with a very different kind of character interpretation and presentation and you haven't got a script to rely on. Meaning can emerge in many different ways, not just from the internal logic of the characters. There are all kinds of things to consider and to play with. How do you keep a scene alive? Can you make it more fluid? Can you make it less static? When do you choose to stand up? When do you sit down? How does that challenge the spect-actor? Can you ask a question and not make a statement? Can you *agree* with the spect-actor who is attacking you, accusing you, commenting, as it were, on your own character? "Yes, I agree I do that. Do you know why? I'm not asking if you like it. I'm asking if you understand it. Do you know what would make you do it too?"

All this is for the actor to absorb. But you asked me about the Joker. As Joker, I have to be constantly checking myself, asking, *Am I doing what I think I'm doing? Am I doing what I claim I'm doing?* But that's about ongoing reflection on your own practice. Before that, if I'm approaching a situation in which I'm going to use TO, I have to start before the actual event: *What kind of antimodel should I use?* Does the coming situation allow me to devise with the future spect-actors or must I research and prepare in advance? Working with young people in schools usually means the latter.

And then, *What are my goals and objectives?* I always like to translate these into something that I developed in my own TIE practice before I was ever working in TO: a framework provided by a *central question* or *central questions* that will guide me. I look for those questions that will help me be more specific in my goals, more specific than "we going to explore . . . such and such." What does that mean?

Another thing that is very important when doing TO with young people is trying to be very specific about the nature of the oppression you are working on. *What kind of oppression is it? Who has what kind of power? How do they use—or misuse—it? What power do the young people posses—individually, collectively, socially, legally—to oppose, address, and break that oppression?* It will not be a successful or useful Forum if the Joker is unclear either about the nature of the oppression or the potential weapons that people can bring to bear on it.

Peter: Can you think of any examples?

Chris: Take the question of young people and their relations with the police. If this comes up, as it frequently does, you have to think very carefully about what you're trying to open up for the young people. Many of the young people we work with see the police as oppressive, racist enemies. That is often borne out by their lived experiences. So, if we create Forum around that idea, what are we looking at? What can actually be done?

What TO tackles best are things that can actually be done, in the face of oppression, in the moment that the oppression is present, being enacted between individuals. But a young person, confronted by what he or she perceives as a racist cop—an enemy out to get them—has limited choices. If one finds oneself in conflict with the forces of law and order—whether it is me, you, or the young person on the street in the Bronx—"in the moment" is not necessarily a very auspicious occasion for confronting the problem. Yes, you need to do *something*, and Forum can still be helpful to explore that, but you have to be very careful, because the dice are heavily loaded against you. So it would be irresponsible to work with this scenario as if it were an open agenda.

This means—and I think in a way this should be true of all TO work, although it operates differently according to the kind and context of the oppression—that you have to be really clear about the kind of dialogue and the critical thinking that you want to engender. How do you, as the Joker, help to develop a deeper understanding about the power the people possess or don't possess? About when to use it or not to use it? About the rights you have? How to assert them, claim them, defend them? About the question of employing appropriate behavior at certain moments? About how to develop opposition and resistance without taking suicidal action with your eyes closed? Sometimes your focus might have to be on how to survive the oppression in the moment, working closer than you might wish to what Boal calls "the point of aggression." And how do you work in this zone without preaching, without issuing warnings and giving answers?

Don't get me wrong, I think it is important for the issues to be explored honestly, without the audience being censored or constrained to act in an approved manner. But there must be analysis: praxis, not just vocalism or activism, as Freire insists. We must help the audience to engage in a critical analysis of the actions that different spect-actors take under those circumstances—and of their possible consequences. And it is our responsibility to make sure that the model contains the opportunities for that critical examination to embrace the bigger picture—beyond the moment of conflict.

This brings me on to something else that I wrote about in the early days when I first encountered TO work and was importing it into my own TIE practice. I think in educational work, in work with all populations but particularly with young people, there is a need for more reflection and therefore discussion than Augusto, certainly in the early days, made room for. He wanted the focus to be on the action. And still today, if you see him work, he is often quick-fire, "OK, next, next, next," in terms of interventions. There is a lot to be said for that, in keeping the energy going, not letting the "debate in action" become bogged down and *obscured* by words. But I think it also has to be balanced out by critical reflection. I don't think it's sufficient to say, "Oh, well, a lot has been thrown up here and our audience will go away and think about it and they will come to the best conclusions for them." This isn't to say we know better than our audiences or our audiences aren't capable of thinking for themselves, but I do believe we have a responsibility to help them analyze their ideas and their moments of inspiration and courage.

This is where the Freirean underpinnings of the work are so important to me—we have a responsibility to problematize with a view to that *conscientization* that Freire talks about. We must provide opportunities for people to understand how the world works. We must help them see beyond and through the superficial appearances, to perceive the structures and the behaviors of people *as social beings*, in ways that will help them to make informed choices and to discover where to go and what to do more readily, more easily, than would necessarily occur to them if left alone to make sense, in isolation, of the interventions they have seen or practiced. I know from experience that young people usually go in one of two ways. Either they think they have totally failed, or they maintain that what they've done was totally successful and the only possible solution! They think it's best because it's theirs! Fair enough! And it's a delicate matter—with them and the audience—to unpick what they've done, reflect on it, project ahead and consider possible consequences, and yet at the same time validate the fact that they have put themselves on the line and are saying something new and brave for them, by getting up and trying out something in front of their peers. It is difficult to help them and everybody else understand that we are working together, that this isn't about "Peter got it wrong and Chris got it right." But nonetheless, if you do get up and do something, people can and will say, "Uh oh, that could lead to problems," and actually, as Joker, you have a responsibility to help the audience think about that. But it can be challenging to help the spect-actor understand that we are not criticizing *her or him* and that this is a collective enterprise, not a competition. This point of view is antithetical to the competitive nature of our education system and the culture of most schools. So it will likely be difficult for the spect-actor to accept that we are, in fact, honoring what she has done, because she has helped us to see something new. She has shown us something to explore and learn about so that the next person can build on that, using the best ideas but trying to avoid the pitfalls we have discovered.

There are no easy answers as to how you handle all this. I try very hard to make it clear that I am separating the deed from the doer, the thought from the thinker, but it is a fine distinction, and success is often a matter of nuance, sensitivity, humor, and the ability to establish rapport and to align yourself with the spect-actor; to simultaneously share the criticisms and highlight the achievements. I do come down very hard on unsupported value judgments and direct or inappropriate criticism of the individual, disallowing phrases such as "She got it wrong" or "That was stupid." I try to direct comments away from "What she or he should have done is . . ." back to "What I would do is . . ."—hopefully followed by a chance to enact the new, alternative action and link the development of the one to the other. But it can certainly be challenging.

Linked to all of this, pervading everything the Joker says, is the question of terminology. How are you going to explain things? What words are you going to use? Is a continual reference to oppression necessarily the most useful way of abstracting whatever the content is before us? I'm not saying we should avoid the phrase, but I think we need to think about the words we choose and the terminology we offer. I've seen people who, presumably having studied TO, know all this impressive sounding language and run around *dynamizing* this, *proposing* that, pointing out *metaxis* here, *breaking oppression* there, and so on, while the audience is becoming more and more bemused. The point is to make the process accessible. It isn't about watering it down. It's just about being in the moment and hearing and seeing what your audience hears and sees.

Also, you have to take your time. Time is very important. So often, when we are working with young people, we do not have time to do all the things that ideally we would like. Working in a community context, we might have two or three hours to play with our Forum, and we can do things that are just not possible in the forty-five-minute class session. So how many sessions have you got? How long are they? How do you structure them so that the passage of time does not dictate that you take the shortcuts that result in you giving the answers that you want to hear. That's frequently the reason that it happens. "Oh, we've got to get through this and we've got to get to our expected 'outcome' and we've only got forty-five minutes to do it." That's why, in our practice at the CAT, we still use techniques such as *simultaneous dramaturgy*, with the audience telling the actors what to do, mixing role-play conventions with Forum methodology. The actor, *staying in role as the character*, also frequently takes on elements of the Joker function, mixing it with that of the protagonist, arguing directly with the audience, eliciting and questioning its advice: "What should I do? Why would I do that? What's wrong with what I just did? What should I do now?" Or problematizing, "I would sound stupid if I said that!" and, "Won't people think I'm a wuss?" and so on. Sometimes these adaptations are necessary to deal with the constraints of time.

Another method we use, rather than the . . . classical antimodel of playing from A to Z and rewinding, is to cut to the chase by showing the moment of sharpest conflict or sharpest dilemma, finding the key moment of choice where the oppressed must respond in some way or another, and determining that he or she will sink farther into the mire or will begin to fight back. Sometimes we have to focus on that and just present that moment because we don't have time to do everything else. So there are questions that I ask myself a lot. What's up for grabs here? Why are we doing this? What do we need to achieve? What time do we have to achieve it in? How are we going to shape the model? What techniques or dramatic conventions are we going to use? Do they all have to come from Boal's arsenal, or can we find what we need elsewhere? And how can we make sure that the constraints (i.e., time, space, numbers, school expectations, etc.) do not derail us pedagogically? It is one thing to cut your methodological cloth to fit your circumstances. It is quite another to compromise your pedagogical process. There has to be a point at which artistic and educational integrity determines that it is not worth proceeding!

So these are the things that I try to think about as I approach TO work with any audience but particularly with young people.

Peter: Would you say something about your views on the nature of TO as an individualistic versus a communal activity?

Chris: One of the criticisms of TO over the years—from the very early days when I first started using it—is that it is so focused on the individual that it doesn't examine the larger picture, that it always pitches one individual oppressed against one individual or group of individualized oppressors, and that it decontextualizes the power structures in society as a whole. That criticism is tied into to a whole range of broader political debates that still surround the efficacy of TO. I don't agree with the general premise. I think you can build models within which there are avenues along which to address the larger social picture, even though drama is essentially about the interactions of individuals. If a group says, "We want to do a Forum about the environment," that's OK, but it has to be about the actions of people. What and where is the oppression? Where is the power? Who are the people who wield it, on behalf of whom and for what reason? Our analysis has to answer these questions in order to create a workable TO model. It has to show the tip of the iceberg, which are the power relationships between individuals, but it should also prompt us to look beneath the surface to examine the larger picture and to see what is at stake systemically.

If it is conceived responsibly, through a thorough analysis of the oppression we are seeking to combat, then I don't believe that TO need only invite individualistic actions or distort reality through a subjective lens. So, to recap, we need to be clear about our central questions; about the realities of the oppression we are fighting; about how power is accrued and the way it is used, individually and systemically, to oppress individuals and groups of people; and about the *real* possibilities for combating it in both the short and long term. None of this is to ignore the very simple and yet profound realization that taking, within the fiction of a Forum Theatre experience, the opportunity to stand up and say, "I object," is in itself extremely powerful. We should recognize that. Sometimes standing up to say, "Screw you," is a first step toward liberation. But, of course, if it is left there, if it is an end in itself, it becomes what Boal talks about *not* wanting his work to be: individual catharsis and a substitute for progressive action.

This work operates on many different levels, providing opportunities for people to find their voices, their passions, and the core of their resistance. But we have to work with that responsibly and analytically, not to tell people what to do, but to help them see what the options are and what the consequences might be. I think over the years, TO and Boal himself have moved toward what he talks about explicitly as a theatre of alternatives. I have no problem with that, but I think we also have a responsibility to find ways of engaging in critical analysis so we can look at the merits of the alternatives. It's all very well to say, "We're here to encourage people to make their own choices," but not all choices are equally effective. How do you make a choice? It should not be arbitrary. You need to have the tools to be able to make choices that will achieve the outcomes you are looking for. It's not for us to tell our audiences what these should be, but it is irresponsible if we don't try to create the conditions in which they can think deeply about their needs, actions, and possible consequences, in a way that helps them to understand that their choices are socially constructed and are not all equally viable or effective. We don't write an agenda saying this is the best choice and this is the worst, but we do need to try constantly to challenge the thinking of our audiences—our spect-actors—to "dynamize" them intellectually as well as physically and emotionally.

Peter: One of the impetuses for developing this text is to critique the range of work I see being carried out that does not adhere to the original pedagogical intentions of TO. As a teacher, I saw Forum strategies being used as a means to influence students into adopting a "party line." For example, I saw some work in which the Joker had many suggestions offered but kept on replaying the scenes, seeking still more offers, until one that was more amenable to the school came up. Then the Joker says, "Hey, that's a great suggestion. OK, we'll do that next time."

So TO can be misused and misrepresented as well. One of the goals of this book is to help people who haven't had the benefit of going to the conferences or working with Boal or other practitioners who are very solid in the work, to understand not only the benefits but also the limitations of the work. Can you comment on this?

Chris: Yes. Again, there's the question of appropriateness. Is TO a method appropriate to your goals? If you decide it is, there are further important questions to address. Because the work has been "popularized" and has become so "sexy," it has inevitably been watered down. It has been taught as a commodity, as a method to be consumed—another way of "doing drama," a set of practices—games exercises, conventions—to put in your "box of tricks," your drama toolkit. I am no purist, but this debases the work and can be dangerous.

One of the things that I do in my TO workshops and classes is to ask the participants why they are there and what they want. Someone will always reply, "Oh, I want some more ideas for my box of tricks." I understand that we're always looking for new approaches, new strategies that we can use, but the issue with TO is that it is more than just a series of games or exercises to be dipped into to enhance the weekly drama class. It is a whole system that is underpinned by a philosophy. Originally, of course, it emerged from an ideological framework infused with a pedagogy that, in turn, contains ideological and political assumptions and aspirations. If we read Freire, we discover his position in respect of what education should be for and how it should therefore be practiced. Boal, talks about the theatre as a weapon and the TO as being a "rehearsal for the revolution." Over the years, his rhetoric may have cooled and his practice changed with the times, becoming more accommodating of varied democratic perspectives, but there is no denying his ongoing commitment to the struggle for worldwide social justice and human rights. So there are a lot of questions begged if you say you want to practice TO. Unfortunately, I don't think that they are always addressed. Certainly, Freire is sadly neglected. Many people are taught TO strategies without the slightest understanding of his pedagogy and its influence on Boal. The same must also be said for the influence of Marxism on both Freire and Boal. It is a difficulty that many choose to ignore. So TO is frequently severed from its pedagogical and ideological roots. Not surprisingly, it is frequently practiced very badly, if not entirely bastardized, as you so rightly say.

Combating this is one of the struggles that we have and one of the reasons that I come back to the question of pedagogy, to asking practitioners to think about what are their goals and objectives and how, pedagogically, they are going to address them. What do you need to understand in order to be intellectually prepared to use TO and what does that mean, in action, in terms of the skills that you need to have and the way that you execute those skills? It's all too easy to hold an answer that you want your audience to arrive at and then to use these strategies and techniques, divorced from their original intention, to manipulate people to articulate the answers that you want to hear. That's bad TO, and it's bad education!

Another thing to reflect on that might seem obvious to us is that the circumstances in which you are doing the work will change it. It will be different according to whether you are working long term with a group that is being encouraged to create its own work or whether you are on a fly-in visit importing work—bringing ready-made work to whatever the group or community is. Those different stances, of course, raise different questions and challenges for the practitioner. How you enter a community and on what terms you enter that community are questions that must be thought about, and they call forth different responses in different circumstances, particularly with adult populations. Many practitioners realize this, whereas, most commonly, when we are working with young people, we are invited to do so by people other than the young persons themselves. If you're working in a school setting, it's self-evident that the invitation is not generated by the students! You are invited to be there, paid to be there, from other sources. And the students have to endure your presence. So can you still make your work student centered? Progressive?

Sometimes the question of what methodology you are going to use isn't the issue; it isn't on anyone's agenda. The adults don't need those details. They know you're going to do something educational using theatre techniques, and that's about as far as it goes. What is usually important to them is the content you are addressing: bullying, HIV/AIDS prevention, or whatever it may be. How you go about doing that isn't the concern of the people who brought you in. They are more likely concerned with out-comes. And there is the trap. Can we get the students to give the answers they and—by extension—we want to hear? Or can we work between the lines, creating the space for students to explore their concerns, inviting authentic responses?

If we are working in more informal settings, we have the opportu-nity of building deeper relationships with the young people enabling us to approach the work differently, much more on their terms, addressing their concerns directly from the outset. But no matter what the context, the pedagogical challenges remain the same. How do we develop authen-tic thinking and build critical consciousness?

Peter: When you're working in this situation—and I think this is a really interesting point—TO work is clearly dedicated to alleviating the oppres-sion of the group. So if you're hired by an outside person—principal, department chairperson, whoever (we're talking about the school context now)—how do you keep your eyes on the prize as far as the oppressions go? How do you remain an honest handmaiden to the process, thinking about the oppression, when you're brought in from the outside?

Chris: I think that returns us to the question of how far TO work, with its original intentions, has now been co-opted and subsumed under broader educational objectives within programs that have educational objectives and goals far removed from the fight against oppression! How far are artists actually using TO to address questions of oppression with young popula-tions? And how far are they using the techniques and strategies in other subtle—or maybe not so subtle ways—as a broader educational tool? Per-haps, if the pedagogy and politics are sound, this doesn't matter. In Freirean terms, good education will always engage with, and connect to, the struggle for liberation. But it is easy to be deceived. We should not presume to police others, but we can be our own watchdogs. We must stay alert.

10

From *I* to *We*

Analogical Induction and Theatre of the Oppressed with Youth

Peter Duffy

A school, like any institution, runs efficiently when all parties involved adhere strictly to its policies and institutional decorum. A school is a complex system of encouragement and detachment, freedom and containment, inspiration and grounding, and imagination and reality (or at least a version of it). These components do not exist in a binary; rather, they are in a relationship with each other and can exist simultaneously. By way of a small example, I witnessed an incident in one school where a girl was in tears as she headed down the hall to speak with a favorite guidance counselor. She was stopped by a teacher and ordered back to the classroom where she came from to get a pass to go to guidance. This one small moment shows the relationships of confusion and power that define schools—they are progressive enough to have places where young people in crisis can go, but they can make that journey a difficult one.

When examining this system of complex power relationships, you can quickly feel like you're in Oz. If teachers and students cast themselves in the roles of the Scarecrow, Lion, Tin Man, and Dorothy in schools, it becomes clear that what we are asking for is permission to use what we already have from a power that exists because we have endowed it so. The four Oz characters became a threat only after they joined forces. We have examples from the start of recorded history that the collective is the strongest force in resisting oppression. To take the metaphor even further, if the people in schools are the protagonists of Oz, then Theatre of the Oppressed (TO) techniques can be Dorothy's dog, Toto, while in the hall of the great wizard. And once the curtain is pulled back, it becomes hard to ignore the man behind it. This can be a difficult reality for both teachers and students to accept, but it's true.

When working with young people to name the powers and oppressions present in their lives, it can be tricky to remember that this is a slow process and can only be done one story at a time. Working as I have as a teaching artist doing long-term residencies in schools and as a high school teacher, naming these powers is a constant endeavor to draw back the curtain and expose what lives behind it.

Before becoming an assistant professor of theatre education at the University of South Carolina, I was the education director for the Irondale Ensemble Project, one of the longest continually running professional ensemble companies in the United States. In that capacity, I had the good fortune to collaborate with a high school English teacher and a dynamic group of young adults between the ages of sixteen and twenty at an alternative high school in the Bronx, New York. Their teacher, Justin (pseudonym), invited me there to use theatre as a means to personalize the curriculum and to encourage students' voices in the development and execution of their program of study. Justin's pedagogy was strongly influenced by Paulo Freire, bell hooks, and Peter McLaren, influences clearly demonstrable in his praxis. During the course of our semester-and-a-half collaboration, Justin and I hoped to co-create with the students a common vocabulary of learning that included intellectual, personal, imaginative, and kinesthetic experiences with the curriculum—a curriculum centered on Frierean principles. Our aim was to work with the students in order to learn and teach in a manner that inspired a *simultaneous consciousness* of world and word (Freire 1970, 62).

Creating the conditions for simultaneous consciousness was indeed a challenge. Naming the world and revealing the fabric of power, authority, and influence that shape our lives and thinking is a huge task that some would rather not engage in. They may feel that it is easier to survive within a system rather than endeavor to change it. Naming the world is a process of recognizing that we all contribute—to use Foucault's term—to a *technology of power*, and though we might not have the power to change it, we have the power to influence it. A student might not have the power to change a draconian detention policy, for example, but she could become more active in student government and discuss the policy with students, parents, teachers, and administrators.

Justin and I were committed to using TO techniques and Freirean principles within the school's curriculum to dissect issues of power and oppression that exist within that school's neighborhood in the Bronx. According to the most recent U.S. Census data available (2002), the neighborhood is well below the national average on many indicators of economic and community stability. The number of families living in poverty was almost 43 percent, where the national average is under 10 percent. The number of twenty-five-year-olds who hold a bachelor's degree is almost 7.5 percent, where the national average is almost 25 percent. The number of young adults sixteen years and older who are in the labor force is almost a full 20 percentage points below the national average of about 64 percent. It is realities like these that make the idea of naming power with young people daunting.

Ensemble Development

It is absolutely essential that the oppressed participate in the revolutionary process with an increasingly critical awareness of their role as Subjects of the transformation.

—Paulo Freire, *Pedagogy of the Oppressed*

The first few weeks of my Bronx residency were focused on developing an ensemble in the classroom. Before we started talking about concepts such as oppression, power, action, and solidarity, I focused on working with the students and the teacher in classroom to create an environment where we could laugh together, play theatre games, and problem solve the group challenges we undertook. This process of playing and laughing together is vital. Laughter and play demonstrate that we are becoming a collective and not merely a collection of individuals. Just because the students had the same English class in common did not mean that they felt like a homogeneous group sharing the same oppressions. I've worked in too many schools were the bullied sat next to the bullies in TO workshops, and because of that dynamic, there couldn't be any progress in dealing with other oppressions. Until that condition is addressed or reframed, the work of confronting institutional oppressions is stymied until the personal oppressions are named.

Sitting next to your oppressor makes the shift from passivity to action a difficult, and sometimes dangerous, one. Boal describes that movement this way: "In order to understand this *poetics of the oppressed* one must keep in mind its main objective: to change the people—"spectators," passive beings in the theatrical phenomenon—into subjects, into actors, transformers of the dramatic action" (Boal 1993, 122).

In his book *Theatre of the Oppressed*, Augusto Boal describes the four requisite stages for "transforming the spectator into actor": knowing the body, making the body expressive, theatre as language, and theatre as discourse (Boal 1993, 126). These stages of transformation are not only good to "warm-up" participants, but they also are essential to create ensemble in the group. Coming into a community like a classroom as a guest artist is an introduction of degrees. The community needs time to work with and assimilate a new member. Because students are polite, they will often be pleasant to guests. But to endeavor to unravel the knot of oppression with a group, more than a distant conviviality is required. Sure, Justin invited me into the classroom, but there is no intrinsic reason for the students to trust me or to want to work with me. It is not enough that I am eager to work with them on issues of oppression and liberation. Just because I have this willingness does not mean that I am the proper person to have in their classroom to do that work. I was brought in from the outside—and not invited by the students themselves. Why should they play along with some random guy who shows up once or twice a week? What reason do they have to put down their Sidekicks to play a theatre game? How will any of this help them?

This introduction of degree is the process that Freire reminds us of; it is a process of deciding whether I, as a facilitator, am looking to forge work *with* or *for* this group of students. Through the playing of games and exercises, this question slowly becomes answered as we forge a common praxis. "To achieve praxis in the educational sphere, practitioners of critical pedagogy must enable students to study and analyze the world and the word critically, and act on their own conclusions accordingly" (Mutnick 2006, 38). Students must have confidence in our ability as a group to act on our own conclusions. This is a difficult task to achieve, since many students only have had the opportunity to enact the school's party line and not to imagine their own. Maxine Greene takes this idea even further when she says, "Young people have not been helped to reflect critically on what dominates and often overwhelms. They have not been enabled to identify their shared concerns as human beings or to challenge, in the name of those concerns, what dehumanizes and compels" (1978, 113). In creating the conditions for this dialogue, it must be clear that all voices in the room will be respected and valued, that whatever comes out of the work will not be used against anyone, and that we are encouraged to all be vulnerable—facilitator and participant alike.

Toward that end, we spent our first eight sessions developing classroom ensemble through games and exercises. We used many games from Boal's *Games for Actors and Non-Actors* and Viola Spolin's *Improvisation for the Theater*. Students were becoming familiar with the language of the theatre and were working through Boal's four steps to transforming a spectator into an actor.

During the course of these sessions, the reluctance faded as we transformed from beginners at our ensemble activities to skilled practitioners. The conversation shifted from "Do we have to play that game?" to "Yo, man, that was sick! Did you see how good we did?" Students began to encourage even the most reluctant game players to join in. Though perhaps not the most appropriate way to encourage a peer, I knew we were on the right track when one student prodded a less enthusiastic player to "put some back into it!" We were still many "I's" playing the games, but it was clear that we had a chance to become a "We."

A week before our Thanksgiving break, Justin said he wanted to look at issues surrounding how we construct the idea of community. We decided to experiment with Image Theatre to see if we could create potent reflections of our understanding of the concept of community. I secretly became a little nervous that the images we would create together would be general and not matter much to the students. I didn't know if we were ready yet as a group to use theatre in ways beyond warm-up activities. I didn't know if we were at a point to use the language of theatre to express our feelings, fears, and aspirations. I feared that, at best, we would spend our ninety minutes together completing an assignment and not creating work.

In class that day, Justin and I explained what we were about to do and how we were going to do it. We had done some simple Image Theatre in class already, so they were fairly familiar with the concept. The students worked silently in groups of four or five and each took a turn constructing images of what community meant to them. Justin and I walked around the room and watched these small groups puzzle through their definition of community. One student asked me, "So, Mister, like what? Do you mean our block, our families, or what?" I replied honestly, "I don't know. That's what we're trying to figure out."

After about twenty minutes, each group settled on an image that worked for them. They showed their images to the class and the students took about a minute to walk around and study them. In a group normally characterized by boisterous humor, their serious demeanor and the solemnity in the room indicated to me that the students internalized their peer's reflections of community. These images were fraught with pain, isolation, and hope. After all the groups displayed their images, we voted on the one that we wanted to spend our time with that day. Boal employs a simple method of having the group raise their hands and vote on the image to which they feel most connected. I make a slight variation and have the students close and cover their eyes during the voting. This seems to remove peer pressure to vote on one image over another.

The students chose the image from Jasmine's (pseudonym) group. As the facilitator, that selection troubled me a bit. The small group she was working with adopted her image as their own to represent their idea of community without a single alteration to make the image more reflective of the group's idea of community. I knew Jasmine was going through a rough patch recently, and I wondered if that might make the image too singular to her situation and not fit in with the broader theme of community. In examining her image with her classmates, I recognized her story of dealing with a terminally ill mother and trying to manage work, school, and being largely responsible for raising her sister's two children. Jasmine was a very popular student at the school, and I suspected her group's image might have been selected because of this. Upon reflection, I can see now that I was more concerned about completing the assignment in that moment than I was in trusting the ensemble. But the students voted, and I, as the Joker, followed their wishes (though with some reservation) and we continued.

The image was an arrangement of four students: three girls and a boy. One student in the image knelt and turned her face away only to look at the protagonist through the slits between her fingers. One of her arms was turned behind her as if she were holding something back.

The protagonist stood inside the clutch of her peers who embodied the collision of her emotions and oppression. She stood, hands at her side, face relaxed, not so much at peace as she was exhausted. Her eyes bored through the two figures in front of her. To her right, a boy stooped over and grabbed the protagonist around her waist. His face, frozen in a pained contortion, looked as if he was screaming the oppression of all human kind. The fourth student stood in front of the protagonist holding a clipboard with a glower of administrative indifference.

We spent some time exploring the initial image. Did she feel as if it captured the sense that she wanted to portray? Was her abstraction meeting the reality of the image? I encouraged her to take herself out of the image for a few moments, to walk around it, to look at her three peers in the image and see if they were capturing the energy and urgency of it. She made a few minor changes here and there, and then Jasmine got to the girl with the clipboard. At first, the girl in the figure had an angry expression. Jasmine took a minute to look at what was not being communicated yet in the image.

Jasmine tried to demonstrate with her own face how the girl with the clipboard should look. She wasn't getting Jasmine's nuance, and finally she said, "Look like you don't care about us." The girl with the clipboard changed her frozen image to indicate she was rolling her eyes at them. Jasmine looked at this alteration.

"No, look like you don't see us and you're just filling out the paperwork." It was in this moment that my interior monologue of doubt in our process vanished. When the girl with the clipboard made the others in the image invisible to her and held her pen as if she were in mid-stroke, several students gasped. That was it. This tableau that I feared was too specific, too individual, too personal, had suddenly become their story of resisting *the man*. One student who recognized a piece of his story in the girl with the clipboard called out, "Oh my god, that's like the cop who stopped me when I was walking home at two in the morning." His friend talked over him, "No, no, no. That's like my Dad. He's there, but he don't see us."

When the image was exact, there was a palpable sense of enthusiasm for working on it. Jasmine's sense of invisibility and her community of school, work, and friends and her home life became a tale that all students found themselves in. Her cast of characters might be specific to her own situation, but the plot was universal.

Jasmine's peers who were not in the image got up from their desks when the image was complete and circled it in silence for several long moments. Once all the students had an opportunity to look at it thoroughly, I quietly asked them to give the image a title or caption. Words and phrases such as *isolation, pain, fear, my bad dreams, home, lost, dreams versus reality,* and *thoughts when I'm alone* came pouring out from the group. I remember feeling spellbound and struck by how long they continued to offer titles to the image. The moment erupted into a laugh when the boy in the image who was stooped over at the waist cried out, "Yo! Will you hurry up? My back is killing me!"

The cooperating classroom teacher wanted to know what the image meant. I took that opportunity to remind the group that precise meaning didn't much matter because we were working on how the image impacted us and what we projected onto it, not on one student's specific story. A young man took that as his cue to kid Justin and said, "For real, Justin, why does shit always got to mean something to you? Can't you just take it for what it is?" Justin laughed and said, "That's some real talk, my friend." The class laughed, and we were ready to move on.

For the next forty minutes, her classmates dynamized the image and created and recreated variations of Jasmine's tableau. They invented idealized images and images of healing. They tag teamed entering and exiting the aesthetic space forged among them and formed one image after the other. Through this participation, the class created a dialectic spoken in English, Spanish, and Image.

This process that was and wasn't language evolved into an action plan that encouraged the protagonist to confront her pressures and to take care of herself in the process. The students worked together to figure out who the girl's allies were and what steps she could take in order to extricate herself from her current situation.

If Jasmine got nothing else from class that day, it was clear that she had a community of peers who "had her back" and the insight that she wasn't solely responsible for everything in her family. In images, the protagonist was working through the feelings of being the only one who could take care of her ailing mother, earn money for the family, raise her sister's daughters, and to go to school. Through their Image work that day, her classmates demonstrated that she had a community of supporters and friends whom she could take the risk of relying on. But more than Jasmine's specific image, the class found a way of working through the constellation of pressures and demands placed on them as students, friends, siblings, sons and daughters, grandchildren, and boyfriends and girlfriends, while living in a community that sags under the weight of poverty and racism.

It was clear that the students were not focused on solving Jasmine's problems; they wanted to interrogate their own problems. Each student in that room felt as if they had a person with a clipboard checking up on them but who really didn't care about them. Several of the students recounted stories of parole officers—either theirs or people they knew—school administrators, social workers, or police. Each young person had a story about a figure who was responsible for paperwork but not to them. So even though some of the students could figure out what Jasmine's image *meant* because they knew her so well, it did not impede their own relationship to the work and projecting their own story onto the image.

Analogical Induction

If an individual's farewell image or scene prompts other analogous images or scenes from colleagues in the session, and if one builds a model detached from the particular circumstances of each individual case using these images, such a model will contain the general mechanisms through which oppression is produced

—Augusto Boal and Susana Epstein, "The Cop in the Head"

The Theatre of the Oppressed is the theatre of the first person plural. It is absolutely vital to begin with an individual account, but if it does not pluralize of its own accord we must go beyond it by means of analogical induction, so that it may be studied by all the participants.

—Augusto Boal, *The Rainbow of Desire*

In his book *Rainbow of Desire*, Augusto Boal suggests that whenever TO workshop participants are from the same group (school, factory, or community) and share the same oppression, the story of an individual's subjugation must transform into a specific example of a common oppression shared by the entire group (1995, 45). As Boal suggests, our work can't be the theatre of *one* oppressed, it has to be the Theatre of *the* Oppressed. It is not enough to hold solidarity through a sense of feeling sorry for the plight of another; we must analyze the offered story in order to find ourselves within it. What might resonate with us about a person's individual story might not be the thrust of that story. It might be a minor point, a subplot, or the experience of another character from the original story. "The function of analogical induction is to allow a distanced analysis, to offer several perspectives, to multiply the possible points of view from which one can consider each situation" (Boal 1995, 45). This process of generalizing from someone's specific story so much that all spect-actors find pieces of their own lives within it is what Boal calls analogical induction. Or, to put it another way, if analogical induction were a verb, its definition would be the process of transforming an *I* into a *We*.

While working with the group of young people in the Bronx, I became concerned that the image the class decided to work on (of the girl's concerns about her ailing mother) was going to become a personal therapy session for her with no relation to the group. But because we offered analogous images, dismantled her image to see what lived within it, Jasmine's singular story became a vessel for us to explore our own analogous oppressions. Her peers did more than help Jasmine out; they faced their own feelings of invisibility, powerlessness, responsibility, and duty.

Through engaging in this Image work with her peers, Jasmine seemed to remind herself that there were specific steps she could take on behalf of her tomorrow. She saw a sliver of hope for herself in an aspect of her life that she appeared to have given up on. What's more, the whole group was working through the image and were projecting their own meanings onto it; each member of the classroom community was able to see themselves in that image and to see their own version of what Jasmine saw—an action plan of hope.

An exciting by-product of our work that day was that my role as a facilitator became less and less important, and less and less helpful, as the session went on. The class saw value and found themselves in the activity, and the students became eager participants. After a while, they didn't need me to challenge their work or to push their thinking. They were doing that by themselves.

One student jumped in when he thought his classmates were moving too quickly through the image action plan and said, "No man, that's whack! You can't go from talking to your teacher to taking to the doctor. There's stuff in between. We ain't done yet!"

"For real, I don't know what to say to a doctor yet," Jasmine scolded, as if to remind everyone that she didn't want to miss a thing in her story—her action plan. The truth was that, by now, the plan belonged to everyone equally.

What became so clear to me that day was a lesson that has been slowly coming to me over the years. I've seen it in bits and pieces, but I think those students in the Bronx solidified its meaning for me. The truth is, in spite of my fifteen years of experience working with young people through theatre, I've been guilty of worrying at times about what young people can handle. I worry that some method we employ or topic we discuss might be too close to their emotional centers. Given the right conditions, young people are no less capable of diving into the complexities of TO forms and content than adults. If I had encouraged the students to work on a different scene that day, I strongly doubt that we would have gotten to the richness or complexity of the work we achieved. If my concerns about doing something that were directed at one student outweighed their interest in Jasmine's story, that would not only have been an oppressive act but one made out of fear. I feared that students would be bored if the image didn't apply to them. I feared the teacher would disapprove of the direction we were working in that day; I feared the material might somehow harm a young person. But that fear was mine. TO is a theatre of hope and trust and never fear.

To operate out of fear while jokering is to discount analogical induction and a person's capacity to handle challenging methods and material. That group of students and I worked together for weeks in the Bronx before we started creating images of oppressive forces in our neighborhoods together. When Jasmine created her image, it was offered after weeks of work and trust. Her image came out of collective risk and support. The group was ready. Looking back on it, I am not sure if I was.

After much training, mentoring, reading, and experience, I've been challenged to trust this work. Almost without exception, if something has gone haywire during my jokering, I don't have to look around for too long before I find the culprit! I must endure the moments of discomfort and fear that come from the little voices in my Joker's head that tell me to abandon an idea, skip a suggestion, and rush through this part of the process in order to tread on safer ground. But this sort of safety doesn't belong in the work. If everyone involved is prepared to participate, Jokers can trust the room's group mind and remember that the work takes care of itself.

The Power of the Image in an Aesthetic Space: Jasmine in Still Life

Though I employ the entire arsenal of TO techniques with young people (depending on the group, our purpose, and my experience with them), I spend the majority of my time exploring Image work with youth. In my experience of working with young people, Image Theatre tends to be the most efficient way into the communication of ideas, longings, fears, and oppressions. Because it isn't "acting," young people seem to be more comfortable getting up and working on an image when that same young person might not hop up to participate in a Forum workshop, for example. With time, patience, and practice, I have seen reticent students open up to even the most challenging TO techniques, and Image seems to be a safe point of departure into more challenging work.

Image theatre is not only a safe and comfortable foray into TO work, but it is also evocative. It allows the body to speak its truth without the mind getting in the way. There is no doubt that the students in the Bronx left our time together that day feeling like they accomplished something important. They spoke of it often throughout the rest of our time together, and many students noted it as their favorite day of the entire residency.

But what, exactly, makes the image work so strong? Why is it that sculpting your body to represent something can be such a powerful tool in the arsenal? I don't pretend to know exactly why, but I have several guesses.

Muriel Rukeyser once noted that the world is not made of atoms, but of stories. I believe this is true. Stories live in our bones and tissue. Our muscle memory is alive with experiences and tales from our pasts. Many people will recoil and grimace upon thinking of a food they dislike. Just imagining an encounter with a food one dislikes will call forth a physical manifestation of that memory in one's body. Our muscles, nerves, tissues, and sinews understand how we feel before we have language for our feelings. Our bodies internalize a "pre-thought known" at an amazing rate. Stories live in our bodies that we can't yet discuss, not due to an unwillingness, but because we don't have the words for the experience yet.

Image Theatre is a way to bypass the cognitive centers of our brain in order to release the stories that live within us through our bodies. Once we have language for an experience, it is concretized, fixed as language. When we use our bodies to talk, then we get the whole story, the known and the yet to be known, the discovered and the yet to be discovered. In his book *The Arts and the Creation of Mind*, Elliot Eisner writes, "Ideas and images are very difficult to hold onto unless they are inscribed in a material that gives them at least a kind of semi-permanence. The arts, as vehicles through which such inscriptions occur, enable us to inspect more carefully our own ideas . . . The works we create speak back to us, and we become in their presence a part of a conversation that enables us to see what we have said" (2002, 12). Though Eisner is speaking about the arts generally, his insight demonstrates the importance of incorporating bodywork into our body of work with young people. Jasmine had an opportunity to create a sort of semipermanence experience with disappointments and trials that she didn't yet have language for. It was her arresting image that allowed her peers to find pieces of themselves in it—even though it was an image etched from the oppressions of *her* life. The image spoke back to her and to the rest of the class, and an action plan was devised from it. Eisner further states, "To be able to create a form of experiences that can be regarded as aesthetic requires a mind that animates our imaginative capacities and that promotes our ability to undergo emotionally pervaded experience. Perception is, in the end, a cognitive event. What we see is not simply a function of what we take from the world, but what we make of it" (2002, xii). When we make possibilities for ourselves, then we are on to something! This act of making the private public holds a galvanizing impact on the entire group of young people participating in the class. The act of naming oppression in action, voice, and gesture creates a liminal space between individuals and community. Once this threshold is crossed, resistance is diminished because it is clear that the work is about the participants and their work for their own revolution.

The crossing of that threshold also transforms the classroom space into an aesthetic realm. As Boal says, "The aesthetic space is the creation of the audience: it requires nothing more than their attentive gaze in a single direction for this space to become 'aesthetic,' powerful, 'hot,' five-dimensional (three physical dimensions, plus the subjective dimensions of imagination and memory). In this space, all actions gain new properties . . . the actor in this space is dualised . . . the objects no longer carry only their usual daily signification, but become the stuff of memory and imagination; and every tiny gesture is magnified, and the distant becomes closer" (Boal 1998, 71–72). Without the creation of an aesthetic space, the students, in my experience, don't endow the exercise with meaning. Also, without utilizing their imaginative capacities, the work is flat—without their heart, passions, and struggles to rename their own world. The classroom transforms from the place where they sit and get schoolwork done into a laboratory of expression and community.

The power of the work created in that Bronx classroom came when the students, the classroom teacher, and I were all able to recognize that each of us has "internalized the image" of our oppressors (Freire 1970, 29). The profoundly humanizing realization that we are all burdened from within took weeks to uncover, and it united us in a way that allowed us to name our oppressions and to work through a few of them. The people in that classroom were united by similar oppressions, and the care and dedication required to name those oppressions were reflected in a comment that one of the young men in the image said while packing up after class: "We did good today. What are we doing next?" Phrases like that are proof of the movement from first-person singular to first-person plural, and confidence in their tomorrows shines through phrases like that.

Final Thoughts

Jasmine was not the only one taking a risk that day. This sort of work always carries risk. Participants risk revealing stories that are perhaps too personal to share in public settings. Facilitators risk dealing with issues that can re-wound participants despite our best intentions. Participants risk providing insights into the inner-workings of their lives that others in the group can use against them. We all risk looking foolish or out of control. TO work must always be done with training, knowledge, and care, because the risks are so great. However, if we don't provide participants—regardless of their age—honest, supportive, nurturing places for exploration of liberation, there are even greater risks: silence, acquiescence, and oppression.

Some might shy away from TO in fear that young people can't handle it. Skeptics might think that concepts such as oppression and liberation are too heady or too political for young people to negotiate. But as Boal and Freire remind us that if we contextualize words and worlds with young people—frame them in their experience—young people will be able to deconstruct concepts such as praxis, liberation, and oppression with the aplomb of an expert. It is an unfortunate reality that many young people are experts in the effects of oppression. So why shouldn't we trust them with a tool to expose it?

This work requires that we develop rapport with the group—the kind of rapport that accompanies truly knowing the names of the people in the room. Knowing names does not mean simply the first and second name signifiers that distinguish one particular person from another; it means knowing what lives within and beneath their names. What are the dreams that got them to the school that day? Who are the heroes in that person's life? What are some of the fears that keep them awake? What fills their time and their minds when they are not at school? These are the names we must know.

Along with learning names can come another essential ingredient to doing this work: trust. We must develop trust within the group—trust among the young people and the facilitator, trust in ourselves. The arsenal of TO techniques demonstrates how we can move beyond being passive receivers of the world to becoming active shapers of it. If we trust that we can shape our world, then that is the first step toward its transformation. In order to get there, we must ultimately trust ourselves, the participants, and the methodology, for it is these pieces all fitting together that brings us from I to We.

TO techniques might not always be the best model to use in every situation working with young people, but their theoretical underpinnings have so influenced my work with youth; in some form or another, it is always there. The work allows the students to create visions of their work and themselves that speak louder than any essay they could ever write. Like Toto, it exposes the man behind the curtain and gives us the opportunity to confront him, face to face, and to recognize that the only reason he is there to begin with is because we allow him to stay there. Like in Oz, TO work brings us the heart, courage, and smarts we seek to lead us home—to the knowing of what has been there all along—and create our own story.

References

Boal, Augusto. 1992. *Games for actors and non-actors*. London: Routledge.

———. 1993. *Theatre of the oppressed*. New York: Theatre Communications Group.

———. 1995. *The Rainbow of Desire: The Boal method of theatre and therapy*. Trans. Adrian Jackson. New York: Routledge.

———. 1998. *Legislative theatre: Using performance to make politics*. Trans. A. Jackson. New York: Routledge.

Boal, Augusto, and Susana Epstein. 1990. The cop in the head: Three hypotheses. *TDR* 34 (3): 35–42.

Eisner, Elliot. 2002. *The arts and the creation of mind*. New Haven, CT: Yale University Press.

Freire, Paulo. 1970. *Pedagogy of the oppressed*. New York: Continuum.

Greene, Maxine. 1978. *Landscapes in learning.* New York: Teachers College Press.

Mutnick, D. 2006. Critical interventions: The meaning of praxis. In *Boal companion: Dialogues on theatre and cultural politics,* ed. Jan Cohen-Cruz and Mady Schutzman, 33–45. New York: Routledge.

Spolin, Viola, Carol Sills, and Paul Sills. 1999. *Improvisation for the theater: A handbook of teaching and directing techniques.* Evanston, IL: Northwestern University Press.

U.S. Census Bureau. n.d. Fact sheet. http://factfinder.census.gov/servlet/SAFFFacts ?_event=Search&geo_id=&_geoContext=&_street=&_county=10459&_cityTown =10459&_state=04000US36&_zip=10459&_lang=en&_sse=on&pctxt=fph&pgsl =010&show_2003_tab=&redirect=Y (accessed December 22, 2008).

11

Ripples on the Water

Discoveries Made with Young People Using Theatre of the Oppressed

Christina Marín

If you have thumbed through the pages of this book, stumbled upon this chapter, and can read the words on this page, then you and I have something in common—in a word, literacy. "In fact," according to Richard Shaull, "those who, in learning to read and write, come to a new awareness of selfhood and begin to look critically at the social situation in which they find themselves, often take the initiative to transform the society that has denied them this opportunity of participation" (1970, 29). The people Shaull refers to in his foreword to Paulo Freire's (1970) seminal text, *Pedagogy of the Oppressed*, are the agrarian farm workers in Latin America who reaped the benefits of the adult literacy projects that Freire conducted in the southern hemisphere. But Freire's philosophical ideas and educational theories have had a much broader impact throughout the world. At first glance, these theories may not seem to apply to the so-called first world, but Shaull points out, "If, however, we take a closer look, we may discover that his methodology as well as his educational philosophy are as important for us as for the dispossessed in Latin America. Their struggle to become free Subjects and to participate in the transformation of their society is similar, in many ways, to the struggle not only of blacks and Mexican-Americans but also of middle-class young people in this country" (1970, 29). It is precisely in response to this observation that I have chosen to examine how Theatre of the Oppressed (TO) techniques, developed by Augusto Boal and directly influenced by Freire's writing, can help us approach an understanding of liberatory pedagogy with young people. How, I have come to ask in my work, can adult educators partner with youths to provoke educational practices in which critical dialogue is the focus and responsibility in the process belongs to all?

Approaching a Literacy of the World

The power to read the written word is a source of educational access. The power to "read the world" is a concept I discovered, and began to negotiate, through reading Freire's book, coauthored with Donaldo Macedo (1987), *Literacy: Reading the Word and the World*. In this text, the authors suggest a reexamination of the definition of the term literacy itself and argue that "literacy cannot be reduced to the treatment of letters and words as purely mechanical domain. We need to go beyond this rigid comprehension of literacy and begin to view it as the relationship of learners to the world, mediated by the transforming practice of this world taking place in the very general milieu in which learners travel" (1987, viii). I believe strongly in the power of theatre as a tool and a weapon for young people to engage in social change; this tool is one through which they can both read and write their own version of the world.

When adolescents are offered a creative forum in which to grapple with issues critical to their communities and their own development as citizens of an ever-changing global society, TO provides a vocabulary of games and exercises that gives them collective ownership of the dialogue. Introducing young people to the techniques of TO to examine their lives and circumstances, to read the world around them, also encourages a critical awareness of their rights and their ability to be agents of change in that world. Like the agrarian farm workers in Freire's literacy projects, adolescents become aware of their positioning as subjects and not objects in the world; they became aware of their capacity for transformation.

But simply giving young people a space in which to converse with one another and allowing them to express their different points of view or share their common perspectives will not be enough. Through dialogue, the participants have the opportunity to come to a collective "epistemological curiosity," in Freire's terms, rather than an individualistic—and too often competitive—fixed experience of the world. In acknowledging this communal process of learning and knowing, we approach an understanding of the Freirean conviction, which recognizes that "every human being . . . is capable of looking critically at the world and in a dialogical encounter with others. Provided with the proper tools for such encounter, the individual can gradually perceive personal and social reality as well as the contradictions in it, become conscious of his or her own perception of that reality and deal critically with it" (Shaull 1970, 32). I believe theatre can be a powerful medium employed to stimulate such encounters because I have witnessed young people using these tools in collaboration and seen them come away with a renewed hope and conviction that they can impact their world.

The premise of this chapter is to highlight some of the many experiences I have been privileged to be part of as a facilitator of workshops with young people. I have worked in rural, private boarding schools; behavioral health and prevention agencies; urban institutions; after-school settings; group homes; thespian festivals; national leadership conferences; and intergenerational programs in which college students have worked side by side with me to facilitate workshops for high school students. Every occasion has engendered new and important discoveries; every workshop has been an opportunity for me to see the work through new eyes. I am indebted to every one of the young people who has ever invited me into their world, shared their thoughts with me, and took risks with other young people in this work.

This is not a case study of one particular group or an attempt to generalize the experiences of the hundreds of young people I have worked with over the past eight years. It is, admittedly, my negotiation of the experiences—experiences that would have been infinitely different if any of the participants had not been involved or if another young person had taken their place. This is a process that I have examined through my own personal lenses and biases, one that might conflict with the perception of an outside observer of the work. I hope to shed some light on the tremendous potential I believe this work has for helping young people discover a collective voice and a critical consciousness.

Theatre Rooted in Pedagogy

The work I do employs Augusto Boal's TO as a foundational point of departure, but, as Boal himself explains in several of his texts, this work is never static. There have been many reiterations of the various forms he developed, originally in Brazil, throughout the world in different contexts; even he himself has adapted and transformed his own methods (Boal 1998, 2002, 2006). Boal explains the transition from a focus on external oppressions and a search for alternatives and concrete solutions in Forum Theatre to the more introspective techniques in the arsenal of his work in both *The Rainbow of Desire* (1995) and in the preface to the second edition of *Games for Actors and Non-Actors* (2002). As my work reflects the education and training that I have had in TO techniques, I choose to refer to the work I do as Theatre for Social Change and acknowledge, as I have done above, the influence Boal's work has had on my praxis. In many workshops, I have introduced the work as rooted in the arsenal of TO; influenced by numerous other applied theatre practitioners, like Johnny Saldaña, Philip Taylor, and Michael Rohd; and colored by my own personal experiences, reading of and negotiation in the world. Even more so, however, I tend to emphasize the impact that Freire's writings have had on the development of my facilitation practices.

I often feel as if Freire and Boal are actually in constant dialogue with one another through my work. Even more curious is the amount of times I have heard a young person who I might be working with utter a response to a game or exercise that parallels something in the writings of both of these men. I recently experienced an example of this literary déjà vu in a talking circle during a workshop that I was leading at a boarding school in the Midwest. When a young woman began to contribute what she would change about the world if she had the opportunity, she echoed closely the words of Antonio Faundez in dialogue with Paulo Freire from *Learning to Question*: "You discover people who are different and, linked with that discovery of other people, the need to be tolerant of them. This means that through the differences between us we must learn to be tolerant of those who are different, and not to judge them according to our own values, but according to their values, which are different from ours. And here it seems to me to be fundamental to link the concept of culture with the concepts of difference and tolerance" (1989, 21). I was truly amazed, as I had read this passage only the night before this workshop.

It is true, I have fantasized about the publication of "the lost talking book,"[1] a text in which Augusto Boal and the late Paulo Freire have the occasion to dialogue about the intersections I find so apparent in their writings and theories. It is sad to me that these two compatriots never had the opportunity to formally address the similarities in their work for the benefit of readers and practitioners in book form, although they did come together on a panel through the Pedagogy of the Oppressed Conference in 1996 in Omaha, Nebraska, before Freire passed away in 1997. For me, this hypothetical talking book represents the manifestation of the theoretical crossroads where Freire and Boal meet. For example, the working definition Freire gave us of the word praxis, in a monograph published in 1970, reads as follows:

> Action upon an object must be critically analyzed in order to understand both the object itself and the understanding one has of it. The act of knowing involves a dialectical movement which goes from action to reflection and from reflection upon action to a new action. For a learner to know what he did not know before, he must engage in an authentic process of abstraction by means of which he can reflect on the action-object whole, or, more generally, on forms of orientation in the world. In this process of abstraction, situations representative of how the learner orients himself in the world are proposed to him as the objects of his critique. (1970, 13)

When I reflect on this passage, I cannot help but relate it to the work approached through Image Theatre. In *Games for Actors and Non-Actors*, Boal explains,

> All images also are surfaces and, as such, they reflect what is projected on it. As objects reflect the light that strikes them, so images in an organised ensemble reflect the emotions of the observer, her ideas, memories, imagination,

desires . . . The whole method of Theatre of the Oppressed, and particularly the series of the Image Theatre, is based on the *multiple mirror of the gaze of others*—a number of people looking at the same image, and offering their feelings, what is evoked for them, what their imaginations throw up around that image. This multiple reflection will reveal to the person who made the image its hidden aspects. It is up to the protagonist (the builder of the image) to understand and feel whatever she wants or is able to take from this process. (2002, 175)

The image in Boal's theatre techniques is a stand-in for the action-object in Freirean terminology, and the participants work as an ensemble in dialogue to determine their orientation in the world with respect to the image. The young people I work with have often come to recognize, through even the most basic Image Theatre work, that every person sees and experiences the same phenomenon in a different light.

In my own practice, I trace the roots of Boal's theatre practices to the fundamental transformative theories of Freire. Of course, Boal recognizes the influence Freire has had on his own work, down to the transparent echo in the very title he chose for his groundbreaking book *Theatre of the Oppressed*. While Boal (1985, 1995, 2006) alludes to numerous other theatrical and philosophical writers, including Hegel, Brecht, and Aristotle, whose work he reacts to in the development of the theoretical framework that he outlines in his books, it is the undeniable connection to Freire's work that comes through, more often than not, when I am working with young people. From my experience, when I ground the theories and techniques of Boal's TO in Freiere's historical, pedagogical influences, it has a tendency to translate into deeper work with young people. Rather than observing only their reflection in the water, I invite the participants in my workshops to dip their hands beneath the surface and create the exponential ripples that affect change through their work together.

A Theatre by Any Other Name

Another reason I refer to the work I engage in as Theatre for Social Change, rather than Theatre of the Oppressed, is one that many practitioners might disagree with me about. I welcome these divergent perspectives, and I invite dialogue regarding these practices. My experiences with young people are particular to the contexts and circumstances in which I work. On several occasions, over the years, when I have introduced the work as TO, young people have automatically jumped to the most oppressive structures and experiences they can muster. They respond with thoughts on HIV/AIDS plaguing the African continent and beyond, they contribute ideas about the abject poverty in some communities in countries like India, and they often imagine the world of oppression to be far beyond their doorstep. Again, I fully recognize this may not be the experience of all adult facilitators employing these techniques with young people in the diverse contexts in which they work, but I can only write from my personal observations. In this chapter, I refer to the work I have done here in the United States. I offer these reflections in the spirit of dialogue and, in doing so, hope to add to the critical discourse regarding these practices both in the United States and abroad.

Several examples from workshops I have conducted might serve to illustrate the importance of language choices that I have made in my own work with young people. During a TO workshop that I facilitated in a high school in a suburb of Chicago, Illinois, I was caught quite off guard. In the interest of adhering to the tenets of the TO outlined by Boal, I invited the student participants to offer themes of oppression they were interested in working on that had an impact on their lives and their community. In *Games for Actors and Non-Actors*, Boal illustrates from his own practice that "the themes to be treated were always suggested by the group or by the spect-actors; I myself never imposed, or even proposed, anything by way of subject matter—if the intention is to create a theatre which liberates, then it is vital to let those concerned put forward their own themes" (2002, 19). When one young woman suggested female genitalia mutilation, I was flabbergasted. On the one hand, I was impressed that some of these adolescents were aware of and interested in topics related to human rights, but I was admittedly taken aback that this was offered as a topic that held personal relevance in the relatively small, rural Midwestern suburb. Not wanting to invalidate any response offered, we spent some time defining the term for the students who were not familiar with the issue. Many of the students seemed as shocked as I had been when they realized what we were talking about. I explained to the workshop participants that, while I recognized the impact of this issue on a global scale and respected the initiative some of the students had in regard to social injustices in a broader context, the time we had together could not possibly afford us the opportunity to unpack this topic effectively. Even Boal admits, "The choice of method depends on the nature of the group, the occasion and the objectives of the work" (2002, 176). I briefly introduced the possibilities offered through the techniques in the arsenal of TO known as Newspaper Theatre (1985, 1998). I reinforced the ideas that with more time and with the proper research and preparation prior to the workshop, the topic itself was not out of the question but that the circumstances governing our work together could seriously limit our outcomes. I also asked the students to be conscious of the fact that this topic was not an issue the majority of the students had exposure to. This was important, I explained, because we wanted to work on an issue that more people had a personal stake in within this particular community.

I then invited the students to refocus the topic of interest to one that they could have a direct impact, one that affected them in their everyday lives and that they could envision having a transformative affect on. When we reframed the work using the term social change, it seemed to conjure up a more local context in which they could see the potential to critically reflect on and influence outcomes to problems closer to home. The issue of sexual orientation and expression came to the forefront, and I respected their communal interest in this topic.

We proceeded with some fascinating work, through Image Theatre exercises, that reflected the media saturated heteronormativity the students collectively decided to interrogate. They created still images related to gay marriage, hate crimes, and popular culture representations of same-sex couples. About halfway through this workshop, it occurred to me that this topic might not be one condoned by the school administration. I looked around at several of the teachers and staff who were observing the workshop and was pleasantly surprised when I noticed intrigue and curiosity on the faces of the adults who were genuinely interested in hearing the youths express their opinions. I experienced the same sense of hope expressed by Jo Beth Gonzalez as she envisions a time when "more administrators and community members might see that high school theatre is a place where students work hard, develop keen insights into humanity, and examine issues that are significant to their development as socially conscious young adults" (2006, 5). Although I don't work with students on high school theatre productions with the same regularity that Gonzalez does in her high school drama program in Bowling Green, Ohio, I have had the privilege of visiting her and her students in the Social Issues Theatre class that she teaches. I worked with some of her students on Boalian games and exercises this past year and believe they, like so many of the adolescents I have worked with, embody the work Boal imagined when he wrote, "Theatre of the Oppressed creates *spaces of liberty* where people can free their memories, emotions, imaginations, thinking of their past, in the present, and where they can invent their future instead of waiting for it" (2002, 5).

Illustrative of this point, and based on the images they had devised, the students in the workshop in Illinois proceeded to discuss the potential changes to legislation they could affect when they legally gained the right to vote at eighteen, the power of the purse strings they held as a viable consumer interest group and demographic, and the celebrity figures and politicians who were already having an influence in the way society addresses these issues. The students were taking risks, I agreed to work with them in solidarity, and the other adults involved recognized the power this form of theatre had to engage young people in controversial yet important dialogues they felt passionate about. On many levels, this workshop was a great success. Not all circumstances are as forgiving.

Learning from Even the Most Difficult Moments

During Hispanic Heritage Month in 2007, I was invited to facilitate three workshops in upstate New York at an all-male youth residence operated through the Office of Children and Family Services. All the young men in this facility had committed some form of crime but had been tried through Children and Family Services, rather than through the penal system. It was a reformatory, supplemented by a fully scheduled school curriculum, five days a week. Many of the other guest speakers that day were either showing PowerPoint presentations or giving a motivational talk of some kind. I appeared to be the only one offering an interactive workshop. Perhaps this was the reason our orientation was not as thorough as it could have been. Working interactively with these young men came with rules and regulations. My intentions were never to break any of these rules; perhaps had I been privy to them before our work began, I would have been better prepared for the situation that arose.

After several warm-up games with the second group of young men I was working with that day, we began some Image Theatre work. We transitioned from the basic handshake exercise—outlined effectively by theatre director and community-based practitioner Michael Rohd (1998) in his book *Theatre for Community, Conflict and Dialogue*, as the "Complete the Image" exercise (60–61)—into a group sculpting exercise in which several participants collectively express their reflections on a particular topic or theme. The model image can be developed in a number of ways. Boal (2002) describes the following, which I employed in this particular instance:

> The Joker asks five or more volunteers to express the chosen theme(s) in a visual form. Each works without seeing what the others are doing, so as not to be influenced by them. One after another they come into the middle of the playing space and use only their bodies to express the theme they have been given. Without talking, they position their bodies in a still pose, to express their opinion or idea or experience of the theme, as it strikes them there and then; having made their image, they need offer no explanation or justification—in itself, it says everything that needs saying, for the moment. (2002, 176–77)

During the brainstorming to select a theme, one young man offered gang violence as a topic.

As all the participants seemed enthusiastic about the issue, I committed to work with them to explore this theme. At the same time, I tried once again to remember and put into practice the sage advice of Gonzalez, applying her work on the production process to my practice in Theatre for Social Change. She suggests, "One reality of promoting the self-agency of minors is that the teacher must remain in control of the learning environment, even if students ostensibly run the show. Hence, the democratic teacher must acknowledge her own self-interest and put it in check, yet also know when to intervene" (2006, 41). Perhaps in a different context, things might have turned out differently. Perhaps if I had been debriefed about the various policies and procedures in place in this institution, I would have proceeded with more caution. But hindsight is 20/20; I have learned from this experience to always thoroughly research the context in which I will be working, especially in my engagement with young people. In the very Freirean sense, I am an educator always in the process of learning and becoming, never completed.

Earlier that morning, in the first class I worked with, I realized that I was one of three adults in the room at all times with these young men. The other two were the subject teacher for each period and a guard who accompanied the class of young men to and from each classroom throughout the day. This figure in the corner was ever observant—the embodiment of authority ready to step in if it became necessary. When the second class entered the auditorium space we would be working in, they followed their guard in a single-file line and seated themselves, according to his directive, one seat apart in the first two rows. The guard took a seat off to the side and settled in to watch our workshop.

He seemed to find nothing contentious in the warm-up games I alluded to earlier, but the controversy centered around the topic the group had chosen: gang violence. The guard did not immediately step in, and what happened seemed to progress so fast that I was genuinely confused when one of the young men was led out of the room as he protested loudly that he had done nothing wrong. The subject teacher approached in an attempt to reassure me that what had happened was not my fault and this particular student would have found some way to cause a ruckus and get himself kicked out; this was apparently par for the course and a daily occurrence. But I was unnerved that something I had brought into the room had been the cause of this problem. I turned to the other young men and asked them to dialogue with me about what had happened. At first, some of them were also inclined to protest:

"Nah, Miss, that ain't right!"
"You told us to make that image!"
"He was only doing what you asked!"
"He got in trouble for doing what you said to do!"

But then, a voice of reason entered the conversation with a rational explanation that made sense. A young man asked his peers, "So how come none of you did it?"

"Did what? What am I missing?" I asked for a replay of what had happened from the workshop participants, giving them the power to process the events and analyze them with me. They reminded me that I had invited them to make an image of their perceptions of gang violence. That much I conceded. One by one, they had stepped forward and embodied rage, hate, anger, attitude, power, allegiance, force, and strength. But the young man who had been removed had stepped into the image in a very calculated way: he had thrown down. Without my knowledge, part of his projected image was the use of his two hands in the formation of a ritualistic gang sign that the guard had picked up on right away. The authoritative figure calmly informed this participant from where he sat that he needed to "put them down." I heard him, but since no one in the image was "holding anything," I moved on with the work, oblivious to the situation that was unfolding. I assumed the guard was referring to one of the other young men behind me who was not directly involved in the image. I chose to let the guard take care of disciplining the students who I weren't working with so as not to lose focus. Again, more emphatically, he raised his voice informing the young man in the image, "Put it down, or you are out of here." Some of the participants seemed to be urging their classmate not to ruin this, but quicker than a flash, he was not only out of the image but also out of the auditorium. Gang signs are against the rules at this school, and any incident in which a resident uses them is grounds for immediate disciplinary action.

When the guard returned without the resident who had broken the rules, I approached him and apologized for any disturbance I had caused in this class. He, like the subject teacher before him, reassured me that I was not the cause of this young man's actions. "Did you notice," he asked, "that even when he dared to break the rules, none of his classmates followed suit? They all know the rules here, and they know what can get them into serious trouble. He made a choice; he makes them every day. This had nothing to do with you." I explained that I had no idea about this regulation and meant no disrespect of the rules, and he responded that he thought the work we were doing seemed really powerful and interesting and that enough time had been wasted on the young man's indiscretion. He urged me to get back to the other young men.

I turned back to the group, and we spent a few more minutes discussing what had happened. Many of them agreed that even though their classmate had made that choice, they knew what the consequences were and didn't want to get in trouble. These were lessons they were learning on a daily basis by living out their "sentences" in this facility. We proceeded to work the rest of the afternoon without any more disturbances. I left having learned so much from those young men, even the one who made the choice to break the rules. I have learned, especially through my work with adolescents, that theatre can be a source of tension—one that we can examine closely in order to make change. In the words of Boal, "Theatre is conflict, struggle, movement, transformation, not simply the exhibition of states of mind. *It is a verb, not an adjective.* To act is to produce an action, and every action produces a reaction—conflict" (2002, 39).

This experience raised many questions for me as a practitioner, and I dove back into my Freirean texts to find myself swimming in the connections between what he describes as critical pedagogy and the methodology employed in Theatre for Social Change. Responding to Donaldo Macedo in *Literacy* (1987), Freire argues, "The role of critical pedagogy is not to extinguish tensions. The prime role of critical pedagogy is to lead students to recognize various tensions and enable them to deal effectively with them . . . I believe, in fact, that one task of radical pedagogy is to clarify the nature of tensions and how best to cope with them" (1987, 49). The arsenal of TO arms us with the tools to engage young people in these tensions. As Freire concludes, "Reading the word and learning how to write the word so one can later read it are preceded by learning how to write the world, that is, having the experience of changing the world and touching the world" (ibid.).

Recognizing that My Liberation Is Bound Up with Theirs

I began working with young people during my doctoral studies. My dissertation examined how Latina adolescents formulate personal identities through the use of Theatre for Social Change techniques with a bilingual youth theatre group in Arizona. My work employing TO methods with youth since that time has been an attempt to make good on the pledge I made in that study: "Through the use of Theatre for Social Change exercises I have made an attempt to give the participants in this study a chance to speak back to this prescriptive labeling, and to redefine their personal identities in relation to the world around them. Although the very nature of a youth program is ephemeral, due to the inevitable fact that adolescents mature into adults, I plan to continue my focus on incorporating theatre methods in educational settings to help students find their own voice" (Marín 2005, 198–99). I welcome the rich dialogue engendered through this volume exploring the different practices and perspectives of my colleagues who also believe in the power of theatre to motivate young people to action; but ultimately, the more interesting dialogue is with the youths themselves.

In Freire's words, "The radical, committed to human liberation . . . does not consider himself or herself the proprietor of history or of all people, or the liberator of the oppressed; but he or she does commit himself or herself, within history, to fight at their side" (2000, 39). Whether I am working with participants in community-based workshops or in university classrooms, I often refer to a quote that has become a cornerstone of my praxis. The words, attributed to an Australian aboriginal collective, read, "If you have come to help me, you are wasting your time. But if you have come because your liberation is bound up with mine, then let us work together." My negotiation of this quote brings me closer to realizing that I cannot operate from any agenda of my own if I am engaged in work with young people; the agenda must emerge out of their concerns. I must, of course, own my own position, but I cannot impose it on others. If I am truly bound to a collaborative process through TO, then the tools I have must be turned over as gifts to those I work with in solidarity.

Note

1. Freire contributed to several such books with international educationalists such as Antonio Faundez, Ira Shor, and Myles Horton and has written in dialogue form with others, including Donaldo Macedo.

References

Boal, A. 1985. *Theatre of the Oppressed*. Trans. Charles A. and Maria-Odilia Leal McBride. New York: Theatre Communications Group.

———. 1995. *The Rainbow of Desire: The Boal method of theatre and therapy*. Trans. Adrian Jackson. New York: Routledge.

———. 1998. *Legislative theatre*. Trans. Adrian Jackson. New York: Routledge.

———. 2002. *Games for actors and non-actors*. 2nd ed. Trans. Adrian Jackson. New York: Routledge.

———. 2006. *Aesthetics of the oppressed*. Trans. Adrian Jackson. New York: Routledge.

Freire, P. 1970. *Cultural action for freedom*. Cambridge, MA: Center for the Study of Development and Social Change.

———. 2000. *Pedagogy of the oppressed*. 30th Anniversary ed. Trans. Myra Bergman Ramos. New York: Continuum.

Freire, P., and A. Faundez. 1989. *Learning to question: A pedagogy of liberation*. Trans. Tony Coates, Trans. Geneva: World Council of Churches.

Freire, P., and D. Macedo. 1987. *Literacy: Reading the word and the world*. London: Bergin & Garvey.

Gonzalez, J. B. 2006. *Temporary stages: Departing from tradition in high school theatre education*. Portsmouth, NH: Heinemann.

Rohd, M. 1998. *Theatre for community, conflict and dialogue: The Hope Is Vital training manual*. Portsmouth, NH: Heinemann.

Shaull, R. 1970. Foreword to *Pedagogy of the oppressed*, by P. Freire. 30th Anniversary ed. New York: Continuum.

12

Let's Rock the Bus

Mady Schutzman and B. J. Dodge

Mady: I arrived that first day in early October 2005 with the usual mix of readiness and anxiety; I was as prepared as I could be but also destabilized by an unfamiliar environment and group of participants. When I arrived, the youth were already engaged in theater games on the stage of this old, highly vaulted, funky and well-worn theater. Within a matter of seconds, I was overcome with fright. I slithered up to B. J. Dodge, who was gadding about with the élan that accompanies fluency and comfort. I followed her like a desperate waif trying to get her attention just long enough to whisper, "I can't do this. I'm very sorry, but they are too young."

B. J.: Mady was probably preparing for this moment her entire professional life, for she always walks into a room with a lesson so carefully constructed as to be matched only by her inner Fool's voice, which asks, "How can anyone [I] ever be prepared for the unexpected?" Although she had been teaching young people at university level for years, she hadn't seen them in this point of development, and it must have been a novelty for her. We have a rather porous border between who is officially allowed to take the class (actors have to be eleven to twelve years old by the time of opening) and who sneaks in (some precocious ten-year-olds have been known to be part of the ensemble).

The Youth Theater Program at Plaza de la Raza was entering its sixteenth season when B. J. Dodge, its longtime director, asked Mady Schutzman, faculty member of the MFA Writing Program at the California Institute of the Arts (CalArts), to be the playwright for the 2005–2006 season. Plaza de la Raza is a multidisciplinary cultural arts center serving the large and growing Latino community of Los Angeles. For the last sixteen years, Plaza has been one of dozens of community sites that have partnered with CalArts within their award-winning program, Community Arts Partnership (CAP). Through CAP, CalArts students and faculty offer workshops for teens in art, theater, dance, music, writing, and film. At the time of this chapter's writing in 2008, CAP works at forty-three sites throughout LA county, hires sixty-one faculty members, teaches four hundred and thirteen CalArts students, and serves over 6,670 middle and high school students both in and after school. The CalArts/Plaza de la Raza Youth Theater Workshop is one of CAP's most renowned and developed programs.

Mady Schutzman wrote *UPSET!* in conjunction with the Latino youths (ages eleven to seventeen) who enrolled in the Plaza theater program that year. Mady met with them once a week, but the youth met a total of three times a week (even more as we neared showtime) with director B. J. Dodge (and the production team) for twenty-two weeks before the play was performed at the Plaza and at a downtown Los Angeles venue, REDCAT. This chapter chronicles the making of *UPSET!*

Ask and You Shall Receive

As a practitioner and scholar of Augusto Boal's work for nearly twenty years, Mady was intrigued by the dramaturgical methodology of the Joker System. The Joker System is a process of rehearsing, writing, and staging a dramatic text. Within Boal's oeuvre, the Joker System preceded the interactive techniques of Theater of the Oppressed (TO) for which he is internationally known, though the philosophical and political tenets were primarily the same.[1] In these early Joker System plays, a story is told as a composite of commentaries, lectures, exhortations, news clippings, and transcripts, as well as dramatic scenes. There is always a Joker, a kind of all-knowing onstage director or MC who interrupts the action to interview characters, offer explanations or critiques, and incite the audience. At times, the Joker, as if inspired or disgusted by what is happening onstage, steps in to play the different characters as he or she pleases. The actors themselves change roles so that no one actor consistently interprets any one character. Everyone gets a chance to tell it as they see it. Scenes are staged in several styles promoting aesthetic eclecticism. There is a Chorus that sings, dances, complains, rallies, and, along with the Joker, talks directly to the audience; Chorus members express their pleasure or discontent (sometimes both at once) with how the story is unfolding and propose, debate, mock, and act out, various alternatives. Paradox, irony, and humor are everywhere. And finally, in spite of the carnivalesque array of opinions, the bad guys and good guys remain easy to tell apart.

A Joker System play is meant to be a spectacular discussion, or a trial, in which different ideas and feelings about any historical character or event can be presented and interrogated. The ultimate goal is to raise questions, offer multiple points of view, and encourage dialogue.

On the very first day that we all met, after the introductions and sizing-ups, Mady asked the youth to come up with a list of historical characters who they wanted to know more about or celebrate. Their original list had as many as forty figures as diverse as Abraham Lincoln and Paris Hilton. It included The Beatles, Marilyn Monroe, Mother Theresa, Jimi Hendrix, Johnny Depp, William Shakespeare, Charlie Chaplin, and Frank Sinatra. After several peda-gogical sessions to educate the youth about the nominees they didn't know (some didn't even know who their own nominees were), we created our A list: Frida Kahlo, César Chávez, Ghandi, Rosa Parks, Fidel Castro, Martin Luther King Jr., Che Guevara, John F. Kennedy, Rodney King, and Tupac Shakur. More lessons and two weeks later, the winners, by democratic vote (i.e., one vote for each young person who showed up that night) were Rod-ney King and Rosa Parks.

Gabriel T., who was later to be cast as the Joker, had nominated Rodney King, it turned out, because he didn't know much about him and wanted to; he had been a toddler when the beating and trial occurred. Because he had a vested interest in the outcome, he campaigned heavily for Rodney just before we voted; it was like watching a lobbyist prior to a legislative session. Rosa Parks ran a close second to Rodney and seemed to be the choice of many of the girls. We learned a few days after the voting that youth had spoken to Donald Amerson, our production manager, at the end of the 2005 season about their interest and desire in playing people of ethnicities other than Latino. "We want to play black people or rich white people." That had an effect on which famous (and infamous) people appealed to the voters.

Most everyone who was of a certain age in 1992 remembers Rodney King as the unfortunate African American man brutally beaten by four white Los Angeles Police Department (LAPD) officers in 1991. Their acquittal, a year later, instigated widespread rioting in Los Angeles. Rosa Parks is nationally renowned as the young activist and seamstress who refused to give up her seat to a white passenger on a public bus in Montgomery, Alabama, in 1955. As we discussed Rosa Parks and her trajectory as a spokesperson within the civil rights movement, Mady shared the story of Claudette Colvin, a fifteen-year-old African American girl who had done the same as Rosa Parks nine months earlier. This less known but courageous character appealed to the Plaza youth. By the end of that particular session, Rosa Parks was replaced by Claudette Colvin as the second main character of our yet-to-be-written play.

The same year in which Rodney King was in the news and when the vid-eotape of the beating played over and over on national television, almost all of the youth in the program at Plaza were born in Los Angeles. Either that or they were born a year later when the four policemen charged with exces-sive force were found not guilty and the city went up in flames. Over our months together at Plaza, the youth listened carefully as the adults in the room told stories of where they were when the riots broke out. They went home and asked their parents, and these teenagers began to envision themselves as infants whisked out of smoke-filled rooms, enveloped by fearful cries, thrown into car seats by desperate parents to pick up siblings unable to get home from school or music lessons. It's not talked about much in Los Angeles now, but the legacy of the uprising of 1992 pervades contemporary Angelenos, no matter what age. From early on in the rehearsal process, these retellings captured the imagination of the youth, as did the mere spectacle of violence and fire that ravaged the city for most of six days.

Claudette Colvin did a very brave thing when she was only fifteen years old, the age of many of the performers. Her courage became a standard, a high one indeed, against which the youth could measure their own courage both in and outside of the Plaza courtyard. Claudette's bitterness as a sixty-six-year-old also may have been instructive, providing an image of dreams unrealized, efforts unrecognized, and pride buried beneath frustration.[2] It was as if they were comparing Claudette to their own grandmothers and teachers, community leaders and politicians, trying to assess how she made sense in their day-to-day world, where her values and actions were or were not echoed. Most of the young Latino actors at Plaza live their everyday lives in Los Angeles aware (with varying degrees of consciousness) of being cast as contested citizens within the general population. The choice of embracing Claudette struck us as healthy, albeit nascent, political defiance: in the spirit of what the theatrical arts have to offer, they wanted "a different part." The youth seemed to intuit that they would glimpse the political potency and burdens of their own history by exploring hers.

We—the adults of the production team who had asked the youth to invest in the process by proffering historical subjects—now had to shoulder the gift of their response. We had indeed received a hefty assignment.

Be Careful What You Ask For: The Task Ahead

If there was anything that assuaged our anxiety about delving into play-making with this particular mandate, it was the techniques of the Joker System. In fact, Mady would not have invited the youth to select the subject matter (i.e., she would not have had the confidence to write about whom-ever they selected) if she and B. J. had not agreed on the Joker System as method and container. The techniques were trustworthy; they embodied the philosophies they were founded on—critical dialogue, multivocality, self-reflexivity, and the endless posing of questions, just what we needed to handle controversial material. In those early days of anticipation, it was a great comfort to know, for example, that if there were contesting visions or interpretations of a particular scene, if we couldn't agree on one, then we would stage them all; the Joker System accommodates, even welcomes, multiple stagings of the same scene.

We were dedicated to making a play that, while telling a historical tale, featured the young people's experiences of learning about the characters they were to portray and the historical events they would enact. Creating *UPSET!* in the mode of the Joker System provided a means to incorporate the teens' curiosity, dismay, outrage, confusion, fear, and inspiration in relation to the subject matter of the play *within* the play. That was its forte—an aesthetic tool that was at once a pedagogical tool. Speculating, collective brainstorming, dreaming, interrogating, and image making joined the facts to become critical characters, dynamic elements, in our representation of the "truth." And because the Joker System was designed from its inception to promote social inquiry and personal agency (by asking, How do I know what I know? Who authored the histories we reiterate? Are those stories relevant to me and my community? Who do they privilege and who do they marginalize?), it afforded us a perfect vehicle to tell not only the story of Rodney King and the ensuing uprising but also a larger, ever-changing and yet ever-the-same history of violence, racism, and resistance in the United States. The inclusion of Claudette, an antihero of the 1950s, not only contextualized Rodney's story in an earlier era of black history, but it also provided the impetus to look back further yet, back to the days of Homer Plessy and then to the Civil War. Our historical timeline, written out in colored markers on a very long unfurled roll of brown paper and filled in weekly with added events and characters, hung on the theater walls for months. It brought the past closer and served as a backdrop to the present.

Before the play was written, we conducted several exercises that would generate the youth's questions and interpretations of various scenes. Later, these would be scripted into the play as "interventions." For example, as Mady relayed in detail the story of Claudette Colvin's act of resistance in Alabama in 1955, she invited them to interrupt and ask questions of any of the historical players at each step in the story's unfolding. We provided them with the critical historical data they needed, such as the prevailing law at the time that designated seats on public buses for black passengers at the back and seats for whites at the front. Black people, we told them, were allowed to occupy the indistinct middle section only if white people did not use them. Sitting around the table listening to the story, they jumped in: "Claudette, why don't you listen?" "Claudette, are you going to let them walk all over you?" "Bus driver, can't you give her a break and just let her sit down?" "White Mask, what makes you better than her?"[3] "Claudette, are you being an uppity black girl?" "White Mask, do you deserve that seat?" "Claudette, do you deserve that seat?" "Claudette, are you brave enough to do the right thing?" "Black Mask, why don't you help her?" And then, after being beaten,

"Is it still worth it, Claudette?" In the final script, the youth hovered closely in real time at the edges of the 1955 reenactment, and, as a chorus of witnesses-*cum*-journalists, they fired these rhetorical questions at the characters as the fateful scene played out on stage.

The literal inclusion of the questions posed by the youth in the rehearsal process into the play itself was a gift proffered by the Joker System; the acuity of the questions themselves can be credited only to the youth themselves.

> *Mady*: I had been working at Plaza for about a month when we decided to meet in the adjacent art building where we could show a video that a group of middle school children in Michigan had made about Claudette Colvin. There was pizza. It was cozy sitting around a big wooden table splattered with dry paint and hardened clay. José V. was sitting just to my left as I began to tell the story of Claudette Colvin and jotted down the various questions they posed to the characters as I relayed each gruesome detail. José was mesmerized by the story, an innocent terror on his face that he was trying and failing to hide. I could sense his body undergoing some elaborate reorganization. He did not ask one question aloud, but when the storytelling was over and we began to pack up to leave for the evening, he tugged gently on my shirt and with a voice full of anticipation asked very softly, "If I were on that bus, where would I have to sit?"

As José V. sat in Lincoln Heights, California, in 2006, traversing time and history, making sense of his identity as a young Latino vis-à-vis the life of a young black girl born over fifty years before him in a place he has never been, he was realizing that he knew the answer to his own question. But more importantly, he seemed to be recognizing that he was part of history, that his life was much bigger than he had ever imagined, and that he had some powerful tools by which to ask and even answer difficult questions. I believe that on that day, the question, "What would I do in her circumstances?" became, for José and others, "What will I do tomorrow when faced with a similar dilemma?"[4]

The youth's connections to a remote historical past were being forged, in large part, by extraordinary current events in Los Angeles. In 2006, the South Central Farm was being threatened (and was eventually razed) by real estate developers. [5] It was also the time of a fermenting immigrants' rights movement: in March 2006, over five hundred thousand people marched in Los Angeles to protest a proposed federal crackdown on illegal immigration. B. J. decided to take the group on a field trip to the South Central Farm and to the site of the Reginald Denny beating, only blocks away.[6]

B. J.: It was a revelation to me to see Michael E. cheer on the speakers at the South Central farm rally we attended and become excited about the plight of the farmers in the face of imminent development of the land. Michael is quiet, shy, but that day he was uncharacteristically passionate in his responses to the speeches. Eddie V., who played officer Stacy Koon, is a vibrant, and challenging young participant, who was given to temperamental outbursts, inappropriate language directed at peers, and fits of pique. The saving graces for the teaching team were his intellectual honesty, acting prowess, and a sincere desire to be a part of a process that he believed in. While strolling on the paths that linked the individual garden plots, Eddie revealed that his mother "made" him garden because getting his hands in the dirt calmed him down.

The early part of the day on this field trip included a visit to the "ground zero" site at Normandie and Florence where the Reginald Denny beating took place. At one point we pulled into the lot of a strip mall that faced the corner. Archival footage of the beating from a documentary played over and over again on the DVD player in Maria Jimenez-Torres's (the CAP site coordinator) Honda Pilot. In small groups, students piled into the car to watch while the rest of the group witnessed life go by on the corner, everyday business—but also police in pursuit, police stopping pedestrians, ambulances racing past—contrasting and reflecting the action on the small screen.

In writing a Joker System play, some scenes are constructed to allow each actor to play an action and a response to that action simultaneously. Just as Michael and Eddie had personal reactions to the events witnessed on the field trip, the actors, of course, had personal reactions to the characters and scenes they were embodying, reactions that we looked to the Joker System to accommodate. In the scene representing the beating of Rodney King, all cast members had an opportunity to become Officer Laurence Powell, the LAPD officer who delivered the most blows to Rodney King; it was an opportunity to perform critical empathy. While in his shoes, baton raised and ready to strike King, the youth expressed what they imagined Powell was feeling or thinking, which, in many cases, was an expression of what they were feeling or thinking: "I am scared to death"; "I'm not sure why I'm doing this, but my buddies aren't stopping me so it must be okay"; "I hate how black people want to move in and take our jobs and change the way we do things"; "It's wrong, but I don't know how to stop it"; "I feel powerful"; "I don't feel anything"; "He looks like a criminal to me"; "I feel like a criminal"; "I hate my job." For each actor, there was an opportunity to bring their contemporary selves into the portrayal of the character. But for the group, and hopefully for the audience, the multiple responses gave breadth to the policemen. Together they suggested that there is no easy good and evil; no one is a monster here. That's what makes it tragic—these characters are human beings, just like us.

During many other scenes of the play, the reactions of the youth to their own characters, while not so explicitly scripted, were evident all the same. That is, the actors were taking personal ownership of the play implicitly, translating the lessons, issues, and queries of the characters into an aesthetic of their own. Some of the most extraordinary moments for the audience came with a recognition of this subtle fusion. "I'm Rodney King. I know I've done bad things. I drink too much. I'd like to turn my life around, I guess. Someone meeting me for the first time, they'd know I'm no Jesus Christ for black people . . . But I'm still the King." When participant Miztli C. delivered these lines, there was an added level of humble pride. Miztli, however subconsciously, identified with the character's status. He was homeschooled for a while and used his participation in the program as a way of connecting with other youth his age. "I'm still the King!" was a declaration that he mattered, not only as the character, but also as the actor playing the character.

Another example of this implicit ownership was evidenced in our Joker, Gabriel T. Gabriel was the natural Joker in the group because of his verbal confidence and his instincts about comedy. When he was given a piece of physical business, he would just do it and then gauge the response from whoever was watching in order to figure out why it worked. He would then build from there and make it his own. He understood that he disappeared inside the large robes and white wig that Lisa Burke, the costume designer, gave him to wear as Judge Stanley Weisberg, so just seeing him struggle to be visible was sidesplittingly funny. The unexpected and brilliant metaphor that came through was that the Joker-as-Judge was struggling to introduce justice into a rigged judicial system. Gabriel was probably not fully aware of the pure genius of his choices, but they are innate in his mind and body and made all the more potent because, as an actor, he doesn't manipulate. He wielded his Joker's "wand" with alarming inventiveness because he enjoyed playing with a cool prop that his brother Mario created for him, not because of some abstract idea about what the wand was supposed to *mean*. As a result, Gabriel's Joker came across as the heart of, not just the conductor of, the Chorus; the others relied on him in a profound way. While the youth may not have understood the Joker as a conceptual figure, they understood what a Joker might be through Gabriel's embodiment. As their onstage director, Gabriel as the Joker was the one who created the tone for each scene (now we are mourning, now we are mocking, now we are terrified, now we are curious). What cast members couldn't understand in the Joker's lengthy speeches, they understood in Gabriel's body. Given the Joker's demanding stage time, whoever played him was in the position of driving or dropping the show in performance. Gabriel's inexplicable intuition and finesse, his energy, will, physical intelligence, and connection to the others as peers, allowed him to take everyone—cast and audience alike—through the show, night after night, in remarkable ways not written into the script.[7]

We noticed that the youth were at times confused and frustrated working in an ensemble, playing one character for only five minutes before moving on to the next. It became clear that this format was a huge challenge for the youth. They were not familiar with plays in general and certainly did not have experience being in (or seeing) plays in which an actor did not play one character all the way through. In a way, playing all these different characters was something like playing no one at all. At first, many missed what they thought all theatre offered in playing a singular character with clear motivations, psychology, storyline, realistic dialogues, and costume. In addition, most of the teens were in the Chorus and onstage for the entire length of the play with no downtime backstage. This resulted in a kind of manic frenzy as if the lack of a consistent character translated—after a certain threshold of time—into bursts of contagious collective attention deficit disorder! (It made for a very dynamic riot scene as the actors' sense of mayhem—that is, desperate need for recess—finally found its calling.)

These concerns notwithstanding, the youth again found ways to step in and make the play their own; that is, they learned *in their bodies* how to change channels without losing the subtleties of each character. "One reason I like these techniques is because they ask you to develop a capability to be 'neutral' so that you can move in all directions," said Levi Brewster, the show's designer (Brewster, cited in Dodge forthcoming). To their credit, the youth intuited early on that they were engaged in an experiment, one that offered them a different set of opportunities than they came in expecting: to convey a recurring and dynamic plot about power, to tell a story that contained within it many stories (including their stories, their questions), and to learn complicity, flexibility, and teamwork. As difficult as this ensemble mode was for them, they embraced these opportunities for the most part.

As work with the youth progressed, it became more and more evident that there was no need to "dumb down," not in language or structural complexity. Whatever stretching or reaching the youth might have to do to meet a sophisticated dramatic text, they were already doing so in rehearsal through their intuition, something the Joker System thrives on. In other words, many of the youth were unknowing taking advantage of the aesthetic generosity of the Joker System. What they didn't fully understand in word or concept was taken as an invitation to interpret and play, rather than as a duty to mouth another's (the characters' or the writer's) words.

This, of course, did not mean there wasn't concern about language.

> *Mady*: At home writing, I pondered a great deal about the words I was putting on the page. Not only did I question the specific terms I was using but also the rhetorical forms I found myself employing in order to express the

complexity of the material. I was struggling to integrate my own experiences and education, stories I'd heard from so many others, all the critical theory and analyses of race and gender politics that I had read over the years. I wanted to do justice to the subject matter, and I did not want to use the age of the cast members as a reason to oversimplify or reduce. At the same time, I asked myself daily, to what extent am I, as writer, necessarily constrained by the depth and breadth of knowledge of our youthful collaborators, those who will be speaking, embodying, the words I write?

Soon after the very first read-through, we spent time working with the youth on language. In early rehearsals, it was evident that they did not understand all the words they were speaking. We spent many hours explaining terms such as "integration," "melting pot," "chokehold," "NAACP," "KKK," "civil rights," and many other terms related to the subject matter of the play, from "Patriot Act" to "habeas corpus." They had less trouble with the words "Vanna White of Civil Rights" (our feminist and historically savvy reincarnation of *Wheel of Fortune*'s Vanna, who narrated the facts throughout the play and capsulized lessons from black history as contestants spun a damning wheel of [bad] fortune).[8] As Roxy R., playing Vanna, repeated the words over and over in rehearsals, most of the cast came to fully understand their importance. They absorbed the horror in the narrated treatment of Fannie Lou Hamer and Emmett Till. While rehearsing other scenes, it was not uncommon to see actors tell each other what words meant in order to help one another remember their meanings.

When it came to a dramaturgical understanding of the entire play—how the language accumulated and made meaning over time—there was a wide range of understanding across the cast in terms of age, sophistication, attention span, interest, and demands from school or home. One might think that those who did understand would have been the handful who played only one character throughout: Gabriel as the Joker, Miztli as Rodney, Roxy as Vanna, and Samantha Q. as Claudette. But this element of consistency would not, in the end, be a determining criteria. Camilo Q.-V. and Eddie V. (two of the oldest members of the cast who changed roles as frequently as there were scenes, and there were many scenes) along with the Joker (interestingly, the youngest in the cast) grasped the dramaturgical dimensions the best. For all three, their interest in the material was keen; they were familiar with and dedicated to the Plaza process, and theatre was a language they loved and knew how to "read" and "speak."

> *Mady*: One of the most interesting challenges in the writing came with my desire to include jokes, satire, double entendres, and turns of phrase. I imagined how a certain line would need to be delivered to convey the layers

of meaning and the comedic potential. Would the youth be able to capture the irony, not to mention the historical significance it all rested upon?

I decided to bring in some masters of lyrical irony from the 1960s: singer-songwriters using their wit to launch a humored critique. We started with Phil Och's 1964 song, "Outside of a Small Circle of Friends":

> Look outside the window, there's a woman being grabbed
> They've dragged her to the bushes and now she's being stabbed
> Maybe we should call the cops and try to stop the pain
> But Monopoly is so much fun, I'd hate to blow the game
> And I'm sure it wouldn't interest anybody
> Outside of a small circle of friends

And then we listened to Malvina Reynolds's "Little Boxes," written in 1962:

> Little boxes on the hillside, little boxes made of ticky tacky
> Little boxes on the hillside, little boxes all the same
> There's a green one and a pink one and a blue one and a yellow one
> And they're all made out of ticky tacky and they all look just the same
> And the people in the houses all went to the university
> Where they were put in boxes and they came out all the same
> And there's doctors and there's lawyers and business executives
> And they're all made out of ticky tacky and they all look just the same

"Little Boxes" was a big hit among the youth and became a huge satirical musical number—Latino youth in a truly brilliant display of hyper-innocence playing white youth in Simi Valley where the trial of the four policemen who beat Rodney King was conducted.

Not all the youth were able to comprehend the innuendoes and double entendres that pervaded the linguistically sophisticated scenes. But most did get the gist; they intuited some creepy fun-house quality whereby words were saying two things (even contradictory things) at once. Hector could understand that the act of showing off the latest weapons in the arsenal of products meant to subdue suspects could be like a Vegematic commercial, so he approached it in that way; José could understand that his character's wild and incompetent swinging of a police baton meant that Officer Powell had issues with control. An even more profound comprehension belonged to actors like Eddie, who, in playing Officer Koon, the arrogant Senior Officer in charge the night of the beating, understood the irony of Koon's line (delivered directly to the audience) contesting George Holliday's amateur video that captured the excessive force used against Rodney King: "You need to know the whole story. People don't understand. I had to write a book to explain it!"

Those who had more difficulty with the satirical innuendoes and humor came to understand them more and more as fellow actors told them why something was funny. And almost all cast members became increasingly aware of what was going on by listening to the reactions of people in the audience who appreciated the subtle sarcasm and contradictions.

While Mady was crafting language, B. J. and her team were exploring the youth's reactions to the characters through theater games.

> B. J.: One day we did an exercise in community cooperation from Michael Rohd (1998) called "Cover the Space." We pass around an object with different intentions: first, with a sense of cooperation and sharing, and then with the purpose of keeping the object away from each another. So, at first, the group moves around in space, passing the object freely. "Now hold onto the object and make your fellow actors work to get the object from you."
>
> The mayhem that ensues at this point is considerable. After the fight over objects, we go back to the original intention: passing the object freely and cooperatively, and then there is a time for commentary and observation. This game was done often, and when it was time to choreograph the riots, we used this exercise to illustrate how random the violence and looting was. We had seen, and been amazed, in documentary videos by the things people took: giant Crayola crayons, piggy banks, TVs, diapers, mattresses.
>
> We also made group tableaux centering on the personal oppression that occurs because of age, skin color, and economic status. All of our exercises were entitled "games" because there was usually a sense of play. Whenever one of the participants directed a group in making a tableaux of personal oppression, afterward they were given a choice: they could say nothing at all about the story, they could share selected details, or they could tell the whole story to the group. These tableaux became part of the choreography of the show.

Working with youth, it is important to consider whether they feel safe enough to express their frustrations, particularly when exploring uncomfortable material in unfamiliar ways. In a very general sense, the youth at Plaza feel as safe as eleven- to seventeen-year-olds ever feel safe performing vulnerable tasks in front of others. The frustrations that we saw acted out were, in fact, not so much in relation to dealing with the difficult material as in expressing how they were feeling about one another. The youth tended to clam up in large groups. For those like Camilo and Eddie, who understood the text and what was meant to happen, frustration boiled up working with people more interested in making friends and securing alliances than in rehearsing a play. Feeling that frustration, one of them might say, "We need to learn our lines and our cues," but would never feel comfortable ratting on someone who was, for example, showing pictures to her friends during a blocking rehearsal. Peer-to-peer frustration manifested in rolling eyes but not in making heads roll.

The uncomfortable material was seen less as uncomfortable than as obscure, more like a history test that they hadn't studied for. For example, the trial of the four officers was extremely complex. The actors had to bear in mind the facts of the trial, the playwright's stylistic rendering of those facts (a commedia rhythm to the trial morphing into the manic conflagration that followed), and the physical logistics of having multiple focal points (five, to be exact) that needed to shift like gears so that the audience could follow.[9] Jurors had to be coached line by line as to where their attention should be and what their reactions to testimony should be.

This said, it was hard at times for the youth to live inside of a performance world where they were being asked to beat each other, destroy property, and portray the more unsavory aspects of human behavior. No matter how well our stylistic stagings provided some aesthetic distance from the rampant violence, there was no way to defend against its effect (and this was not our goal). While the youth never expressed outright frustration about the subject matter of the play, the returning students had, in the year prior, finished a season of celebrating the fifteenth-year anniversary of the program with a play involving tuxedos, big cakes, and beautiful gowns. The contrast between waltzing and beating couldn't have been more stark.

Making a play with youth about Rodney King and Claudette Colvin obviously required deliberation over how to stage violence, not just physical violence, but also the violence embedded in language, law, and the media that functions to deny people their constitutional rights on the streets every day. One way of handling the violent and racist nature of the material of the show was to have students step into the imagined bodies and voices not only of outraged and frustrated rioters but also of the racist police, commissioner, and the Ku Klux Klan. The earlier rendering of the beating scene exemplifies one approach whereby the youth could express their personal feelings about violence within a highly stylized choreography. In another scene, four actors portraying white supremacists decided what character they thought would best convey this political ideology to the audience. They chose Hitler, a cowboy, a housewife (in a clam bake apron), and a Viking. Delivering their lines in rap style to a pounding electronic beat, they mock Rodney King's infamous line ("I felt like a crushed can.") and rant proudly about crushing cans: "Afro-*kans*, Jamai-*kans*, Domini-*kans*." Meanwhile, a Klan member dressed in full KKK regalia, performs a wild stomping dance, literally crushing aluminum cans scattered across the stage. They loved it—the permission to be as violent as they liked.

But there was more to it than that: they were speaking to racism *as racists*. They understood this sophisticated kind of acting in which they were critiquing violence precisely as they embodied it. Part of that sophistication came from violence being a necessary aspect of maturation in public schools.

B. J.: During a text analysis rehearsal with a small group, we started talking about times when we had been either the oppressor or victim in a violent encounter. Essentially, we were trying to figure out the emotions on both sides of the equation. José E. talked about fights after school, how in fighting somebody he was defending himself; one on one, for José, was a vital act of survival. Recently, however, he experienced what he thought someone in Rodney's position might feel. His school field trip group had been jumped by gang members in the parking lot of Magic Mountain. His teacher, who tried to intervene, was beaten by the gang members, and José was unable to do anything to help her. All he wanted to do was run away in the face of an implacable force. It was the numbers that tipped him to the oppressive quality, and this informed the way he approached his roles in *UPSET!*: José played Hitler, the worst bully with the biggest gang in the history of Western Europe; he also played Darryl Gates, who you could say was the gang leader of the biggest, baddest gang in LA history!

Samantha, playing Claudette, talked about that incredibly powerful feeling you get when you're winning a fight, when you overpower your foe and get your licks in; she fully realized that she was the oppressor when she was on top. She then talked about how it feels when you're on the losing side. She made a tableau of oppression: a time when she and her mother were questioned when they made a second visit to the buffet table to get desserts. That embarrassment, for her, was more violent than the toe-to-toe fighting between peers that she felt she had to engage in to be safe at her school.

Both José and Samantha not only enjoyed the role of oppressed other in order to comment on evil, but they also enjoyed *being evil* in a safe, fictive, imaginal context. Especially for those participants who experienced violence in their everyday lives, the play offered a catharsis with every performance of the beating scene, counting aloud the fifty-six blows to Rodney's body by the police batons. As a handful of actors rotated into Rodney's position, curled up on the floor, the rest of this very large cast, in a highly rhythmic display of violence run amok, became the "evil gang." Over time, there was a growing sense that perhaps they should not have to expect violence as part of everyday existence, that violence should be an aberration, not ubiquitous.[10]

While plays written in the Joker System style engage a constant shifting of point of view and character (allowing for empathy even toward the antagonists) and an eclectic use of style that breaks narrative flow (*UPSET!* included dramatic styles of documentary reportage, musical theatre, realism, tragicomedy, commedia, and musical styles of folk, rock 'n' roll, gospel, and rap), these plays also take clear political stands. While problematizing easy "us-versus-them" positions, *UPSET!*, like Boal's plays, was somewhat Machiavellian: while it invited sympathy for the role of the accused policemen, it expressed a firm accusation of their behavior, as well as the behavior of the courts and the press. The play did not even try to pretend neutrality: Rodney was the underdog, the victim, and the antihero (as was Claudette) who the audience was urged to root for while the police rarely escaped serious scrutiny. Interestingly, the youth were not confused by this rather sophisticated and characteristic synthesis of seemingly incompatible positions within the Joker System. On the one hand, they had empathy for the police (most of the youth could relate to the idea of competition, the need for power and attention, and the desire to be on the winning side). On the other hand, they had no trouble with condemnation (the youth also understood something about victimization). While the Joker System techniques encouraged a certain humanizing of the police that allowed everyone to recognize that "we are all potential oppressors," the techniques also convey that empathy does not have to compromise one's sense of right and wrong or the readiness to take a stand in the face of injustice. The Joker System seems to have taught, on some level, that in the face of complex, hopeless, or overwhelming circumstances, being confused, conflicted, and terrified is normal. And that once this is accepted, they might next ask a lot of questions, reflect on their own experience and those of others, exercise compassion, and, in the end, with diligence and playfulness at once, assume a firm and always flexible stand.

Words in Context

Mady: It took me the entire process of working at Plaza to fully comprehend what constituted my fear that first day when I entered the theater. I knew it had something to do with the fragility of their age and a sense of my responsibility. I now regard my assumption of responsibility as a form of conceit: I was intimidated by the youth, I didn't know who they were or what they were capable of, and, in my ignorance, I underestimated them. I was already busy compensating, positioning myself as caretaker, protector, and controller of a process that hadn't even begun. In the end, the youth took on more responsibility than I ever could have imagined that first day in the midst of my own private crisis.

So I return to that question, To what extent are we, as writers, constrained by the depth and breadth of knowledge of our youthful collaborators? And I now ask in response, How do we *know* the depth and breadth of knowledge of our youthful collaborators? And even though we might get a glimpse one day—this one's talent, that one's limitation—these elusive measures are not fixed. Once a collaborative process begins—one predicated on dialogue, interaction, play, and mutual respect—these glimpses start shape-shifting way faster than a girl can write.

Another way to consider the important question of a writer's mandate and benchmark in relation to the skills (across any number of skill sets) of their teen collaborators might be by taking a closer look at a few of the Plaza participants themselves. There was tremendous diversity in the cast of *UPSET!*, a diversity not only reflected in how much they comprehended the events and themes depicted in the text but also in how much they understood the process of theater. On one end of the spectrum might be Misael S., new to the Plaza group that fall in 2005. It was glaringly evident from the start that Misael was very nervous and self-conscious about his body in front of others, about being touched and touching. He giggled a lot and spoke very little. B. J., who has the rare ability to turn a postmortem into a circus, joked with him, cajoled and inspired him, held him in a way that obliged everyone else to do the same. In early rehearsals, Misael had very little idea what he was saying or what was going on around him. By the end of a long rehearsal period and seven performances, his body was just beginning to reflect some wit and some depth, as well as a feel for the tragedy of it all. He would make a gesture or sing a line with an intelligence that was not evident before. He wasn't laughing in inappropriate places. He grew in spite of, perhaps because of, his earlier ignorance. But that ignorance would have made an unfortunate benchmark for a writer.

Camilo, we might say, represents the other end of the spectrum at Plaza. He was in his second year of the program, and he absolutely understood Mady's sense of humor, outrage, and irony. He also had enough sophistication theatrically to synthesize the layered ideas of the script. In an interview for a book about this program (Dodge forthcoming), Camilo talked about how this experience was different from other CAP theater projects in terms of investment in the writing process: "*UPSET!* was a lot different for me than the first project I was involved in because the play had a lot more substance and personal resonance for people in the show . . . Growing up in the neighborhood, and seeing things like [the beating] happen to family members and people I know—things like that gave me a greater stake. Also, it was really interesting that even though it happened in Los Angeles, very few young people know about it." For Camilo, the words he was given to speak—he had the longest and most provocative monologue in the play—provided an opportunity to say aloud what he already knew. If there were to be any benchmark for the writer provided by the youth, it would be the one set by Camilo. But then, we want Camilo to grow and be challenged as well.

The writing of the play became a kind of terrain on which each performer might find his or her own arc of growth; we put words in their mouths, so to speak, but words to chew on and digest, not to recite and swallow whole. The Joker System encouraged each cast member to spit out, savor, or chomp their lines over and over in search of some flavor. And while there was, of course, some constraint in the writing (limited time, diverse group, untrained actors, performers with short attention spans and demanding lives), it was not determined by any presumed lack of depth or breadth of knowledge.

Mady: By the end of the process, while I never forgot about the vulnerability of the youth, I was far more struck by their resilience, versatility, and capacity to learn—that is, their inclination to be creative (to employ guesswork, intuition, playfulness) in order to "fill in," or make sense of, whatever seeming gap existed between their everyday world and the imagined world of the play. Ultimately, it wasn't the language I used that would allow or disallow this from happening but rather the pedagogical and artistic environment in which the play was being brought to life. Language was a vehicle, not an end. And with that recognition, the onus shifted from the words on the page to the context of their speech—that is, the Joker System and Plaza as well.

B. J.: Sometimes, when working after school with students between the ages of eleven and seventeen, training takes a secondary place to immediate demands around communication, teamwork, respect, and responsibility. There was one occasion when I needed to conference with two actors under the seating area of the theater because one had called the other a particularly ugly name. It turned out that they had been sniping at each other for several weeks, and the most that could be accomplished was a kind of truce in which they promised that they would avoid contact except when necessary and tone down the rhetoric for the sake of civility. The conflict had little to do with the subject matter of *UPSET!*; these kinds of interactions are givens among the population, especially when the stresses of school, home, and production come together.

In the years between 1995 and 2002, my assistant director in the workshop was Chris Anthony, who taught me a lot about the benefits of introducing "safety in the workplace" training to the youth. The afterschool nature of the program meant that by the time classes began at 6:00 PM, everyone's civility was taxed by emotional, physical, and mental exhaustion, so having some ground rules became increasingly helpful. Check-ins and checkouts became de rigueur as part of the ritual of opening a class.

There was also periodic brainstorming with regard to appropriate behaviors that moved the work forward: behaviors that grew in the "Garden" were listed side by side with behaviors piled in the "Junkyard," ones that undermined forward motion. The youth added to the list based on their own observations, and we referred to the list whenever they were practicing one or the other without entirely realizing it.

The truth is that oppression, of a sort, is built into the tradition of theatre making. Technicians and designers who have had very little exposure to the actors come in and demand a series of tasks as a part of technical and dress rehearsals: wear this costume, stand in this light, speak up, say it again, do it again, quiet backstage—not so much as a please or thank you. It sounds a great deal like the verbal behavior we piled into the junkyard. Not to mention the fact that rehearsals closer to performance bring out the anxieties in everyone, and each person has a particular way of manifesting that stress in usually unattractive and bizarre ways. Where training ends and human relations begin is utterly indecipherable.

> B. J.: A fairly typical scenario: a fourteen-year-old girl comes to rehearsal hiding her new buzz cut and freaking out about what her mother will do. Later, she (wrongly) accuses a gang of backstage actors at Plaza, girls she is intimidated by, of forcing her to stand still while they cut off her hair. The same girl doesn't show up for the final performance at the downtown venue, and several actors—twenty minutes before curtain—figure out what to do with her various roles and lines of dialogue.
>
> Perhaps this is illustrative of how the student actors bring all their training to task, how they function in the face of a crisis after having spent so many months of their lives in the company of people who write down how important good behavior is while working closely with others. They felt that the performance was theirs to save, to keep safe, and they didn't spend one moment pondering the junkyard behavior of their erstwhile colleague; they just turned it into manure for the garden.

The challenges the youth faced with the seriousness of the text—its demands of language, history, and irony—were all in the mix of challenges they were facing with algebra homework and errant boyfriends, sick grandparents, or troubled siblings; they saw it all in the context of a mostly fun and sometimes boring adventure that ended spectacularly with public performances, live music, dancing, and tamales. There was a community safety net as much as a human relations one: they were creating another family with the same sense of obligation and respect for elders who they grew up with in their homes. The push and pull between the outrageousness of what the play was asking and the outrageousness of what theatre requires gave them a place to settle down inside of the storm and ignore some of the demands of teenage life for a while. They cultivated tolerance and respect for each other and, in some cases, enduring friendships, which are fairly positive outcomes in any group activity of such longevity and gravity.

While Plaza is dedicated to creating the most professional performance experience possible given the nonprofessional agenda of the program (Plaza is not a conservatory for theatre training), the subject matter of each play becomes a pedagogical site: they learn about scripts, acting, rehearsing, working together, performing, but, just as importantly, they are introduced to new perspectives through which to envision their lives, their communities, and the lives of many people they will never meet. Simultaneously, they introduce into the theatrical site the perspectives, values, and readings of their everyday life. We consider these dialogic objectives as integral to a youth theatre program as learning a theatrical language and acquiring dramatic skills.

During the year of *UPSET!*, the adult team trusted that the Joker System techniques could hold the subject matter of the play and all it would provoke. We found that it did. It also promised to provide an environment in which several different agendas could commingle: pedagogical, artistic, therapeutic, and activist. Boal's entire oeuvre, in fact, is founded on the false distinctions between these domains. Plaza itself provided another context that only enhanced this interactive agenda. The learning was erratic and immeasurable, different actors awakening to different things (in the realm of history, art, politics, family, self, communication, and, really, who knows what else) at different times. In the end, the goals of artistic training and the goals of human relations were reciprocally beneficial. And on the best days, they were inseparable.

From the opening scene, or *Dedication* to Rosa Parks, to the very final scene of the piece, *UPSET!* tracked a bus motif that, borrowing from Tom Wolfe's famous line from *Electric Kool-Aid Acid Test* ("You're either on the bus or off the bus."), suggested that there is no middle road, that one must act without compromise in accordance with the right set of principles, or you are off the bus. In *UPSET!*, we were lucky to have a real bus in the story to more literally drive home the point. The cast, along with the audience, were being asked—among other things—what they would do if they were in Claudette's shoes. They were also asked to consider larger questions that inform many of our decisions: How do I make choices amid contrary information? Who do I trust in moments of crisis? Am I getting all the information I need from the media, teachers, parents, and community leaders in order to make the right decision? Are the police (and others designated as peacekeepers) around to protect me or to suspect me? Do I have the courage to make the "right" decision given what might be painful consequences? What is the difference between agency and heroics? When is it foolish to perform acts of resistance, and when is it courageous?

For nearly ninety minutes of show time, the teens waited for this bus to arrive having embodied just about every perspective to the riddle of responsibility and ethics that its eventual arrival posed. By the time the bus appeared, most everyone on and off the stage was aware of its significance, but not necessarily certain how they would answer the question, What role do I want to play when this speculative moment on stage manifests itself in my real life? For most of the youth, the "bus" comes by just about every day. What we think the Joker System taught, if anything at all, is that the "bus" is a social predicament; we can only hope that upon "boarding," the youth have a few more aesthetic and critical skills so that they might better recognize, reflect on, and maybe even rock the bus.

Notes

1. The roots of TO lie in carnival and circus, Brechtian theory, and the pedagogical philosophy of Paulo Freire. In carnival and circus, Boal found public engagement, merriment, multiple voices and interpretations, inversions and reversals, clowns, irreverence, and popular forms of satire. In Brecht, he found outrage, critical distance from (and analysis of) the social roles we play, and an invitation to live in the ambiguous and fertile terrain between thought and action, reality and illusion, the ordinary and the strange. In Freire, Boal found dialogue, the belief that the marginalized are central to the structure of society, and a pedagogy predicated on an ever-changing, performative reality. Boal shared with Freire an understanding of praxis—the inseparability of reflection and action, theory and practice—in pursuit of social change.

2. Colvin was quoted as saying, "What closure can there be for me? There is no closure . . . We still don't have all that we should have . . . They took away my life. If they want closure, they should give it to my grandchildren" (Colvin, cited in Younge 2000).

3. Handheld neutral masks were used to identify the black and white passengers on the bus and to purposefully signify the harsh racial duality of mid-century Alabama.

4. It may be helpful at this point for readers to get a synopsis of the play: Claudette Colvin, who has never received acknowledgment for her act of resistance, comes to hijack the show from Rodney King, someone who is getting a lot of attention for having done, in Claudette's opinion, nothing very remarkable for the civil rights movement. As each of their stories unfold, the audience learns about the historical complexities of racism and resistance in U.S. history and meets a slew of characters including Homer Plessy, Rosa Parks, Emmett Till, Medgar Evers, Fannie Lou Hamer, Malcolm X, and Donald Rumsfeld, just to name a few.

   The primary scenes in Rodney's story are the beating, the trial of the four policemen, and the ensuing uprising when a not-guilty verdict came down a year later. The primary scenes in Claudette's story are her defiance on the Montgomery bus, her relationship to Rosa Parks, and her being abandoned by black leadership for being too young, too black, and too outspoken.

   Every scene is witnessed by a Chorus that interrogates the characters; no one is immune to a cross-examination. The Joker, as commentator, actor (he plays the judge), and member of the Chorus, interviews, lectures, mocks, talks to the audience, and offers biting and trenchant repartee about the historical past and current state of social injustice.

   By the end of the play, Claudette receives her due with a full-cast 1950s rock-gospel number honoring her courage in 1955, after which she and Rodney, united as the odd couple in their status as antiheroes, give the audience a lesson in civil disobedience. Well, Claudette does, and Rodney, giving activism a try for Claudette's sake, follows her lead.

5. The South Central Farm refers to fourteen acres of vacant land in South Central Los Angeles, offered by the City of Los Angeles to neighborhood citizens as a site for community healing after the riots of 1992. Over fourteen years, the land

was cultivated by local residents into what was presumed to be the largest urban farm in the nation.

6. Reginald Denny was the white truck driver who was pulled from his cab and brutally beaten during the uprisings in 1992.

7. An interesting sidenote is that the understudy Joker, Hector C., understood that Gabriel was the person who got the role that he didn't get and wanted, and Hector's natural sense of competition added a frisson to their encounters on stage, underscoring the notion that the Joker's position, like everyone else's, had the possibility of shifting.

8. The black history lessons were embedded in a dramatically modified simulation of the TV show *Wheel of Fortune*. Rather than a pie of dollar amounts and prizes, our wheel was a demographic pie of the United States divided by skin colors, the largest slice being white. Contestants would spin, and a character named the Spin Doctor appeared out of nowhere to assure that the pointer always landed within the black sliver. Vanna White's character would then narrate another miserable saga of racial injustice. It was, indeed, a very long scene.

9. The five focal points were (1) officers and their attorneys, (2) Rodney and his lawyer, (3) the Judge and Claudette (as court recorder) and whoever was on the stand, (4) the enormous jury that changed nightly as people missed rehearsals (though rarely performances) and who wore extremely eye-catching masks (held on dowels) painted in black, and (5) the screen on which the video of the beatings played.

10. Interestingly, many youth were able to translate their understanding of this gang-like violence to systemic violence. They came to understand that when the Spin Doctor spins history, *everybody* is oppressed—police, citizens, courts, media, privileged, and marginalized alike—and that we all lose when we don't acknowledge and challenge how poverty, ignorance, and racism distort the functioning of a democratic society.

References

Boal, A. 1979. *Theatre of the oppressed*. Trans. C. A. and M-O. L. McBride. New York: Theatre Communications Group.

Dodge, B. J. Forthcoming, 2010. *Plaza de la Raza*. Valencia, CA: Community Arts Partnership, CalArts.

Rohd, M. 1998. Theatre for community conflict and dialogue: The Hope is Vital training manual. Portsmouth, NH: Heinemann Drama.

Schutzman, M. .2006. *UPSET!* Los Angeles, CA: REDCAT (Roy and Edna Disney/CalArts Theater), Community Arts Partnership, CalArts.

Schutzman, M., and others. 2006. Unpublished roundtable interview, Los Angeles, CA.

Younge, G. 2000. She would not be moved. *Guardian Unlimited*, November 7, 2008. http://www.guardina.co.uk/lifeandstyle/2000/dec/16/weekend.garyyounge.

13

The Human Art

An Interview on Theatre of the Oppressed and Youth with Augusto Boal

Peter Duffy

When I first read *Games for Actors and Non-Actors*, I was a young high school English and drama teacher in rural Maine. My practice was heavily influenced already by Paulo Freire, so when I read Boal, it felt more like a homecoming than an introduction to a stranger. *Games for Actors and Non-Actors* and Boal's other books gave me a much-needed vocabulary to attempt what I always surmised theatre had the potential to achieve, though I didn't have the personal experience or the vision to imagine myself.

When, at the end of the preface, I read, "Theatre is a form of knowledge; it should and can also be a means of transforming society. Theatre can help us build our future, rather than just waiting for it" (xxxi), I knew I was reading a book that would change my practice and myself. Boal's words ignited a specific sense of purpose and practice to a more generalized hunch that I had about theatre up until that point. I was moved to apply the work not just to oppressive situations in adult lives but to question how these same techniques could be used with youth as well. I started handing the book around to a couple of juniors and seniors at the school where I taught, and through this reading and sharing, a group of students and I formed an interactive theatre troupe based on Theatre of the Oppressed (TO) in 1999.

Our goal was to expand the discourse beyond what was the traditional "interactive theatre" model I was seeing at schools around the country. The discourse norm at the time was to have troupes of young actors perform scenarios for student audiences and the audience would then have a chance to interview the actors, still in character, about why they did what they did. It ended up like a Jerry Springer show with the audience members enjoying the ability to verbally assault the choices of the characters. Little was unearthed about how to go about the same situation differently, how to explore alternatives that came from the audience in any sort of meaningful and liberatory way. I had a deep sense that the theatrical experience could be different from this, and I was desperate to find other practitioners who were doing similar work with teens.

In an effort to move our troupe's work beyond feel good, "why can't we call just get along" school-based drama, I went to the TO conference in Omaha, Nebraska, in 1997. I found few other like-minded people whose sole focus was on youth. I briefly met Andrew Burton, who does some truly remarkable work with teens in Canada with a troupe called Street Spirits Theatre Company. After I met him, I knew not only that TO could be done with teens but it must also be done with them. The more I steeped myself into the theory and spoke with Boal and other practitioners, the more it became clear that working with teens was fairly new to the language of TO work.

The following are excerpts from two interviews I conducted with Augusto Boal. The first was in April 23, 2004, in Omaha, Nebraska, and the other was a phone interview conducted on May 9, 2008, between New York and Brazil.

Peter: You speak often about the power of the metaphor. How do you see TO as a method or tool to help students metaphorize their own lives?

Augusto: I believe that all of those techniques of Image Theatre are extremely effective to work with children. Why? Because the children, even if they learn a lot, they have a very limited vocabulary. And sometimes they don't know how to articulate their thoughts well. If you ask them a question in English, though they know many words, they will tell you only approximately what they mean. But if you ask them in image, they are going to build their own vocabulary. They don't have to learn a vocabulary because they have to invent a vocabulary. The image is invented. And then, as the image is invented, it's more precise because they say exactly what they want to say in image whereas they can only approximate in words. Many times I made Forum Theatre beginning with images. And only at the end are they going to speak. For instance, I remember one day I was working with fifty children that came from all over Brazil in a congress of children that were organized by adults evidently and financed by adults. But the children held the meetings, the round tables among themselves.

We started by talking, and it was very difficult to talk, because we did not know exactly who came from where, the conditions of life. They were children of the street. But the streets are different. In the south, it is very cold; in the north, it is very warm, so it makes it difference—the climate, the wealth, or the poverty of the city where they live. And then I asked them to make images of family. And they started making images of family, and, in some way, they looked very much alike—the north, the south, the west, and the east. While they made their image of their representation of family, I asked them to stand still and start speaking their inner thoughts. Each child in an image impersonated someone else in their image—a father, a mother, a brother . . . Each one could think about what that character is thinking at that moment and speak out loud their thoughts. Then I said, "Now, action!" like a photo that becomes a movie. And they did it, and then we saw the family that exists inside the family. Then I said, "OK, let's take that as a model and let's make a Forum about that."

It was very easy because we used the image. If I started by saying, "Look, let's discuss his family," the discussion, relying on words, would be so intense and people would not understand. If you use the word "mother," for example, you might intend to communicate the mother that you had or the mother that you know. If everyone has a different construction of the word "mother" in their minds, the discussion would take a long time and never say precisely what they wanted. So I think the image—the Image of the Word, the Image of the Counterimage, all those techniques—are a shortcut to go to what they really feel and think. It is a shortcut from emotional to communication.

Now, not too long ago I was in England and I was having difficulty [facilitating a group of young people]. There were children there with mental challenges, which made it even more difficult. I was working with Julian, my son, and Julian proposed, "Why don't you use Image Theatre with them?" And then we started doing the Great Game of Power, which is a game that is, I would not say is complicated, but is a game in which you have to look at each part of the image and try to feel that part of the image. You have to play with the whole image, sometimes a complex image. The young people played it very easily, whereas before they were having problems expressing their ideas through words. So all the techniques that you use, predominantly images, as they are the creators of the images, they don't have to remember what does that image mean. It means what it is, it is there. The signifier is the signification at the same time—that's what I believe, that Image Theatre is the best to start with.

Peter: One question that students asked me on the way home from a workshop we held with students from another school is, "We've created these images. The students from the other school were excited about what they were able to communicate about their school to their teachers through the image. But the kids are still in the same system. How much can really change if they are still in the same institution?" So, Augusto, what would you say to the students I work with about the dilemma they feel about the limits of the change the students in the school can create?

Augusto: That's a problem of not just those children but of all those people who do Forum Theatre or TO in general and then they don't have the means of extrapolating real life—what they have found or discovered to be their desire, their needs—there is not a ready answer for that because you're talking about a school, but the schools are so different from one another. Sometimes by talking to the principal, to their parents, or to their neighbors, I don't know, you might get allies.

What we feel always is that sometimes the oppressed allow themselves to be oppressed, or they facilitate the oppression because they insist on being alone, in fighting alone. But what I would tell those children, those young people, is try to find allies. Where can you find allies—among the teachers, among the parents, the family, the neighborhood, among whom? It's the idea of finding allies, because if you are alone, you are much more easily dominated. I don't like to give advice very much, but if I had to give advice, I'd say, look for allies and then fight together. It's not you and me; it's us and them. So, in order to be able to say "we," you have to first be able to say "I," but you cannot say "I" or "me" alone without going to "us." You have to go to "we" and "we" can include other people who are not students. The parents, the teachers, and the principal could all be allies. Because if it's a situations that's bad for the children, it's going to be bad for the parents of the children, the family of the children, and for the school. It's bad for everyone, not only for children. It's not an antagonistic conflict in which the children, if they have their will, are going to make the principal or teacher lose power; no, it's not antagonistic. When it's antagonistic, yes, one or the other has to win over their opponent. But in this case, I don't use the concrete case, the concrete situation, but that's generally speaking. The only thing I can do is to speak generally because I don't know the school, I don't know the kids, I know the wonderful kids you brought to Milwaukee last year, Peter, but generalities are all I can use without knowing a specific situation.

Peter: You've said you don't work all that often with children, but when you do work with children, do you find yourself having to think about the exercises differently, or do you have to change what you do at all in order to reach them? How do you find yourself working differently?

Augusto: No, with children, I only avoid games in which they have to touch each other's bodies too much. Because sometimes they are in puberty, their bodies are changing, and they are very much ashamed of their bodies. Their bodies are not yet what they want them to be yet they are no longer what they were before. They don't want to be touched. And adults sometimes have the same problem, but mostly they accept more easily. So the only thing I avoid is the touching—excessively touching—exercises.

But what I learned working from a group of children with physical challenges is that we should not censor ourselves in proposing exercises or the game. We should say, "Look, no one is forced to do it. You're not obliged to do anything, but try."

But there is one difference. There is a game, a very intense game, of pushing against one another frontally, then in the back, and then sitting down and standing up—always pushing against one another. It requires some strength and some ability. And I had many people in the group who were in wheelchairs. The organizer of the workshop, Tim Wheeler, who is a friend of mine who directs a group for disabled people in Bradford, England, said to me, when I told him I'd like to do that game with them but I was afraid, Tim said to me, "Don't be afraid. They're going to adapt the way they can." And then I proposed the game. I said do that the way you can, and, to my astonishment, even the people in wheelchairs did the exercise.

The point of the exercise was the same for these students. Of course they did not have the same dexterity, the same force, as those without these physical challenges had. But I don't censor myself. If I feel that the majority has a big problem [with a certain activity], I don't propose that. But, generally, as they have total liberty to accept or not to, I've never asked why you don't want to do it. If they say, "I don't want to do it," then I say, "Don't do it. Sit down and observe the others." I prefer that everyone participates, and sometimes I insist a little bit but I never force participants. And then they feel that I respect them and then they respect themselves too. And I respect myself also.

Peter: Have you ever used Rainbow of Desire Techniques with children?

Augusto: Rainbow? No, but I will, I will. Especially those techniques like the Analytical Image, Image and Counterimage. These are techniques that do not provoke people emotionally too much. I will do it, certainly.

Peter: Do you see any distinction between TO with adults and TO with youth? And what direction do you see your work with children going?

Augusto: No, I don't, I don't. I think it's theatre. I don't separate it. Like I said, some games you don't use because they are not so useful, but no matter with whom you're working, you always have to choose the games that you believe the group is going to profit from. Even if they are only adults, you have to choose; you don't pick any kind of exercise at any moment; you see the moment then you say, "Now it's good to do this exercise," [you observe] the atmosphere [and judge what's most appropriate]. I don't say, "For children it's only this special arsenal." We don't have a special arsenal for children, a special arsenal for women, an arsenal for men, an arsenal for white people, an arsenal for black people. There is no difference, because it is a human art. It's for everyone.

What I have found more interesting—and this is not specifically for adults, but for children as well—is to work with children in prison. If you see a child in prison, he usually comes from the slums where he is a participants in [drug] gangs and trafficking. The problem for many of these children is that from the time they are born they hear, see, and experience things that show them that their lives are not important. And if they believe that they are going to die before they are twenty-five years old, they don't appreciate being alive. Many of these children feel, OK, now you are alive but you're going to die soon. They don't have the horror of dying that most of us have. We don't want to die. But they take that as a fatality. So when they do plays, the first ideas that come to their heads are plays of killing—killing the judge, killing the prosecutor, killing the guard—because that's what they are used to. Then, a few days ago, the chief of a gang—one of the biggest gangs in Rio—was killed by the police. He was twenty-six years old. He was a big chief and had enormous power because it's a lot of money that's circulating through his gang. Of course, the big ones that get the money, they do not live in the slums. Maybe they are living here in the United States, in Paris, in other countries where they are secure. But the people there also manage lots of money, and they know that they are gong to die at any moment. So it's very difficult to work with them. From them came the idea of the Subjunctive Theatre. Of course, when you present a Forum model, you subjectively ask them, If it were to be like this, how could it be otherwise? In case the Forum is only about killing the guards or the prosecutor, we use the subjunctive model. We pose the idea, if killing the guard were never an option, how else could you fight your oppression? We don't tell them that their alternatives in the Forum are wrong. We question our model, not their solutions or alternatives. But as I don't have very frequent work with children, I don't have many specific examples. But whatever I would do with adults, I would do with children too.

Peter: How do you approach about using TO with young people in systems that are top-down and often oppressive?

Augusto: We never change the methodology. We explain, we dialogue, we have a conversation, then we start the exercises, the games, the techniques of Image to Forum, and then we prepare the real Forum. That's always the same; in the beginning, in those cases. Now we also use Aesthetics of the Oppressed. In this, [young people] have to paint and make sculptures, which are the images. But they also have to use sounds and make rhythms, whatever music they can create and the words. They have to write poetry. These methods are always the same. It doesn't matter if we are working, for instance, with children or the Royal Shakespeare Company. The work is the same. That's the way the TO is, and they are free to say yes or no, to go away; the doors are open.

When I work with children who've been arrested, I know that whatever they are going to say in the presence of the guards can be used against them. So I avoid doing anything or making them do something that can be taken against them. So we try to discuss not exactly the conflict they have with those people, but there are indirect ways in which we can deal with that. You can use fables, you can use metaphors, but you cannot to talk directly so that they are beaten by the guards. They cannot really talk directly in front of the guards because they are going to be beaten even more. We will try to show them their suffering and how to fight against their suffering. We cannot point at the guards and say, "You are the ones." That is the only precaution I take with them.

In *Don Quixote*, there is a scene in which the boss is beating a child. And then Don Quixote comes in. The boss stops, and Don Quixote tells the man to stop that and to never do that again. He makes a big speech about not beating children and that children deserve our respect. The man kneels down and asks for forgiveness and says, "I'll never do that again." And then Don Quixote is very happy because he has obtained what he wanted—a promise from the man to never beat a child again. Then Don Quixote goes away, and, of course, the man beats the child again. So we don't do like Don Quixote. We go there [to the jail] and are happy that we have done a good deed, but this good deed could be against the children. So, you have to take those precautions. Not with the method, because the method cannot change. There is a method; you cannot change that. So it is the way it is, no?

Mostly, in those cases, we stick to the TO method of Forum Theater and Aesthetics of the Oppressed. I don't go beyond that. I don't get into Rainbow of Desire or other techniques that are more complex. But if we work with peasants about land disputes, we work the same way. We don't make a different TO for each category of people. We have a method, but the method is for the people to use and not for us to impose.

The important thing in the TO is the oppressed. The theater is the Theater of the Oppressed and not the Oppressed of the Theater. So we have to take care of the human beings with whom we work.

Peter: Sometimes, in Forum work, when young people can't think of alternatives, all they can think to do is to replay the oppression. Is that something that you've come across or witnessed? And if so, what have you done about it?

Augusto: No, I haven't encountered that. When we work with young people, sometimes we don't even use the word *oppression*. Many times, they don't know what oppression is. It's useless to tell them "Define oppression," or to say that oppression when dialogues become monologues. If you talk too much, maybe they won't understand what you're saying.

I remember one day in France when I was using the word *oppression* with children. I asked, "What are your oppressions?" And one child said, "I don't have any oppressions." So I said, "So your life is OK and you don't have any problems?" And the child said, "*No, oppressions I don't have, but I have a lot of* [French expression that means something like "shit on me"]. Yes, that is what I have." So I said, "OK, let's talk about it. Who shits on you? Let's talk about that." I think that we have to use words that maybe they don't know but that they can learn. Because it's not that I think that you should limit yourself only to the words that they know. Sometimes their vocabulary is very small. Take a word like protagonist. If they are twelve years old, they might not know what a protagonist or antagonist is, or what contradiction is, but they can learn those words. They can master them. So we explain what a protagonist is, what an antagonist is. But we cannot expect them to keep in their minds what catharsis is—it's more difficult. As long as you can use words that they can apprehend, and then *use*, that's what we will do. So we want to enlarge their vocabulary, but we don't want to enlarge it by putting words in their heads by force. If we feel that they understand, it's good because every word is irreplaceable, every word has a meaning. In fact, I always say that words are means of transportation—like a plane or a truck. They transport meaning. But, you know a truck is a truck, and a plane is a plane. Every word has its own personality. You can change the meaning, but every word has its personality.

So this is what we do. We try to explain to them that nothing in the world is so easy. And so maybe they have uneasiness. What are the moments of uneasiness for them? Or maybe they feel that they are limited, so we try to find the words that they understand and then we introduce new words that they can come to understand and utilize.

But in Forum, we speak through metaphor. A Forum scene is a metaphor of reality; it is not reality—and that's why you can use violence in a Forum scene without really being physically violent. You can talk about violence without the violence. In the past in cave paintings, when people painted a lion, the painting was not dangerous. They could understand the painting and the lion without having to look at the lion face to face. So the theatre is the same. You make a metaphor that is a scene. You look at that scene, you understand what the represented reality really means. And so if you do your work well, there is no danger at all that they are going to reproduce the oppression. The audience is going to understand the oppression in a metaphorical way—which is the art. All art is a metaphor. We have to make sure that the production of the Forum scene should be really correct, should be gratifying for them—be they children or peasants, workers or teachers, or whoever.

Peter: So suppose you're working on a Forum scene about bullying. What do you do if the people offering alternatives cannot come up with an alternative that will break the cycle of harassment or violence? What can you do to help expand the imagination of the moment to explore alternatives aside from the ones that have already been tried—which might look more like bullying than a ceasing of the bullying?

Augusto: Well look, I believe the method itself helps them because if one person goes there and tries to break the oppression and is not successful, another person is going to try another idea, a third one a third idea, and so forth. Remember that the idea of the Forum is not necessarily to get a really good recipe, but how can you make a good recipe for those situations? Sometimes we have arrived at a very good idea like *if this happens, you do that*. But Forum, most of the time, is a way to make them think—not to take anything for granted, but to think that everything is changing, everything is modifiable. But I trust the method. The Forum is conducted by the Joker. If the Joker allows the people to come onstage and act out their ideas, then the Joker must stimulate the thinking of the children to find a new solution. The Joker should encourage the spect-actors to explain the meaning of the intervention. If you do good joker-ing, I believe that, inevitably, the audience will get much more excited. That's the main difference between the normal theatre and TO. Because usually, you go to a theatre, you see an image of the world, and that's the way it is. You cannot modify it. And so we do the opposite. In Forum Theatre, we say, "Look, this is the way it has been up until now. How would you like it to be from now on?" So some ideas always come. I have never seen a Forum in which people get depressed. Sometimes it's exactly the opposite. They get too excited, too euphoric, that you have to stop and calm everyone down so that you can analyze each idea slowly so that you can understand them.

Peter: What do you want young TO practitioners to know or learn about TO when they use it with groups of young people?

Augusto: I want them to know everything! That's why I wrote all of those books! But I'd want them to read the first draft of *Aesthetics of the Oppressed*. But it was a first draft, and now I am working on a better version, a bigger version. I am trying to make the real book, and it's very hard to put into words the experiences I've been having now with the Aesthetics of the Oppressed.

It is true that, if you are going to use TO in therapeutic work, I say, "OK, you go to *Rainbow of Desire* because that's where you have most of the techniques that are introspective techniques, no?" Now, right now, my company is working on developing new techniques. Just a few weeks ago, we finished creating a new technique, a totally new technique, in which you go from the most inner technique like "Cop in the Head" into the Forum Theatre. We follow it the whole way.

But anyway, if there are people interested in the psychology and inner life of people, I say *Forum Theatre* is OK, *Invisible Theatre* can be OK,

Legislative Theatre can be OK, but mainly go to *Rainbow of Desire*. If you are a politician or work politically, then you go to *Legislative Theatre* and *Forum Theatre*. If you are more in school, for instance, I often use *Image Theatre* and all the techniques of *Image Theatre*; sometimes the simplest ones are the most effective. But TO is like a big tree. It has many branches, so it depends on what you want. For teachers, I would say mostly *Image Theatre* and *Forum Theatre*, but not *Rainbow of Desire*. It's not so useful. *Legislative Theatre*? I don't know, it may be helpful. If you have a teacher in a concrete situation in which there are oppressions, maybe you want to fight against them, maybe you want to change the law, so go to *Legislative Theatre*. In this tree, you have to see which fruit you want to pick up because it produces many different kinds of fruits.

Peter: I've been speaking with people recently who are thinking about ways of using TO as a means to engage the oppressor as well. They are thinking about ways to use the techniques that will both illuminate the oppressor's actions as well as give the oppressed alternatives for how to work their way through a given situation. Chen Alon, a former Israeli soldier and now member of Combatants for Peace, was telling me recently that there was a time that he didn't see himself as an oppressor. And once he saw that, he was able to move with more awareness toward not acting oppressively in working in the Israeli army. I know that there has been some conversation around engaging the oppressor. What is your thinking about that now?

Augusto: A few months ago, I saw a DVD that was done in Israel by Chen Alon. This man is a refusenik and was an officer in the army who left the army because he said he would not massacre the Palestinians. And then he was arrested, of course, like many other refuseniks, but when he came out, he got in touch with TO and he decided to make Forum Theatre about checkpoints and take those plays to schools for young people. By young I mean ten, twelve, fourteen years old. It is marvelous because you see young children, they take the place of a woman who is pregnant and she wants to go to the other side of the checkpoint to have the baby. But when she gets to the checkpoint, they have so much bureaucracy there that she almost has the baby there, at the checkpoint. And then he takes this scene, which is based on real facts and has happened more than once, and asks the children to replace the woman. And they do! They replace the woman. It is very beautiful to see how they can understand the other side. So, they are not the oppressors themselves, the children, of course not, but they belong to a system that is oppressive for the Palestinians who have to go from here to there. They have to go from checkpoint to checkpoint to checkpoint. So, in this case, I believe that it is something very wonderful.

There is a group here in Brazil that uses TO with men who have beaten their wives or partners, and the group helps them try to understand why they did that and use TO to help them do that. So they are the oppressors, but they make Forum Theatre to try to look at their situation and to ask, What would you have done? And they are, all of them, oppressors. The only one who is not an oppressor was one of my assistants who works with me here, and the oppressors play the situation out and the other men who are also oppressors or have been oppressors of their wives or partners replace the oppressed and try to analyze what happened to them that makes this monstrosity that is to beat a woman whom you supposedly love. So this, I believe, is perfect to work with oppressors of that kind who are willing to change. The examples from Israel, from this men's group, and from other places like in prisons shows excellent work with oppressors. Sometimes you work with prisoners, sometimes you work with guards. The guards are the oppressors, but by playing prisoners they understand the situation, they humanize the relationship, and that, I think, is OK. It's good, no?

But, at the same time, I know of some groups, and happily there are not so many, who use some games and techniques of the TO to reinforce oppression. For instance, they tell workers they should feel grateful because they have a job—even though they are exploited, they have a job. They use the techniques in favor of the enterprises, of the corporations. And this, I believe, is treason. That is something abominable; I hate that.

You see, psychoanalysis is a beautiful, wonderful form of helping people. But it can be used to oppress as well. Psychoanalysis was used in dictatorships in Latin America, and perhaps in other places too, where they had denounced the patients. That is treason. You cannot do that. That is something horrible. I despise those kinds of people. Why is it wrong? Because they take formalized elements and they forget that if the TO is a tree, it has roots. And the roots are in the ethics. That's where they get their nutrients for the tree; it's from years of ethical behavior. If you don't have ethical behavior, then you are a traitor. Maybe people exploiting the techniques is something that can't be avoided, but it is something I despise.

Peter: There is another way to be a traitor to the techniques, I think, and that is to give up on them. I've been doing a lot of work with teachers recently in New York City. These teachers work in economically depressed neighborhoods and are feeling the weight of a dysfunctional system pressing down on them. They are tired of having to fight so hard to help kids "make something of their lives." I was doing an Image Theatre workshop with teachers recently, and they kept on talking about the apathy of young people and how young people just don't care. What would you say to teachers who feel like they are working so hard, but their students just don't care about changing their lives?

Augusto: Look, remember those experiments that were done on mice, where a mouse is put a meter away from a piece of cheese? Then the mouse smells the cheese and runs toward it to eat it. When it gets close enough, something blocks the mouse's way, and he cannot eat the cheese. The second time the experiment is done, the same thing is done, but the mouse will try a new way to get to the cheese. This time he goes up the middle now, and when he gets close to the cheese, it gets blocked again. After a while, you could show the mouse all the cheese you want, and if it gets blocked often enough, the mouse does not move toward it anymore.

So those children who are *apathetic* in reality are having almost a Pavlovian reaction. They try, they try, and they try, but they never get anything. Why should they believe these teachers now? That's why we always start with small games, simple games. Because if they do a simple game and they like it, they start wanting more. But if you come to them and say, "You have to change your lives!" and you make a big speech about transforming the world, they are going to look at you like the mouse looks at the cheese and say, "OK, the cheese smells very good, but I can't ever get there. Why should I care?" But if you start with things that give them pleasure, all children like to play. Even if they are sick, they like to play. They don't want to accept what the teacher proposed to them. But they have their own ways of playing. If you go to their ways playing and see what they are playing and you try to modify to make it clear to them what it means, and slowly and lovingly make them understand what you are proposing, I believe that they will come with you. I believe but that is only in our experience. Even when we worked with children who were sent away from the school to a special school for those who had failed, we have seen it work. We worked in France with kids with drug addiction and who were mentally and psychologically challenged. It is much harder than if the people come to you and they want to do everything that you say, they jump on it—that's wonderful. But sometimes they look at you and they don't trust you. You have to give them a reason to trust you first.

References

Boal, Augusto. 1992. *Games for Actors and Non-Actors*. London: Routledge.

Afterword

Snacking on the Moment

The Drama of "Working Through" Oppression with Kids

Glenn M. Hudak

First of all, I want to thank Peter Duffy for inviting me to provide a final comment on the manuscripts in this volume on Theatre of the Oppressed (TO) and youth. As Peter and I discussed my contribution, we thought it would be helpful to give the reader another "take" on TO from someone outside the theatre community. As a philosopher of education, my task is to investigate diverse systems of thought to aid the contributors and readers alike in our efforts to reconceptualize what we mean by education and, more specifically—as Paulo Freire would affirm—to humanize schooling for children in particular. In this afterword, I do not intend to review the chapters but rather to address the text from my current research interest: psychoanalytic theory and its relevance for TO.

Besides being a philosopher, I have also been trained at the Harlem Family Institute (HFI) in New York City and received a diploma in psychoanalytic psychotherapy. I bring in these biographic facts as they help frame my discussion of TO and its relevance for humanizing schooling for children, especially children in economically poor neighborhoods, like Harlem. When I interned at HFI, the curriculum consisted of three interrelated components: the study of the classics and contemporary psychoanalytic thinking; self-analysis (if one is going to be a therapist, one needs to work through his or her own transference issues); and a clinical component where interns worked with students in Harlem under careful supervision. The motivating idea behind HFI, as I understand it, is that kids in economically poor communities (the oppressed) would benefit from the therapeutic setting, allowing them to work through the oppressive and often traumatic effects of poverty. At the time I attended, there was no tuition at HFI; rather, faculty and staff donated their time and efforts to train interns, and, in turn, we donated our time to work with kids within the school setting. In short, the mission of HFI was to bring therapy into the social justice arena—by working with children in oppressive school, family, and community situations.

Clearly, there are similarities and differences between my HFI experience and TO. One similarity is the clear commitment by TO and HFI to work with kids in oppressive situations; one can say that alongside a theatre of *the* oppressed, there is also a therapy of *the* oppressed exhibited by the mission of HFI. Regarding the differences, TO is political and public, while HFI is personal and private; the obvious difference in this undertaking with kids is that TO is more overtly political in its orientation as its efforts are directed at unmasking "oppression" in a public forum with an audience. HFI's encounter with kids, on the other hand, is personal and private, focusing exclusively on the events of the child's life, which often times revolved around "traumatic" personal events; and while poverty is oppressive, seldom did I employ the term "oppression" in our private sessions. All this is to say that, as Peter Duffy illustrates, TO moves from an "I" to a "we," while, for the most part, the therapeutic sessions at HFI focus primarily on the "I"—enabling the kids to successfully navigate through their daily lives at school and home.

At HFI, I worked primarily with adolescents: mostly children of color, all facing the harsh realities not only of economic poverty but also the trauma of substance abuse in families, physical abuse in foster homes, and violence in school, such as bullying and beyond. Unfortunately, in my experience I found that there were teachers and administrators who unjustly labeled many adolescents as "trouble makers," "losers," and so on; fortunately, however, there were many committed teachers and principals who were glad to work with HFI interns like myself.

While it would be wrong to say that the adolescents I worked with experienced no joy or laughter, often times, however, they endured serious challenges and struggles in silent despair without adult guidance. Often they "internalized" (to employ a term used both in TO and HFI sessions) their oppression in concrete ways—manifesting it as rage, anger, and violence aimed at themselves and others. I remember one adolescent who had been working with me. Over the course of her life, she had "internalized" a great deal of anger and rage over school and family situations where she felt she had little or no control. Often, she would be brought before the assistant principal for disciplinary reasons. Initially, our sessions were difficult, to say the least, in that they focused around issues of trust. Why should she trust me, her therapist, with the personal details of her life story? As the semester went on, we worked through the "transference" of her mistrust of me and her mistrust of any adult in her life. As she began to slowly articulate, or name her world—to work through the transference—it became evident to her that those closest to her denied her a "voice" in many matters in her life. Her foster parents and her boyfriend often told her what to do, giving her little room to express her own needs. At one meeting toward the end of our sessions, she declared that she would break up with her boyfriend and that she needed some "space" to take control over her own life. After this pronouncement, I remember a long silence between us. At some point, I stated, "I hear you." She looked at me and began to cry. Then said, "You're the first person who has ever really heard me!"

This was a breakthrough moment for her as she experienced being heard—really being heard—in a meaningful manner, perhaps for the first time in a long while. For myself, I realized intellectually and emotionally just how rewarding and valuable my work was: to stand with those oppressed, those traumatized by hard social and economic conditions; to work through with them the unconscious structures of their lived-experience; and to allow them to articulate their "truth." That is, the point of our therapeutic encounters was not only to provide a simple cognitive understanding of oppression and trauma but also to "unconceal" (as I shall explain later) the structure of their lived-experience as a moment of truth about their lives.

What is one's lived-experience? While the term "lived-experience" is often used as a *descriptor*, a term to describe the events of one's existential world, it is important to also note that "lived-experience" has *structure* to it, and this structure reveals the "moment of truth" of the event. Within the psychoanalytic tradition, we can say that the psychic dimensions of lived-experience are framed within concepts such as "transference" and the "working through" of, for example, bullying. Indeed, this notion of "truth," while said differently within the psychoanalytic tradition, is nonetheless evident in Johnny Saldaña's chapter as he states that the goal of his project with kids, "was to provide children opportunities through TO to explore how their personal oppressions, such as the victimization from bullying, could be recognized and dealt with in the classroom and on the playground" (p. 45, in this volume). The "truth" of one's lived-experience structures one's experience of schooling and where—if not addressed—one may relive this trauma over and over again throughout his or her adult life.

What is this subjective "truth" that I'm making reference to? In *Dialectic of Freedom*, Maxine Greene quotes a verse from poet Muriel Rukeyser: "What would happen if one woman told the truth about her life? The world would split open" (1988, 57). Indeed, when the children and teachers in this text on TO and youth tell their "truths," the world does split open, as Elinor Vettraino, for example, writes: "Watching her [Dana] sitting on the floor, hugging her knees to her chest, reminded me of all the times that I had felt squashed as a child, unable to move, trapped by my own fears, and without my own voice. And yet here she was, aged nine, more eloquent about her pain in her stillness and silence than I am in the writing of this. If I needed another example of the power of Theatre of the Oppressed (TO), then here it was, in Technicolor" (p. 63, in this volume).

Here the complete picture is complex and multilayered, yet, as a reader, I felt myself empathizing with her experience, as I too have felt "squashed as a child," and I felt myself sympathizing with her desire to face her own experience as she worked with Dana. For me, Vettraino's experience was poignant as it expressed how painful and perhaps disorientating it is to face one's own subjective "truths" about one's life, even as new spaces of understanding are "unconcealed" within the TO setting.

Maxine Greene writes, "To 'unconceal' is to create clearings, spaces in the midst of things where decisions can be made. It is to break through the masked and falsified, to reach toward what is also half-hidden or concealed. When a woman, when any human being, tries to tell the truth and act on it, there is no predicting what will happen" (1988, 58). Psychoanalysis James Grotstein also writes on the trauma of "truth" as a moment of "unconcealment." Goldstein asks, "How much truth can the subject tolerate at any given moment?" (2003, 223). Here he tells us, far from a philosophical proposition, that we can only emotionally process the truth of the moment in small doses. Unconcealing, lifting the mask of one's experience of being bullied (see, for example, Saldaña), is both disorientating and painful and is most likely to be avoided, if possible. From another perspective, Buddhist nun Pema Chodron observes, "When the bottom falls out and we can't find anything to grasp, it hurts a lot . . . We might have some romantic view of what [this] means, but when we are nailed with the truth, we suffer" (1997, 7). Indeed, to process trauma—the trauma of schooling—we need some "falsehoods" to aid in digesting the truth of the event. I found in the chapters of this book many examples of TO providing just enough dramatic "falsehood"—imagination to allow the kids to reexperience their traumas at a safe distance.

Now as I read Augusto Boal's *Rainbow of Desire* (1995), I discern many places of confluence between the work of TO and my work at HFI. Not only do both programs work within the school context to address the oppressive (and traumatic) in the lives of kids and adolescents, but they also share at places a common political-therapeutic goal: to work through the internalization of oppression (and trauma). Indeed, Boal draws upon the therapeutic discourse as he employs such terms as internalization, introspection, and projection (1995, 23–25, 68–69). Likewise, as I read this manuscript, I found many passages that mirror, in my estimation, the spirit of HFI. In particular,

I was moved by Peter Duffy's (Chapter 10, "From I to We," in this text) heart-felt realization that

> the power of the work created in that Bronx classroom came when the students, the classroom teacher, and I were all able to recognize that each of us has "internalized the image" of our oppressors (Freire 1970, 29). The profoundly humanizing realization that we are all burdened from within took weeks to uncover, and it united us in ways that allowed us to name our oppressions and to work through a few of them . . . Along with learning names can come another essential ingredient to doing this work: trust. We must develop trust within the group—trust among the young people and the facilitator, trust in ourselves . . . If we trust that we can shape our world, then that is the first step toward its transformation. In order to get there, we must ultimately trust ourselves, the participants, and the methodology. (p. 214, in this volume)

Duffy's "trust" in the TO methodology provides me with food for thought or, perhaps, the opportunity to snack on the moment: As a philosopher, I conceived of my task in this chapter to bring together diverse ideas from diverse contexts into one conservation, that is, a conversation between TO and psychoanalytic thought.

More to the point, throughout my reading of the text, I kept wondering if the concept of "transference" has a place in TO methodology. Polly Young-Eisendrath writes that, within the therapeutic setting, transference means "sustained projections of certain states, images, and feelings into another, in a way that prevents the recognition of the other as different from the projections . . . I will use 'transference' to refer to a projective state and 'countertransference' to refer to the affective reactions to the transference" (2003, 304). In the therapeutic setting, there is both transference as projection and countertransference as reaction, a felt affective reaction. Reflecting on Duffy's narrative and especially on TO's methodology, I couldn't help but feel that the transference–countertransference dynamic was functioning between himself, the teacher, and the students he worked with. Young-Eisendrath makes clear that not all transference reactions are negative projections onto another. In fact, she identifies "containing-transcendence transference" as the source of a patient's hope and perhaps trust in the therapist and her methodology. She writes,

> This form of transference is filled with the hope of transforming one's suffering and one's life, as well as transcending other kinds of limitations in a way that is similar to spiritual transcendence. This containing-transference is experienced first in the patient's hope that this therapist or analyst is knowledgeable and caring enough to be helpful in alleviating suffering . . . [As such] over time, both analyst and patient deeply appreciate the discovery in which they have

engaged, and recognize how they depended on each other in the most unlikely moments when things felt tense or frightening. (ibid., 305–6)

It is clear to me that Duffy's remarks regarding the Bronx classroom experience captures the essence of containing-transcendence transference. However, in Duffy's case, rather than the patient transferring onto the analyst, there is containing-transcendent transference on Duffy's part aimed at the students—the hope that they will help in alleviating not only their suffering but his as well. Duffy writes, "It is an unfortunate reality that many young people are experts in the effects of oppression. So why shouldn't we trust them with a tool to expose it?" (p. 215, in this volume). It is at junctures like this where I find TO and the psychoanalytic setting begin to converse and dialogue. From Duffy's account and others in the text, it is clear that the students become teachers, and the teachers become students. This reversal is interesting, as Boal (1995) claims there are no spectators in TO. However, by extending our conceptual framework and including containing-transcendence transference into the picture, we see that this reversal is not a simple reversal of roles or power. Rather, in a profound way, Duffy's hopes about the children as experts begins to play an important role in a process of mutual discovery and, I might add, compassion for each other.

It has been my intent to highlight only a few moments from the larger text as well as to draw from my experiences at HFI. My closing point is that transference is a powerful conceptual tool that is not only helpful in understanding, concretely, interpersonal dynamics in a clinical setting; both within the context of psychotherapy and TO, but also the dynamics of transference allow us to focus also on the adults, the writers of these chapters, and the "truths" of their lived experience of schooling that is repeated, relived, over again. By locating the psychic process of transference in the lived-experience of TO, perhaps it becomes possible for kids and adults to work though the truth of schooling—its traumatic (and oppressive) effects and how this trauma is relived again and again until addressed. Indeed, only after we have worked through the truths of our lived-experience of schooling can we address another question: when does "education" end? To explore the context of this "end" is, of course, another conservation between TO and psychoanalytic thinking.

References

Boal, Augusto. 1995. *The Rainbow of Desire: The Boal method of theatre and therapy*. Trans. Adrian Jackson. New York: Routledge.

Chodron, Pema. 1997. *When things fall apart: Heartfelt advice for difficult times*. Boston: Shambala.

Greene, Maxine. 1988. *The dialectic of freedom*. New York: Teacher's College Press.
Grotstein, James. 2003. East is east and west is west and ne'er the Twain shall meet. In *Psychoanalysis and Buddhism*, ed. Jeremy Safran, 221–29. Boston: Wisdom.
Young-Eisendrath, Polly. 2003. Transference and transformation in Buddhism and psychoanalysis. In *Psychoanalysis and Buddhism*, ed. Jeremy Safran, 301–18. Boston: Wisdom.

Contributors

Peter Duffy has worked as a teacher, director, writer, and actor for almost fifteen years. As a high school and middle school teacher in Maine, he founded Maranacook Community School Interactive Theatre (MCS IT, pronounced "mix it"). He and the high school members of the troupe traveled from Maine to New York to Wisconsin using Theatre of the Oppressed (TO) with public school students. He also wrote and composed the book and music for the interactive musical *Nothing Again*, which played off-Broadway for a week for high school audiences and families. He has used theatre as a means of self-expression and problem solving with incarcerated youth, recent immigrants, families, teachers, and students. Peter received his MFA in Theatre for Youth from the University of North Carolina at Greensboro. He is currently the head of the Master's in Arts and Teaching program at the University of South Carolina.

Elinor Vettraino is head of Creative Arts at Adam Smith College in Fife, Scotland. Until recently, she was head of Expressive Arts and head of placement coordination within the teacher education programs at the University of Dundee and convenor of the Learning, Teaching, and Recruitment strategy group for the School of Education, Social Work, and Community Education within the University of Dundee. Prior to this, she was a primary class teacher in Livingston, Scotland. Her current research interests include the link between Boalian pedagogy and the experience of teaching or facilitating, and in particular the link to image as a tool for reflective practice. She is also engaged in research around the development of the use of Rainbow techniques to explore creative writing, engaging reading pedagogy and primary education. Elinor has published in the *International Journal of Special Education* and in *Forum Qualitative Social Research*. She is currently undertaking doctoral studies.

Chen Alon is a doctoral candidate and serves as a facilitator and a lecturer of "Activist-Therapeutic Theatre" in the Theatre Department at Tel-Aviv University. In recent years, Alon has been conducting community-theatre projects within a state prison, drug addiction and homeless rehabilitation centers, and the Israeli-Palestinian theatre group Viewpoints. Alon was a cofounder of the movement Courage to Refuse, a movement of officers and combatant soldiers who refuse to serve in the occupied Palestinian territories, an action for which he was sentenced to three weeks in a military prison. Alon is also a cofounder of the movement Combatants for Peace, which is a movement of combatants from both sides, Palestinians and Israelis, who have abandoned the way of violence.

Brent Blair is an actor, director, voice instructor, therapist, and TO practitioner who founded the Applied Theatre Arts (ATA) emphasis at the University of Southern California (USC) School of Theatre, where he is a senior lecturer. He has worked with Augusto Boal and taught training workshops for cultural fieldworkers all over the world since 1996. His workshops explore TO techniques for labor rights, homelessness, youth justice, education, homophobia, racism, and recently for communities affected by trauma, specifically work in Rwanda with survivors of the Tutsi genocide. He is a former Fulbright scholar to Eastern Nigeria specializing in community-based theatre and its response to social and political rupture. He created the ATA emphasis and ATA Minors Program at USC and is launching a master's program in Applied Theatre Arts at USC where he designed and teaches the courses "Theatre and Therapy," "Theatre in Education," and "Theatre in the Community." He conducts professional development workshops in TO in the United States and around the world.

Augusto Boal is a writer, theatre director, and politician. Founder of TO in the 1960s, Boal continued to adapt and develop his techniques throughout the world. He is most commonly known for his Forum Theatre work, which he further developed into Legislative Theatre when serving one term as a vereador in Rio de Janeiro. In 2008, Augusto Boal was nominated for the Nobel Peace Prize. His revolutionary approach to politics and theatre continues to inspire practitioners across the globe.

Julian Boal is a member of the Group of Theatre of the Oppressed–Paris, a group that works mostly with the oppressions linked with the salary relations. He has led workshops, alone or as Augusto Boal's assistant, in more than twenty countries. He is also the translator of *The Rainbow of Desire* into French and the coordinator of the new French edition of *Games for Actors and Non-Actors*. He is also the author of *Images of a Popular Theatre*.

Diane Conrad is associate professor of drama and theatre education in the Faculty of Education at the University of Alberta in Edmonton, Alberta, Canada. Her research program combines critical pedagogy, applied theatre, and participatory research with youth deemed "at risk." Her most recent project, *The Transformative Potential of Drama in the Education* *of Incarcerated Youth*, was funded by the Social Sciences and Humanities Research Council of Canada (SSHRC) and won the SSHRC Aurora Prize.

Andrea Dishy is currently an educational theatre consultant with thirteen years experience developing and implementing drama education programming in New York City's five boroughs and professional development workshops in and outside of New York City. Andrea is a member of the adjunct faculty for Creative Arts Team at the City University of New York (CAT/CUNY) Paul A. Kaplan Center for Educational Drama. She has led credit-bearing graduate level courses for CUNY and New York University (NYU) as well as weeklong drama-based learning intensives (institutes) for early learning teachers and partnering artists. She has developed and facilitated a number of customized training workshops for organizations such as the Lincoln Center Theater, New York City Head Start, New York City Very Special Arts Festival, the Center for Arts Education (CAE) in New York, and the Alliance Theatre in Atlanta, Georgia. She has presented at regional and national conferences including the American Alliance for Theatre and Education, the National Association (and the New York State Association) for the Education of Young Children, New York City Arts-in-Education Roundtable, and the Wolf Trap Institute for Early Learning through the Arts in the greater Washington DC area. Andrea holds a bachelor's degree in French and drama from Tufts University and a master's degree in educational theatre from NYU.

B. J. Dodge is the faculty coordinator for the California Institute of the Arts' (CalArts) Community Arts Partnership Youth Theater Workshop at Plaza de la Raza in Lincoln Heights. She has been making theater with youth, students, and alumni from CalArts and community-based artists for nineteen years and has taught at CalArts since 1984. In addition to these activities, she works as an artist educator and mentor for the Center Theater Group's (CTG) PLAY (Performing for Los Angeles Youth) programs and has codesigned a template for collaboration between CTG and LA's BEST (Better Educated Students for Tomorrow). She teaches mask, movement, and acting for the California State Summer School for the Arts; is a founding member of the Center for Theatre of the Oppressed and Applied Theatre Arts, Los Angeles; and is a board member of Fringe Benefits, an organization whose mission is to teach tolerance through theater making. A student of Suzuki and Viewpoints, she studies with Burning Wheel in Los Angeles, and she has participated in SITI Company's intensive training summer programs in Los Angeles and at Skidmore College. She has participated in REDCAT's (Roy and Edna Disney/CalArts Theater) NOW (New Original Works) Festival and Studio Series as director and performer.

Sanjoy Ganguly is the founder of Jana Sanskriti, the largest TO movement in the world. After experiencing the culture of monologue inside the communist party he belonged to, Sanjoy went to the villages of West Bengal, India, to promote the organization of independent peoples. His experience with the folk artists there allowed him to discover the theatre person within himself. In the beginning, he was engaged in propaganda theatre, but he later realized that the intellectual ability of the people needs to be respected. In 1991, while searching for a form that can democratize theatre, he came in touch with Augusto Boal. Sanjoy and his group see Boal from an Indian philosophical perspective. During the past few years, Sanjoy Ganguly has become the most prominent figure of integration in the world's international TO movement.

Linda Goulet is an associate professor of education at the First Nations University of Canada where she teaches aboriginal pedagogy and antiracism education. Dr. Goulet facilitates workshops where drama is used as a tool for elementary and high school students to examine social issues in their lives. She incorporates aspects of Forum Theatre in her teaching at the university to analyze controversial issues in health education and racial dilemmas in social justice, so students connect the personal to the social and vice versa. Dr. Goulet has published in various education journals such as the *Alberta Journal of Educational Research*, the *McGill Journal of Education*, and the *Canadian Journal of Native Education*. She wrote more than one chapter in and coedited *Recreating Relationship: Collaboration and Educational Reform* (State University of New York Press, 1997). She also cowrote a chapter in *Aboriginal Education in Canada: A Study in Decolonization*, edited by K. P. Binda (Canadian Educators Press, 2001).

Glenn M. Hudak is professor and program coordinator for the doctoral program in cultural foundations of education, University of North Carolina–Greensboro. He has written about the philosophic, psychoanalytic, and cultural dimensions of education. He is coauthor of two books, the latest, *Labeling: Pedagogy & Politics* (Routledge, 2001), with Paul Kihn, and he has recently been guest editor for a special issue on spirituality and leadership in the *Journal of School Leadership* (2005).

Sonja Arsham Kuftinec is associate professor of theatre at the University of Minnesota. She has published widely on community-based theatre including her book *Staging America: Cornerstone and Community-Based Theater* (Southern Illinois University Press, 2003), which received an honorable mention for the Barnard Hewitt Award in theatre history. Professor Kuftinec also works professionally as a director and dramaturge. Since 1995, she has developed collaborative theatre projects with youth in the Balkans and the Middle East. Her coproduction, *Where Does the Postman Go when All the Street Names Change?*, won an ensemble prize at the 1997 International Youth Theatre Festival in Mostar. Professor Kuftinec also works as a conflict resolution facilitator with Seeds of Peace, an organization that brings together youth from the Middle East, South Asia, and Balkan regions. Her new book, *Theatre, Facilitation, and Nation Formation in the Balkans and Middle East*, is contracted with Palgrave Macmillan.

Warren Linds is an assistant professor in human relations and human systems intervention at Concordia University, Montreal, Canada, where he teaches courses on diversity, leadership, and ethical practices in community development. For the past twenty years, he has been a popular theatre facilitator and community educator using TO in antiracist education programs. His doctoral dissertation (2001) was on the facilitation and development of TO in a North American context. His articles have been published in a wide range of drama, theatre, and research journals. Warren was a coeditor of *Unfolding Bodymind: Exploring Possibility through Education* (Holistic Education Press, 2001) and author of a chapter in *The Boal Companion*, edited by Mady Schutzman and Jan Cohen-Cruz (Routledge, 2005), as well as collaborator on a chapter in Richard C. Smith (ed.), *Sounds and Gestures of Recollection: Art and the Performance of Memory* (Routledge, 2002).

Christina Marín is an assistant professor in the Program in Educational Theatre at New York University, where she teaches courses in applied theatre, TO, research methodology, and diversity. She also supervises the Master of Arts in Educational Theatre for Colleges and Communities. Her research interests include the employment of theatre pedagogy in human rights education. She has published in national and international journals such as *Gender Forum*, *Youth Theatre Journal*, and *STAGE of the Art*. Her work has been presented at the annual conferences of the American Alliance for Theatre & Education, the American Educational Research Association, the American Society for Theatre Research, the Association for Theatre in Higher Education, the United States Hispanic Leadership Institute, and Pedagogy and Theatre of the Oppressed. She has also conducted workshops in Colombia, Ecuador, South Africa, Ireland, Singapore, and Mexico.

Karina Naumer, MFA, is a freelance educational drama specialist living in New York City. She is currently a master teaching artist for the Wolf Trap Institute for Early Learning through the Arts and implements drama-education clinics and training seminars to teachers nationwide. Karina is the founder and, for thirteen years, served as the director of the CAT/New York City Wolf Trap Program: Early Learning through the Arts, a drama-education program in residence within CUNY. One of her highlights as director of this program was developing and fostering an extensive teacher-mentoring project in collaboration with the New York City Administration for Children's Services/Head Start. For ten years, Karina was also an instructor within NYU's Paul A. Kaplan Center for Educational Drama where she taught credit-bearing courses in drama education and storytelling and implemented professional development seminars and workshops in early childhood drama both nationally and internationally. She has worked as a teaching artist and instructor at Maui Academy of Performing Arts in Hawaii, Seattle Children's Theatre, Youth Theatre Northwest, and throughout the Seattle Public School District. In 2001, she was awarded the American Alliance for Theatre and Education's Creative Drama Award for outstanding excellence in the field. She holds an MFA degree in child drama from Arizona State University in Tempe, Arizona.

Johnny Saldaña is a professor of theatre and associate director for the School of Theatre and Film in the Katherine K. Herberger College of Fine Arts at Arizona State University (ASU), where he has taught since 1981. His books include *Drama of Color: Improvisation with Multiethnic Folklore* (Heinemann, 1995), *Longitudinal Qualitative Research: Analyzing Change through Time* (2003), and *Ethnodrama: An Anthology of Reality Theatre* (2005; both published by AltaMira Press). He has written articles for such journals as *Multicultural Perspectives*, *Qualitative Inquiry*, the *Journal of Curriculum and Pedagogy*, *Research in Drama Education*, and the *Youth Theatre Journal*. Saldaña is a recipient of the American Alliance for Theatre & Education's 1989 Creative Drama Award, 1996 Distinguished Book Award, and the 1996 and 2001 Research Awards; the Burlington Resources Foundation Faculty Achievement Award in 1991; the ASU College of Fine Arts Distinguished Teacher of the Year Award in 1995; and the ASU Katherine K. Herberger College of Fine Arts Research Award in 2005. He received his BFA in drama and English education in 1976, and his MFA in child drama in 1979 from the University of Texas at Austin.

Mady Schutzman is a writer and theatre artist. For over twenty-five years, she has worked as a freelance practitioner and scholar of Augusto Boal's TO. She is coeditor with Jan Cohen-Cruz of two collections of essays, *Playing Boal: Theatre, Therapy, Activism* (Routledge, 1994) and *A Boal Companion: Dialogues on Theatre and Cultural Politics* (Routledge, 2006), and author of *The Real Thing: Performance, Hysteria, and Advertising* (Wesleyan, 1999).

Schutzman has published her essays in several critical anthologies and journals including the *Drama Review*; *Women and Performance, Theatre Topics*; and the *Journal of Medical Humanities*. She is currently working on a film about the Socialist City—a utopian collective started in the desert of California. She teaches in the MFA Writing Program and the School of Critical Studies at the California Institute of the Arts.

Chris Vine is an artistic and education director. He has worked for over thirty years in the related fields of theatre in education (TIE), professional community theatre, and young people's theatre. He was a founding member of the Perspectives Theatre Company (now called New Perspectives) in England and the artistic and education director of Greenwich Young People's Theatre (GYPT) in London, one of the foremost educational and youth theatre companies in the United Kingdom. Chris's directing and teaching have taken him to many countries worldwide, including Canada, the Czech Republic, Denmark, Germany, Poland, Japan, and Tanzania. Since coming to New York in 1993, he has responded to many requests for workshops and seminars from across the United States; his specialties include TIE, creating original theatre with young people, teaching through drama, and Augusto Boal's TO.

Index

9/11 attacks, 98, 105

aboriginal, 135; people, 159; youth, 128
Academy of Healing Arts (AHA), 98,
    108
achievement standards, 25
acting: as social action, 147
activists, 147
actor, 230; forum, 191, 194;
    professional, 190, 192–93
actor-teacher, 18, 20, 21, 23, 24, 36, 38,
    39, 40, 41, 42
Adam Institute, 92
Adams, M., L. A. Bell, and P. Griffin,
    166
aesthetic engagement, 104
aesthetic experience, 152
aesthetics, 70, 97, 104, 152
Aesthetics of the Oppressed, 110,
    256–57, 259
aesthetic space, 64, 103, 104, 170, 209,
    212, 213, 214
aggressor, 25–28, 32, 37
Alexander, Jacqui, 117
allies, 167, 192, 254; definition, 166
Alon, Chen, 84, 260
alternative space, 164
analogical induction, 165, 210–12
Analytical Image, 255
Anansi, 100
antagonist, 48, 56–60, 72–73, 110–12,
    118, 122, 167, 189, 258; replacing
    of the, 89
Anthony, Chris, 245
antimodels, 111–16, 120, 189, 193,
    195, 198

antiracism: education, 161; group, 167;
    program, 159–81; theatre projects,
    162
Anzaldúa, Gloria, 99, 100
applied theatre, 126
Arab citizens of Israel, 88
Aristotelian empathy, 87–88
Aristotle, 88, 116
Arnold, R., 163
Arts and the Creation of Mind, 213
ascesis (Augusto Boal), 195
"at-risk," 99, 125, 126, 127, 128
"at-risk teens," 98, 100

Bacon, Francis, 63, 69
Banaszewski, Charles, 47
Barone, T., and E. Eisner, 126
Bauman, Zygmunt, 87
Beatles, The, 231
Bedouin Arabs, 91
Bishop, A., 181
Boal, Augusto, 85–87, 91–94, 110–11,
    139, 166, 188, 205, 207, 210,
    213–14, 220–21, 223, 230, 242,
    247, 251, 266, 268; adaptations of
    Theatre of the Oppressed work,
    219; catharsis, individual, 200;
    choice of workshop method, 222;
    Forum Theatre, 48; Image Theatre,
    explanation, 71, 220–21; maieutics,
    170; metaxis, 66; philosophical
    links with Paulo Freire, 42, 66,
    128–29, 201–2; point of aggression,
    196; psychological forum, 118; role
    of dialogue, 162; three levels of
    connection, 72

Boal Companion, A, 121
Bohm, David, 106
Bosnak, Robert, 112
Brecht, Bertolt, 93, 154, 248
Brewster, Levi, 237
Buber, Martin, 93
bully, 39, 46, 205
bullying, 39, 45, 161, 165, 202, 205,
    258, 264–65
Burke, Lisa, 236
Burton, Andrew, 252
bystander, 167

California Institute of the Arts, 229
Carousel of Antagonists, 111
Casdagli, Penny, 74
caste: discrimination, 148; hierarchy, 145
Castro, Fidel, 231
catharsis, 88, 155, 200, 258
Center for Theatre of the Oppressed, 145
Cesaroni, C., 127
Chaplin, Charlie, 231
Chávez, César, 231
Cheng, Spica, 40
child as puppeteer, 30
child-learning objective, 25
Chodron, Pema, 266
Chorus, 230, 237, 248
City University of New York (CUNY), 18
civil rights, 238
classroom equality, 35
coaching, 34
cofacilitate, 101
cognitive reframing, 109
Cohen-Cruz, Jan, 121
collective action, 150, 152–53
collective witnessing, 147
colonialism, 101
Columbian Hypnosis, 91
Colvin, Claudette, 231–33, 241–43,
    247–49
Combatants for Peace, 93, 260
combating the oppressor, 149
commedia, 241
Community Arts Partnership (CAP),
    229, 230, 244

community-based theatre, 116
concretization, 85
conflict, 25, 43
conflict: intervention, 22; resolution,
    20, 25, 38, 87
conscientization/conscientizacao
    (Paulo Freire), 77, 86, 104, 118,
    121, 197
containing-transcendence
    transference, 267
Cop in the Head, 110, 259
countertransference, 267
Cover the Space, 240
Creative Arts Team (CAT), 17, 18, 39,
    42, 43, 58
Creative Arts Team/New York City
    Wolf Trap Program: Early
    Learning through the Arts (Early
    Learning Program), 17, 18, 19, 34,
    38, 39, 41, 42, 43
Creel, G., 166
Cree Nation, 130, 132, 135
critical consciousness, 219
critical dialogue, 232
critical pedagogy, 139, 227
cultural workers, 100, 112, 117, 122
curriculum: personalizing, 204

Dean, M., 127
De Castell, S. and J. Jenson, 135
dehumanized, 98, 109
Dei, G., 161, 174
Delhi Sramik Sanghathan (Delhi
    Workers' Organisation), 148
democracy, 154, 172, 180
democratic space, 153
democratization, 85
democratizing process, 148
demonstration, 47
demythicisation, 36
Denny, Reginald, 234–35, 249
Denzin, N. K., 126
Depp, Johnny, 231
de-role, 38
Dialectic of Freedom, 265

Diamond, David, 133, 135, 165, 166;
    Power Plays, 160, 166; Your
    Wildest Dream, 133, 165
Dimona, 91–92
discrimination, 159, 165
dismantling oppressive social and
    political structures, 37
Dodge, B. J., 229
Dominion Institute, 159
Donoho, B. H., 162
Don Quixote, 257
Doob, A., and C. Cesaroni, 127
dowry system, 150–51
drama: embodied experience and
    reflective explanation, 164
drama education: enactment of trust, 163
dramatic truth, 194
Dream Theatre, 112, 122
Duffy, Peter, 181, 264, 267–68
Dwyer, P., 167
dynamize, 51, 72, 198–99, 209

Early Learning Program. See Creative
    Arts Team/New York City Wolf
    Trap Program: Early Learning
    through the Arts
Edmonton Journal, 136
educational drama, 67
educational objectives, 74
educational outcomes, 74
Eisner, Elliot, 213
Electric Kool-Aid Acid Test, 247
El Khader, 88, 89, 90
Elm, Steve, 20
empathy, 108, 109; Aristotelian, 87–88
ensemble: development of, 205
epistemologies, 116
ethics, 260
ethnographic fieldwork, 46
ethnography, 126
Evers, Medgar, 248

facilitation, 21, 22, 24, 33, 36, 39, 42,
    47, 83, 94, 176–79, 219
facilitator, 18, 24, 26, 36, 39, 45, 48, 61,
    73, 76, 94, 97, 102, 117, 173, 179,

189, 194, 206, 214–15, 218; Israeli
    and Palestinian, 91; Palestinian,
    95; role of, 211
family health, 144
fantasy, 98
Faundez, Antonio, 219
Felman, Jil Lyn, 66
female genitalia mutilation, 222
First Nations youth, 128
First People, 132
Fischer, Trina, 42
Forum Theatre, 21–24, 47–49, 53–56,
    59–60, 86–90, 92, 97, 99, 101,
    110–15, 119, 133, 136, 146–47,
    149, 151–56, 166–68, 170–71,
    175–81, 189–90, 193–95, 198–99,
    252, 257–61
Foucault, M., 87, 127, 204
Freed, Jennifer, 98, 108, 118–19
Freedman, Rendy, 98
Freire, Paolo, 106–8, 112–13, 197,
    204, 217–21, 248, 251, 263;
    action-objective, 221; banking
    education, 162; human
    liberation, 227; praxis, 196, 220;
    problematization, 36

games, 104–5, 129, 163
Games for Actors and Non-Actors
    (Augusto Boal), 70, 104, 121, 163,
    206, 219–20, 222, 251
Ganguly, Sanjoy, 95
gang violence, 225–26
Gates, Darryl, 242
gay marriage, 223
Gaza, 92, 93
geography of Theatre of the
    Oppressed, 110
Gerein, K., 132
Gestalt technique, 69
Ghandi, 231
Ghost Stallion, 132–33
Gilligan, Carol, 100–101
Ginwright, S. and T. James, 179
Giroux, H., 178
Goffman, Erving, 47, 59, 60, 61

Gonzalez, Jo Beth, 223–24
governmentality, 127
Great Game of Power, 253
Green, S., 166
Greene, Maxine, 206, 265, 266
Griffin, Maura, 23
Griffiths, Rudyard, 159
Grotstein, James, 266
group dialogue, 106
Guevara, Che, 94, 231

habeas corpus, 238
habits of being, 87
habits of thinking, 87
Hamer, Fannie Lou, 238, 248
Hardwick, Gwendolen, 19
Harlem Family Institute (HFI), 263
hate crimes, 223
Head Start, 19
healers, 99
healing, 99, 100, 116; as coparticipants, 98; as a process, 98
health, 143, 148, 156
Hebron, 92
Hendrix, Jimi, 231
Henry, F., and C. Tator, 161
Heron, J., 176
Hillman, James, 115
Hilton, Paris, 231
Hitler, Adolph, 241–42
HIV/AIDS prevention, 202, 221
hooks, bell, 66, 77, 120, 204
hot-seating, 48, 52, 56
Huff, D. J., 160
humanization, 86, 89, 110, 113, 121–22, 214, 243, 263; of the Other, 85
Hyslop, F., 65

ideal image, 58, 59, 134, 135, 209
ignorance, 87
Iktomi, 100
image: of healing, 209; ideal, 58, 59, 134, 135, 209; of liberation, 72; as narrative, 164; of oppression, 71, 72, 73, 164, 165; of power, 164; of racism, 164; of reality, 134

Image, Complete the, 111, 164
Image and Counterimage, 255
Image of the Counterimage, 253
Image of the Images, 71, 74
Image of the Unspoken Word, 111
Image of the Word, 253
Image Theatre, 45, 47, 58, 64, 70, 74, 84, 111, 112, 133, 207, 212, 221, 252–53, 260–61; Boal's explanation, 220–21
Image to Forum, 256
Improvisation for the Theater, 206
improvisation, 34
incarcerated youth, 125–39, 256
Indian Supreme Court, 145
indigeneous students, 160
inner monologue, 48
Innovation Center for Community and Youth Development, 173
in-role, 19, 23, 24, 41
inside facilitator (IF), 24, 25, 28, 30, 33–35, 41
Instant Forum Theatre, 48
Integrated Child Development Services (ICDS), 144–45, 156
interactive, 166
interactive narration, 20
interactive scenarios, 85
interactive theatre, 83
intervention, 18, 21, 22, 24–26, 32–34, 36, 37, 39, 73, 85, 87, 89, 151, 172, 177, 196
intervention facilitation, 23
intervention sequence, 41
introspective action, 150
Invisible Theatre, 259
IPSOS-Reid survey, 159
Irondale Ensemble Project, 204
Israeli and Palestinian facilitators, 91
Israeli Defense Force, 89
Israeli soldiers, 89
Israeli youth, 83–95
Izraty, Igal, 84

Jackson, T., 162
Jana Sanskriti, 95, 143–56

Jerusalem, 88
Jewish Israeli youth, 83–95
Jimenez-Torres, Maria, 235
joker, 21–24, 48, 49, 60, 63, 66, 73,
    89, 109, 110, 118, 149, 150, 153,
    177, 194–98, 208, 236, 248, 259;
    explanation, 230; jokering, 212;
    Joker System, 230, 232–37, 242–47

Kahlo, Frida, 231
kaleidoscope of images, 110, 111
Kaplan, Paul A., Center for
    Educational Drama, 19, 43
Kennedy, John F., 231
Kent, G., 136
Kershaw, Baz, 125, 129, 138, 139, 179
King, Dr. Martin Luther, Jr., 231
King, Rodney, 231, 233, 235–36, 239,
    241–43, 248, 249
Kirk, P., and A. Shutte, 176
Koon, Officer Stacy, 235, 239
Kruger, Kathryn Sullivan, 100
Ku Klux Klan (KKK), 238, 241
Kumashiro, K., 161, 179

Lakota people, 100
Learning to Question, 220
Legislative Theatre, 115, 119, 260
liberation, 69, 70, 72, 73, 75, 85, 114, 151
liberation arts, 99
liberation of the oppressed, 85
liberation of the oppressor, 85
liberation psychology, 99
liberation theology, 99, 100
liberatory pedagogy, 217
Lightning Forum, 59, 76
Lincoln, Abraham, 231
Linds, Warren, 74, 166
Lipsky, Jon, 112
literacy, 217–19
Literacy: Reading the Word and the World
    (Freire and Macedo), 177, 218, 227
"Little Boxes," 239
London, J., 172
Lopez, Alexandra, 23
Lorenz, Helene, 100

Los Angeles, 229
Los Angeles Police Department
    (LAPD), 231, 235
Los Angeles riots, 1992, 231

Macedo, Donald, 112, 177, 218, 227
magical solutions, 25, 30, 38, 56
Magic Mountain, 242
maieutics, 170
Malcolm X, 248
malnutrition, 145, 151
Marcos, Subcomandante, 106–7
marginalization, 108; marginalized
    groups, 161
Martin-Baro, Ignacio, 116
McLaren, Peter, 204
message theatre, 116
metanarrative, 116
metaphorize, 252
metaxis, 66, 78; Boal's definition, 175, 198
mirroring, 49
modeling, 47
Monroe, Marilyn, 231
Morales, Aurora Levins, 99, 100, 109
multivocality, 232
Murtagh, C., 77
Museum of the Unspeakable, 112
Mutnick, D., 206

NAACP, 238
Naseeruddin, Mullah, 155
National Family Health Survey, 144
Native American Counsel, 98
Native program, 127, 129
Naumer, Karina, 20
Neelands, J., and T. Goode, 48
Negev, 90
Neith, 100
New Delhi, 148
Newspaper Theatre, 133, 136, 222
Ng, R., 161
Nicholson, H., 163, 180
Noam, G. G., 176
non-actors, 166
nongovernmental organizations
    (NGOs), 146

normative citizen, 84
nutrition, 143, 145, 148, 156

objectives, 25, 41
occupation, the, 89, 91, 95
Occupied Palestinian Territories, 84
Occupied Territories, 84, 88, 89, 94
Och, Phil, 239
OPCC/Sojourn—Ocean Park
    Community Center, 101, 107, 120
oppressed, 37, 85, 86, 151, 198, 254;
    poetics of the, 205
oppression, 37, 43, 45, 47, 49, 53–55,
    58–59, 61, 68–71, 83, 86, 95, 112,
    115–18, 125, 143, 146–47, 176,
    195–96, 199, 202, 222; breaking,
    198; institutional, 205; naming,
    204, 213; reinforcing, 192
oppressor, 37, 76, 85, 86, 93, 108, 109, 116,
    122, 167, 188, 191, 194, 242, 261
oppressor-oppressed contradiction, 117
Other, the, 83, 85, 87, 88, 90–92, 133
outside facilitator (OF), 23–35, 40, 41
"Outside of a Small Circle of Friends,"
    239
Oz, the land of, 203, 215

Palestine, 95
Palestinian youth, 83–95
Palotai, Ada, 107, 117
pantomime, 20, 21, 31
Park, P., M. Brydon-Miller, B. Hall,
    and T. Jackson, 126
Parks, Rosa, 231, 247, 248
participatory drama, 125
Pasquino, P., 127
patriarchy, 148; oppression, 148;
    patriarchal society, 149, 151
Paul A. Kaplan Center for Educational
    Drama. *See* Kaplan, Paul A.
    Center for Educational Drama
Pedagogy and Theatre of the
    Oppressed, 48
Pedagogy of Hope, 126, 134
Pedagogy of the Oppressed (Paulo
    Freire), 36, 117, 170, 205, 214, 217

Peres Center for Peace, 84, 94
Petkewich, Emily, 48
play, 205
playing space, 104
Plaza de la Raza Youth Theater
    Program, 229, 243–47
Plessy, Homer, 233, 248
poetics of the oppressed, 205
political action, 85, 154
political awareness, 97
political oppression, 95
polyrhythmic realities, 162
poverty: effects of, 264
Powell, Officer Laurence, 235, 239
power, 47, 49, 172, 195, 199; have
    power over, 165; naming power,
    204; technology of, 204
power dynamic, 189
powerless observer, 166
power relationship, 37, 85, 161, 193,
    199, 203
power structures, 193, 199
Pratichi Trust, 144, 156
praxis, 48, 66, 73, 102, 170, 196, 204;
    Freire's definition, 220
Prentki, T., 126
Preston, S., 126
privilege, 161
problematizing, 36, 42, 191, 198
problem-posing education, 170
protagonist, 48, 56–60, 73, 122, 149,
    167, 189, 198, 203, 208–9, 258; in
    image of oppression, 63; replacing
    in a Forum, 149, 151
protagonist-antagonist models, 117
puppeteering, 39–41, 42
puppet intervention, 42
puppets, 18
puppet scenarios for intervention
    purposes, 22
Pye, C., 173

racism, 241; structural causes of, 161;
    victims of, 159
Radical in Performance, The, 125

Rainbow of Desire, The, 63, 110, 111, 112, 121, 165, 210, 219, 255, 257, 259, 260, 266
read the world, 36
realistic image, 58
re-creation, 106
REDCAT, 230
reenactment, 24, 33
Refuse Soldier, 84
rehearsal for the revolution, 129
Renk, H., 164
replacement, 33, 34
resistance, 67
Resolving Conflict Creatively Program, New York City, 19
Reynolds, Malvina, 239
ritual, 103–4
Robinson, K., 65, 77
Rohd, Michael, 219, 224, 240
role-play, 28, 31, 33, 34
role-reversal, 48
Royal Shakespeare Company, 256
Rukeyser, Muriel, 213, 265
Rumsfeld, Donald, 248

Saldana, Johnny, 219, 265
Salverson, Julie, 67
Sanders, V., 162
Sandoval, Chela, 101, 116, 117
scaffolding, 34–35
Schissel, B., and T. Wotherspoon, 160
Schutzman, Mady, 121, 162, 229
sculpting, 49
Seebaran, R. B., and S. P. Johnston, 162
Selby, D., 163
Selman, J., 126
sexual orientation, 223
Shakespeare, William, 231
Shakur, Tupac, 231
shared image, 72
shared leadership, 176
Shaull, Richard, 217–18
Sheared, V., 162
Silver, J., and K. Mallett, 160
Silver, W., 128
simultaneous consciousness, 204

simultaneous dramaturgy, 53, 198
Sinatra, Frank, 231
single-sex groups, 71
social change, 218
social justice, 172, 201, 264
Social Sciences and Humanities Research Council (SSHRC) of Canada, 126
Socratic, 24
solidarity, 71, 94
Sonar Meye, 150–51, 157
Sounds, 132
South Central Farm, 234, 248
space: aesthetic, 64, 103, 104, 170, 209, 212, 213, 214; alternative, 165; for as-if world, 159, 175; classroom, 69, 73; democratic, 153; emotional, 75; empty, 104; for engagement/reflection, 147; free, 65; liminal, 213; physical, 68, 71, 75, 104; playing, 104; safe, 163, 175; transformative, 126
space between, the, 97
spaces of liberty, 223
spect-actor, 17–18, 24, 37, 49, 51, 59–60, 63, 66, 86, 110, 113, 147, 149, 151–54, 156, 167, 189–97, 259
spectator: transformating into actor, 205–6
Speigelman, Marvin, 110
spirituality, 97
spiritual practice, 109
Spolin, Viola, 206
Springer, Jerry, 251
standards, 25
Status Lineup, 167
St. Denis, V., 161
stigma, 50, 60
stigmatization, 45, 46, 47
stigmatize, 50, 52, 56, 58–62
Stop! Don't Go!, 148
Street Spirits Theatre Company, 252
student voice, 165
sympathy, 87

tableau of oppression, 242
tableaux, 240

tableaux vivants, 111, 112
talking circle, 107
Taylor, Philip, 219
teacher-in-role, 48
Teachers as Cultural workers: Letters to Those Who Dare Teach (Paulo Freire), 180
teaching artists, 18, 41
technology of power, 204
Tel Aviv, 90, 94
theatre: as analytical tool, 168; as a shared language, 162, 205, 207; as tool for liberation, 85
theatre for activism, 85
Theatre for Community, Conflict and Dialogue, 224
Theatre for Social Change, 219, 221, 224, 227; techniques, 227
theatre in education (TIE), 19, 41, 48, 195–96; curriculum, 20
Theatre of the Oppressed (TO), 45–46, 48–49, 59–61, 63–64, 66–70, 73–77, 83–85, 89, 91, 93–94, 97, 101–4, 107, 109–11, 116–20, 121, 126, 128–29, 138–39, 143, 153–54, 159, 166, 170, 181, 187–89, 195, 200–201, 205, 211, 215–18, 221, 230, 251, 257, 260–61, 263–64, 266; arsenal, 146, 215, 219, 227; curriculum, 47; in education, 75; efficacy, 199; methodology, 267; misuse of, 200; practitioners, 117; in therapeutic work, 259
theatre of the oppressor, 118
Theresa, Mother, 231
third space, 118
thought balloon, 48, 50, 52
Till, Emmett, 238, 248
transference, 263–68
transformation: capacity for, 218
transformative space, 126
trauma, 85, 86
Tsuchigumo people, 100
Turnbull, D., 175
Turner, Victor, 104, 121

University of Alberta, 126
UPSET!, 230, 233, 242–47

Vegematic, 239
Vettraino, Elinor, 265
victim, 167
victimization, 45
Viewpoints, 85, 86, 87, 88, 89, 93
Viewpoints, an Israeli-Palestinian Interactive Theatre Group, 83; Viewpoints Theatre, 83
Vine, Chris, 19, 36, 58
violence, 21, 99
Violence Intervention Program (VIP), 101
violence prevention, 20
visual literacy, 131

warm-up, 205
warm-up games, 163, 170
Watkins, Mary, 99, 100, 112
Watt, Maureen, 66, 77
Weisberg, Judge Stanley, 236
West Bank, 86, 88
West Bengal, 143, 144, 145, 150, 156
Wheeler, Tim, 255
Wheelock, Helen, 41
Wheel of Fortune, 238, 249
White, Michelle, 48
White, Vanna, 238, 249
Williams, Martin, 78
Wilson, P., 160
witness, 167. See also powerless observer
witnessing, 85, 87; collective, 147
Wolfe, Tom, 247
Wolf Trap Institute, 43
Wright, D., 164

Yeroham, 90–93
Yeroham Community Center, 90
Young-Eisendrath, Polly, 267
Young Offender Centre, 126
Youth Criminal Justice Act, 127, 129
youth exploitation, 146

Zapatista, 106–7